NO Man PUT

ASUNDER

The Complete Series

LASHANDA MICHELLE

L.M. Ink, LLC

L.M.Ink, LLC

Copyright © 2015 by LaShanda Michelle

ISBN-10: 0996491414

ISBN-13: 978-0-9964914-1-9

The Pharisees also came unto him, tempting him, and saying unto him, Is it lawful for a man to put away his wife for every cause?

And he answered and said unto them, Have ye not read, that he which made them at the beginning made them male and female,

And said, For this cause shall a man leave father and mother, and shall cleave to his wife: and they twain shall be one flesh?

Wherefore they are no more twain, but one flesh. What therefore God hath joined together,

let not man put asunder.

~Matthew 19:3-6 (King James Version)

Let No Man Put Asunder

(The Complete Series)

ONE
DANA

Lord, please bless this food that I have prepared. Please make it delicious to those who eat it, and let it be nutritious, too. In your name I pray... Oh—Please keep me from laying unholy hands on that witch—oops, I mean... my mother-in-law. In Jesus name I pray, amen.

I tried to calm my nerves as I emptied a pot of freshly prepared mashed potatoes into a serving bowl and placed it on the dining room table, but it was to no avail. I was an emotional wreck. The Bible said to be anxious for nothing, but Sylvia Gardner was on her way to my house. How could I be calm?

Everything is going to go smoothly, Dana... Just don't attack anyone...

"Don't forget the big spoon, Mommy."

"Huh?" I snapped out of my anxiety-filled thoughts long enough to acknowledge my step-son. "What'd you say, Jonathan?"

"Don't forget the big spoon."

I nodded and placed a kiss on his cheek before I retrieved the utensil. My sweet child had been by my side for the majority of the last nine hours, working hard to help me prepare an over-the-top meal for his grandmother. At this moment he was setting the dinner table, which I greatly appreciated. "The table looks good, honey," I told him as I placed the spoon beside the mashed potatoes. "You're doing a fantastic job."

"Yeah, okay. But I'm *starving up in here.*"

I chuckled at the anxious seven-year-old now rubbing his stomach. He was so dramatic, looking just like his father with his light brown skin and adorable dimple on this left cheek. He'd been snacking all day as we cooked. There was no way he could possibly be famished.

I helped him lay out the rest of the silverware, then straightened his clothes and sent him into the living room to watch TV until his grandmother arrived. As soon as he sat on the couch he loosened his necktie. If I hadn't stopped him he would have kicked off his shoes, too. I knew he hated the semi-formal attire I'd dressed him in, but this dinner was important to me and I wanted him to look his best. I was just about to tell him not to get his clothes wrinkled but became distracted by the sight of my husband entering the living room.

"Oh, shoot," I sang as he crossed into the kitchen and joined me in the dining room. I nearly drooled as the tall, handsome man I was lucky enough to call my husband proudly spun around and showed off his clothes. *"Looking good, Mr. Gardner."*

He placed a kiss on my forehead before fawning over the food in front of us. "Dang, baby. Look at all of this!"

"I told you I was gonna do it big," I reminded him.

"Yeah, but... Don't you think this is a little much? It's just Mama."

I looked at the ten-pound pork roast sitting in the middle of the table and the surrounding side dishes. Mashed potatoes, spiced carrots, pan-seared asparagus, corn on the cob, peach cobbler, German chocolate cake, and lemon pound cake. There was also a tub of vanilla ice cream in the freezer. Maybe I did go a little overboard. But this meal was for his mother. I should have made a twenty-pound roast.

"I didn't want to leave room for any complaints," I told him.

"The only person you need to worry about impressing is me," he claimed, and squeezed my behind as he pulled me close to him.

"Yeah, right." I rolled my eyes and moved away, then went over the table setting again. Satisfied, I went into the kitchen and began to prepare the bread basket for the dinner rolls that were still baking in the oven.

"What was that?" Gavin asked from the spot I left him in.

"What was what?"

"You rolled your eyes at me."

"Did I?" I asked, knowing fully well that I had. He knew exactly what it was about, but I wasn't in the mood to entertain his intentional denial. We both knew his mother was an overly cynical, manipulative, envious, destructive, cold-hearted vampire behind the faux smile she laced her venomous attacks toward me with. I was just the only one truthful enough to admit it. Sylvia Gardner was *the* thorn in our marriage, but he refused to put her in her place the way a protective husband should have. I felt like Paul, repeatedly asking the Lord to take her away. She hadn't learned to accept me yet, nor had she moved away or croaked over in death, so I had no choice but to put up with her for the time being. Her, and the disgusting way my husband acted like she could do no wrong. Every time I expressed to him the way she made me feel, he disregarded my complaints as simple misunderstandings and encouraged me to try harder to get along with her. But how was I supposed to get along with a woman who criticized me every chance she got and told me to my face that the only reason her son married me was because he needed an in-house caregiver for his son? Never mind the fact that Gavin and I had been together for months before he got full custody of Jonathan. Or the fact that her son actually loved me and wanted to spend the rest of his life with me. Nope. According to her, the only reason he asked for my hand in marriage was because he needed a full-time babysitter. How could that possibly be a "simple misunderstanding?"

"Dana?"

I continued to prepare the bread basket and kept my mouth closed. If I verbally expressed my frustration with him over the way he continuously allowed his mother to openly berate me, things were going to get ugly. Right now I had to focus on the tasks at hand.

"Something on your mind?"

I sighed wearily. He wasn't taking my silence as a hint that I didn't want to talk, and I really needed him to. I wasn't in the mood to argue. My feet hurt from standing up all day, and I was beginning to get a slight headache.

"Let's just stay positive, okay? Your mother will be here in a few minutes."

"I am positive. But I don't like it when my wife rolls her eyes at me. What's that all about?"

"You really don't need me to tell you, do you?"

I'd been saying it for the past two and a half years. He wasn't an ignorant person, and I didn't appreciate him pretending to be one now. He knew what was bothering me. His mother and her fat mouth. But I suppose he wanted me to just pretend everything was fine and that I wasn't putting on this ridiculous dinner to please him by getting back on good terms with her. She and I hadn't seen each other in six weeks, and while I was perfectly fine with it, the silence on her end drove him crazy. Big ol' mama's boy. He just had to have her approval in everything, even if she treated me like a glorified girlfriend who needed to be replaced. He begged me to invite her over for dinner so we could make amends. Granted, he didn't tell me to go over the top with what I prepared. No. The grandiosity was my idea. Since Sylvia always complained that I didn't cook, I wanted to make a meal that would knock her socks off. Hopefully they'd end up in her mouth and shut her up for good.

"Can you get the pitcher of tea out of the fridge for me, please, and set it on the table? Thanks so much, babe."

He did as I asked, then inquired, "Your attitude isn't about that whole 'in-house help' comment Mama made, is it? I thought we'd moved on from that?"

"I'll move on when I get an *apology*," I told him. "And please don't disregard my feelings again. I *hate* when you do that. I have a very valid reason for being upset."

I prepared the butter dish and took it into the dining room, and immediately felt guilty for using the tone that I'd just taken with my husband. I shouldn't have to apologize, though. He was wrong for letting things get to this point, and he knew it.

As I stood at the dining room table, Gavin approached and wrapped his arms around me, then kissed the side of my face.

"We're not fighting tonight," he whispered softly in my ear as he stood behind me. "We know what we have together, and it doesn't matter what anyone else says. Let's just pray for a good evening tonight. You've made this wonderful dinner, and I want us all to enjoy it. Okay?"

I leaned against him and wished that I believed him, but my gut told me not to let my guard down. When I called Sylvia and invited her over, she put on a sweet front, as if nothing had ever happened between us. From our past battles, I knew that meant she had something planned. There was always a calm before her storms.

"I'll behave if she will," I told him.

He sighed, not happy with my response. "I thought this was supposed to be a peace offering?"

"It is," I assured him. "But both sides have to want peace, Gavin. I can't do this on my own."

He knew I was telling the truth, and it saddened him. I turned around and gave him a kiss on his lips.

"What was that for?" he asked.

I shrugged. "Just wanted you to know that I still love you."

"I love you, too."

"I know," I said, and kissed him again. "Your mom will be here soon and I still need to run upstairs and get dressed."

He released me from his embrace and I hurried toward the stairs.

"If I come back down here and find any fingerprints in the frosting of my German chocolate cake, you will have problems," I called to him over my shoulder. "Understand? And don't try to blame it on Jonathan, either."

Gavin was silent. I already knew that as soon as I hit our bedroom floor he was going to sneak a sample.

"Just don't make it obvious," I compromised. Halfway up the stairs I remembered the dinner rolls were still in the oven. "Shoot!" I fussed, and scurried back to the kitchen.

"What are you doing?" Gavin asked when he saw me. He had the lid of the cake tray in one hand and was licking frosting off the index finger of his opposite.

"Forgot the dinner rolls."

"Go upstairs and get dressed. I'll get them."

I made a u-turn and headed toward the stairs again. As I rounded the corner I glanced out of the living room window and saw Sylvia's Lincoln parked in the driveway. A second later she peered into the window, directly at me.

Dang it!

I knew she was going to say something about my clothes. I was dressed in a pair of old dingy sweats and a muscle top that I purchased during the ridiculous week I tried to implement a workout regimen into my daily routine. Slaving in the kitchen all day had left me a complete mess. Why was she here already? Our meal wasn't supposed to start for another fifteen minutes.

She rang the doorbell.

"Grandma's here!" Jonathan announced loudly, and ran to the front door. "Grandma!" he shrieked, and pounced on her with excitement as soon as he opened it.

"Jonathan!" I fussed as she struggled to hold herself up. "Get down, boy! You're too big to keep jumping on her like that!"

"Oh, it's all right," the short and stocky woman told me, even though he was almost as tall as she was, and laughed. "I'm gonna hold him as long as I can, while I can. Soon he'll be a man, and too in love with some woman to pay ol' Grandma any attention."

That last comment was a subtle dig at me, retaliation for marrying her son and taking him away from her, even though he was the one who proposed to me.

Let it slide, Dana... Let it slide...

"Hey, Mama," Gavin greeted her as he joined us in the living room. He leaned over to give her a hug and a kiss on the cheek, then took her purse from her and put it in the closet.

"Jonathan, baby," she said. "Go on out there to the car and get Grandma's bowl of banana pudding. It's in the back seat, and I made it just for you."

"All right!" the child hooted, and took her car keys from her and rushed out of the door.

I cleared my throat. "Sylvia, you made banana pudding?"

"Yes," she smiled innocently. "You all know how much my grandbaby loves my banana pudding. I thought I'd make him a batch."

"Yes, but when we talked on the phone I specifically told you not to bring anything," I said as calmly as I could. "We have plenty of sweets here."

"Oh, don't make such a big deal about it," she told me, and flung her hand in the air as if I were overreacting. "A little banana pudding never hurt anybody. It's for the baby."

No, it wasn't. It was her devious way of sneaking *her* food into *my* dinner. As soon as someone ate one spoonful she was going to comment on how they chose her dessert over mine. Or worse, she'd demand that Gavin eat her dessert instead of one that I prepared, then boast that no one could ever satisfy his belly the way that she did, no matter how hard they tried. I wasn't being paranoid. She had a plan, and a vicious one.

"It's fine, babe," Gavin told me from the closet door.

Sylvia smiled at me in a taunting fashion, proving what I already knew. She wasn't innocent like she pretended to be. Gavin took her side, yet again, and she relished the victory.

"Yeah, it's fine," I pretended to agree.

"That's right, dear. What you should really be focused on is your clothes," she stated with a frown. "I thought this was semi-formal? Here I am in my Sunday best, and you have on this frump wear."

Embarrassed, I explained that I'd been in the kitchen all day and was on my way upstairs to get ready when she arrived—fifteen minutes early.

"Uh huh, I see." She pretended to understand, and tucked the ends of her curly wig behind her ears. "Dana, do you really think what you have on is appropriate to wear in front of your son? That shirt is a little revealing, don't you think?"

Surprised, I looked down at my shirt for the inappropriateness, but found none.

"Why? Because it's sleeveless?"

"I can see your navel," she frowned.

I looked again and realized that half an inch of my stomach was exposed. I hadn't noticed it before and looked to Gavin for support, but he chose to remain silent as he waited at the door for Jonathan to return.

"It's pretty hot in the kitchen," I told her. "I wanted to be as comfortable as possible."

"Really? I've been cooking my entire life, and I've always managed to do so without being half naked in front of my child. But I suppose you *modern women* are a bit different."

There she went again with that stupid argument. Was I supposed to feel bad that I was born in the 1980s? She always tried to make it seem like my age was something to be ashamed of. It wasn't my fault she was an old hag. Gavin was only a few years older than me, but did he get called a "modern man?" No, of course not.

Ugh! She made me sick! Besides, my belly button barely peeked over my sweatpants. It wasn't like I was showing my entire body. Jonathan had a navel, too. Didn't we all?

"As I said, I'm on my way upstairs to change," I told her, and quickly retreated to the bedroom. On the way I rolled my eyes at my husband again for being so silent while his mother tried to ridicule me.

Once upstairs I heard the front door close.

"Here you go, Grandma," I heard Jonathan say.

"Thank you, baby. Why don't you go ahead and take it into the kitchen for me."

A moment later Gavin asked, "Did you really have to bring banana pudding, Mama? This is Dana's dinner, and she made it clear that she didn't want you to bring anything."

"Please don't tell me that you're offended," she replied back. "I thought you would be happy I decided to bring something extra. It's a safety dish, just in case what Dana prepared doesn't turn out good."

I knew it!

I grumbled under my breath, but told myself not to worry about it. At least this time my husband spoke up for me.

I took a quick shower to get the smell of sweat and food off of me, then put on the midnight blue sheath dress I'd laid out when I first got up this morning and a pair of low heels. I whipped my shoulder length hair into a bun, smeared a little makeup across my face, and put on a pair of earrings and a bracelet. The entire process took fifteen minutes—the exact amount of time I needed to get ready before Sylvia was supposed to show up.

I made my way back downstairs and found my family sitting on the sofa. Jonathan was sitting in Sylvia's lap, and Gavin sat beside them, flipping through television channels with the remote.

"What's that smell?" I asked as the stench of something burning filled my nose.

They seemed not to notice at first. Suddenly Gavin gasped and ran into the kitchen. I followed behind and watched as he pulled out the pan of charred dinner rolls he was supposed to take out of the oven a long time ago.

"Gavin!" I fussed.

He coughed as smoke filled the kitchen. I opened the window, then used a potholder to fan the smoke alarm that began to ring.

"Sorry, babe," he apologized. "I forgot to take them out. The doorbell rang and I got distracted."

I groaned and continued to help him. When the smoke cleared we looked up to see Sylvia standing at the entrance of the kitchen.

"Is something wrong?" she asked.

"Everything's fine," I told her. "We're about to eat in a minute."

"Everything doesn't look fine. Do I need to call the fire department?"

Why would you call the fire department? Do you see a fire?!

"No need."

"You sure?"

"Absolutely positive. We're just getting everything together, that's all. You and Jonathan can go ahead and sit at the dinner table if you'd like."

"I hope you're not bringing those to the table." She twisted her face in disdain as she pointed to the dinner rolls. "They look burnt."

"Of course not," I said with a fake laugh. The last thing I wanted was for her to know she was getting under my skin. Gavin had already given her a small victory. I was not about to let her have any more.

"Just making sure. I know you're new to this whole cooking thing. I didn't want you to think that was suitable."

I opened my mouth to snap at her, but quickly returned it to a smile. Snapping was what she wanted me to do. I refused to give her the satisfaction.

"We'll be right out, Sylvia," I said as nicely as I could.

She hesitated for a moment, but finally left Gavin and me alone. I snatched the pan of burned dinner rolls away from him and threw them in the trash.

"It's starting already," I grumbled. "She's giving me a hard time already, after I slaved in this kitchen all day to feed her evil behind."

"Will you relax already? Goodness. You're just tense because you've made such a big deal about this dinner, and it's making you overreact."

"Don't try to act like that wasn't malicious. You know that it was. And I heard what she said about her banana pudding, too. Her safety dish? *Really?*"

"Well..."

I turned around slowly to face him, a warning to be careful with his next words.

"She kinda has a point," he stupidly agreed.

"You must want to eat those burned dinner rolls. I will take them out of the trash and put them on your plate."

"Don't start acting crazy. I'm just saying—"

"You're just saying, once again, that she's right and I'm wrong. I gave her very simple instructions, and she refused to follow them out of spite. You know I can cook. I've taught myself very well since we've been married, despite working sixty plus hours a week. But do you tell her that? No. You just agree with her that this dinner needs a safety dish, even though you were dipping your fingers in the dessert before she got her."

"No one makes you work all those hours."

I dropped the empty pan into the sink with a loud clang. "We're not talking about work right now," I told him. "We're not starting that argument."

"You're the one who brought it up."

"I was making a point. You know, the least you could have done was told her that you were the one who burned the rolls. You know she's going to find some way to antagonize me about them. She'll use them as yet another example of how I fail at being a wife and mother to you and Jonathan."

He sighed heavily and rubbed his temples the way he always did when I started to get on his nerves. He was tired of hearing the drama between his mother and me, which I understood. However, it would all go away if he corrected Sylvia the way he needed to.

"Fine, I'll be pleasant," I told him. "For the sake of this dinner that *you* suggested I put on. But if she starts acting crazy and disrespecting me, you better have my back. I mean it. I'm sick of her crap."

"Yeah, yeah," he said, and gave my behind a firm smack of correction for being so short with him as I walked out of the kitchen.

I wanted to be mad at him, but the surprise of it made me blush. I both loved and hated being so weak for him. It made it difficult to stay angry with him when I needed to—like right now, because he burned the dinner rolls. But he was my husband, and being quick to forgive him proved how much in love with him I really was. They were, after all, just dinner rolls. Remaining peaceful with him was more important.

When Gavin and I entered the dining room, I was irritated to see that Sylvia was sitting in my seat. Gavin didn't seem to mind. He took his usual position at the head of the table, and Jonathan sat across from her, trying to be as patient as his little body would allow in front of a table full of food. He was nearly salivating.

"Dana, this spread looks absolutely wonderful," Sylvia told me.

"Thank you," I said, a bit surprised that she actually gave me a compliment. That was nice of her, but she still had to move. "I'm sorry, Sylvia, but you're in my seat."

Her face fell. "Your seat?"

"Yes, ma'am. I always sit next to Gavin. I was thinking you could sit here," I told her, and tapped the remaining available seat.

"But I want to sit by you, dear," she pouted at Gavin.

He smiled at her then gave me sad eyes, as if to plead with me not to break his mother's heart.

I decided to play the guilt game, too.

"Baby," I whined with a pout of my own, "don't you want to sit next to me?"

He turned to Sylvia. "Mama, would you mind—"

"My knees, baby," she complained. "And my back..." She winced as if she were in pain and began to rub herself. "You not gon' make me get up, are you? Not after I drove all the way over here. You know how old I am. These bones are weary, son."

He looked at me with the same pitiful eyes, but I pierced my own back at him. He saw that I was annoyed and suggested that Jonathan trade seats with me so that he and I could sit next to each other.

"Don't make the boy move," Sylvia stopped him. "He's already seated. There's no point in disrupting the child. Dana can sit where she is. It's only one meal. What will it hurt?"

Evil witch!

Gavin didn't object. He shrugged as if there was nothing more that he could do and motioned for me to sit down. Feeling outnumbered, I reluctantly sat across from him.

"There you go," Sylvia smiled at me. "See? Isn't this nice?"

I gave her a fake smile and placed my napkin in my lap.

"Grandma, I set the table," Jonathan boasted.

"You did?"

"Yeah. But Mommy made the food."

"*Yeah?*" Gavin asked. "Is that how you talk to your grandmother?"

Jonathan leaned back in his seat and stared at Gavin with his face twisted, not understanding at all what his father was talking about.

"Remember the discussion we've been having about manners?" I tried to remind him. He always took correction from his father hard, and I wanted to spare his gentle feelings. He shook his head at me, though, not knowing what I was talking about, either.

"*Yes, ma'am,*" Gavin corrected him. "Your grandmother is not your homeboy. Speak to her with respect."

"Oh," he said. "Sorry, Grandma."

"That's all right, baby," she said, and gave him an encouraging pat on the back. "Grandma knows your heart, sweetie."

"So you know I'm hungry, too, right?"

We all laughed. I was thankful. His cuteness released some of the tension in the air.

"Yes, baby. I am, too," Sylvia told him. "Let's say grace so we can eat!"

We all joined hands and Gavin instructed us to bow our heads. Before he began to pray, Sylvia asked him if she could. He agreed.

"Dear Lord, thank You for being You," she began. "Thank You for allowing us to gather here today, in the lovely home that You have allowed my son to live in with his son and the woman that he married."

My head snapped up and my eyes popped open. Everyone else continued to pray as if they hadn't noticed that she just insulted me to Jesus.

"Let this food be nourishing to our bodies, Lord," she continued. "And tasty, too, because we know that Dana really doesn't know how to season all that well. We don't want the meat to be too dry and choke us Lord, so please let it have some tenderness."

Gavin's head came up, too. He looked at me, then stared at his mother with disapproval, but she kept praying as if she hadn't said anything offensive.

"We know she's not a great cook, like me. But bless her for trying, Lord. Please protect our stomachs from anything that would harm us. In Jesus' name we pray. Amen."

"Amen," Jonathan said.

I kept my eyes on Gavin. If I looked at Sylvia I was going to slam her face into the bowl of mashed potatoes sitting in front of her.

Gavin cleared his throat. "Mama, that was an... interesting prayer."

"The Lord knows my heart, dear," she said firmly. "Shall we eat?"

Gavin was annoyed, but told her yes and stood up to slice the roast. I passed her the bowl of carrots sitting in front of me, then began to fix Jonathan's plate.

"How's the food, Mama?" Gavin asked once we all began to eat.

She frowned. "It's a good try, but it's a little bland."

My eyebrows went up at her claim. "Excuse me?"

"Don't be offended, Dana. It's nothing that a little salt and pepper won't fix. It'll actually go a long way, if you use some."

I dropped my fork and let it clang against my plate. "Salt and... Sylvia, this food is not bland," I snapped. "I got this pork recipe from Emeril Lagasse, and the mashed potatoes from Gordon Ramsay. They're world-renowned chefs, and I followed their recipes perfectly. All of the ingredients are organic and fresh."

"Okay, and that's fine, dear," she told me. "I'm just saying that *my plate* could use a little salt and pepper."

Angry, I picked up the salt and pepper shakers from the center of the table and sat them down firmly in front of her.

"Thank you," she said a moment later, and began to douse her food with salt. "Would you like some, Gavin?"

"No," I answered for him, and dared him with my eyes to defy me.

"I'm good, Mama," he told her.

Jonathan tapped my hand. "I think it's really good, Mommy."

I thanked him. I really wanted to hug him, but didn't want to fall apart completely at the table. He was the sweetest kid I knew, and always knew just what to say to make me feel better.

"I think it's good, too," Gavin told me. "Thank you for working so hard to make this meal for us, babe."

"Yeah, thank you," Jonathan added.

They both looked to Sylvia to do the same, but she only continued to season and sample her food as if she still weren't satisfied. Finally she gave up and put her fork down, content with not eating, and asked Jonathan what he'd learned at school recently. While he gave her an elaborate answer I focused on my husband. My glare made him uncomfortable. He continued to eat nervously while I bit my tongue to keep it from becoming unruly.

Sylvia became excited once Jonathan finished talking to her. Her face lit up and she grabbed Gavin's hand. "You will never guess who I ran into the other day!"

"Who?"

"Tanya!"

"Tanya...?" He waited for her to give a last name.

"Tibideaux. From back home," she beamed.

Gavin's face grew long, but he remained quiet while Sylvia continued to smile.

"Who's Tanya?" Jonathan asked.

"One of your father's friends from high school," she answered.

"Eat your food, son," Gavin told him quickly, and shook his head at me, discouraging me from asking any questions.

I knew then who she was talking about.

That Tanya.

"Yes! I was at Macy's, and I looked up, and there she was," Sylvia continued. "She's looking good, too, son. Just as beautiful as she's always been."

"Mama..." Gavin's voice cracked as he looked down at his plate and continued to shake his head. He was clearly bothered, but Sylvia didn't care to notice. She kept smiling as if she'd just delivered the best news in the world.

I was uncomfortable, too, and wondered about her mental state. What woman in her right mind would go on and on about her son's ex-girlfriend in front of his wife? How could she possibly think that was okay? She probably thought she was going over my head and covertly relaying information to my husband unbeknownst to me. But that was stupid, because Gavin and I knew each others' pasts. I knew all about Tanya and the way she broke his heart. She was his first love. They were high school sweethearts and he wanted to marry her, but she broke up with him to be with someone else. Gavin shared with me that Sylvia had always treated her like a daughter up until that point.

"Isn't it such a small world?" Sylvia continued, despite how uneasy he was. "It's amazing how God will fix things for you. Just when you think you've lost it all, God will provide a ram in the bush."

I stared at her in bewilderment. Did she even know what she was talking about? Or was this another instance of her cherry-picking scriptures and twisting them to fit her own ill-meaning interpretation?

"I haven't lost anything, Mama," Gavin said, to which she responded with a face full of doubt. "There's no need for any rams in bushes because nothing is being sacrificed."

"Well, not literally. But you know what I mean."

"No, I don't. But I can tell you who did sacrifice, though. Dana sacrificed her entire Sunday to make this meal for us. You know she has that big presentation to make at the hospital in the morning, and she could be focusing on that, but she went out of her way to make this meal for us."

Sylvia looked my way, and for a split second I thought she was going to give all of my effort some type of positive acknowledgement, but she only sipped her tea and told us that it needed more sugar.

Gavin cleared his throat. "Dana, why don't you tell Mama about your presentation in the morning?"

"Oh yes," I agreed to with a smile, and proudly sat up straighter in my seat.

Last year I decided to expand my interior design business to include architecture as well. I became interested in it shortly after Gavin and I got married and decided to become licensed. Since then not much opportunity had come up in the area for me, until last month when it was announced that the local hospital was looking to reconstruct their west wing. I pounced on the opportunity, but because so many other firms in the area wanted the job, I had to put a bid in. The hospital was interested, and since they let me know I'd been working tirelessly on the presentation I would give them tomorrow morning.

"I have come up with the most brilliant design for Daytown Memorial," I told Sylvia. "You will love it. Everyone's going to want to get sick just so they can see how spectacular it is. Honestly, it's so fantastic, I wish I could just rebuild the entire hospital. When it's finished, it's actually going to look like a—"

"That's nice, dear. Can I *please* have some sugar for my tea?" She took another sip of her drink and frowned. "Now, please? This honestly tastes like brown water with a few drops of lemon juice in it. You know, I keep a bowl of sugar on my table all the time when I have guests over."

Of course you do, because you're perfect and I'm not.

I couldn't help but slouch. Sylvia wasn't interested in reconciling with me at all. The woman hated me, and it showed.

"I'll get it for you," Jonathan told her.

"Thank you, sweetie," she said, and waited patiently for him to get the bowl off the kitchen counter. "He loves his grandmother so much."

He proved it by placing a kiss on her cheek, then return to his food.

The doorbell rang suddenly. Gavin and I exchanged inquisitive glances as we tried to figure out who it could have been. We weren't expecting any more guests.

"I'll get it," Gavin said.

"No, no. Let me," I nearly begged, and stood up quickly. "You stay here and entertain... *her.*"

I ignored Sylvia's offended scowl and went to the door. Through the peephole I observed a stranger standing on our porch. She seemed harmless enough. She was well put together and her long hair fell lightly around her shoulders and blew softly in the breeze. But why was she ringing my doorbell? Was she selling something? She couldn't have been a Jehovah's Witness. Not in that tight fitting dress. She was showing too much cleavage to be holy. Maybe she got into an accident off the main road and needed help. She looked like she had money, though. She was carrying a designer handbag. A woman with a bag like that surely had a cell phone inside. And AAA. Maybe she was simply at the wrong house.

"Yes?" I asked through the door as I watched her.

She stood up straighter when she heard my voice, and leaned closer to the door. "Sylvia? Is that you?"

Sylvia? Who in the world is looking for her at my house?

I opened the door slowly and poked my head out. "Can I help you?"

"Hi," she smiled at me. "I'm not sure I'm at the right address. Is Sylvia Gardner here?"

"Tanya!" I heard Sylvia cheer from behind me.

I froze in horror as I realized who was standing on my doorstep.

Tanya.

That Tanya.

Here.

At my house.

My mother-in-law rushed to the door and pushed me to the side so she could eagerly wrap her arms around this woman who had the nerve to show up at my house in full glam mode. Everything about her was fashion forward—from her makeup and full hair extensions to her dress and open-toed pumps. She had the nerve to have a fresh pedicure, too. And she was wearing Spanx. She had to be. Her arms were too fluffy for her waist to be that tight.

"Hi, Sylvia," the intruder said as she hugged her back. "I made it."

"It's so good to see you, dear. Come on in," Sylvia said, and pulled the woman into the house.

Tanya eagerly agreed, and smiled at me as they passed.

I stood at the door with my mouth open and felt like a complete fool as I tried to figure out what the heck just happened. Did my husband's ex-girlfriend from high school just show up at my house? Had my mother-in-law invited her? Did she really just *push* me out of the way to present her to my husband? *In my own house?!* After I slaved in the kitchen *all day for her?!* And did this chick just strut past me, ready to prance in front of my husband with painted toenails and Spanx on?!!! *Without even introducing herself to me?!!!!!!*

I closed the door and returned to the dining room. Everyone was standing, except Jonathan, who was too busy eating to be bothered.

"Mama, what's going on?" Gavin asked nervously. As brown as he was, his face seemed to grow paler with each second that passed.

"I know I surprised you, son," Sylvia told him, and pulled Tanya close as she stood beside him. "But I thought it would be good for you two to see each other again. Isn't this such a nice surprise?"

"Surprise!" Tanya beamed, and wrapped her arms around Gavin and gave him a strong squeeze, pressing her boobs that were big enough to feed the entire continent of Africa against him. He moved away quickly, but she was so happy to see him that she didn't notice.

"Wow," was all he could say, and he diverted his attention to me. He immediately saw how unamused I was. More like enraged. I was so angry that my ears burned. I could feel heat radiating from me, and it threatened to disintegrate the entire room the longer Tanya kept her grabby hands on my man. The sickening part was that Sylvia smiled with pride as if she'd just saved the world. She took special delight in the appearance of my husband's ex. She was so thrilled that she could barely contain herself. I'd never seen her so pleased.

"Mama, what's going on, here?" Gavin demanded to know.

Sylvia played coy by not answering, which angered me more. Loud thumps burst into my ears each time she batted her wicked eyelashes. I could feel my heart beating faster the angrier I got, and I begged the Lord to keep me from jumping on Tanya and wrapping my hands around her throat.

She's trying to replace me.

It had never been more clear to me than at this moment. Sylvia didn't want me to be a part of her family. She wanted things back to the way they were before I came into the picture. There was no point in me even trying to form any type of relationship with her. I'd been married to her son for two years now, and it still hadn't happened. I was never going to be good enough for Gavin in her eyes. I'd spent the entire day slaving in a hot kitchen to feed her, her son, and her grandson, and she thanked me by insulting the food and bringing a whore into my house. I didn't deserve this. I was not a horrible wife, nor was I a horrible person, but she was for trying to destroy my family.

"Tanya's been living in Dallas for about six months now," Sylvia told Gavin. "After Katrina she and her family relocated to Houston, but now she's in Dallas. Isn't that something? This whole time she's been so close."

I cleared my throat to get their attention, but the attempt was ignored.

"She's been here for a few months, but she still doesn't know much about the area. I told her that you wouldn't mind taking her around and showing her everything the area has to offer. I know you're busy with work and the baby, but you can make time for an old friend, can't you?"

"I, um... I..."

You better stand up for me, Gavin! You're my husband! Put her in her place! Tell her you wouldn't dare take this woman anywhere because married men don't do disrespectful things like that!

"I... Mama, that's..."

Ugh. He'll never go against his precious mother.

Rage came over me. I wanted to grab both of these scallywags by their hair and drag them all over the house while they kicked and screamed and begged for mercy and forgiveness. They committed the ultimate crime, and I would see to it that they suffered the painful consequences. Sylvia, especially. She should have been on her knees every night thanking God for me. I was a good wife to her son. I was loyal, and faithful, and committed to our marriage, and had done absolutely nothing to deserve being treated this way. If she thought I was just going to stand to the side and watch while she tried to set my husband up on a date, she had another thing coming!

Sylvia continued to dote over Tanya while I watched, nearly seething, with clenched fists. Tanya was just as bad, pretending to simply be an old friend. Clearly she came up to get Gavin back. No woman showed up unannounced at an ex's house dressed like that if she wasn't trying to get him. I wasn't worried about her, though. She didn't have a chance with Gavin. I was confident that I was the only woman he would give his devotion to. But Sylvia... She needed to be put in her place. *Now.*

I cleared my throat again to get their attention, but the only person who noticed this time was Jonathan. Though he was a child, he seemed to be the only one bright enough to realize that I was about to go off. He watched me with extreme worry and caution. I knew all of my bearings were about to escape me, so I sent him upstairs to his room, allowing him to take his food with him, and told him not to come out until I told him he could. At this point Gavin looked concerned, but not enough to tell Tanya to keep her hands off of him, or to chastise his mother for bringing her into our house.

"Excuse me, Tanya?"

She faced me and smiled like an idiot. "Yes?"

"You need to get out of my house."

Her smile slowly went away, along with Sylvia's. They both stared at me with shock.

"Excuse me?" she asked.

I moved closer so she could hear me better. Apparently, not only was she a home wrecker, but she was deaf, too.

"I said *you need to get out of my house.*"

"That is not the way you speak to a guest," Sylvia scolded me.

"She's not a guest. I didn't invite her. You did, which is why you need to get out, too. Now."

She gasped loudly while Tanya asked Gavin what was going on.

"Wait a minute," Gavin tried to stop me. "Everybody, let's just keep a cool head about this. Obviously there has been a misunderstanding, and before we let our emotions take control, let's just—"

"Who are you?" Tanya asked me.

"I'm his wife."

The news caught her off guard. Her eyes flared with shock, and she quickly turned them on Sylvia, accusing her of betrayal. Unable to handle it, Sylvia chose to focus on me.

"Don't you dare take that tone of voice with me, young lady! Have some respect!"

"Respect?!" I nearly laughed in her face. "After you brought this tramp to my house? Are you *freaking serious?!!!* Are you trying to pimp your son out now, or what?!"

"I didn't know you were married," Tanya whispered to Gavin.

"Of course you didn't," I told her. "She thought she was going to be able to slide you in right under my nose because she thought I didn't know you were my husband's ex-girlfriend. But what she refuses to accept and *respect* is that we are married. We know each other's pasts."

Sylvia was frozen by her own horrific embarrassment. Her wicked plan was falling apart right before her eyes, and we all watched with severe judgment.

"Do something!" she pleaded to Gavin a moment later. "Don't let her talk to me like that!"

He moved closer to me and tried to place his hand on my shoulder. "Let's just try to be rational about all of this, okay?"

I swatted his and away. "Don't you dare. Not after this. You should be just as mad as I am!"

"There's no need to become aggressive."

"You want her here?" I asked, pointing to Tanya. Before he could answer, I warned him, "You better remember who you're married to. I'm not playing this game with either one of them."

"I'm just gonna go," Tanya excused herself, and tiptoed toward the door.

"Wait," Sylvia stopped her. "You don't have to go."

"Yes, she does!" I declared. "Both of you need to get out!"

"You can't talk to my mama that way," Gavin fussed at me.

"You heard what I said!" I yelled at them both.

Tanya rolled her eyes and threw her hands up in the air as she left. Sylvia continued to beg her to stay while Gavin told me to let him handle things from now on.

"Are you happy now?" Sylvia snapped at me once it was clear Tanya wasn't coming back. "She's gone."

"I'm half happy. You're still standing here."

"Dana!" Gavin rebuked me.

"How dare you talk to me like that!" she ranted. "Tanya has done nothing to you, and neither have I. If you are not secure enough in your marriage to meet one of his old friends without falling apart at the seams, then maybe you're not as good a wife as you'd like to think. But don't you ever try to take it out on me!"

"Oh, it's my fault now?"

"You're the one acting crazy."

"Let me handle this," Gavin begged me again, but I ignored him.

"I'm not crazy," I continued. "You are if you thought I was just going to sit back and let you get away with that. You can play dumb all you want, but nobody believes that was innocent. If it was, you would have told us she was coming, but you didn't. Why? Because you were trying to be slick, and I don't appreciate it. It was asinine, and deplorable, and disgraceful, and disgusting, and downright sickening."

"Ugh!" she screamed. "Who do you think you are?!"

"I *know* that *I am* his wife!" I screamed back.

"For right now! But I will always be his mother!"

Gavin gasped. *"MAMA!"*

I took a step back, wounded by her words. She may as well have kicked me in my face and spit on me.

"There it is," I said as I clapped my hands and tried not to cry. "After all this time, you finally admit how you really feel. You want him to divorce me."

"Dana, let me handle this," Gavin begged.

"Well, you can forget about it," I told her, "because nobody over here is getting divorced!"

"Dana!" Gavin yelled at me. "Let me handle it!"

"You never handle anything!" I snapped at him.

"You need to calm down!"

"NO! I will not calm down!" I screamed. Of all the times he should have had my back, right now was it. "Get her out of my house! RIGHT NOW! I'm sick of trying to be nice to her! TELL HER TO LEAVE!"

"Lower your voice," he demanded, and grabbed me by my arm to show me how serious he was. "Don't talk to me like that. I'm your husband."

"But she can say whatever she wants to me?! What is wrong with you?!"

"DANA!"

"ENOUGH!" Sylvia screamed.

The outburst startled us into silence. She'd said and done a lot of nasty things before, but I'd never heard her be so forceful before.

"Son, I love you," Sylvia told Gavin as he let go of me. "I really do. But I will never allow a woman like this to talk down to me, so I'm leaving. I've tried to be nice, but I'm done trying to save you from your bad decisions. If you had any sense, you'd leave with me."

My mouth hung open as she got her purse out of the closet and slammed the door behind herself as she walked out of the house.

"We will talk about this when I get back," Gavin said sternly, and followed her outside.

When the door closed again, I buried my face in my hands and screamed. I tried hard not to, but I was too angry to keep myself from crying. I knew Sylvia wanted me out of her life, but I never would have imagined she'd go to this extent, nor did I ever dream that Gavin's would openly reprimand me for trying to defend our marriage. He swore up and down that I came first in his life, but instead of standing beside me, comforting me like he should have been, he was more concerned with his mother and her feelings. As. Always. Even after she did something so atrocious.

I forced myself to stop crying and began to clear the dining table. Dinner was most definitely over. After all the slaving I did, the food was only going to end up stored away in various containers in the fridge. Most of it would probably spoil and end up getting thrown out. Prayerfully, my marriage wouldn't, too.

As I brought the food into the kitchen, my eyes fell on Sylvia's bowl of banana pudding. I emptied it into the trash, then tossed the bowl in as well, and took the bag to the garage for Gavin to get rid of in the morning.

"No one in this house is ever eating banana pudding again!"

I went back into the house and washed my hands, then finished putting all of the food away. The sink was now piled high with stacks of dirty dishes from all of the labor I'd done, but I was in no mood to clean them. Twenty minutes had passed, and Gavin was still outside talking to his mother. The longer he stayed outside with her, the angrier I became. I felt like I was being cheated on. I was supposed to consume his love, loyalty, time, and dedication, especially after I was attacked. But instead he was giving all of that to her. What was wrong with him? Why couldn't he see that he was just as wrong as she was?

Emotionally overwhelmed, I prepared a slice of cake and a glass of milk and sat down at the table.

"This is good," I told myself after taking a bite, and thanked my brother Sean, the greatest baker I knew, for giving it to me. Over the past few years we'd grown closer to one another, and he knew how important this meal was to me and gave me his secret recipe. He really wanted me to wow Sylvia. For one, he knew how often she tried to criticize me for not being a great cook in her eyes, but he also loved Gavin and wanted our marriage to last. Both he and Leah, my sister, did. They were the only family I had, and they loved Gavin, and it hurt to know that his mother didn't feel the same way about me.

I ate more cake and wished that Sylvia had gotten the chance to taste it. I'd had her banana pudding before, and it didn't have anything on the chocolate goodness I'd baked. She would have bent over with envy and taken that ridiculous so-called "safety dish" and thrown it away herself. The humiliation she felt would have been so satisfying. But then again, she probably would have come up with something even more extreme than bringing her son's ex to my house to get even with me. Maybe the German chocolate cake, as good as it was, wasn't worth it.

"I'm not doing this anymore," I said out loud, and tried to enjoy my cake as hot tears fell from my eyes. I couldn't help but be hurt. How could she do something so mean and evil to me? What had I ever done to deserve my husband divorcing me? Nothing. She'd crossed the line, and I was done trying to make her happy. From now on I would only concern myself with Gavin, the person I shared a covenant with before God, and Jonathan. I was done with her.

The front door opened. I was too disgusted to even look at my husband. I dried my tears and ate the last of my cake, then asked, "Is she gone?"

He didn't answer me. He was angry, which made me even angrier. How could he have the audacity to be upset with me? I didn't bring that woman into this house. His mother did. But of course, I was in the wrong. I always was when it came to her.

"I really wish you had let me handle it," he finally said.

I turned my nose up at him and drank the rest of my milk.

"Don't be rude."

"Did you tell her that? Because what she did was definitely rude."

"I'm not talking about her right now. I'm talking about you."

"Sure you are. Because it's my fault, isn't it? She brought another woman in here, but I'm getting the lecture. Okay."

"I understand why you're upset. But you could have handled that better. She's my mother. You didn't have to talk to her that way."

He'll never get it. He'll never understand.

I covered my face and screamed in frustration. I couldn't talk to him anymore. Not right now.

I stood up and put my dishes in the sink, then walked past him and made my way to the stairs.

"We're not gonna talk about this?"

"No," I said, but then thought for a moment. "Tell me something, Gavin. How would you feel if my brother or sister brought J. Kameron to dinner, unannounced?"

The mention of my ex-fiancé left him speechless. He only stared at me with apologetic eyes, but his lips didn't render the request for forgiveness that they should have.

"Thought so," I said, and sadly walked up the stairs. "I cooked all day, so you wash the dishes," I called over my shoulder, and went into our bedroom and closed the door.

TWO
GAVIN

I didn't realize how much better I slept with Dana lying against my chest until she spent the entire night on the other side of the bed. We argued for hours after Mama left, and she vowed never to speak to her again, which broke my heart. I love my mother very much, and I couldn't stand feeling like I had to choose between them. But I couldn't blame Dana for feeling the way she did.

When Tanya walked into the dining room I thought my mind was playing tricks on me. I hadn't seen or even thought about her in years, and I was so shocked to see her that I didn't know what to say. There was no telling what Mama said or did to have her show up like that, but clearly none of it was honest. She didn't have a clue what she was walking into and was lucky she got out without getting hurt. Dana didn't play when it came to protecting our marriage, and I could see she was ready to drag Tanya. Poor girl. She didn't know I was married, which was why I kept trying to tell Dana to calm down, but she was over it. Now I realized that had the situation been reversed, like she suggested when she mentioned J. Kameron, I would have been just as angry.

A chill went through me just thinking about that guy. Dana reunited with him for a while during a breakup we had before we got married, and that was all I needed not to like him. I'd never like any man that got to hold and kiss her before, no matter who they were. Yeah, she had her past, just like I did, coming into our marriage with an ex-wife and a kid. But that didn't mean I wanted it thrown in my face. She knew it, too, so bringing his name up let me know for sure that I was in the dog house.

The situation with Tanya really wasn't my fault, though. I didn't tell Mama to invite her over. I didn't even know they were communicating with each other. Dana knew I would never condone that. She was upset because I didn't overreact the way she wanted me to by kicking Tanya out and going off on my mama. Since I didn't, she felt like I was taking their side, which wasn't the case at all. I was just as blindsided as she was, but before I could handle things she started going off on everybody. Even after I asked her to let me take care of things, she ignored me, then she went off on me for being outside with Mama for so long instead of in the house with her. Was I supposed to just let Mama leave as angry as she was? The only reason I was out there so long was because she started talking crazy, saying she was going to try to get custody of Jonathan because Dana was a bad mother. I could never let that happen. But I could never tell Dana about that. Oh, no. Things would certainly get out of control then.

I just didn't understand why there had to be all of this drama. It was Mama, really. The whole world could see that I was in love with Dana, but she refused to accept it. She insisted that we were wrong for each other. Yes, we had our problems, but what married couple didn't? I didn't even recognize her last night. The woman who raised me had never been that vicious. To say I should get a divorce was extremely hurtful, especially after the horrible separation my first wife and I went through. Mama was a divorced woman herself. Why would she want to inflict that type of pain onto another woman—especially as a Christian? She knew God hated divorce, and Dana hadn't done anything to warrant it.

I was partly to blame. I didn't introduce them to each other until two days after we got married, but instead of being angry with me about it, Mama chose to blame Dana. She claimed that as a woman, Dana should have insisted on meeting her, out of respect. That started them out on the wrong foot, and unfortunately things never got better between them.

Honestly, I knew Mama wouldn't like Dana. She'd always been very vocal about her disdain for independent, spirited women like Dana, and I wanted to enjoy my relationship with her without any negativity. Had I known that Mama would hold it against Dana forever, I would have made a different choice. It wasn't like she didn't know who Dana was. She knew of our relationship. But I decided to pop the question spontaneously, and after Dana said yes we went straight to the courthouse. That explanation was never good enough for Mama. To this day she unfairly held it against her.

The problem was that Mama had an old-fashioned mentality about women and their role in the family structure. She felt that a wife's main duty was to give her husband children and serve her family relentlessly by cooking and taking care of the house while the husband worked. As she put it, Dana didn't know how to take care of a man. She said she was too modern, too independent, and didn't know how to run a household. Granted, Dana wasn't the best housekeeper, and she didn't even know how to cook when we met. But, in her defense, the woman did work sixty hours a week, and sometimes even more. As great as my mother was, if she worked that many hours outside of the home, her house wouldn't be immaculate either. But Dana didn't have to worry about that because she had me. I took up the slack. I loved my wife and didn't have a problem balancing out her shortcomings. She did the same for me. That was what being married was all about.

I personally liked that my wife was career driven. Sure, I wished she were home more. Jonathan and I needed her, and I was growing weary of being at home alone all the time. It left me bored, and at times I felt like I was still single. We hadn't been on a date in months. She was always either swamped with work or too tired to go out. I had to suck it up, though, and be supportive. Things were going to be worse when she got the job remodeling the hospital. Besides, it wouldn't be fair of me to hold her career against her. She had her business before she met me, and I knew her responsibilities as an entrepreneur placed a lot of weight on her shoulders.

I would never tell my mother these things, though. I could only tell her that I loved that Dana found a way to turn her passion of interior decorating into a very lucrative business. I had no room to really complain at all. Financially, we didn't have to worry about a thing. Sadly, I believe that was my mother's real issue with Dana.

Unlike my mother, Dana made her own money, therefore she didn't have to depend on me for anything. If she wanted something, she went out and bought it on her own. She made twice as much money as I did. A lot of men would be intimidated by that, but I wasn't. Her success allowed us to live comfortably and enjoy many things in life that others couldn't. Our home was set to be paid off in half the time that I mortgaged it for when I initially purchased it. It was furnished with all of the latest in home appliances. Only a crazy person wouldn't love living here. Both of our vehicles were paid off, and even though Jonathan was only seven, he already had a college fund. Who wouldn't be happy for a family in that position? My mother, that's who.

Though she appreciated that I purchased a home for her here in Daytown after she lost everything in Hurricane Katrina, I think the financial security Dana's success allowed us to have was a painful reminder of all the bad choices Mama made in her own life. She married my father right after high school and became the dutiful housewife she'd always been taught she was supposed to be. I was born a year later, and a year after that my dad left. Because she depended on him to take care of her, we were forced to move in with my grandmother. She never remarried, and they always struggled to make ends meet. Now she had this daughter-in-law running around in ridiculously expensive clothes, constantly reminding her that she could never afford any of it, and she passively aggressively took it out on her by inviting my ex to dinner. Crazy. But I could never voice this revelation. Mama would go off, and Dana would say instead of being mad, Mama should ask her to teach a class on how to be fabulous. Mama would then call Dana arrogant, and another argument would follow.

That was because Mama hated Dana's shopping habit. She said it was stupid and wasteful. I had to agree with Mama on this, though I initially appreciated that she liked to present herself well. When I found out how much money she spent on her clothes and accessories, I realized she had a problem. Her shoe collection was worth thousands of dollars, and some of them she didn't even wear. They were either too beautiful to get scuffed, or she didn't have the perfect outfit to wear with them yet. I was the type of guy who would wear anything as long as it was clean and fit well. Not my wife. She had to have the best of everything, no matter how much it cost, regardless of if she really needed it or not. She actually spent five hundred dollars on a sweater, and she only wore it once. What a waste! That money could have been used to feed the homeless, or buy school supplies for an underprivileged child, or even given to a scholarship fund to help someone go to college. I've suggested these things to her in the past, but she never seemed interested. I didn't get it. Granted, she worked hard, and she always made sure our household expenses were taken care of, which was a lot more than I could say about other women I've been with. She could afford everything that she purchased, but I just didn't think that because she *could* meant that she *should*.

The issue Mama was the most vocal about was the fact that Dana hadn't got pregnant yet. It was a sensitive subject that I tried desperately to avoid talking to her about, but she brought it up every month like clockwork, as if the pain of Dana getting her period didn't bring me enough heartache. She argued that in this day and age, a woman in her thirties who didn't have a baby yet didn't have one because she didn't want one. In her opinion, Dana should have been trying desperately to have a baby, but she wasn't, which meant that she didn't want one.

I tried to tell her that she had my wife all wrong, but she insisted I would see it for myself one day. She didn't know that Dana and I had been trying our entire marriage to have a baby. We just hadn't been able to conceive yet. It was frustrating, but we prayed together and asked God to bless us with children, and we believed that He would. We just had to be patient and keep the faith. I was getting pretty desperate for a baby, though. I was thirty-eight now, and she was thirty-three. I'd always wanted five kids, and I'd wanted to have them by the time I was forty. That didn't leave us with a lot of time, which was why I wanted to visit a fertility specialist, just to make sure we both were healthy. But whenever I brought it up, Dana always resisted, saying she wanted to conceive the natural way. The idea of needles, Petri dishes, test tubes, and doctors in lab coats all seemed too scientific and gave her a Frankenstein vibe. I understood, but I would feel better about it if she would at least have bloodwork done. I told her I would get checked too, but she wouldn't hear of it, so I chose not to pressure her about it anymore. She had enough on her plate and didn't need to hear me whining about our reproductive systems. She didn't seem to be too worried. She only brought up having a baby when I did.

But I didn't want to focus on that right now. I didn't want to be mad, or fight, or get fussed at. Right now I just wanted to have sex.

I rolled over and watched my wife snore. At least one of us got some sleep. Even with curlers in her hair and a scarf on her head, she was more attractive than anyone else in the entire world to me. I wanted to prove it to her, too, before she jumped out of bed for work. But I doubted she'd want to have sex with me after the epic fight we had last night. Then again, she'd never turned me down before. She loved being intimate just as much as I did.

I told myself to let her sleep. She had her presentation at the hospital in a few hours and she needed her rest. I needed mine, too. I had a full day of work ahead of me, as well.

I closed my eyes and tried to fall asleep, but it wasn't happening. Unable to resist, I scooted closer to Dana and tugged at the blanket covering us as we lay on our California King bed. Her shoulder became exposed, but she only stirred at the surprise of cold air being blown against her skin from the ceiling vent directly above her. She pulled the blanket back over her and continued to snore.

I chuckled and slowly moved across the bed and pressed myself against her. Her eyes opened as I kissed her shoulder, but she moved away and teetered against the edge of the bed.

"Leave me alone," she fussed with a groggy voice.

She didn't threaten me. I still had a chance.

I pulled her into my waist and kissed her neck. She knew what I wanted.

"I'm sorry, baby," I apologized, and prayed the words would make her more receptive to my advance. For added emphasis, I ran my hand over her hips and thighs.

"Move," she moaned.

She wasn't mad anymore. I could tell. If she was she would have shoved me. She wanted me just as I wanted her.

"Please, baby," I whispered into her ear. "You know what I need."

She stopped my hand from sliding beneath her nightgown.

"I'm still mad at you," she claimed.

What she meant was that she still wanted to be. I understood. But she felt too good against me for us to continue last night's argument.

"I'm sorry," I told her again, and nibbled on her ear.

She quickly pulled away. "I'm for real," she snapped. Her hand immediately went over her mouth to protect me from her non-existent morning breath. The antic was silly, but she insisted on it every time we talked in bed before she got up and brushed her teeth.

"I know you are," I said, and kissed the back of her hand as I pulled it away.

She covered her mouth with her other hand. "You have to do something about your mother."

"I know. And I am."

"Today."

"Today?"

"Today. Not later, like you always say but never do. This craziness just can't go on," she told me.

"I know."

"Do you really?"

"Yes," I insisted, and covered her with more kisses.

She pulled away. "Are you sure? Because when it comes to her, you like to treat me like I'm your girlfriend, and I'm not your girlfriend. I'm your wife. You are supposed to cleave to me, like the Bible says, and you're not cleaving."

"I'm trying to right now," I whined, and buried my face in her neck.

"That scripture is not about sex," she scolded me. "It's about life. You and I are one now. In everything. It's not just about you anymore. It's about us."

I grumbled and rested against her chest. Now was not the time for a sermon.

Right now we needed to be fruitful and multiply.

"I know," I told her, and let my hands roam up and down her body. She became distracted, but continued to fuss.

"You better talk with her and lay down the law, and if she doesn't want to listen you need to make her. As a woman, I demand respect. But as my husband, you should demand that for me. I don't care who it's from. Your mother, the pastor, those little bad kids running around at Jonathan's school. Everybody. And I mean everybody. Your mom is just—"

"Bae," I finally hushed her. "You know what I'm trying to do right now. You wanna kill that by talking about my mama. Really?"

"I'm just saying that—"

"I'm just saying that right now all I wanna do is make love to you. Why don't you let me?"

"You're *such a perv*. I ought to not give you anything after what happened last night."

I pulled her completely beneath me and laid on top of her. "You know if you do that you'd only be punishing yourself."

She was too prideful to admit it. "Let me go to the bathroom first," she said.

I held on to her tightly and told her no. Every time we got ready to be intimate she jumped up and ran to the bathroom to freshen up. I appreciated the sentiment, but it always ruined the spontaneity of the moment. I wanted to make love to her without any interruptions.

"Move," she moaned after I refused to allow her to get up. "I need to brush my teeth."

"No, you don't," I told her, and kissed her through the squirming protest she gave. "Just make love to me."

She turned away and covered her mouth.

"I don't care about your breath," I insisted, and chuckled at how silly she was being. She was my wife, for goodness' sake.

She tried to get up again. "Let me go to the bathroom. While I'm in there you can go make sure Jonathan is asleep."

"Stop making excuses and fulfill your wifely duties."

She giggled. "I hate you so much."

"I love you, too," I told her, and wrapped her legs around me.

"*Ggggaaaavvviiiinnnnn...*"

Yep. I won.

****

"Oooohhh... *Baby,"* Dana breathed heavily as she wrapped herself in one of the sheets from the bed. "That was..." She couldn't finish her sentence. Her eyes seemed to smile as they rolled to the back of her head in satisfaction. Thank God I managed to put a smile on her face. There was nothing more torturous in the world than her being upset with me.

"I enjoyed it, too," I said proudly, and kissed her sweaty forehead.

She snuggled against me and rested her head against my chest as I wrapped my arm around her and let my hand settle on her backside. "What time is it, babe?"

"Relax. You got time."

"Good," she said with a sigh. "I love you so much, baby. I hate when we fight."

"Me, too," I agreed, and squeezed her tightly. She felt so good against me. We hadn't had a morning like this in a while.

"You know... I've been thinking."

Oh, Lord. Please not any more about Mama...

"'Bout what, babe?"

"The whole thing with your mom."

I sighed under my breath. "Can we please just enjoy our morning?"

"I'm not picking a fight," she promised. "I was just gonna say that I thought about it a little, and even though your mom was totally wrong last night, I may have been a little unfair, too. I think maybe I expected too much from her. I came into our marriage super excited that I was going to have a mother again. You know, since my mom died, there's always been this void." Her voice began to quiver. "It was hard growing up without her. Leah and Marcus were wonderful, and did the best they could, but they were kids, too. It was hard not having a mom and dad. But then I met you, and we got married, and I just assumed that she'd take me in and love me as her child, too. But that may not have been fair. She didn't even know me."

She stopped suddenly and dabbed at her eyes. My heart broke seeing her cry. She had a good point, though, one I never considered, and it made me feel even worse about what happened. If she'd been looking for Mama to fill the mother role that she lost as a child, surely the way Mama treated her had to be doubly hurtful.

"Don't cry, baby."

"I'm not," she tried to tell me as I rubbed her shoulders for support. "I'm fine, it's just... Urgh. I hate thinking about it."

"I understand," I said, and gave her a hug. "And I promise I'll talk to Mama today, okay? What happened last night can't happen again."

"Oh, it won't, because I'm never speaking to her again."

Before I could voice my concern, she continued.

"I've done all that I can do to try to make our relationship work, Gavin. I really have. I honestly just can't be around someone who's trying to break up my marriage. Like I said before, she's not my mother. She's yours. *I* have no obligation to her whatsoever, other than to love her, like the Bible says, and I can do that from a distance.

"What about forgiveness?"

Her face fell. I knew she felt convicted.

"I'm gonna have to pray about that," she confessed a few moments later. "And if I'm wrong in any way, I'm sure the Lord will show me. But for right now, for my own peace of mind, I can't be around her. Not unless she agrees to respect me and our marriage. Until then, she won't have the opportunity to mistreat me anymore. I love myself more than that."

She shifted in the bed and turned away with nothing more to say.

I cringed, hating that she felt the way she did. Somewhere along the line I'd allowed things to get this bad, and as a husband I'd failed at being her protector.

"I'm sorry, baby," I apologized as she settled against me again. "I'm gonna have a talk with Mama and get all of this straightened out."

Her silence proved that she didn't believe me. She gave me a kiss anyway and scurried out of bed.

"Where are you going so fast?"

"I gotta go to work."

"You're just gonna sex me and leave? Can't you just lay with me for a few minutes?" She didn't seem to understand. "Lay?"

"Yeah. You know... Just lay down and enjoy being with me."

"Aw, babe," she pouted. "You make me feel so bad. But I gotta—"

"Get back in the bed," I told her, and lifted the comforter so she could return to me. "I promise you won't be late for work."

"What time is it?" She froze, as if she didn't trust me.

I turned the clock on the nightstand around so she couldn't read it. An intense standoff followed. She stared at me with eyes that warned if I wasn't telling the truth I'd greatly regret it. Instead of cowering, I returned the glare with a threat of my own. If she didn't get back into bed, I was going to get up and give her another round of what she just had, then she'd *really* be late for work.

"Just a few minutes," she finally backed down, and returned to her previous position against me.

I was thankful. "See how nice this is," I said. "Just me and you in bed. Neither one of us rushing to get up. Can't you get used to this?"

She was trying her hardest to relax, but I could tell not being in control of the situation was driving her crazy.

"When was the last time we just stayed in the bed all day?" I asked her.

"Who has the time to do that?"

"You have to make the time. We should go somewhere nice that we haven't been before. And we'll do nothing but stay in the bed all day and make love. Doesn't that sound nice, instead of jumping up to work all the time?"

"You want to take a vacation?"

"Yes! We never got to take that honeymoon we planned. That's what we need. A nice honeymoon. A full week of love and intimacy. Then a baby will come."

She stiffened against me. So much for relaxing. I shouldn't have mentioned a baby.

"What time is it? It feels like it's late."

"It's not late."

"It feels like it," she insisted, and pulled back the blackout curtains hanging over the window behind our bed. She gasped at the sunlight that now beamed into the room. "Gavin!"

My stomach dropped. Apparently we'd made love for longer than I thought.

She reached over me and snatched the alarm clock. "OH MY GOD!" she gasped, and sprang out of bed. "GAVIN! I'M LATE!!!"

I caught the clock midair as she hurled it at my head. It was 8am.

"Will you calm down?" I pleaded as I watched her run into the bathroom. The bed sheet that was wrapped around her fell to the floor, leaving her completely naked, but she didn't care. I wasn't offended in the least. I loved the view, but she was overreacting. "You have plenty of time to get to work."

"No!" she yelled as she stepped into the glass shower, then yelped as the cold water hit her. "I have my presentation at the hospital in an hour. It's all the way across town! There's no way I'm going to get dressed and make it through traffic that fast. Gavin, you've messed up my morning! Messing around with you is gonna cost me the biggest job of my career!"

I watched her scramble to get clean in the shower. The scarf that protected her hair while she slept was lying on the bed next to me in the same spot it fell to during our makeup session. She had to be really frazzled. Dana never stepped foot inside the shower without it on her head unless she was washing her hair. If she didn't, it would be frizzy and unmanageable throughout the day, and she was too polished to have that. She always presented a pristine physical appearance, even if it was to simply step outside to check the mail.

"I'm sorry, baby. I didn't mean..."

She grunted with frustration as she continued to shower. "Just... Leave me alone..."

I watched her for a moment. She looked good with soap running down her body. *Real good.* And the water made her glisten as it trickled down her body. I wanted to join her, but not to get clean. I wanted to—

"Stop staring at me! You're not getting anything else this morning!"

I forced myself to calm down, then told her I was going to check on Jonathan. She thought it was a good idea, so I put on a pair of shorts and my robe, then went to his room. It was empty, but his bed was made, so I figured he was downstairs already. I found him in the kitchen eating a bowl of cereal.

"Good morning."

"Good morning, Daddy," he said. His eyes stayed glued to the television mounted on the wall the entire time. It was a wonder he even noticed me.

"How's the cereal?"

"Fine."

"Did you brush your teeth?"

"Yeah. And washed my face."

"Yeah?"

"Yeah, Daddy."

I cleared my throat. He finally pulled his attention away from the television and looked at my stern face.

"I mean, 'yes, sir.'"

"Good. Ready for school this morning?"

"Yes, sir... I think so."

I gave him a fist bump for realizing his mistake, then prepared myself a bowl of fruit to start my day. A few minutes later Dana bustled down the stairs. She'd swept her hair into a bun and applied a little makeup to her face. She wasn't as made-up as she usually was, but she still looked good, although I knew as soon as she got in her truck and checked her makeup she'd fuss at herself for cutting corners.

"Good morning, Mommy," Jonathan greeted her.

"Hey, baby," she said, and hurried to kiss him. "You have a good day at school today, okay? I'm sorry I can't spend any time with you right now. I'm running late."

"Aw, man."

"I know, sweetie. I'll make it up to you, okay? Promise."

"Yes, ma'am," he consented, then returned his attention to his cartoon.

"I love you, baby," Dana said quickly as she kissed me good-bye. "Wish me luck."

Before I could offer to pray with her, she ran out of the house, grabbing her keys and her portfolio on the way.

"She's gonna be tired, running like that," Jonathan said.

I chuckled and told him to finish eating his breakfast.

THREE
DANA

I jumped into my brand new Cadillac Escalade, then frantically pulled my cell phone out of my bag to call my assistant, Wendy. When the screen lit up I saw that I had a missed call from Leah. She was more than likely calling to see how my dinner with Sylvia went last night. I couldn't wait to tell her, but that conversation was going to be long, and I needed to call Wendy first.

"I'm at the hospital," she said as soon as she answered the call I gave her through the truck's media system. "And I have your coffee, too."

"Good," I told her as I backed out of the driveway. "But you may as well drink it. I'm gonna be late."

She was silent, undoubtedly shocked.

"Wendy? You there?"

"Yes, I'm here. What's wrong? Are you okay?" she asked.

"Yeah, yeah," I answered hurriedly. "I just got a late start this morning."

The explanation was juvenile, I knew, especially for one of the most important days of my career. But she would have to be satisfied with it. It was all the she was getting from me.

"What do you want me to tell them?" she asked, panic in her voice. "People are already here, ready to make their presentations, and we're up first. Do you want me to start for you? I can give them a little bit of information. You know, just until you get here."

"No," I said quickly, and prayed that my snappy reply didn't hurt her feelings. There was no way I could let Wendy speak on my behalf. I could see her now. Smacking on bubble gum and popping her lips, all the while butchering the English language as she told everyone she worked for me. "Just tell them I'm in traffic."

"Okay," she replied. Her worry was obvious.

"Everything will be fine. Don't worry," I said, talking more to myself than to her. "If they say it's a problem call me back."

"All right," she agreed, and hung up.

I forced myself to slow down as a stray dog crossed the street. The last thing

I needed to do was feel guilty all day about killing an animal. That was one of the downsides of moving out of the city. Random wandering animals without enough sense to move out of the way when thousands of pounds of machinery were barreling down on them.

"Move out of my way!" I screamed at the dog, then remembered I needed to return Leah's call.

"Hey, you," she greeted me when she answered the phone. "On your way to work?"

"Yes, my presentation is today. I'm on my way to it right now."

"Oooohh. Are you nervous?"

"Now I am, because I'm running late," I told her, and cringed when I checked my makeup in the rearview mirror. It didn't look right. It never did when I cut corners.

"*Oh*... That's not good, sis."

"I know..." I muttered.

"So.... Tell me, how did your dinner go last night?"

"GIRL!" I screamed, and became angry all over again just thinking about it.

"That bad?"

"You will not believe what that woman did!"

"Wait, wait, wait... I'm making my morning cup of tea. I can already tell whatever you're about to say is going to be crazy. Let me get to the couch first, so I don't miss anything."

I waited in silence, nearly fuming as I thought about Sylvia. I hadn't talked to Leah about my her in a while, but she was fully aware of the animosity between us.

"All right, dear," Leah said. I could hear her grunt as she sat down on her sofa. She was six months pregnant, and her expanding midsection made it challenging for her to get around. "Start from the beginning, and don't leave anything out."

I took a deep breath, then filled her in on what happened, including my decision to no longer communicate with Sylvia for the time being. She gasped and screamed throughout the story.

"That's so crazy!" she howled once I finished. "Why is she even bringing up old girlfriends? You and Gavin are married. That's just flat-out rude! I don't usually condone violence, but in this case, if you had slapped her I honestly don't know if I would blame you. What in the world is going on with Gavin? I can't believe he sat there and let you be disrespected like that."

"It's crazy, girl. I just don't get it. He's so strong when it comes to everything else, but turns into a little boy whenever she comes around. It's like he's scared she's gonna send him outside and make him get a switch."

"She's wrong," she told me with sympathy. "No one is ever supposed to try to break up anyone's marriage. That's between them and God, and she needs to respect that."

"Amen."

"And she needs to realize that Gavin is a grown man. Shoot. He asked you to marry him, not the other way around. He's nearly forty years old. If he's not capable of managing his own life by now, there wouldn't be anything she could do anyway. Lord, that woman needs to get a life and get over herself. No, she needs to get her own man."

I'd thought the same thing myself on several occasions, but never said it aloud.

"I'm for real," Leah continued. "That's what she needs. Her own man to keep her busy so she'll be too occupied to worry about her grown son who already has a wife taking care of him. Girl, I do not have the patience to deal with a woman like that. And she has the nerve to always want to call you silly? No. She's the one who is silly. She doesn't even realize she almost arranged a murder having that woman come to your house."

I laughed at the exaggeration. "I'm telling you, you're lucky your in-laws love you, girl. Because my mother-in-law..." I let out a frustrated grunt.

"Woosa, girl," Leah told me. "Jesus is just a prayer away. But if I were you I wouldn't fester on this too much."

Suddenly I felt as if I was being judged. It wasn't exactly her nature, but from time to time I felt she was biased when it came to Gavin. She rarely uttered a word of fault against him. She looked me square in the face once and told me, "God has blessed you with a good husband. Don't screw it up." It didn't keep me from seeking her advice, though. She'd been married for nearly twenty years, even though she was only a few years older than me. Obviously she knew how to make a marriage last.

"I understand why you're upset," she continued. "Forgive your husband for not defending you, okay? I know it hurts, but some men are just like this when it comes to their mothers. It doesn't mean that he doesn't love you. We both know that he does. Just try to focus on that, okay? You guys will get through this. You have bigger and better things to worry about. Like your presentation. *Rriiiggghhhttt?*"

I envisioned her giving me a big smile and a thumbs up sign. Thankfully, it brightened my mood.

"Yeah. I guess you're right."

"You know I'm never wrong. But if it'll make you feel better, I can ask Marcus to talk to him."

"No, that's all right." Leah meant well, but telling her husband about my frustrations with Gavin wouldn't do any good. My overprotective brother-in-law would have stern words for him, which would only lead to us bickering even more.

"You sure? You know Marcus doesn't play when it comes to you."

"I'll keep him in mind," I answered honestly. Gavin had a lot of respect for him, even though they were the same age, and he took his advice for the most part when it was given. Over the past two years he'd become his father figure as well. "Hopefully we'll be able to work things out in-house."

"I hope so. And I'll be praying for y'all."

Uh oh. I already knew what was coming next.

"Speaking of prayer..."

"Leah, please... Don't."

"What?" she whined. "I haven't even asked you yet."

"I already know what you're going to say. I don't want to go."

"Oooooooohhhhhh," she fussed. "Jesus is going to be mad at you."

"No, He won't."

"Dana!"

She wanted me to come to her home Bible study. I hadn't been in over a month, yet she consistently called every week with an invitation she already knew I was going to turn down. I knew rejecting her again was going to hurt her feelings, but I could not deal with the snotty women who gathered in her house every week, nor their ill-behaved children. I understood that Leah was striving for a family friendly atmosphere, especially since her third child was on the way, but I was the only one in the group who didn't have a baby, and the other women never let me forget it. Like Sylvia, they judged me because I was a career woman who hadn't ever given birth. They all considered Jonathan to be my son, but apparently I wasn't a real woman until I pushed someone out of my uterus. The more Leah's stomach grew, the more they pressured me. It really angered me, too. What if I was a woman who couldn't conceive? How painful would that be? They hadn't even considered that, but they continued to run their mouths, even when Leah told them to leave me alone about it. I didn't feel like saying anything else to those women. I was stressed enough and didn't need any more drama in my life.

"I want you to come to my Bible study," Leah finally said.

"Can't. I have plans."

"Don't lie, Dana."

"Not lying. I do."

"Plans to do what?"

"Not be there," I quipped.

"Please? I really want you to come. You can just ignore everyone else."

"Sorry, sis, but I just can't with those women."

"What if you come early? Just to see me, and then you can leave."

I gave a long sigh. We both knew that wouldn't work, either. She'd only try to convince me to stay, or someone would come early and judge me for leaving.

"All right, fine. I'll leave you alone about it for now," she finally gave in. "But just in case you change your mind, I'll make some extra food for you and Jonathan if y'all come by."

"Thanks, but I—"

"I'll save some for you."

I grinned. She couldn't bear to hear me tell her that I wasn't coming over.

"Do whatever you need to do," I told her with a laugh.

"I'm not mad at you," she told me. "But I really miss seeing you. I hardly get to see you anymore."

"I know. Business has been booming, sissy. But once I land this account and make all of this money, things will be even better than they were before.”

“Are you ready to go in there and knock ‘em dead?”

“I think so,” I said, then became nervous as I thought about presenting my ideas to the hospital. “I don’t know. Sometimes I feel like I’m crazy.”

“Well... You are.”

“Leah!”

“ I meant that as a compliment,” she insisted.

“It surely didn’t sound like one.”

“You are crazy, because no woman in her right mind, who comes from where we come from, and has been through all of the things that we have been through, would ever try to attempt to go after the things that you go after. Not unless they’re crazy.”

I smiled. In her own roundabout way she was saying she was proud of me. She was right. We had come a long way since our parents died in a car accident when I was in the eighth grade. She and Marcus were only high school students at the time, but since he was eighteen already, the state granted him permission to marry Leah and they became the legal guardians of my brother and me. Life was hard for us, but by the grace of God we all grew up to become successful adults.

“You’re gonna do well,” she told me. “You always do.”

“Thanks,” I said, and tried to breathe away the anxiety growing in my stomach.

“I gotta get back to my housework,” she told me. “Just think about reconsidering my invite. And don’t be too hard on my brother-in-law. I love that man and want him in our family.”

“Yeah, yeah, yeah,” I said, then told her I loved her and disconnected our call. The radio came on, but I quickly switched to my phone’s playlist and prayed the rest of the ride to the hospital.

FOUR
GAVIN

I was glad Dana and I had makeup sex this morning, but the festivities, combined with not sleeping all night, left me exhausted. It was only one o'clock in the afternoon and I was so tired that my body was actually sore. I felt like I'd just run a marathon and could barely keep my eyes open. Luckily my reputation as the best physical therapist assistant at Daytown Physical Therapy & Wellness Clinic gave me enough leeway with the rest of the staff to keep them off my back. They pretty much let me come and go as I pleased, which was a relief on days like this, though they hardly ever came.

"You ready to go?"

I turned away from my computer to see Deitrick standing in the doorway. Though he worked on another team, he always managed to sneak to my side of the clinic to chit-chat about whatever random thing was on his mind—mainly sports, his baby mamas, and God. As flawed as he was, he knew a lot about the Bible, and ever since I transferred to this clinic six months ago, we'd always had intellectual conversations about the scriptures. Dana met him a few times and shared with me that he wasn't the type of person she wanted to be around, mainly because she saw him as a womanizer. I found him to be pretty harmless, though. I liked that he didn't hide his shortcomings, and I preferred his honesty over the other Christians in the clinic who could never admit to their shortcomings. They were just flat-out creepy.

"Yeah, man. I'm ready," I told him, and locked my computer. A staff meeting was starting in the clinic's cafeteria in ten minutes, and we always went to them together.

"Man, you look beat!" he observed. "Making love to that fine wife of yours all night?"

"Watch your mouth before I have her come in here and kick your butt."

We left my office and made our way down to the basement, where the cafeteria was located. Several of our colleagues were already gathered, but instead of making conversation I went straight to the coffee stand in the back and ordered a double espresso.

"*Hello,*" Deitrick said to himself, and nodded in the direction of a young woman standing a few feet away from us. "Who is that?"

I shrugged after watching her for a moment. "I don't know. I've never seen her before."

"She is *fine.*"

Others in the room seemed to agree. Their gawking made it obvious. She was okay. Petite. Decent face. But she didn't even come close to what I had at home.

"I'm about to go introduce myself," Deitrick declared, and made his way over to her while I shook my head and watched. He had no self-control, which was why he had six children by five different women, none of whom he'd ever been married to. He often complained about the drama they all put him through, and when I suggested he get a vasectomy to avoid repeating the same cycle, he told me he wanted to have more children when he got married in the future. As crazy as it sounded, I understood. I couldn't wait to knock Dana up. I guess any man who really loved his woman and wanted to spend the rest of his life with her would feel that way, so I didn't argue with him about it. However, I had concern for the woman he was putting the moves on now. She wasn't like the women of his past. She actually had a job, and she didn't need to get linked to Deitrick and have his baby mamas drain her for his child support.

Run, girl! Run!

"Attention, everyone," someone called out from the front of the room. "If you all could please take your seats so we can get started."

Everyone shuffled to sit in one of the chairs arranged in the conference style setup, but I opted to remain in the back. I laughed to myself as I watched Deitrick whisper into his new crush's ear. She shook her head, gave a frown that he couldn't see, then scurried to the front of the room. Deitrick seemed disappointed, but shook it off and rejoined me by the coffee stand.

As soon as our chief of staff began the meeting, my thoughts drifted to Dana's presentation. I doubted if she made it there on time, but I knew if they were willing to see her, she got the job. She was great at what she did, and everyone knew it. She deserved it, too. I didn't know anyone who worked as hard as her.

"Before we get too far into this," our chief said, "I'd like to take a moment to introduce you all to our newest PTA. Parker Knight, will you please step forward?"

Deitrick's crush stood from her seat and made her way to the front of the room.

"Knight is from Houston, right?"

She nodded.

"Don't be shy, now," he told her. "Tell us a little about yourself. We hired you, so we want you here. We won't hurt you."

We chuckled at the humorous welcome.

"My name is Parker Knight," she said as she smiled and waved. "I just moved here from Houston. I've been a PTA for three years now. I worked at Woodland Heights before transferring here."

"Do you have family in the area?"

"My daughter," she answered, still smiling. "Her name's Madison."

He smiled back at her. "No ring. Are you married?"

She blushed as nervous laughter went throughout the room. Our chief of staff was old, but clearly he knew better than to ask that. He was a sexual harassment lawsuit waiting to happen.

"No, I'm not married," she told him.

I looked over at Deitrick, who confidently nodded my way. He was a lawsuit waiting to happen, too. He'd already been in relationships with two other women in our clinic. Luckily they didn't end up pregnant.

"Well, it's nice to have you here," our chief told her. "I think you're on the blue team," he said, and looked over to his assistant for confirmation. "Yes," he said, once he got it. "Gardner is the lead assistant on your team. Have you two met yet?" He turned and searched for me. "Gardner?"

I lifted my hand so they both could see me. "I'm right here."

"All the way in the back," our chief said as he pointed to me. "That's Gavin. He's a good guy. Very well respected here. He'll help you out in any way that he can, and everyone else will, too. Thank you for joining us."

"It's a pleasure to be here," she told us all, and returned to her seat.

My mind began to drift again. I quickly downed more of my espresso to regain my focus, but it didn't help. My thoughts were on Jonathan. That son of mine was something else. I continued to be amused and amazed by the hilarious things that came out of his mouth. At times I thought he was too clever to be my child. If he didn't look exactly like me and display some of my mannerisms, I wouldn't believe it. He was imaginative and often came to conclusions about things that most kids his age wouldn't, and often ended up in trouble because of it.

He loved Dana, too. Always had. From the moment he met her, I knew he wanted her to be his mother, which is how I also knew she was the woman for me. His biological mother hadn't seen him in over a year. I hated that she treated him that way. She claimed it was because of her schedule, but I knew she wasn't that busy. She was just jealous of the relationship he had with Dana, and also of our marriage. But she was the one who walked away from us, so I didn't have any sympathy for her at all. The one who was hurt the most by it was Jonathan. The other day he asked me if he could call her. I allowed him to, but she didn't answer the phone. He looked me in the eye and said, "I don't want her to be my mommy anymore." I was so surprised and so hurt that I didn't even know what to say to him. Dana did, though. I told her what he said and she had a talk with him the next morning. She always knew what to say to him, which was another reason why I wanted her around more.

The chief of staff continued to talk, and to my surprise he ended the meeting quickly. I think we were all grateful. He often rambled on and on about things we could have read in a quick email. But at least he thought highly of me.

Once we were dismissed, Deitrick and I made our way back to my office. He was telling me of his plans to woo Parker when my phone began to vibrate in my pocket. I pulled it out and frowned.

"Uh-oh. Wifey?"

"Stop worrying about my wife, man. It's my mama."

"Could be worse."

"How?"

"Could be a *baby* mama."

I shuddered as he walked away. My ex-wife definitely would have been way worse. I guess I really didn't have room to complain after all.

"Yes, Mother," I said as I answered, quickly ducking into my office and closing the door for privacy.

"Hey, baby," she said, sounding happy to hear my voice. "How is your day going?"

"A little busy," I subtly rushed her.

"Okay, I won't keep you. I was just calling to invite you over for dinner tonight."

"Is Tanya going to be there?" I asked sarcastically.

"Do you want her to be? I can call her."

"You better not," I warned.

"No, Tanya isn't going to be here. I'm just trying to be nice. I know your wife isn't making anything for you and your son to eat."

I couldn't help but roll my eyes. "You sure you're trying to be nice?"

"All I'm saying is that I figured you could use a nice home-cooked meal."

My mama. She drove me crazy, but I loved her.

"Yeah, Mama. I'll come over after work."

"I know you're bringing my grandbaby. Especially after that woman didn't allow me to spend any time with him yesterday."

"'That woman is my wife. And yes, I'll bring Jonathan."

"All right, boy. Bye," she said, and hung up the phone.

I stared at it, surprised by her abrupt ending.

Lord, can I please get some relief?

FIVE
DANA

Wendy and I were all smiles as we walked out of the hospital's conference room. The presentation went smoothly, and the board seemed very impressed with my design ideas. I was sure I got the job, but didn't want to jinx myself by boasting too soon.

"Money in the bank, money in the bank," Wendy sang under her breath.

I hissed at her to hush, but as soon as we made it into the elevator and the doors closed behind us, I joined her in a squeal.

"Girl, you did that," she beamed, and gave me a big hug. "Congratulations. You deserve it. You've worked so hard!"

"I haven't gotten the account yet," I told her, pretending to be humble.

"You're gonna get it. Stop playing. You know that you are."

I grinned. "Yeah. I am."

We got off the elevator and danced our way outside to my truck.

"Let's go out and celebrate," she suggested. "Somebody is serving cocktails somewhere, and I want one."

I shook my head and took the oversized portfolio she was carrying for me and put it in the back seat. "Naw. We got work to do. Did you get the laptop?"

"It's right here," she said, and undraped its bag from her shoulder.

"The extra presentation packets?"

"In my bag."

Something felt slightly off.

"My phone!" I gasped.

Wendy held it up for me.

"Oh," I said, and placed it in my purse.

"What's the matter with you?" she frowned.

"I feel like I'm forgetting something," I explained, and wracked my brain trying to figure out what it could have been.

"It's probably just your nerves, which is why we need to go get some drinks! Come on, let's relieve some of that stress."

"You better be at work in thirty minutes," I told her, still trying to figure out what I could have forgotten. "But I'll buy you lunch. It's the least I could do for all the hours you've been putting in."

"That's cool."

I gasped. "My wallet!" I screeched, and opened my purse. To my surprise, it was where it should have been.

"You didn't forget anything," Wendy assured me. "Will you relax already? Goodness. You're getting my nerves all riled up, and I'm the cool-headed one."

"Maybe I am losing my mind," I concluded with a frown, and got in my truck.

"Relax. You did good today. No need to stress. The hard part is over."

I told her she was right and started the engine. She went to her vehicle, which wasn't far away from mine, and I led us to my studio. I told myself she was right the entire drive there, but my gut was still troubled. I forgot something. Something important. I just couldn't figure out what it was.

SIX
GAVIN

Jonathan became excited as soon as Mama opened the front door of her house.

"Grandma!" he sang as he danced beside me.

My eyes were facing forward, but I heard his seatbelt unbuckle.

"Jonathan."

"Sorry, Daddy," he apologized, and immediately fastened the safety restraint around himself again.

I was relieved that he'd been listening to the recent wave of lectures I'd been giving him about the importance of waiting until the car was parked before taking off his seatbelt. Lately he'd been trying to jump out of the car before it even stopped.

"Grandma is right there," I told him. "She's going to wait for you to get out. No need to risk your life trying to get to her."

Jonathan continued to bounce in his seat, watching me intently, trying his hardest to be patient and wait for me to shift the truck into park. Out of amusement I waited a few moments. His anticipation had him squealing and his face began to turn red. After letting loose a good laugh, I finally parked the truck and gave him permission to get out. He did so in a flash, and ran to his grandmother.

"Grandma! Grandma!" he screamed as I got out and joined them. "I missed you!"

"I missed you, too, sweetie pie," she said, and gave him kisses on both cheeks and a loving swat on the behind. "Have you been a good boy?"

"Yes, ma'am."

"Well, let me ask your dad and see what he says."

I kissed her cheek. "Hi, Mama. "

"Hi, son," she said, and led us into the house.

"I know you're hungry. I cooked dinner for my two boys, and it's just about ready."

"Did you make some more banana pudding?" Jonathan asked.

"You're just gonna have to wait and see. But not until after dinner, okay?"

"Okay," he agreed with a frown.

I locked the screen door behind us but left the main door open, and told Jonathan to go to his room so his grandmother and I could talk. She gave him the space as soon as she moved in, and furnished it with a bed and too many toys for him to play with. He loved it, and I especially appreciated that it was upstairs and out of hearing range.

Mama and I went into the kitchen. Her arthritis was bothering her, but she managed to make it to the stove just as its timer went off. She silenced it, then used potholders to pull out a covered dish.

"How was your day, son?"

"Rough," I answered honestly. I was dog tired, and really wanted to be in my own house relaxing on the couch, waiting for my wife to get home. Prayerfully, two hours here would be enough for Mama. That was all I could give her today.

"You'll be better once you get this food in you," she said confidently. "You know can't nobody cook like your mama."

I knew she wanted me to agree, but I chose to say nothing.

"I talked to Tanya this morning."

Here we go with the nonsense. I sat down at the kitchen table and prayed it wouldn't last too long.

"She asked about you," she continued. "Wanted to know if she'd caused any trouble between you and your wife after she left. I assured her that she hadn't."

She was fishing for information, trying to see if Dana and I were arguing. I wasn't about to entertain her.

"Why are you hanging around my old girlfriend?"

"What do you mean? We're friends."

"Y'all are not friends. She's twenty years younger than you."

"That doesn't mean anything. We happen to enjoy each other's company."

"Y'all have absolutely nothing in common except me. And I don't want y'all hanging around each other. It's not right. Women your age don't hang out with women her age unless they want them to be their daughter. You already have one, and her name is Dana—and by the way, you've never gone out for breakfast with her."

"Your wife doesn't eat breakfast. Remember? Ain't that what she told me?" she snapped. "When you brought her over here the first time. Ain't that what she said?"

I was confused. "When y'all first met? You expect me to remember something she said two years ago?"

"Of course you would easily forget," she laughed through her frustration. "But it doesn't matter. You have your wife, and I have Tanya, and we'll be at IHOP tomorrow, eating all the pancakes and eggs we want."

"No, you're not. You're going to cancel it," I told her.

She stopped fussing over the food she was preparing and faced me with a long face. "Since when do *you* tell *me* what to do?"

"Since you started bringing uninvited women you want me to marry to my house."

"I didn't say I wanted you to marry Tanya. I know you're with that other woman."

I didn't hide my scowl. "I'm not here to play games, Mama."

She stood flat-footed and crossed her arms, daring me to correct her.

"Dana is my wife."

"I know that."

"If you know it, you need to accept it."

"I have."

"Then why are you pretending that you have another daughter-in-law? Bringing Tanya to dinner, Mama? Really? That was foul. Do you know how badly that hurt Dana?"

"Oh, she's the only one that matters?" she sassed, and rolled her eyes. "Don't forget the way she talked to me."

"You had it coming!"

I could see the anger rising within her. She didn't like that I was being so stern. She seemed trapped, unable to come up with an excuse, and took frustrated steps around the kitchen as she tried to escape my judgment. She finally slammed the potholders she was holding down on the counter and grunted.

"Stop hanging out with her. It's not going to do anything but cause trouble. Now if you love me you'll respect my wishes, and respect my wife, too. Why are you so intent on hanging out with my ex-girlfriend? How can you not see that it's inappropriate?"

"Oh, please," she sassed, and rolled her eyes. "She's inappropriate."

My face fell.

"She is. Running around here calling herself a wife, and ain't a bit suited. I don't know why you married her. She don't cook, she don't clean. She ain't never at home. She don't halfway spend time with Jonathan. All she wants to do is prance around in clothes that are way too expensive, just so everybody will know how much money she makes."

"That's *enough, Mama!*"

"No! You don' come in here after I done cooked all day, telling me that she feels disrespected. Well, I feel disrespected that she had the nerve to say she feels disrespected. I feel disrespected that she ain't taking care of you. Men are supposed to get fat after they get married. Not you. Look at you—all skin and bones. I know that woman ain't feeding you. And that *sad* dinner she tried to make last night. What kind of pitiful mess was that?"

My head lowered. Mama was tripping. Maybe she did need medication, like Dana kept suggesting. Something to calm her mood. Maybe a bottle of wine or something? No. Prayer. Definitely more prayer.

"Dana worked very hard on that dinner, and it was delicious. You would have known that if you had at least tried to enjoy it."

"If that was her best attempt..." She held up her hands. "Let me watch my mouth, before the Lord come back and catch me in the middle of a cuss word."

Suddenly she started to cry. I didn't respond. I wasn't sure if the tears were sincere or not, but even if they were, I refused to be moved by them. Mama needed to get her act together. Now.

"I hate it when we fight," she finally said, and dried her eyes with her wrinkling fingers.

"No one is fighting. We're just having a talk."

"Well, I hate it when you're mad at me."

"I'm not mad. Just... disappointed."

"That's the same thing, boy."

"It may feel like it right now, but it's not. I know you're better than the way you've been acting."

She took a deep breath to collect herself. "I just want you to be happy," she told me. "And I know you ain't."

"Yes, I am."

"I'm your mother. I know everything about you, and I know you ain't."

"I am happy," I said sharply. My patience with her was just about gone. I was a grown man and didn't need her to tell me how I felt.

"Fine. I'm not going to argue with you," she fussed, and pulled out a few plates from the cabinet. "If you say you're happy, then you're happy. But one day you're going to be able to admit it to yourself, then you'll be able to admit it to me. Then I'm going to tell you what you should do—send that woman you have on her way, and call Tanya."

"Mama," I growled with disappointment. "Stop it! I'm not interested in Tanya. I have a wife already, and she's the only woman I want."

"But Tonya is perfect for you. And she has a child, too. Just a little younger that Jonathan, but they can play together. You know Jonathan has been dying for a sibling."

I started to tell her that she just proved she didn't know what she was talking about. I didn't want a woman with kids, because I didn't want to put up with another man being around. But if I did, she'd only use the comment as an excuse to go on another tirade about Dana not giving her any more grandchildren yet, and I didn't want to hear it.

"We're not talking about this anymore," I told her. "Dana is my wife. You may not like her, but she is the woman that I chose to spend the rest of my life with, and to help me raise my son, and you will respect her."

Mama's eyes tried to pierce me, but I refused to be moved.

"I'm serious, Mama. Don't bring Tanya up anymore. Or any other woman. *Ever.* "

"All right," she snapped. "When you realize you aren't happy, just give me a call. I'll be here for you, just like I always have been."

She held up her hand to keep me from protesting, then pointed to the plates that were sitting on the counter.

"Come make a plate for you and the baby. After y'all eat, make a plate to take home to your wife. This way she'll know what a real pork roast tastes like."

I joined her at the stove and looked over all of the food she prepared. It was the exact meal Dana prepared yesterday, including the desserts.

Lord...You're gonna have to fix this...

SEVEN
DANA

I tried to remain positive as I stirred the pot of chicken boiling on the stove, but it was impossible. I hated cooking. Standing over a hot stove just wasn't my thing, but I got off work early and told Gavin I'd help him out with dinner. He appreciated it, but after working all day I didn't feel like coming home and working again. That's what restaurants were for. If only Gavin would change his mind about hiring a chef. We had the money to afford to keep one full-time, but he wouldn't hear of it. Not even on the weekends. What was the point of busting your butt all day only to come home and not have what you really wanted? Shoes and a chef. Gavin didn't see things that way, though. He insisted we take care of our own meals, which was why he was at the store right now, picking up fresh tomatoes for our salad.

"I finished number seven, Mommy," Jonathan told me from the kitchen table.

"That's good, baby," I told him. "How many more do you have to go?"

"Just three more. And then we can talk about my party, right?"

This child had the attention span of a toddler. I wasn't sure how he made it through class every day without getting in trouble. We'd been working on homework for the past ten minutes, and I must have reminded him to focus twelve times. He could care less about his math assignment. His little mind was entirely consumed with his upcoming birthday party, which was three months away, and his new friend Madison, who I was sure he had a crush on.

"Yes. Then we can talk about your party. But then and only then, okay? Now focus on what you're supposed to be doing."

"Yes, ma'am," he told me. "But before I finish this problem, I need to tell you something."

I saw the smile he was trying his hardest not to express and burst into laughter. This kid was something else. Anything to avoid math.

"Jonathan, you better do your work."

"I just have to tell you this *one thing.*"

"What is it?"

"I just want you to know that I already invited Madison to my birthday party. I probably should have asked you and Daddy first, but... I kinda didn't think about that when I asked her. It kinda just slipped," he confessed bashfully.

"Back to work."

"Okay. But I think you should know that I want MJ to come, too. And the new baby, because Aunt Leah said it will be out of her stomach by the time I have my party. You know who else I want to come? Cousin Jessica. But I don't know if she will, because, you know, she's been acting kinda weird lately. Aunt Leah says that it's because she's a teenager, but then MJ told me that Cousin Jessica said Aunt Leah was acting weird because she's having a baby. I think they're both weird, because..."

*...Oh... ****!!!!*

THAT'S WHAT I FORGOT!!!!!

I turned off the stove and ran upstairs to my bedroom.

*****!!! ****!!!! ****!!!! ****!!!!*

"Mommy, are you okay?" Jonathan yelled after me.

"Stay down there! I'm fine!" I called over my shoulder just before I shut the bedroom door, then locked myself in the bathroom and dove for the cabinet beneath the sink. I continued to curse as I frantically knocked over all of my hair and skincare products to find the box of tampons my birth control pills were hidden in. Once I located the compact, I popped one of the pills into my mouth and swallowed it.

Lord, please don't let me be pregnant!

I took two extra pills, just to be on the safe side, and swallowed a handful of water from the sink to help the tiny doses of hormones slide down my throat.

Jesus, please... PLEASE!!! Please don't do this to me, Lord! I don't want a baby!!!

I leaned against the counter and trembled at the memory of the sex Gavin and I had three mornings ago. How could I have been so stupid and so careless?! I knew I had to take these things like clockwork in order to avoid getting pregnant. The slightest slipup could result in a baby. I should have jumped up from the bed and locked myself in the bathroom and popped a pill in my mouth, just like I did every morning when he woke up wanting to be intimate with me. I knew what to do. But no, I got weak because he's fine and he promised to stand up to his mother, and I got sloppy. I fell off my routine, and all the stress at work with trying to land the hospital's account had my mind going in a million and one different directions, and I forgot to take my pills.

Not now, Lord. Not now... Please, not now...

In a panic, I frantically fell to the floor and cleaned up the mess I'd made. Gavin was due home from the store any minute, and if he saw the bathroom in this state he'd know something was wrong. I couldn't take the chance of him finding the pills in my tampon box and discovering I never stopped taking them when we got married, like I told him I did.

Once everything was back in its place, I splashed cold water on my face and told myself everything would be okay. I wasn't pregnant, and Gavin would never find out about my secret.

I tried to check my appearance in the mirror, just to ensure I didn't look as frazzled as I felt, but I was too ashamed to even look at myself. I felt like a disgrace to both God and my husband. I begged God to send me a man who would love me and cherish me, and when He gave him to me I spent our entire marriage lying to him. Gavin was a good man. He loved me so much and would never mistreat me. He supported my career when most men would be envious and intimidated. All he wanted me to do was give him more children. Why couldn't I do it? Why couldn't I be a good wife and pass on his lineage?

I didn't purposely set out to lie to him. Before we got married, I had no idea that he wanted so badly to have more kids. I didn't find out until a few days after we got married and he took me to meet Sylvia for the first time. She proudly told me he wanted five kids while I sat there feeling like a hoodwinked idiot. I didn't want any more kids. The fact that I could be so loving and kind to Jonathan was a testament of God's grace and mercy and guidance. I didn't want any of my own. I never did.

Before we got married, Gavin mentioned to me that he wanted to have more kids. It was only once, and I didn't take him too seriously. Once I told him that I didn't, he never mentioned anything else about it. But as soon as we got married, all he talked about was creating babies with me. I tried to tell him plenty of times that I didn't want any more kids and that I was happy with Jonathan. But Gavin claimed I was only nervous and would change my mind as soon as I got pregnant.

A few months into our marriage I started to believe him, so I decided to stop taking my birth control. I couldn't take seeing his heartbreak and disappointment every time I got my period. But I became so anxious about it that I thought I was going to have a nervous breakdown. I couldn't sleep, and I threw up every time we were intimate. I decided I couldn't do it yet and started to take the pills again. Until a few days ago, I hadn't missed a day since.

Gavin would be devastated if he knew. I could still remember the day he suggested we visit a fertility specialist. He was so sweet and gentle when he brought it up, afraid that my feelings would be hurt. I hated to lie to him, but pretending that I wanted to wait on God to bless us instead of going the in vitro route was the only thing I could think of on my feet. I never intended on keeping the lie alive this long, but Gavin never gave up. All he talked about was knocking me up. I wished that I wanted to make his dreams come true, but I loathed the thought of being pregnant. The big belly, the mood swings... The... stretch marks. Plus, if I got pregnant, there would be no way that I could carry the full workload that I did now, and I was not ready to give up my career. I'd worked too hard to get to where I was now, and I didn't want to just dump the child off on Gavin. That wouldn't be right. He was already struggling with having to do so much for Jonathan. Why couldn't we just leave things the way they were? Was it selfish of me to feel that way? I didn't feel selfish. I felt smart. It wouldn't be fair to have a child and not make it my priority. But then again, life wasn't all about me and what I wanted, especially now that I was married.

"Mommy?"

Jonathan's worried voice startled me out of my thoughts.

"I thought I told you to stay downstairs."

"You did. But... I just wanted to make sure you were okay."

I slumped over to the door and opened it. "I'm okay," I insisted as I looked into his sweet face.

"You don't look okay," he said slowly. "Why are you crying?"

I quickly wiped the tears that had managed to escape my eyes.

"I'm okay," I assured him, and forced myself to smile. "Did you finish your homework?"

He shook his head. "I need your help on the last problem."

I took him by the hand and together we returned to the kitchen just as Gavin made it back home from the store.

EIGHT
GAVIN

It was ten o'clock, and I was already buying another cup of coffee from the cafeteria. I was tired, but I didn't know why. It wasn't like I stayed up all night making love to my wife. If I did, I wouldn't have been annoyed. I loved Dana, but I was honestly getting tired of being at home alone at night. Life was supposed to be fun. Not mundane. Every night proved to be the same old tasks. Help Jonathan with his homework. Put him to bed. Fall asleep on the couch waiting for Dana to get home. I was bored, and becoming frustrated, too. Last night she fell asleep right as we were about to make love. That was the third time that happened in the past two weeks. I understood that she was tired, especially now that she actually got the job at the hospital. The schedule was very demanding, and she was already working more hours than usual. I was supportive, but I wasn't interested in being celibate anymore. I needed my wife to make love to me.

She disrespects herself. Running around here calling herself a wife... I know you ain't happy...

I tried to shake away the harsh words Mama spoke a little while ago, but they haunted me. Was she right? Was I really unhappy?

No, that wouldn't be a fair assessment. I honestly wasn't thrilled. Maybe more like disappointed. Marriage the second time around wasn't nearly as exciting as I thought it would be. I was starting to feel... lonely.

"Good morning, Gavin."

I looked up and saw Parker standing at the end of the coffee counter. She was alone.

"Good morning," I greeted her, and paid for my drink. The coffee stand worker handed me my large coffee and thanked me for my business.

"How are you doing today?" she asked as I joined her by the condiments.

"I'm good. About to be better, as soon as I get this in my system. You're a coffee drinker, too, huh?"

"Yeah." She lifted her drink. "But today I'm drinking tea."

I frowned. "Gross," I said, and began to pour milk and sugar into my own drink.

She chuckled. "You doing all right?"

"Yeah, I'm cool."

She seemed doubtful. "You sure? You seem a little off your game."

"Oh, yeah? Why do you say that?"

"Because you're pouring salt into your coffee instead of sugar."

I gasped and looked at the jar in my hand. Sure enough, it was labeled SALT with big bold letters.

"Dang it!" I grunted and slammed the bottle back into its place. "Why is this even here, anyway?" I griped. "Who puts salt in their coffee?"

"Apparently you do," she teased. "Hey, don't feel bad. It's happened to me before."

"Really?"

"No. I just... *didn't want you to feel stupid.*"

We both laughed and she insisted on ordering another coffee for me. When she wouldn't take no for an answer I thanked her.

"No problem. And just so you know, some people add salt to their coffee to take away some of the bitterness."

"Oh. I didn't know that."

"It's true. But judging from all the sugar you thought you were pouring into your first drink, I'd say you wouldn't know a good cup of coffee if you had one."

"Coffee is just coffee, isn't it?"

"Oh, my Lord. What have you been drinking?" She took the coffee cup the barista prepared for me. "Let me make this special for you. I know just how to hook it up, and I promise you it'll be better than anything you've ever had before. Just trust me, okay? I know what I'm doing, and you won't be disappointed."

"Sounds like you're pretty confident in your skills. Go ahead."

She smiled as she pulled various spices from the condiment stand and began to go to work on my drink. Midway through she blocked my view with her body.

"You're not adding vodka to that, are you?" I joked.

"Ha! That would be funny, wouldn't it? But no. I just don't want you to see my formula."

A moment later she stirred the drink with one of the plastic straws from the stand, then presented the cup to me. "Enjoy."

I took a sip, and sure enough, it was delicious. "Not bad."

"Not bad? More like perfect, buddy," she sassed, and gave me a playful nudge to the shoulder.

"It's pretty good," I agreed. "Thanks for the hookup."

"No problem," she said, and took up her tea again. "Gotta get back to work. Have a good day, okay?"

"Yeah. You, too. And thanks again for the coffee."

She walked away, and I stood in place, grinning for some reason.

"Hey, Gavin?"

I looked up to see Parker poking her head into the room.

"Whatever's bothering you will get better," she smiled, and left again.

I continued to smile, and had a feeling that she was right.

NINE
DANA

I was in my new office at the hospital, hanging a piece of artwork on the wall, when I heard a knock. I looked up to see Warren Bronson, one of the hospital administrators, standing at the door.

"Hi, Mr. Bronson," I greeted him. "How are you?"

"I'm well. Do you need some help with that?" he asked.

I told him no, but he rushed over to the couch I was standing on and helped me hang the picture. Once we got it into place he held my hand so I could step down easily.

"Thank you."

"No problem at all," he told me. "I was just coming by to congratulate you on the job again, and to welcome you to Daytown Memorial."

"Thank you. That's very sweet of you."

"Just want to be hospitable. We're really glad to have you here. We've been trying to get funding for this remodel for years, and now that we have it, we couldn't be happier that someone of your caliber wants to work with us. I have to tell you, we were just blown away by your designs. They're really quite stunning."

"Thank you. It's what I do," I said as modestly as I could.

"I just know you're going to do a fantastic job. I'm excited, and really can't wait to see the finished job. I'm pretty sure by then everyone will want you to redesign the entire hospital."

I laughed, but only because I didn't know how else to respond to all of his compliments.

"Sorry, I don't mean to embarrass you," he told me when he realized I had become slightly uncomfortable. "I'm just really fascinated by your work."

"Are you interested in design?"

"Now that I've met you, I am," he said, and smiled at me. "I was hoping that maybe we could talk about it over a cup of coffee. Or maybe even dinner. My treat."

I realized what his visit was all about. He wasn't interested in design. He was interested in me. The grin on his face and the way his eyes began to roam to different parts of my body said it all.

"I don't think that'll be a good idea, Mr. Bronson," I told him. "We're colleagues now, and I'd like to keep things professional."

"Oh, what's a little friendly conversation between friends, huh?"

"Friendly? Conversation?" Who did he think he was fooling?

"Yeah, you know. So we can get to know each other better."

I wanted to crouch under my desk to get away from his lustful eyes. His perverted look was making my skin crawl.

"I'm happily married," I told him.

"Aren't we all?" he asked, and licked his lips while he twirled his wedding band around his finger.

Was that supposed to entice me? Please. I had a man at home whose lips were way juicier.

"Not all of us, but I am," I assured him.

"Well, you know—"

"Thank you for your warm welcome. I have to get back to work now. Got a lot to do."

He seemed to be offended that I cut him off, and stared at me with sudden disapproval. When I didn't back down, he forced another smile.

"Maybe some other time, then."

Not on your life, dude.

"You have a good day now," he told me as he turned to leave. "Welcome to Daytown Memorial."

"Thank you, and you have a good day, too."

He smiled at me one last time before he left. I shook away the creepy feeling his stares left me with and got back to work.

Well, well, Mrs. Gardner. You still got it.

TEN
GAVIN

I was in a better mood when I got to work the next day. I still didn't get to spend much time with Dana when she got home last night, but we had a nice conversation this morning before she left for work. It wasn't much, but enough to get me through the day, and I appreciated it.

When I sat down at my desk a small gift bag was waiting for me, with a note attached to it. I pulled the note off the bag and read it.

Gavin,

    Here's to a great day. ~ :-)

I peeked inside the bag and pulled out the small package of sugar that was inside. I smiled, knowing the gift was from Parker. I laughed as I remembered the salt mishap and put the gift in my desk drawer, then got to work.

****

I was in the middle of filling out progress paperwork for a patient when Deitrick stuck his head into my office door.

"You ready yet?"

He was anxious to go to the staff lounge. The clinic was having a potluck, and we'd been hearing how good the food was all day. Deitrick claimed to be starving but didn't want to go alone out of fear of being blasted for not bringing a dish. I didn't bring one either, so if I went with him we both could take the heat.

"Come on, man," he rushed me. "Those forms will be there after we eat. I'm hungry."

"All right, I'm coming," I said, and put the files away. "Good Lord. You sound worse than my son."

"I doubt that very seriously."

"Not too far from it."

"Just come on, man. You can criticize me later."

I put my things away and walked with him to the lounge. As soon as we went inside Deitrick dashed for the food. There wasn't a line, which I appreciated. The food looked and smelled delicious.

"Is that jambalaya?" I asked Deitrick, who was already preparing a bowl.

"Yeah, man. And I'm about to *tear it up.*"

"You better find out who made that before you eat it," I advised. "Everybody can't cook."

"No, this is right," he said, and inserted a small spoonful into his mouth. "Say, man..." he started after tasting it for a moment. "This might be better than yours."

"Why are you playing? You know nobody can cook New Orleans food better than me," I boasted, then ushered him to the side so I could try the dish for myself. I made a small bowl, and to my surprise, the recipe was more pleasant than my own. I was shocked. Annoyed, too. Everyone knew jambalaya was one of my specialties. Every time we had a party, I was always requested to bring it. Who would so rudely step on my toes like this?

"Whoever brought this clowned you," Deitrick teased. He knew how competitive I was when it came to cooking.

"Who made this jambalaya?" I asked everyone as I looked around for the culprit.

No one said anything. Just as I was about to repeat the question, I spotted Parker on the opposite side of the room. She watched me with a smile.

"No," I said, pleasantly surprised. "You made this?"

She nodded as Deitrick snickered. Feeling a bit embarrassed that she'd outdone me, I finished making my bowl and joined her on the couch. We'd seen each other in passing over the past few days, but hadn't spoken to each other since last week when she saved me from my cup full of salty coffee.

"Young lady, I know you're new here, but I make the jambalaya in this clinic," I joked. "I'm gonna give you a pass this time, but don't make this same mistake again."

"You better step your game up then. No one has mentioned your pitiful jambalaya all day. Must not be too special."

"Ouch," I laughed. "Good one. And the food is good, too, by the way."

"I know," she said confidently.

"Where'd you get the recipe?"

"I will never tell," she said, and licked her spoon.

Dang... That was... kinda nice...

I knew she didn't mean to be that way, but I couldn't help but notice her lips. They were full, and quite appealing with the gloss she had on them.

"Gavin?" she asked. "You okay?"

I realized I was staring and turned away. "Yeah, I'm cool," I told her, and tapped my bowl against hers. "Cheers."

She laughed and continued to eat her food.

Oh, Lord. I'm in here tripping...

****

After the potluck I worked with three patients, and none of them had kept up with their home exercises, which made therapy especially difficult for me and painful for them. I felt drained, but I knew I had to get myself together before I picked Jonathan up from his after school program. I needed to make dinner and help him with his homework, and the laundry needed to be done, too. Dana was working late again, so it was going to be a long night.

"I need some help, Lord," I whispered as I walked out of the clinic. "I'm tired. I feel like I'm doing this all by myself..."

"Hey, Gardner! Wait up!"

I stopped so Parker could catch up with me.

"Got something for you," she said once she was next to me, and pulled a large food container out of her shoulder bag. "It's the leftover jambalaya from earlier. We aren't really into leftovers at my house, so it'll just sit in the fridge and waste. I figured since you liked it so much, maybe you and your family could enjoy it."

"Aw," I couldn't help but say. I was completely caught off guard by her kindness. Free food? And it tastes good? Man, yeah! "Thanks, girl! We surely will. My son will love this. Thank you. You saved me from the kitchen. I was just trying to figure out what I was going to make for dinner tonight."

"Your wife doesn't cook?" she asked, surprised.

"Yeah, she does sometimes," I answered. "But she has a really demanding job, so often it's left to me."

She seemed disappointed. "Pity. Well, there you go," she said, and tapped the container she'd given me. "Enjoy," she added, and walked away.

I stood and watched her, wondering if God had just answered my prayer, or if the devil had slyly presented me with temptation. I wanted to get to know Parker better. She seemed really nice and down to earth, a really cool girl to hang out with. Plus she could cook. Jonathan and I would never be hungry with her around.

"Can't play with it," I told myself, and rejected the thought. I was a married man. The only females I could hang around were the ones my wife were related to. Anyone else would be inappropriate.

I was thankful for the food, though. *Really thankful...*

ELEVEN
DANA

Work was torturous. I must have been crazy to think I could take on a project as big as the hospital. Not only was the workload massive, but I found out today that part of the budget was being slashed, which meant adjustments with the materials had to be made, which meant I was going to be behind schedule. No one wanted to hear that, though. They still wanted everything completed by the original deadline, which was absolutely crazy. Mr. Bronson was still sniffing around for a date, too, which was annoying. After two weeks, he still didn't want to back down. All of it stressed me out, so I took a quick trip to the mall for a little retail therapy before I went home for the evening.

It was a little past seven when I walked into the house.

"Mommy!" Jonathan screamed when he saw me, and jumped up from the dinner table. "You're home!" He ran over and gave me a hug.

"Hey, baby."

"You went shopping," he observed as he looked into my shopping bag.

"You did?" Gavin frowned as he looked up from the table.

"Yeah," I told him, closing the front door behind me.

"What'd you get?" he wanted to know.

"Just something pretty for me." I noticed the irritation of his face all the way across the room. "Something wrong, babe?"

He didn't answer at first, but finally said, "No," then told Jonathan to return to the table and finish his dinner.

"I'm finished, Daddy."

"Go upstairs and wash your hands and face, then go to your room."

Jonathan could tell his father was bothered by something, so he didn't protest. He gave me a kiss and went upstairs.

I took my shoes off and left them at the door with the rest of my things, then went into the kitchen and tried to give Gavin a hug, but he resisted.

"Are you okay?"

"I'm fine," he huffed under his breath, and moved me to the side so he could stand up from the table.

"You don't act like it," I said with a frown, and watched as he began to clear the table. "You wanna talk about it?"

"For what?" he mumbled. "It's not like it's gonna change anything."

What in the world? Where is this attitude coming from?

"Did I do something?" I asked. "If I did, tell me. I'm too tired to try to read your mind tonight."

"You weren't too tired to go shopping, were you?" He bit his bottom lip suddenly as if he were trying to keep himself from saying too much.

"You may as well go ahead and say whatever it is that's bothering you. I can't do this passive aggressive stuff right now," I let him know.

"It just would have been nice to have you here at home," he told me. "It bothers me that instead of rushing home to spend time with your family, because you never do, you chose to go to the mall and spend money on stuff you don't even need. What'd you buy? Another pair of shoes?"

Offended, I told him, "Yes, I did. But why does it matter? I bought them with my money. What's the big deal?"

"The big deal is that while you were lollygagging at the mall, I was here alone, again, with our son, helping him with his homework, and cooking, and cleaning, and taking care of everything on my own."

"I told you we could get a chef," I snapped at him. "And a housekeeper, too, if you want one."

"I don't want a housekeeper and a chef! I want a wife!"

My mouth fell open. "Are you saying you want me to be your chef and housekeeper, or that you don't feel like you're married? Make it plain, because this attitude is too much for me."

"You act like you don't have any responsibilities outside of yourself."

"No, I don't," I said. "And I don't appreciate you trying to make me feel guilty. I didn't even do anything for you to be upset about."

He laughed. "Yeah, right," he said, and went to the front door and picked up my shopping bag. "Let's just see how much you spent on these precious shoes, huh? I know you have the receipt in here. How much? Five hundred? Six hundred?"

I grimaced as he pulled out the receipt. He was about to go off.

His mouth rounded with rage as he stared at the thin piece of paper in his hand. He looked over at me and screamed. "DANA! I KNOW NOT!"

I threw my hands in the air and hurried upstairs to our bedroom. He was impossible to talk to when he was in one of these moods. He was about to go on yet another tirade about how I spent too much money on shoes and should instead donate to different charities for needy children.

"Twelve hundred dollars?!!" he yelled as he followed me. "For some shoes?! I know you didn't spend that much money on shoes!"

"Stop screaming at me!" I fussed, and snatched the bag and receipt out of his hand. "These are Giuseppe Zanotti boots! I got these at a very good price! You'd know that if you dared to pay attention to anything, you fashion delinquent!"

I went into the closet and put the bag on the shelf with my other unboxed shoes, but he picked them up.

"No. These are going back to the store," he told me. "You're not wasting any more money on this crap."

"You can't tell me how to spend my money," I reminded him. "You don't own me or my pocketbook. I make my own money and do what I want to with it. You're not going without anything you need, nor is Jonathan, so why are you so upset?"

"Because this is STUPID!" he yelled at me. "Do you know how many kids in the world you could have fed with the money you spent on these shoes? How many school supplies you could have bought? This money could have went to a scholarship fund."

"Ugh!" I grunted. "Look, I gave to the United Negro College Fund already! Okay? Dang it! Why is it my responsibility to provide for all the children in the world when I didn't help to create any of them?!"

The remark disgusted him. "You're so selfish," he told me with disdain. "And vain. There's so much more to life than what you wear and Debonair Designs by Dana."

"I know that!" I snapped.

"Well, while you were out shopping, your husband and your son were at home alone. Again. Just like we have been for the majority of this marriage, and I'm sick of it. Every night I'm doing it all by myself. I'm tired of it."

"You're not doing everything by yourself. I help out when I'm home."

"When?"

"When I'm home."

"When is that?"

"It's not often during the week," I hated to admit. "But it happens occasionally."

"We need more than an occasional wife and mother."

That was low. It felt like a kick in the stomach. "Are you trying to tell me that you're not happy?"

He sighed. "I'm telling you that you need to do better," he said, and walked out of the bedroom. "Take those damn boots back to the store, too," he called out once he was downstairs.

I stared at the box in my hands. I was so happy when I purchased these boots an hour ago. They were so beautiful. How could they now be the cause of so much contention?

TWELVE
GAVIN

When I woke up this morning Dana was already gone. Normally she gave me a hug and a kiss before she left for work. Not today, though, and I felt horrible about it. She was my wife and the love of my life. What if, God forbid, one of us didn't make it home this evening? I would feel awful if the last things we said to each other were hurtful words over a stupid pair of boots. An expensive pair of boots, but stupid boots, nonetheless. So I decided to pursue peace by surprising her at work with lunch and a bouquet of flowers. She was always thrilled when she got them. She told me once they made her feel like she was in the movies or the popular girl on a television sitcom that all the guys wanted.

"Mrs. Gardner!" I called out when I spotted her across the room. One of her crew members had to help me hunt her down. It took us nearly fifteen minutes.

She turned and began to blush when her eyes landed on me.

Good. She's not mad anymore.

I tipped the hard hat the crew member insisted that I wear and made my way over to her, holding up the food and flowers that I brought with me. She smiled as she waited for me to reach her.

"I'm sorry, beautiful," I apologized, and gave her a hug and a kiss. "Do you forgive me?"

"Yes," she said quickly, and stood on her tiptoes to get another kiss, which I eagerly supplied.

Dang! Her lips. So...freaking... soft... How could I ever take the chance of not having these things against mine? So succulent! Oooohh, I could just take her right now and—

"Wwwwooooo hooooooo!!!!"

Dana pulled away as a few members of her crew howled at us. She was embarrassed, and rightfully so. She was running the show and her man was ramming his tongue down her throat in front of everyone. Not professional at all.

"Show's over," she told them. "Get back to work."

Most of them did, but someone standing in the corner stared at us like he had a problem. He was jealous. I could tell by the way he watched us.

"Come on. Let's go to my office," Dana said, and began to pull me away as she took the flowers from me.

We still had an audience. The guy continued to watch us. Just to irritate him, I grabbed a handful of her behind and squeezed it, making her giggle.

"Stop, Gavin," she fussed, as she led me past the organized chaos that was her work. Piles of wood and dangerous equipment surrounded us, but we finally made our way to the sectioned-off room that was her temporary office. True to her style, it was decorated to perfection, even hosting a sofa and matching chair.

As soon as we were inside she placed the flowers on her desk, then shut the door and closed the blinds.

"What you doing?" I asked as she pushed me against the wall.

She grinned, then planted a kiss on me that was so passionate I had to force myself to remember that we weren't at home.

"You better stop," I warned as she continued kissing me. "They're gonna know what we're doing."

"At this moment, I don't think I care."

I was so glad she was mine, and so glad I didn't have to repent after I touched her. She was my wife, and too beautiful for me to regret ever being with. I had to force myself to let her go. If I didn't, she wouldn't stop me, and I didn't need her getting in trouble on the job.

"I don't want to fight anymore, baby," she said, pouting her lips.

"Me, either. So let's not, okay?"

"Okay," she said, and tried to hug me again. I restrained her, letting her know with my eyes not to tempt me.

She agreed to wait until we got home, then thanked me for the flowers. "They're beautiful," she said.

"They pale in comparison to you, my love."

She winked. "You better get out of here if you don't want me to get fired."

I laughed. "All right."

"Ooooh—first let me show you the place," she said eagerly. "You haven't been here yet, and I want you to see the work that I've done. Do you have time?"

"Yeah, I got a few minutes."

"Great," she said, and grabbed me by the hand again and pulled me to the door. When we opened it, we were surprised to find someone standing there. It was the same guy who watched us earlier.

"Mr. Bronson," she gasped, startled.

"Ms. Gardner. You have a visitor," he responded, eyeing me.

"*Mrs.* Gardner," I corrected him. "I'm her husband, Gavin Gardner."

I didn't like this dude. Something about him was off, but I played it cool and gave him a handshake.

"Yes," Dana said nervously, sensing I was annoyed, and cleared her throat. "Mr. Bronson is one of the hospital's administrators."

"Yes. I'm the person who gave your wife her job," he told me.

"Is that so?" I asked. I wanted to laugh. I guess that small bit of information was supposed to impress me. It didn't. Nor did it cause me to worry. He clearly was a simple man, and he probably thought Dana owed him something outside of professionalism. Fool. He didn't have a chance with my wife. She'd shut him down as soon as he tried. He better not, either. His position probably forced him to handle a lot of problems, but I was one that he didn't want.

"It is," Dana told me. "And I'm enjoying working here," she added, more to me than to him. "I was just about to show my husband all of the work that I've been doing."

He stared at me for a few moments, but finally said, "All right," and walked away.

As soon as he was gone Dana pinched my arm. "You are something else."

"I don't like that dude."

"Really? I never would have guessed," she said sarcastically, then took me on my tour.

THIRTEEN
GAVIN

I woke up in a good mood. It was Saturday, and Dana was taking Jonathan to a birthday party, so I had the afternoon to myself. This was the first time in months that I had absolutely nothing to do, and I looked forward to catching up on some reading.

"I think there's going to be monkeys at the party," Jonathan told me as he ate his breakfast. "And a lion."

"A lion?"

"Yeah."

"Excuse me?"

"A lion. I think that's what he said."

"Yeah?"

"Yeah. I mean, yes, sir."

"I don't know if a lion will be there," I told him. "I don't think they can have lions in the park."

"Maybe if it's in a cage."

I read the party invitation myself, and nothing on it said anything about a monkey or a lion. Where did my child get this stuff?

"Finish eating," I told him.

"Yes, sir," he said, and forced a spoonful of cheese grits into his mouth.

A few moments later Dana walked downstairs, fully dressed, and joined us in the kitchen.

"Good morning," she yawned, and kissed Jonathan on his cheek before making her way over to me at the stove.

"Where are you going?" I asked, surprised by her appearance. She looked like she was headed to work.

"I have to go in today," she said, and poured herself a cup of coffee. She must have been exhausted. The only time she drank the Maxwell House I prepared was when she was about to pass out. Normally her assistant picked up her needed dose of caffeine and had it waiting on her when she got to work.

"I thought you were taking Jonathan to the birthday party?"

She gasped and covered her face. "Oh no," she pouted, and turned to Jonathan, who had overheard. "Oh, baby, I'm so sorry," she apologized to him, and put her coffee down so she could run over to him and give him a hug. "Mommy is so sorry, baby. I have to go to work, so I won't be able to take you to the party."

Jonathan was disappointed. He'd been looking forward to the party since he got the invitation two weeks ago.

"Mommy, you promised," he frowned.

I shook my head, disappointed in her, too. He loved spending time with her, and after working all week, the least she could do was give him a few hours on the weekend. And why was she just now letting us know that she had to work? Why didn't she say anything last night before bed?

"I'm sorry, baby," she apologized to him. "I really am, but I have to go to work. Do you forgive me?"

He continued to frown, but said, "Yes, I forgive you, Mommy. I just wanted you to come."

"I know, and I'm sorry. I'll make it up to you. I promise. Maybe Daddy can take you," she added.

"Daddy has no choice now, does he?" I mumbled under my breath. She knew I hated birthday parties. They weren't my thing. I always ended up being the only guy there, listening to a bunch of catty women talk behind each other's backs and complain about the men in their lives. Then they'd get turned on watching me be a good father to my son and try to flirt with me. I wasn't up for it.

Dana returned to the stove and hugged me from behind. "I'm sorry, baby," she apologized. "Things are falling behind at work and it's really important that I stay on schedule. You understand, don't you?"

"I pretty much have to," I said with a sigh.

"I promise, I'll make it up to you, too," she whispered into my ear, and gave me a nice, lengthy kiss. "Soon as I get home."

Jonathan giggled. "You guys are so gross."

Dana winked at me. "Maybe just a little," she agreed with him. "You guys have fun at the party. Love you both," she told us, and dashed out of the door.

"Mommy always has to work," Jonathan complained. "When I get big I'm gonna make a whole bunch of money so Mommy can stay at home."

I chuckled. "What about me?"

"You'll be okay. You get paid enough."

****

Jonathan ran away from me as soon as we got to the park. I let him go, content with periodically checking on him for the next two and a half hours as he played with his friends, and made my way over to the gift table to drop off the present we picked up before coming to the party.

"Gavin!" someone nearby waved at me. I remembered her face, but couldn't recall her name. I'd met her at the school play Jonathan was in a few months ago.

"Hey," I waved.

She made her way over to me and placed a cup of punch in my hands.

"It's from the adult bowl," she told me, and made her eyebrows dance, hinting that the drink contained alcohol. "If we have to be out here with these kids, we may as well enjoy ourselves," she laughed, and took a long swig from her own cup.

"Thanks," I said, but didn't drink the juice she gave me.

"Where's Deena? That's your wife's name, isn't it?"

"It's Dana," I told her. "And she's working."

"Again?" she pouted. "Wasn't she working during the PTA meeting? And the play? And the—"

"Yes, my wife works a lot."

"Yes, she does," the woman said. "Man... All that working... Must get pretty lonely at home," she added, and batted her eyes at me.

Not that lonely.

"Daddy!"

Jonathan and a little girl raced toward me.

"Excuse me," I said to the possibly intoxicated woman beside me, and advanced toward the children approaching me.

"This is my friend, Madison," Jonathan told me. He was out of breath from running.

"Oh, hello, Madison," I said to the little girl beside him, and shook her hand. "I'm Mr. Gardner."

"Hi," she said, and bashfully pulled her hand away. "Nice to meet you, sir."

"Well, you are very polite, aren't you?"

She nodded.

"Madison said there aren't any lions here," Jonathan said with disappointment. "But they have horses, so... I don't know. I guess that's cool. Can we ride them?"

"Let's see what safety precautions they have in place, first. You've never ridden a horse before."

"I have," Madison told me. "I can ride with him. I will take care of him. I won't let him fall."

I chuckled. "I was thinking someone slightly bigger than you."

She stood up taller. "Look, I'm growing," she said, and laughed.

I laughed, too. "I was thinking someone who has already finished growing. Like an adult."

They both laughed, then Jonathan pointed and said, "Look, there's your mom."

"Pointing is rude, son," I said, and looked over my shoulder to see someone approaching. To my surprise, it was Parker.

"Gavin?" she asked as she got closer. "What are you doing here?"

"What are *you* doing here?" I asked in return.

"That's my mom," Madison informed me.

"You don't say?"

"Yes, I do say. Because that's what I said."

"Madison," Parker warned. "What did I tell you about your mouth?"

Madison shrugged. "What did I say?"

"Go play," Parker instructed sharply, and shooed her away with her hand.

Madison grunted, then pulled Jonathan by the hand to join her.

"Don't ride any animals without asking me first," I called after him. "You hear me?"

"Yes, sir," he called back, but I doubted he would listen. I didn't want to spoil his fun, but the last thing I wanted was a sudden trip to the ER because he got thrown off a horse.

"Madison is your daughter?" I asked with a laugh. "What are the chances of that?"

"A small world, huh?" she laughed with me. "And I'm assuming Jonathan is your son? Your little boy's name has been all over my house every since we got here."

"Same with your little girl. I know so much about Madison. I hear her name every day. I can't believe I didn't realize she was your daughter. Our kids are best friends, and I didn't even know it."

"Well, you wouldn't have known. This is my first time really going out with her. We've been so busy with unpacking and getting the house in order. This party invite was just what we needed."

"Honestly, this isn't the way I wanted to spend my weekend," I admitted.

"No? You didn't want to be surrounded by seven-year-olds?" she asked sarcastically. "By the way, don't drink the punch. It's spiked, unless you got that out of the kiddy bowl."

I poured the drink out and crumpled the cup in my hand.

"They have bottled water, too."

"Let's go get some. It's hot out here."

"My thoughts, exactly," she said, and led me to the food area. "I'm so surprised to see you here. I don't know why, but for some reason I thought you were married."

Confused by the statement, I said, "I am married."

Startled, she said, "Oh. I thought you were. But then..."

"But then, what?"

"Nothing. Foolish of me to just assume things. It's just that I see you here at a birthday party with your son, and you're alone. Normally the dads who show up at these things aren't married. If they were, the wife would be the one at the party."

"Is that how it usually works?" I pretended not to know. "I've gotta tell my wife when I get home. We're doing this whole birthday party thing wrong."

She rolled her eyes as we continued to walk. "Forget I said anything."

"Don't worry about it. Yes, I'm married. And normally my wife does handle these types of things, but she had to work today, so that's why I'm here."

She nodded, but clearly didn't want to say anything more about Dana.

"So, how are you adjusting to Daytown?" I asked. "Does it feel like home to you, yet?"

"No," she said bluntly.

"You don't like it here?"

"It's okay," she told me. "Just not Houston."

"Well, no place will truly be like home. I'd hate this place if I constantly compared it to New Orleans. But you're here now, so you gotta make the best of it."

"You sound like my mom," she fussed as we reached the food table. She dug two bottled waters out of a cooler and placed one in my hand, keeping the other one for herself. "You hungry?"

I shook my head as I took a drink. "Nah. Not right now, but maybe later."

"So you're from New Orleans?" she asked. "I've been there a few times. Not since the storm, though. You?"

"Only to handle property issues. I had to move my mother and grandmother out. They lost everything when Katrina hit."

"I'm sorry to hear that," she said with a saddened face. "Are they okay now?"

"Mom is cool. Grandma passed away a little while ago."

"Oh, Gavin." She looked even sadder. "I'm so sorry."

I shrugged to keep myself from thinking about it. As I did I felt someone grab my arm.

"Hi, Gavin! How have you been?" It was Jonathan's first grade teacher, Mrs. Parks. "Is this your lovely wife I've heard so much about?" she asked as she extended her hand to Parker. "It's so nice to finally meet you."

"Oh, um..." Parker stammered as Mrs. Parks shook her hand eagerly.

"Mrs. Parks, this isn't my wife," I told her, and separated their hands. "This is Parker, one of my co-workers."

"Oh," she pouted, and eyed Parker with suspicion. "Have you and your wife separated?"

Awk... ward.

"Nope. No, still married," I clarified, and held up my hand so she could see my wedding band. "My wife is at work, and Parker and I were just here chatting. Her daughter and Jonathan are in the same class."

"Oh, I see," Mrs. Parks said, and seemed a bit relieved. "Well, it's good that she's working. So many aren't," she added. "My apologies. I didn't mean to be rude or insinuate anything inappropriate between you and your co-worker, here. I just saw you speaking with this young woman and thought I was finally about to meet Dana."

"It's quite all right, ma'am," my mouth said. My mind, though, told her that she needed to mind her own business.

"So, how is Jonathan doing in school this year?"

"He's doing well. Still one of the top students in his class. Still talking too much."

She laughed. "A good imagination is always encouraged, Mr. Gardner. Especially in little boys. He has a creative side."

"I guess," I chuckled, and nodded at Parker, who seemed to be feeling out of place as she sipped her water.

"Okay. Well, I won't hold you two up. It was nice meeting you," she said to Parker.

"Likewise."

"Good seeing you again, Gavin," she said, then walked away.

"Sorry about that," I apologized to Parker. "She's a nice woman. A bit nosy, but harmless."

"Maybe I should move away from you," she suggested. "At this rate, by the end of the party I'm going to have a big scarlet letter attached to my clothes."

I chuckled, but said, "Don't leave. Stay and talk to me. If you don't, I'm just going to be bombarded with kid talk and questions about the whereabouts of my wife. Don't really feel up to it."

"Sure, we can talk," she said, and suggested that we sit at an unoccupied picnic table. It was under a large pine tree, which promised shade and protection from the sun. I obliged, and before I knew it, was engrossed in a conversation that I found to be surprisingly pleasant.

****

Parker and I ended up talking for over two hours. In that time I learned a lot about her. She was the same age as Dana, which was a surprise. They looked the same age, but Parker's conversation was much more mature. She lived for her daughter, which was attractive. It made her happy, and she didn't seem to feel as if she were missing anything in life. She was divorced, and even though she wanted to get remarried one day, it wasn't a priority, although she wanted more kids. She loved to cook, and also loved to work out. It showed, too. I could see the muscles in her thighs through her tight jeans. She had nice arms, too. Back home she would have been described as a "bad yellow bone": attractive with light skin. I hated the terminology, basically because it derived from the way slave masters divided our ancestors during the oppression of our people. Still, she was beautiful, and any man would want to be with her.

"Can you believe they have all of this for a seven-year-old's birthday party?" she asked, looking around.

"I think the birthday boy turned eight today."

"Whatever," she said. "I'm grown and I've never had anything like this. I hope Madison doesn't get any ideas. Last year for her birthday I bought her a cake, then took her and two of her cousins out to the nail shop. After that they had a sleepover. I can't afford all of this."

"You don't have to," I told her. "I don't believe in extravagance either, and especially not with kids. Most of the time all of this extra stuff is for the parents, anyway. Kids find joy in the simple things. I learned that the hard way."

"How?"

"When Jonathan was two," I recalled. "It was Christmas day, and I must have spent nearly a thousand dollars on clothes and toys for him. Do you know what that child of mine did? He spent the entire day playing with the plastic casing of one of the toys. You know, the hard plastic that the toy is wrapped in when it's in the box. That's what he played with, and his grandma let him eat the candy canes from the tree. He had a ball."

She laughed.

"He kept that plastic for three whole weeks. He slept with it and everything. Bathed with it. He took it outside and used it to mold dirt in the sandbox. I could have saved all of my money."

Parker continued to laugh. "Kids are so funny, man," she said. "Serves you right for overcompensating."

"Who said I was overcompensating?"

"You did, in so many words. You told me you and his mother split right before his second birthday. You felt bad for not being there for him the way you previously were, and tried to make up for it by spoiling him at Christmas. It's pretty obvious."

She was smart. That is exactly what happened.

"I take it the same happened with Madison and her father?"

She hissed. "Madison hasn't seen or heard from her father since the day he left. She was only one."

"Oh," I said, feeling bad for them both. That was horrible. "That's rough. Sorry to hear that."

"Don't be," she said. "I put him out. He was a cheater."

"He still has a responsibility to his daughter, though."

"I refuse to worry about it," she replied. "I learned a long time ago that a person can do bad all on their own. But I'm better without him. My daughter is happy when I'm happy, and that's all that matters to me."

I smiled, encouraged a bit by her outlook. She was stronger than she realized.

"Does Jonathan get along well with his new mom, your wife?"

"Does he? He loves her. From day one, she was his mommy, and I hadn't even asked her to marry me yet. It was like he just knew."

"Aw, that's so sweet," she beamed.

"Sometimes I think he loves her even more that me."

"You think?"

"If he told me he did, I wouldn't be surprised. Of course, I'll never ask him. But if the information leaked, it wouldn't be a shock."

She smiled. My eyes locked with hers, and for a second I felt a connection with her that I didn't expect. I forced myself to look away and saw both Jonathan and Madison running toward us.

"Look what Madison did to her face, Daddy," Jonathan said when he reached us.

Madison turned to the side to that her mother and I could get a good look at the face painting on her left cheek.

"Can I keep it, Mama?" she asked. "Please don't make me wash it off."

"You can keep it until tonight," Parker told her. "Are you guys ready to eat yet? You've been playing all day."

"I could eat," Jonathan told her.

I chuckled. "You could?"

He nodded, to the amusement of Parker and me.

"Let's get some grub," I said, and stood up, then helped Parker get down from the tabletop where she'd been sitting.

The kids ran off in front of us, and Parker and I walked behind them. Once we caught up, Parker shared hand sanitizer with us all from her purse, then began to prepare her daughter's plate.

"You two are just so cute," I heard someone say.

Parker and I looked up to see an older woman smiling at us.

"Excuse me?" Parker asked.

The woman continued to smile. "I just love to see young couples in love. Are you married?"

"Eeewww, no!" Jonathan fussed at the woman. *"She's not my mom! That's gross!"*

"Boy," I hissed, and swatted the back of his head. He rubbed it, but didn't say anything else. Madison snickered.

The woman in front us nervously began to rub her necklace. "Oh, my," she said with a heavy sigh. "I'm so sorry. You two have just been over there talking so long, and you seemed to be enjoying each other's company so. It reminded me of my late husband and me when we first got married. I just assumed... I'm so sorry."

Madison laughed. "That was kinda funny."

"Sssshh," Parker quieted her.

"We all thought you were together," the woman continued, and pointed to a group of women sitting around a table. They waved when we looked their way. "We've been saying what a cute couple you are."

I shook my head at her. "We are not a couple. I'm a happily married man," I told her, and grabbed Jonathan by the hand and pulled him away from her, then quickly began to prepare his hotdog. The woman tried to apologize again, but I didn't want to hear anything else that she had to say. This was exactly the reason I didn't like going to these type of events. As usual, all the women found a way to get in my business.

"Are you okay?" Parker asked me.

"Yeah, I'm fine," I said, and hurried to finish preparing Jonathan's food. Once I did I ushered him away from her, determined not to have Parker confused with Dana ever again.

FOURTEEN
DANA

I sat in my office and stared at all of the work in front of me with a heavy frown on my face. I was supposed to be at the park with Jonathan, suffering through baby talk with other mothers while he and his friends enjoyed a birthday party. Things had fallen behind at work, though, so here I was, thinking about everything except work. Mostly Gavin and the fight we had the other day, my strained relationship with his mother, Jonathan, and the boots I forced myself to return out of respect for my husband's wishes. I was frustrated, too. I really, really, *really* wanted those boots! Even worse, my period was two days late. It wasn't time to panic. At times it became irregular, but knowing that I missed a few days of birth control did not calm my nerves. I would feel a lot better about it if I could go home and put on those Giuseppe boots...

Stop thinking about the boots!

I did the right thing by taking them back to the store. Gavin was right. I didn't need them. I had several boots. One extra pair didn't matter, no matter how beautiful they were.

So why was I still upset? Especially after we made up about it already?

Because he hurt my feelings. He called me selfish and vain, and insinuated I wasn't a good wife and mother. Those were awful things to say, and even though he apologized, the words still stuck with me. It was like he turned into his mother all of a sudden.

Ugh. That Sylvia Gardner. I could not stand that woman! I had been nearly four weeks since we had dinner, and I still hadn't talked to her. She hadn't bothered to get in touch with me, either, which proved she fine without me being in her life. But why was I sitting here thinking about a woman who clearly wasn't thinking about me?

Because maybe she had been right about me this entire time. Maybe I really wasn't a good wife. I was nowhere near as good as the virtuous wife of Proverbs 31. She would never go to the mall and spend a ridiculous amount of money on a pair of boots. She was smart with her money. That was the kind of wife Gavin needed. One who was disciplined with her shopping and only purchased what she needed. One who was attentive and always gave him love, intimacy, and support. One he wouldn't have to lecture. One who would want to have his children.

My heart ached thinking about it. I loved my husband so much. But becoming pregnant just wasn't something I could see myself becoming. It wasn't in my DNA. I was a career woman. Running my business made me who I am. He knew of my dislike for children before we got married. He couldn't have thought that putting a ring on my finger would somehow transform me into a miniature version of his mother, could he? Surely he knew better.

Maybe in a few years I would change my mind. I know of several women who didn't have the mommy bug at all, and then suddenly, out of nowhere, their maternal switch came on. Gavin and I were technically still newlyweds, and there were still things I wanted to achieve in life. Like... redesigning the White House, or... completely making over a chain of private hotels. Maybe then I'd get excited every time I saw a Huggies commercial and want to procreate. Yes. After a few years, I could consider it.

Then again, I wasn't getting any younger. Shoot, I was already close to the danger age. Maybe the White House wasn't a part of my destiny. Maybe the hotel chain wasn't either. I wouldn't be able to live with myself knowing I denied my husband's dream in order to chase something I was never meant to have. Would Gavin ever be able to forgive me? Would he even still want me? Maybe I should just suck it up and give him a baby and not worry about the morning sickness, or the stretch marks, or the constant crying it would do, or the way it would spit up all over my clothes. I can't give him four, though. No. One. That would be a nice compromise. Just one to keep him satisfied for now. That should fix things between us, and Sylvia too. A new grandbaby would be just the thing to shut her up.

Wait. What was I thinking?! I could not put the responsibility of fixing my marriage on a baby!

I slumped over on my desk and began to massage my forehead. I was feeling stressed and now was not the time to get a headache. My stomach was already bothering me. Prayerfully these ailments were only symptoms of PMS and my period was about to come soon. Either that, or I was possibly under too much stress. Maybe Gavin was right. Maybe I needed to stop working so hard.

Maybe I was just crazy.

FIFTEEN
GAVIN

I was on my way to retrieve a patient's x-rays when I saw Parker standing in the hallway, talking to one of the interns. It was my first time seeing her since the party this past weekend, and I felt the need to apologize for the awkward and childish way I walked away from her.

"Excuse me? Ms. Knight?"

She turned at the sound of her name, then quickly wrapped her conversation with the intern and began to walk toward me.

"Hey," she said once we were in front of each other. "How are you doing today?"

"I'm good. You?"

She gave a modest nod. "Good, I guess. Can't complain. I shouldn't, anyway."

"That's good."

She waited patiently for me to tell her whatever it was I called her over for. As I looked into her eyes, though, I lost my train of thought. Every time I looked at her, she seemed to become more beautiful.

"Gavin?" she asked. "Is there... Something you needed to tell me?"

I was confused. Why did I call her over?

"Gavin?"

"Yes," I said, snapping out of it. "Yes, about the park. I just wanted to apologize for the way I kinda walked away from you like that. You know, when that lady thought you were my wife."

She chuckled, but said, "No apology needed."

"Um, yeah... Pretty much."

"No, I understand. The situation was awkward."

"It was," I agreed. "But I could have handled it a lot better. I apologize."

"It's okay," she assured me. "No hard feelings. Everything is cool between us."

I studied her for a moment to see if she was telling the truth. She was, which was a relief.

"Cool," I said, and began to laugh.

"Cool?"

"Absolutely. Yes. Cool. Very cool."

"Good," she said. "You didn't think I was mad or upset or anything, did you?"

"Nah. I just wanted to be sure, though."

"Well, rest assured, Gavin. Everything is fine between us. And don't call me Ms. Knight anymore. I know I'm grown, but that's reserved for my mama. Parker will do."

I nodded, then she returned to the intern who appeared in the hallway again, needing her assistance. As she left my eyes went to her round hips. I fussed at myself for not being stronger, then hurried to get my patient's x-rays.

SIXTEEN
DANA

Gavin was in the kitchen making dinner when I got home from work. Jonathan jumped from the dinner table where he was doing his homework when he saw me, and Gavin had a smile on his face as well.

"Mommy!" Jonathan yelled as he hugged me. "You're gonna eat dinner with us today!"

I smiled at his excitement and kissed his cheek. "Help Mommy take her shoes off."

He agreed, but then pouted. "Oh, man. You have on these strappy shoes again."

I laughed as Gavin came over and helped him. They struggled to remove the shoes from my feet, but once they did I felt instant relief.

"Yeah, maybe I won't wear these to the hospital anymore," I told them. "My feet are killing me."

"You look like you're getting a corn," Gavin told me. *"Is that a bunion?!"*

I gasped and looked down at my foot, then shoved him playfully when I saw he was only teasing.

"Corn?" Jonathan asked. "And onions? In your shoes?"

Gavin and I laughed at his misunderstanding.

"Don't worry about it, baby," I told him, then allowed them both to escort me into the kitchen.

"Jonathan, take your things upstairs to your room so I can talk to Mommy," Gavin instructed.

"Can I watch TV?"

"After you finish your homework."

"Okay," he said, and gathered his things, then kissed me on my cheek before he ran upstairs to his room.

"Dinner smells good, baby," I told him. "Are those fried pork chops?"

"Yep," he said, and sat down at the table beside me. "But that's not what I want to talk to you about." He leaned over and kissed me, then told me to stay seated and went into the laundry room. A moment later he returned with a bag from Nordstrom.

"What you got for me, baby?" I asked as he sat next to me. "It's not even my birthday or our anniversary."

"You've been working really hard, and I wanted to give you a little something to let you know how proud I am of you."

"You got me something from Nordstrom," I sang, and danced in my seat as I placed the bag on its side and pulled out a shoe box. *"No... You got them for me?!"* I gasped, and squealed as I opened the box. Laying inside were the boots I'd returned after our fight last week.

"I take it you still like these, then," he joked as I squeezed him as tightly as I could.

"Yes!" I squealed, and covered him with kisses. "Oh, my goodness! Baby, I love you so much," I told him as I stared in awe at the beauty before me. "They're magnificent."

"Well, go on," he encouraged me. "Put them on. I know you're dying to."

I stared at the boots but didn't move. After watching me for a few moments, Gavin took one out of the box and kneeled before me.

"May I have your foot, please, my Cinderella?"

I smiled and lifted my foot. He slid the boot on with ease, and we both admired it.

"Yeah. These are nice," he smiled.

"They're beautiful. But... I can't take them."

"What?" He placed his head on my forehead, then peered into my eyes deeply. "You don't have a fever. Have you been drugged?"

"Ha, ha," I frowned and rolled my eyes.

"You don't want these?" he asked, not believing me. "After all I went through to get them back for you?"

"Did you have to jump through hoops?"

"My bank account did," he joked. "Shoot, girl. After all the money I spent on these? You *are* accepting them. As a matter of fact, you're never taking them off. You're gonna sleep in them and everything."

I took his hands into my own and kissed them. "The thought was really sweet, and I appreciate that you went out of your way to get them for me. But you were right. I don't need them."

He gasped and clutched his chest as if he were having a heart attack.

"Don't play. I'm trying to be serious," I whined.

He smiled and hugged me. "I know, baby. I'm just surprised, that's all."

"Why? Because you think I'm selfish?"

"No, not that. It's just that... You know... They're your beloved boots."

"I know," I said as I stared at the impeccable creation on my foot. It was absolutely divine. So much detail was given to each accent, and the structure was exquisite. These were the kind of things I dreamed about wearing as a kid. When Leah and I went to the mall, I'd stand in department store windows and drool over them, then fantasize about becoming a successful business woman who could afford to wear them. Now I was that woman. But maybe I was overindulging to make up for my poor childhood.

"You sure you don't want them?"

"No, I do want them. But I thought about what you said the other day, and I can make the sacrifice for our family. There will always be more shoes that I can buy later. I can cut back for right now. You know... Just until the end of the season. When the weather changes, I'll be sure to buy an extra pair."

He laughed with the sweetest sense of pride. "You are so awesome, girl."

"I know," I said confidently, and winked at him.

He kissed me and told me that he loved me.

"I love you, too."

"Hey, let me ask you something. Can I still return these shoes if they're worn?"

"As long as there's no visible wear and tear on them."

"You don't have to worry about that. They won't even touch the floor."

I stared with confusion at first, then realized what he meant.

"Ol' mannish boy," I smiled, and gave him another kiss.

SEVENTEEN
GAVIN

I was working with a patient when one of the physical therapists stuck her head into the room.

"Excuse me, Gardner," she said. "You have a phone call on line two. It's your son's school."

My son's school?

Worried, I told my patient I would be back momentarily, then went into my office to pick up the phone, praying the entire time that Jonathan was okay.

"This is Gavin Gardner," I said into the receiver.

"Hello, Mr. Gardner. This is Mrs. Luke, the counselor at your son's school. I'm calling to let you know that Jonathan got into a fight today, and he has been suspended for the next three days. We need someone to come pick him up."

"WHAT?!!"

I didn't mean to yell in her ear, but what in the world was going on with Jonathan? It was totally out of his character to fight. Who could he have been fighting with, and what for? And where was I supposed to put him for the next three days while his mother and I were at work?

"Yes, Mr. Gardner. Unfortunately, it's true," his counselor told me.

"Shoot," I fussed aloud. "All right. I'll check with my boss and see if I can take an early lunch to come get him. If not, I'll have to send his mother to get him. Either way, someone will be there shortly."

"I understand," she said, and explained to me where her office was before we disconnected.

I found my boss and told him what happened. He excused me to take an early lunch and gave me permission to bring Jonathan to work with me for the rest of the day. I thanked him, then hurried toward the parking lot. On my way I saw Parker leaving the building, too. I didn't think anything of it at first, but when she stopped walking and gave me an inquisitive stare, we both laughed.

"Are we going to the same place?" she asked.

"I'm afraid so," I said, and held the door open for her. "Your kid suspended for fighting?"

"Yep," she said with a sigh. "I don't know where she gets it from."

I chuckled. "I wonder who won."

"Clearly your kid started it. My child is perfect," she joked.

****

Parker and I sat in the principal's office and exchanged looks of astonishment as he and the counselor explained what happened between our children. They got into a tussle that left Jonathan's face bruised and Madison's eyeglasses broken, but neither child wanted to explain why. I could tell that Jonathan was embarrassed and trying his hardest not to cry, so I didn't pressure him to talk. But as soon as we were alone, he was going to let me know what was going on with him.

"Mr. Gardner, our school has a very strict policy against fighting and bullying," he told me.

I looked at him like he was crazy. "My son isn't a bully."

"Well... He did hit a girl."

Keep your cool, man...

"My son isn't a bully," I repeated. "What he did was wrong, yes. And he knows it. Don't you, Jonathan?" I asked as I looked down at him.

He nodded.

"Jonathan has been at this school for two years, and this is the first time he's ever had to come see me," Mrs. Luke told the principal. "I don't think it's fair to label him a bully."

"Thank you," I told her, and eyed the principal with sternness. He needed to watch the way he talked about my son.

"Fine," he said a few moments later. "But he's still going to be suspended."

Parker gasped. "Suspended?!"

"Yes," the principal told her. "And your daughter will be, too."

"They're just kids!" she protested. "It's not like they brought a weapon to school and tried to hurt anybody!"

"Look at what your daughter did to this little boy's face," the principal told her.

"Kids fight all the time," she insisted. "Keeping them out of school isn't going to solve anything. They have to be here to learn."

"That's right, Ms. Knight. They come here to learn, not fight. The suspension will be for three days," he told us. "Their teacher has also advised that they will miss recess for a week on their return."

"HEY!" Madison screamed, and stood up angrily. "NO RECESS?!!! ARE YOU

CRAZY?!!"

"That's not fair!" Jonathan declared with her. "For a whole week?!"

"Sit your little behind down," Parker said sharply to her daughter, and pulled her into her seat by the bottom of her dress. "I don't know what has gotten into you today, but you better get it out of you real quick. Do you understand me? You know you don't talk to grown people like that."

Madison folded her arms across her chest and stared angrily at the floor.

Lord, have mercy... Parker's got a diva...

"You might want to simmer down, too" I told my son. "You're in enough trouble as it is."

He lowered his head and began to fiddle with his hands.

"Isn't there something else we can do?" Parker asked the principal. "I'm a single parent, and I have to work. I don't have anyone here who can keep her."

"That's not our problem," he told her plainly.

She grunted. "Sir, I'm trying to tell you that I—"

I held up my hand to stop her. There was no use in begging this man for anything. He was heartless, and I doubted that he was compassionate enough to work with children.

Parker eyed me with confusion, but then understood why I stopped her when she looked me in the eye. She sat back and crossed her legs, allowing me to take the lead, which I appreciated. Dana would have kept arguing.

"When does the suspension start?" I asked him.

"Immediately," he said, and gave Parker and me each a sheet of paper. "Once you sign these, you are free to go. But please keep in mind that your children will still be required to keep up with their work load. Their teacher has it for you in her room.

Parker was visibly upset, but she kept her mouth closed and signed the paper. I did as well, then we excused ourselves to our children's classroom with them in tow. Once we had their work we went our separate ways.

"Can we listen to the radio?" Jonathan asked once we were in my truck.

"No. You're gonna ride in silence so you can think about what you've done. Now what happened between you and Madison? I thought you were friends. How did you end up fighting?"

"She didn't do what I told her to," he answered, as if that warranted him breaking her glasses.

"I need a better explanation than that."

"I told her to be my girlfriend, and she told me no."

What the...?

I took a deep breath and told myself to tread lightly. If I came down on him too hard, he'd never tell me anything ever again, and I didn't want us to have that type of relationship.

"How did you end up breaking her glasses?"

"Because she pushed me."

"Why?"

"Because she got mad at me."

"Why?"

He huffed, irritated with my questions. "I told her to be my girlfriend. She said no, she didn't want to. I told her she had to be my girlfriend, and she said she didn't want to be my girlfriend because her mama said she can't have a boyfriend until she is old. So I told her that I didn't want to wait until I was old, I wanted her to be my girlfriend now, and then we can get married when we get old. She said no, and I told her she was going to be my girlfriend no matter what, and I kissed her, and she got mad and punched me in my face. So I got mad because she punched me, and I pushed her down, and she fell and broke her glasses. I didn't hit her like the principal said. I pushed her. I didn't break her glasses on purpose. But she—"

"Wait a minute," I stopped him. "This whole ordeal is because you wanted her to be your girlfriend?"

"I still do," he told me. "She's pretty, Daddy."

I looked out of my window to keep from laughing in his face. Once I regained my bearings I turned to him again.

"You know that you are supposed to be nice to women," I told him. "Don't I teach you that?"

"Yes, but she's not a woman. She's Madison."

"She's a girl, J. You gotta treat her with respect."

"Respect?"

"Yes, respect."

"Like... Call her ma'am, and stuff?"

"No, not like that. What I mean is that you have to be polite. You can't force a girl to do what you want her to do, son. You can't make Madison, or any other girl, be your girlfriend. It has to be consensual."

He frowned with confusion. "Con... what?"

"*Con-sens-u-al.* It means that both of you have to agree to it. You want Madison to be your girlfriend. She said no. You agree to it and just stay friends. That's it."

"But I like her."

"*It's not all about you, Jonathan,*" I scolded. "If you want her to be your girlfriend, then she has to want you to be her boyfriend. She told you that her mother said she can't have a boyfriend right now. You should have listened. You didn't, and that's why she popped you. And since when did you start kissing girls?"

He blushed and covered his face with his hands.

"Answer me."

"I don't kiss girls," he said, his face still covered. "I just really want her to be my girlfriend. I love her so much, Daddy."

I had to turn away again.

Wait until I tell Dana. She is gonna fall out laughing!

"Well, you gotta be nice to her," I told him once I gathered myself, and pulled his hands away from his face. "You can't just bogart your way into a girl's heart. That's not nice. You can't force her to like you."

"That's what you do to Mommy," he claimed.

Surprised and slightly offended, I asked him what he meant.

"That is what you do to Mommy," he insisted. "You say, 'Come here and kiss me,' or, 'Come here and get a kiss,' and she does it. And you do tell her what to do. You tell her she can't buy her shoes anymore, and that makes her sad, but you still do it, and she's a girl."

His little chest swelled before my eyes as he talked, and his eyes pierced with further accusations. My feelings were actually hurt. I didn't know that he heard Dana and me arguing, or that it had affected him so much. I had to be a better example.

"I'm sorry," I apologized to him. "You're right. I haven't been as nice as I should be to Mommy lately. But I'm telling you the truth. You have to be nice to Madison. Not just because you want her to be your girlfriend, but because it's the right thing to do. You have to be a gentleman at all times. You remember what a gentleman is, don't you?"

"Yes. A gentle man," he answered.

"Yes, sir. Now, were you gentle with Madison earlier? Trying to kiss her when she didn't want you to, and pushing her to the ground? Do you think a gentleman would do that?"

"No," he admitted.

"Madison's a great friend to you, right? Didn't you tell me she's the only girl in your class that's not scared of spiders? She's pretty cool. She didn't deserve that, did she?"

"No, sir."

"No, she didn't, so don't treat her like that anymore. And you keep your hands to yourself from now on. I shouldn't even have to tell you that. You already know not to hit people."

"She hit me first. I was defending myself. You said I could do that," he reminded me.

"Yes, I did. But you know you can't hit girls."

"I didn't hit her. I *pushed* her."

"You can't *push* girls, either. That's not nice."

"Well, what was I supposed to do? She punched me! And it hurt!"

I held onto his face and studied the bruise.

"She clocked you, huh?" I chuckled. "She got you good."

"She hit me so hard I fell on the ground."

"Serves you right. But you'll be all right. I'll get you an ice pack when we get to work," I told him, and started the truck. "And you will be paying for Madison's glasses."

His face fell. "How? I don't have any money. I'm just a kid."

"Should have thought about that before you went around kissing a girl with glasses."

He gave a depressed sigh and leaned back against his seat. "Maybe I can ask Mommy for the money. I remember she bought me some glasses at the mall one time, and they were twenty dollars, I think."

I laughed. "Were they sunglasses?"

He nodded.

"Yeah... Madison's glasses weren't like those. They were special. She has to go to a doctor to get her glasses. And they cost a lot of money."

"Oh," he said, and became visibly worried. "Like, forty dollars?"

"Probably more than that," I told him. "We'll find out when we ask her mother."

"But all I have is five dollars," he told me as we advanced out of the parking lot. "You think Grandma will give me the rest of the money?"

"Nope," I declared. "You, son, are going to do what a man does when he doesn't have the money to pay for the things he needs."

Jonathan was confused. "I said ask Grandma."

"Nope. You're going to work."

He gasped. "Like... *a job?*"

"Yes, sir."

"How? I'm not old enough to have a job!"

"We'll start with extra chores when we get home this evening."

"Aw, man," he frowned, and angrily turned to face his window.

EIGHTEEN
DANA

I tried not to yawn into my sister's ear as she gave me the latest happenings from her home Bible study gathering, but the rudeness escaped me despite my effort. We'd only been on the phone for fifteen minutes, and what she had to say wasn't boring at all. I was just tired. I'd hadn't slept well all week, and the constant nausea I'd had the past few days was draining. It was a wonder I could remain standing.

"Girl, that is the fifth time you've yawned," Leah complained.

"Thanks for counting."

"You're working too hard. You need to sleep."

"I'm trying to," I said through another yawn. "Just have too much stuff to do."

"I keep trying to tell you that you aren't young anymore."

"I'm not old."

"You're not twenty. You need to eat right, exercise, and get enough rest."

"Yes, *Mother.*"

She sighed. "Just answer me this, smarty pants. When was the last time you had a good bowl of mixed vegetables? And coffee beans don't count."

"I don't know... Last night?"

She was surprised. "Really?"

"Yes. You know Gavin cooks."

"Right, right..." she remembered, pondering. "How long have you been feeling like this?"

"About a week," I told her. "It's probably just stress."

"Did you get your period?"

I didn't answer, which was all the answer she needed.

She gasped. "Oooh, girl. You're pregnant."

"Hush. No, I'm not," I declared, but I really wasn't sure. The thought of it was frightening, and I'd been avoiding dealing with the fact that my period was now eight days late.

"That would explain everything," she said happily. "The grogginess. Your fatigue. Girl, you're pregnant. I'm not telling you what I think, I'm telling you what I know."

"Well, you don't know what you're talking about, because I'm not pregnant," I said with fake confidence. "I just need stronger coffee, that's all."

"You and Gavin are still trying, aren't you?"

"Yes," I told her, knowing full well that I was still taking my birth control pills.

"You need to take a test."

"I'm not pregnant. I probably just need a detoxifying massage at the spa or something. Or maybe go on a cleanse. That'll fix me."

"You need to quit playing and take a pregnancy test. You need to start taking prenatal vitamins as soon as you find out, and how else will you know until you take the test? Go take one. Right now."

"Girl, I just got home after working all day. I'm not running back out to the store to pick up a test I don't need to take because I'm not pregnant.."

She paused a moment. "You don't have one?"

"No," I said, and frowned at the phone like she was crazy.

"You've been trying to get pregnant for the past two years, yet you don't have a pregnancy test at your house? Are you even having sex, Dana?"

"*YES!*" I snapped. "Goodness, Leah. Boundaries!"

"I'm not convinced," she continued. "When we were working to get MJ, I had a *slew* of tests at my house."

Annoyed, I said, "Great for you, boo."

Leah gasped. "I'm bringing you one."

"*What?!*"

"I'm bringing you a test. I have one in my bathroom. I'll bring it over and you can take it while I'm there. Then we'll both know."

"Leah, *do not* come to my house."

"I'm coming," she said, and began to squeal. "Marcus is here. He can watch the kids. Give me thirty minutes, and I'll be there. I'm so *excited!* Oh, you're pregnant! I already know. *I can feel it!* I've been waiting on this baby *forever!*"

"Leah, don't you come to my house!"

She'd already hung up.

"Dang it!" I fussed, and put the phone on the counter. I did not need Leah all in my business. I was going to take the test, it was going to come out negative, then she was gonna be all dramatic and give me a sermon about the biblical story of Sarah and how she had to wait a long time for her baby. Sarah wanted a baby. I did not.

Jonathan looked up at me with surprise. "Aunty Leah not listening to you again?"

I pointed to the sheet in front of him. "Homework."

He frowned, but did as he was told.

****

Leah walked into the house without even knocking or ringing the doorbell.

"Girl!" I scolded when she wobbled into the kitchen with her big belly. "I know you didn't just sashay in here like you pay bills or something."

She went over to Jonathan and gave him a kiss on his forehead.

"Hush all that fuss," she told me, and placed the pregnancy test she had with her in my hand. "If you're so worried about people walking in, lock the front door. Now stop stalling and take the test."

"What test?" Jonathan asked.

"Go in the living room and watch TV," Leah told him.

As Jonathan walked away I gave the test back to Leah. "I don't feel like taking that test right now. I wish you had listened to me before you drove all the way over here."

She studied me for a moment, then said, "I know what this is. You're afraid of being disappointed. You've been trying so long to get pregnant, and you don't want to be let down again."

I rolled my eyes. Pregnancy was making her deaf. "That's not it."

"It's a normal feeling," she insisted. "I've been where you are. But the sooner you find out, the better, for both you and the baby."

I sighed deeply and snatched the test away from her. "If I pee on this thing, will you leave me alone?" I asked impatiently.

"Maybe," she said, and winked at me. Her exuberance was sickening.

"Uuurrggghhh," I groaned, and went to the bathroom with her close on my heels. "Don't follow me in here," I snapped, and closed the door behind me.

"I need to make sure you do it right," Leah insisted as she knocked on the door.

"I can read the instructions! I'm not a baby!"

She waited a moment, then said, "Maybe not. But you're about to have one," and giggled.

"Don't make me come out there," I warned as I read the back of the box. The instructions weren't difficult. Pretty much, all I had to do was urinate on the stick. I did not need supervision or further instruction.

"I don't hear any tinkling," she rushed me.

"All right, already!" I hollered back, then prayed to God to please not allow me to be pregnant.

Dang it. I should have picked up one of those morning after pills. No. I could never do that. I didn't want a kid, but I could never abort it.

"I still don't hear anything!"

"I can't with you breathing down my neck! Go watch TV with Jonathan. I'll just be a minute."

I knew she wasn't going to go anywhere until she heard the sound she was waiting for, so I went ahead and took the test. Once I finished I washed my hands and joined her on the other side of the door to wait for the results.

"Aren't you excited?" She bounced and clapped her hands with anticipation. "Clearly, you are."

She hugged me and began to sing that she was going to be an aunt.

"Daddy's home!" Jonathan yelled at us from the living room.

I gasped as I heard the garage open. A moment later the hum of his truck's engine reached us. Leah's entire face rounded as she grew even more excited. My heart sank. I didn't want Gavin to know that I thought I might be pregnant. He'd only get excited, and I didn't want to talk about babies all night like I knew I would end up having to do if he got wind of this.

"Shoot!" I fussed, and stomped my foot. I should have kicked Leah out as soon as she gave me that stupid test!

"Sister-in-law is in the house!" Gavin said as he came inside and saw Leah.

"Hey, Daddy!" she squealed.

He was confused, but before I could say anything she squealed, "Dana's pregnant!"

"No! Dana is not pregnant!" I yelled, and pinched her arm. "Leah thinks I'm pregnant and she's making me take a test," I told him. "But don't get your hopes up. I'm just a few days late. Probably just because of stress, that's all. We're just waiting for the results."

I could feel the happiness pouring out of him. He flung his bag into the corner and stood behind me, wrapping his arm around me in a hug. I cringed. He was going to wait with us for the test results. Ugh, this day was never going to end.

"We'll know in a minute," Leah told him. "I'm so happy for you guys!"

"Leah, don't you think this is a private matter?" I asked. "You know, a husband and wife thing?"

"She can stay," Gavin told me.

"It should be ready now," she said, and nudged me toward the bathroom door.

"The box said three minutes."

"It's been three minutes."

"No, it hasn't," I denied, afraid of what the test would say. I didn't want a baby! My life could not be all about bottles, and breast feeding, and day care centers, and diapers, and pacifiers. I wasn't ready!

Jesus, please don't let me be pregnant! PLEASE!!!

"Well, just go check," she told me, and opened the bathroom door for me.

I looked to Gavin for an escape plan, but he offered none. He wanted to know the results more than my sister did.

I moaned and slumped to the bathroom counter where I'd left the test. A pink plus sign showed on the results display.

"Oh," I gasped, and horrified tears filled my eyes.

Leah came into the bathroom with me and peered over my shoulder.

"Yes!" she screamed, and hugged me from behind. "I knew it! I knew you were pregnant!"

I continued to stare at the test as Gavin joined us. Tears flooded down my face as everything began to register.

I was pregnant. I was going to have a baby. A baby. A live... screaming... baby.

I was going to get fat...

And be forced to wear maternity clothes...

And *flat shoes*...

I felt sick. Literally sick. Like I was going to throw up. Or pass out. Or both.

"I'm so happy for you!" Leah beamed.

"We did it!" Gavin bellowed. "We did it, baby! We're going to have a baby! We finally did it!"

I turned to face him and saw the elation in his eyes. He was so happy, but I was horrified.

"Aren't you excited?" he asked when I didn't say anything.

I looked at the test again, just to make sure my eyes weren't playing tricks on me. They weren't.

I was pregnant.

"Dana? You okay?"

I fainted.

NINETEEN
GAVIN

The longer Leah and I watched over Dana as she laid in her hospital bed, the more concerned I became. We'd been at the hospital for over an hour, and the longer we stayed, the more irritated she became. She talked more to Leah than to me, and whenever I said something to her she refused to make eye contact with me.

"Are you sure you're okay, baby?" I asked as I leaned in close to her.

"I'm fine, Gavin!" she snapped, and lifted the bed sheet over her head. "I just want to go home."

I looked to Leah for help, but her patience was running thin, too. She pulled the sheet away from Dana and popped her on the arm as if she were disciplining a small child instead of a grown woman.

"Stop being difficult," she fussed.

"Can you just leave me alone, please?" Dana begged.

We all knew that wasn't about to happen. I'd already asked Leah to sit in the waiting room with Jonathan so he wouldn't be a bother to the nurses watching over him at their station, but she wouldn't hear of it. Dana was her baby sister, and she'd always been very protective. Her overbearing love was only going to be intensified now that she finally had a little niece or nephew on the way.

"We have to make sure the baby is okay," Leah said. "You're a mother now. Start acting like it."

Dana flinched. When she saw that I noticed she tried to disguise it by shifting to her side on the bed.

That's what bothering her. The baby...

Suddenly I remembered her face when she read the pregnancy test results. It wasn't full of joy and elation like it should have been, considering that we'd been trying to conceive for so long. There was no relief at all, or gratitude to God for finally blessing us with a child. She was horrified. I hadn't realized it until now because everything happened so fast. One second I was celebrating our good news, and the next second I was shaking her into consciousness. Now that I thought about it, I could have sworn I heard her say, "Oh, no," before she hit the ground. Yes, she did.

And why wasn't she as concerned for the new baby as Leah and I were? She hadn't said anything at all about it. As a new mother, shouldn't she be worried?

Leah adjusted the pillow behind Dana's head to try to make her more comfortable, but all it did was annoy Dana even more. When she began to adjust the bed's incline, Dana shoved her hands away and threatened to have a nurse throw her out of the room.

Once Leah finally left her alone, Dana put all of her energy into staring at the needle piercing through the back of her hand that pumped saline through her veins. After watching her for a few minutes, I determined her behavior was too unsettling not to talk to her about and asked Leah to give us some privacy. Just as she was leaving, a heavyset bald man with glasses came into the room.

"Mrs. Dana Jeffries-Gardner," he said as he reviewed her chart, then looked up at her and smiled. "What are you doing passing out, girl?"

Surprisingly, Dana smiled back at him. Apparently they'd built some type of rapport with each other where he felt comfortable enough to become unprofessional. He gave her an encouraging pat on the leg as he stood beside Leah.

"Hi, Steve. This is my husband, Gavin, and my sister Leah," she introduced us, and pointed halfheartedly. "You guys, this is Steve Kohl."

"Lucky man," he said to me, and extended his hand "I had the pleasure of having your wife design the mother-in-law suite of my home. She did a fantastic job."

I shook his head, which he offered to Leah, too, but she didn't have time for niceties.

"Is the baby okay?" she demanded to know. "Did you run tests on the blood you took? Aren't you guys gonna do an ultrasound or something?"

"*Leah...*" Dana grumbled and slowly lifted her hands to her temples as she laid her head back on the bed.

Dr. Kohl laughed. "Baby? There's no baby here. Dana isn't pregnant. She's on birth control."

Confused, Leah and I exchanged glances, then stared at Dr. Kohl for an explanation.

"Are you trying to pull my leg?" he asked when we didn't laugh with him.

Dana slid her hands over her eyes.

Suddenly, his face fell. I realized then that he'd said too much. They shared a secret, and I was out of the loop.

"*Dana...*"

She turned away from my voice and stiffened in the bed.

What the... is going on? I was her husband. How did this guy know something about her that I didn't?

"What's he talking about?" Leah asked. When Dana didn't answer, she turned to the doctor and placed her hand on her stomach as if she were suddenly scared for her own baby that she was carrying. "What do you mean, she's on birth control?"

Birth control...

Intense pressure weighed against me the longer Dana refused to deny it. She didn't say anything at all. She just laid in the bed with her face covered, too ashamed to admit how deceitful she'd been.

I was becoming angry. How could she be on birth control and I not know about it? Why would she do such a thing behind my back? I was her husband. Why would she not tell me? Why would she take birth control, anyway? She wanted a baby, didn't she? If not, why did she pretend to for two and a half years? She wasn't that foul, was she?

"What's going on?" Leah asked Dr. Kohl.

"Uuugghhh..." He backed away cautiously. "Perhaps I should leave," he suggested.

"Perhaps you should stay right here and tell me what you're talking about," I warned. "One of y'all better say something, and since she's all of a sudden mute, *you* better start talking."

Leah gasped and watched me with alarm. I realized my hands were balled into fists, and my jaw was tight, too. Learning I'd been deceived had me mad enough to hurt someone.

"I, uh..." He stammered and pushed his thick glasses up on his nose, but didn't say anything more.

"What's he talking about, Dana?" I asked her, and held on to the railing of the bed to keep from putting my hands on someone.

She said nothing.

"Dana!"

"Gavin, calm down," Leah told me, and began to rub Dana's shoulder as she started to cry.

"This doesn't concern you," I said through tight teeth. "This is between me and my wife."

"Yes, but this isn't the place. Not until you calm down," she told me, and shifted her eyes toward the doctor. "If they have to call security, you know where you'll go. *Now calm down.*"

I listened to my sister-in-law's advice and forced myself to calm down. This wasn't worth going to jail over.

Dana continued to cry and wiped her eyes with her hospital gown. I backed away from her, disgusted by what was happening before me.

"Can you talk to us, please?" Leah asked Dana.

She curled her knees into her chest and continued to cry with her head down.

"What's going on?" Leah asked the doctor. "How can you say she's not pregnant? She just took a pregnancy test and it came back positive."

Dr. Kohl saw that we were concerned, and his sympathy for us showed on his face.

"Dana, you're not pregnant," he said, even though she wasn't looking at him. "There are times when a home pregnancy test can give a false positive. It happens all the time. We tested your blood. You're not pregnant. All of your symptoms—the fainting, fatigue, upset stomach, and the headaches, are all likely due to stress and dehydration. I'm sure this is a relief to you, seeing that you listed Ortho Tri-cyclen as the only medication you are currently taking."

His eyes darted over to me, and I realized he was saying all of this for my benefit. As a man, he put himself in my shoes, and knew he would feel the same way that I did if he were me. I received his message loud and clear, and the information began to clear my confusion.

"Are you sure?" Leah asked. She was disappointed and couldn't believe her sister would keep such a secret from her.

"Positive."

"Oh..." Leah turned to me with concern, but I couldn't face her sympathy and turned away. "Will she have to stay for more tests?" she asked the doctor.

"No. She's fine. After her IV bag finishes she can go," he told us. "If you have any more questions, you can see one of the nurses up front. I suggest that you keep an eye on her throughout the night. If she faints again or has any serious discomfort, come back."

He gave us a grim nod, and we thanked him before he left the room.

Dana's fear was evident once he was gone. She stared down at her hands and continued to cry while we waited for her to explain. Her inability to do so made the air tight with tension.

A few moments later Leah told us she would returned to the waiting room to keep an eye on Jonathan. She gave Dana an encouraging kiss on the forehead and left us alone to talk privately.

"You gon' talk to me now, or what?" I asked.

She straightened her legs out and wiped her eyes with the back of her hand. "I'm sorry," she finally said.

Normally I would have had compassion for her and rushed to console her. Not this time. Not about this.

"Birth control?" I asked. "Really?"

She didn't answer.

"Why?"

She still couldn't say anything. It only made me angrier. My mind raced with more questions, and her silence taunted them. How could she do something like this to me?

"You need to start talking."

"Baby, please," she begged. "Don't be mad at me."

"It's too late for that!" I yelled at her.

"I'm sorry!" she cried.

She probably was, but I didn't care.

"You've been lying to me. Taking birth control behind my back? I can't believe you, Dana! Why would you do that? And I have to find out about it here, in front of your sister and the doctor? That should have been between us."

"I'm sorry," she apologized again. "I wanted to tell you. I promise you, I did."

"Then why didn't you?" I asked, and fought to hold back the tears that were coming to my own eyes.

"I tried to," she cried. "But you wouldn't listen."

"It's my fault you lied?"

"No, that's not what I'm..." She covered her eyes again with hopelessness.

I took a step back and told myself to keep it together. If I yelled and screamed the way I wanted to, things would get out of hand. But I was furious. She'd stabbed me in the back, and this wasn't an overpriced pair of shoes or a ridiculous purse purchase that I could overlook. This was betrayal.

"How long have you been taking them, Dana?"

She sank into herself and started holding her breath. My eyes closed in agony as I understood what her silence actually meant.

"You've been on them the entire time, haven't you?"

I didn't have to wait for an answer. I already knew.

She erupted into uncontrollable sobs. All I could do was stand there and try to figure out what had actually been happening over the past few years. My wife, who up until now I thought was the love of my life, had been lying to me for our entire marriage. For two and a half years she'd pretended to be down for me. She pretended to want the same things I wanted, and to actually be on my team. She knew the only additional thing I wanted out of life was to have more children, and she promised me she would do that for me, but she was nothing but a fraud. All the times we made love and prayed for God to bless us was just a front. She didn't want to have my children.

She was a liar.

"Baby, let me explain," she begged.

I was a fool. How could I be married to her and not see how fake she really was? This woman played me like I was the simplest fiddle. And I actually picked her to be a mother to Jonathan...

The sight of her tears repulsed me. They weren't because she was sorry. They were because she got caught. She was embarrassed that she'd been exposed.

"I'm out of here," I said, more to myself than to her, and walked out of the room. She called out to me, but I ignored her and continued to the waiting room to get my son, leaving her alone for her sister to deal with.

TWENTY
DANA

To my disappointment, the house was empty when Leah brought me home. I'd called Gavin repeatedly since he left my hospital, but each attempt to connect went ignored. I'd hoped he would be home when I arrived so we could talk about what happened.

"He'll be back soon," Leah told me when she saw how hurt I was. "He may just need a little time to think. That's all."

"He's so mad at me," I told her as we sat on the couch. My voice shook with anxiety. "I've never seen him that upset before. I think I really messed up this time."

"You did," she confirmed. "You can't blame him for being upset. You were lying to him about something that meant a lot to him, and you embarrassed him. That's something that a wife should never do."

I didn't have a right to cry, but I couldn't help it. All of this was overwhelming.

"I never meant for any of this to happen."

"Don't get yourself all worked up, now. Everything's gonna be alright," she told me.

"Can you stay with me, sis?" I begged. "Just until Gavin gets home. I really don't want to be alone right now."

She sighed, then said, "Yes, I can stay. Marcus is with the kids, so they'll be alright for a little bit. You're gonna have to feed me, though. Me and my baby are hungry."

"Thanks," I told her, and together we made our way into the kitchen. I was starving, too.

The dinner I was in the process of making before I fainted was still on the stove. It'd been simmering for hours now, and was severely overcooked. I thanked God that the house didn't burn down, threw the food away, and made turkey sandwiches for my sister and I to eat.

"Are those chocolate cupcakes?" she asked as she strained her neck to look into the pantry. She was nearly salivating as she eyed Jonathan's snacks.

"Do you want one?" I asked, nearly laughing at her excitement.

"Two, please," she told me with no shame.

I grabbed the bag of potato chips I'd originally opened the pantry to get, as well as the cupcakes, and joined her at the bar.

"Since when do you eat food like this?" I asked. Leah was a cook. She rarely ever ate anything processed.

"It's not me. It's the baby," she said, and took a big bite out of her sandwich. "She's so greedy, I tell you."

I chuckled as I watched her stuff her face. My sister. Where would I be without her?

"Can I ask you something?" she asked after we ate in silence for a few minutes.

I popped a chip in my mouth. "Shoot."

"Why'd you do it?"

I really didn't want to talk about it, but after Dr. Kohl, who I was *never in my life* speaking to again, blabbed all of my business, it made no sense to hide anything. Besides, I could be free with Leah. We had that type of relationship and she'd always been a safe haven for me. If I told her the truth, I knew she wouldn't hold it against me.

"I really don't want to have a baby," I confessed. It felt awful to actually say it out loud as a married woman. But it was true. "I never have."

"You know, I figured that. Even when we were kids, you never expressed a desire to be a mother. I was just hoping that being married would change your mind about it all, especially since you have Jonathan."

"I love that little boy," I said honestly, and felt some relief as I thought of his sweet face. *"He's* my baby. I don't want any more kids. I'm happy with just the three of us. And honestly, after I got married and Gavin told me how bad he wanted more kids, I thought after a while I would change my mind. But I never did."

"Well, what's so wrong with being a mother?" she asked me.

"Nothing. It's just not for me. I don't want to do the whole pregnancy thing. I feel blessed that God gave me a child through another woman. Sometimes I feel like the only reason Gavin was with Sabrina was to make Jonathan for me, because God knew that I never wanted to get pregnant. That may sound a little vain, but that's what I think sometimes."

"You don't have to try to explain the way God has blessed you to me," she assured me, though she did roll her eyes at my logic.

"Do you think I'm a bad wife, Leah?" I asked a moment later.

"Do you think you are?" she asked in return.

"I don't know. I don't think I am, but... The way he looked at me..." My eyes watered just thinking about it. "I just don't understand why everything has to depend on having a baby."

"No one is saying that."

"That's how it feels. I'm constantly being judged for it. You should hear the way he allows his mother to talk to me, and he just goes along with it without saying anything. The women in your bible study, too. Everyone acts like my sole duty in life as a wife is to produce children. None of who I am as an individual matters anymore. Not my career, or even my goals in life. It's all about popping those babies out."

"You shouldn't care so much about what his mother thinks. She just uses those things against you because she doesn't like you. What you and Gavin do isn't any of her business."

"Yeah, but when he found out I was on birth control, he just looked at me like everything she ever said about me was true."

"He was just upset. And you would be, too, if the situation were reversed and he mislead you for months."

"Years," I corrected her.

"Years?"

"Yes. Years, Leah," I confessed. "I've been on my birth control the entire time. I never stopped taking it."

She gasped. *"Dana!* No wonder he hasn't come home yet! Girl! It'll be a miracle if you see him at all tonight!"

"I know," I moaned with a deep sigh, and explained to her that Gavin and I didn't talk in depth about having children before we got married.

"That's a problem."

"You think?" I asked sarcastically.

"It wasn't good to lie to him about it, though," she continued.

I slumped over on the bar and picked at my sandwich. "I know... I tried telling him how I feel, but he's not the best listener."

"I don't know any men who are. That doesn't excuse deceiving him."

"Well, what am I supposed to do? Just give him everything he wants and be miserable? Does it all have to be about him?"

"No. But it's not supposed to be all about you, either, Dana. Marriage is give and take. You both have to put forth an effort to make each other happy. Now I know you love your husband, and I know he loves you. You both are going to have to find some common ground on this issue and do what you have to do to make your marriage work. Right now your ground is shaky, dear. However you may feel about it, the truth is that you lied to your husband about something very important, and he's upset about it. You're going to have to make it up to him."

"How?" I asked after trying to figure it out myself for a few minutes. "He won't even talk to me."

"Girl... I don't know. I give my husband all the children that he wants, so I don't have your problem," she joked.

"Ha, ha," I sassed, and rolled my eyes.

"Seriously, sis, if you want your marriage, you're gonna have to fight with all you have to keep it. Gavin is hurt. You're gonna have to go above and beyond to make it up to him."

I groaned. "Do you think it's actually possible?"

"Yes. You know why?"

I waited for the answer.

"Because you have God on your side. He's got you, and Gavin, too. You just keep praying for your husband through all of this. Don't be surprised if it takes him a while to trust you again. You lied to him for a long time. Most people would never be able to get over that. But I believe he'll come around. Just remember you made this bed, so you have to lay in it."

The truth hurt, but I accepted it. We continued to eat our food, and I prayed that it wouldn't take Gavin too long to forgive me.

TWENTY-ONE
GAVIN

Other than killing me, I'd always thought cheating was the worst thing a woman could do to me. Now I wasn't so sure. Would I rather Dana be intimate with another man than lie to me for our entire marriage? If it happened once, maybe. A one-time betrayal would be easier to get over than her lying to me the thousands of times she told me she wanted to have my child. The memories felt like darts of poison being shot through my heart.

This was killing me. I'd been madly in love with her since the day we met. I thought I knew her, but obviously I didn't. How could she do this to me? How could she lie like that, over and over again, directly to my face? And how did I miss her taking a pill every single day? *For two and a half years?* Was I dumb, or was she just extremely sneaky? How could I possibly trust her after this?

Her face...

I just couldn't get over the expression she had when she thought she was pregnant. She was scared out of her mind. I should have known right then. She didn't want a baby, and she never did. I should have known. *I should have known...*

"Are you okay, Daddy?"

I took my eyes off the road long enough to look over at Jonathan. He sat in the passenger's seat and wore a frown too heavy for his small face to carry.

"Yeah, son. I'm alright. Just tired."

"Is Mommy okay?"

"Yes, she's fine. Aunt Leah's staying with her at the hospital."

"Why couldn't we stay?"

"Because Mommy needs to be alone right now."

"Then why did Aunty stay?"

"Because."

"Because what?"

"Because she just wanted to, okay? Stop asking so many questions."

"Where are we going?"

"To Grandma's."

That brought him some relief. He hadn't seen his grandmother since the day she recreated Dana's dinner, which was nearly a month ago. I hadn't either, though I called every day to check on her. Things had just gotten too hectic with her constantly berating Dana, and I had to take a break from her for a while. Now I regretted it. She'd been telling me the truth about Dana the entire time. I was just too blinded by love to see it.

"When we get there, I need you to go upstairs to your room and play," I told Jonathan. "I have some grown up things I need to talk to Grandma about, and you don't need to hear."

He agreed to, and I told him to pull his video game out of the glove box to keep him occupied. We rode the rest of the way to Mama's quietly.

As soon as we walked in the house she knew something was wrong. Jonathan hugged her and went directly upstairs the way I told him to.

"What's the matter, baby?" she asked with worry on her face. "I haven't seen you in so long, and when you show up you look a mess. What's going on? You okay?"

I slumped over to the couch and flopped down. "It's Dana," I confessed with a heavy groan.

She stared at me blankly and waited for details.

"Something happened."

"Is she all right?"

"Yeah, she's fine. Physically, anyway, which is... *The problem.*"

"I'm an old woman now, baby," she said with an impatient sigh. "I ain't got all the time in the world. Spit it out already."

I sat up straight and rubbed my eyes. Mama was probably the worst person to talk to about this, but I needed to confide in someone trustworthy who supported me, and no one ever had my back the way Sylvia Gardner did.

"Well?" she asked. "What happened? She didn't leave you, did she?"

"No, no. Nothing like that," I assured her. "We just left the hospital, and... I found out that she really doesn't want to have my kids."

I waited for her to go on a full rant, but to my surprise she remained calm.

"Okay... Why were you at the hospital?"

I was suddenly getting a headache, but I gathered my strength and confided in her the evening's happenings. She gave me a hug, but didn't seem surprised at all.

"Did you know about this, Mama?" I asked. Why wasn't she as upset about this as I was? Didn't she want more grandchildren?

"Boy, you know that woman don't talk to me. Don't get to actin' foolish, now. How would I know that?"

"Then why aren't you surprised?"

"Because I'm not," she said plainly. "Honestly, I don't see how you even are. What do you expect from a woman like that?"

"Mama..." I recoiled at her remark. She may as well have slapped me and called me stupid.

"I'm not trying to make you feel bad," she alleged. "I just want you to think. Now you know I have always told you to believe people when they show you who they are, and all Dana has shown is selfishness and disrespect. Everything is always all about her. Not once has she ever showed you that she's about family. The girl don't even want to fully carry your last name. Why would you think she would want to have your baby? She didn't even have the decency to meet me before you got married."

Mama was telling the truth, but I didn't drive all the way over here for her to dog Dana. I needed her to be my mother and support me. Dana was still my wife, and that had to be respected.

"Don't talk about her like that, Mama," I warned.

"I ain't tryin' to make you upset. You mad enough, I see," she said. "I was jus' tryin' to answer your question."

My head started to pound. I covered my face and rested against the couch. She gave me an encouraging pat on the back and told me that I was going to be okay.

"I know," I whined. "I'm just..."

"Hurt," she finished for me. "And that's understandable. She deceived you."

Yeah. She did.

"So are you getting a divorce now?"

"What?" I sat up and looked at her like she was crazy. "What are you talking about? Nobody's getting a divorce."

She stared back at me like I was just as crazy as I thought she was. "Why not? Don't you think it's time to, after all this?"

"She didn't cheat on me. She just lied."

"Oh, that's excusable?" She scoffed. "That girl don' put roots on you. Whip appeal or something. 'Cause I don't know how you still wanna be with her after all this. Don't you know that you are a good man? You deserve someone who will love you the way a wife should love her husband, and that girl there don't. Do you know how many women out there would be more than happy to give you the children you want? And they cook and clean, too!"

"Marriage is about more than cooking and cleaning," I told her. "It's about love and sacrifice."

"Seem to me like you the only one sacrificing."

"Uuugggghhhh... Mama..."

I hated to admit it, but she had a point. A really good one, too. I couldn't remember the last time Dana sacrificed anything for me. Maybe she really didn't love me the way I thought she did.

"Now look," she continued. "I ain't never been one to break up no happy home. Or home, period, because yours don't seem to be too happy. And I ain't trying to make you feel no worse than you already do, so I'm gonna leave this alone for now. But—"

"Thank you," I cut her off.

She understood that I wanted her to shut up. She got up and walked slowly into the kitchen while I kicked my shoes off and stretched out across the couch. My headache was growing stronger and I desperately wanted to rest.

"I just gotta say something," she said a few minutes later.

I opened my eyes to see her standing over me with a glass of iced tea in her hand. "What, Mama?"

"I know you want some more babies, and that's fine. But you need to think about the child you already have upstairs. He needs a good mother."

"Dana is a good mother. Stop trying to rag on her, Ma."

"Don't get mad at me. You're the one who came over here complaining. I'm just trying to tell you that maybe, just maybe, she ain't the one you need to be having babies with. Just 'cause you married her don't mean nothing. Sometimes God has a way of answering our prayers by not giving us what we really want. That's all I'm trying to tell you. If you ain't happy, baby, you can always leave."

I sat up straight and looked her directly in the eye. She had absolutely no conviction at all about the hurtful and dangerous words she just spoke. I couldn't take this blatant disregard of respect any more. I had to put my foot down.

"If you even *hint* one more time that I should divorce my wife, you won't see me again," I told her. "You're my mother, but you don't make those decisions for me. *Do you understand?*"

In all my years of living, I'd never been so stern with her. She was offended, but she believed me.

"Fine," she said, and tears came to her eyes. She blinked them away and whispered with a shaky voice, "I'll let you be the man that you've become."

She walked slowly into the kitchen with her shoulders hung low. I hated to see her wounded like that, but returned to my lying position and let the promise I made resonate. I couldn't go back on my word.

"Y'all eat yet?" she asked me about ten minutes later. She pretended to be fully recovered from the heavy blow I'd given her, but I could still hear the pain in her voice.

"No," I answered.

"That's probably why you have a headache. It's after seven o'clock. I got some meatloaf and mashed potatoes in here my boys can eat. I'll heat this up and go upstairs to get the baby," she told me. "You have a headache, so just lay on the couch until it goes away. I'll fetch you some Motrin, and some water, too."

"I'll get it, Grandma," I heard Jonathan say quickly.

I rolled over on the couch and saw him trot down the stairs. There was no way he'd been in his room playing like he was supposed to have been. Had he been listening to our conversation the entire time? How much did he hear?

I eyed him suspiciously as he walked past me into the kitchen. A moment later he brought me a glass of water and a bottle of Motrin. He was sad. He didn't even look at me. He'd heard something, for sure, and needed a swat on his behind for being disobedient.

"Go back upstairs until I call you down for dinner," I said sternly. The last thing I needed was this child in my business.

He did as I said, and I took a dose of the pain reliever and drank the glass of water.

As I laid back down again, I couldn't help but think about what Mama said. She was nosy, yes, and demanding, and too controlling. But one thing she had never been was stupid. She was not surprised at all by what Dana had done, and that said a lot. Not once had she ever faltered on her opinion of her. Maybe I really had made a mistake in marrying her.

No.

Noooo...

I prayed before I proposed to Dana, and I could remember distinctly hearing the Lord tell me that she was the woman for me.

Or did I?

If I did, would I really be in this situation right now? Would the woman He told me I could marry really not want to have my children? How did that make sense? Mama was right. We weren't perfect for each other after all. I needed to be with someone else. Someone like...

Parker.

TWENTY-TWO
DANA

Leah was only able to stay with me for a couple of hours. Around nine o'clock she had to return to her own family, and since then I'd been calling Gavin nonstop, worried sick about where he could be and what he was doing out with Jonathan so late at night. He refused to answer any of my calls, and I became so desperate for him that I resulted to calling his mother. She told me it wasn't her job to keep up with my husband and hung up the phone in my face.

It was after one o'clock in the morning when I finally heard the garage open. I leaped from my spot on the living room couch where I'd been perched ever since Leah left and ran to the door. Gavin didn't greet me when he saw me. In fact, he seemed annoyed that I was still awake.

He got out of his truck, then hoisted Jonathan over his shoulder as he struggled to gather their things. The child was in a nearly comatose state of sleep and didn't stir out of his slumber at all.

"Hey, baby."

Gavin didn't respond, but I knew he heard me. I moved to the side so he could walk into the house and tried to take Jonathan from him, but he jerked away quickly and threatened me with eyes that yelled, "DON'T YOU DARE TOUCH MY SON!"

My mouth gaped with alarm, but Gavin didn't care to apologize. He rolled his eyes and continued into the house, leaving me at the door completely crushed by his coldness. Did he really think I was going to hurt Jonathan? Did not wanting to birth children make me no longer suitable to even touch him? Was he no longer my son?

I brushed the hurtful thoughts away and set our home's security alarm, then hurried upstairs. Gavin was in Jonathan's room, putting him in his bed.

"I can put him in his pajamas," I offered, and went to his dresser.

He held up his hand to stop me. "If you change his clothes, you'll wake him up."

We both knew that I wouldn't. He just didn't want me to be around his son, and it hurt. He knew that it would, too, which was why he did it.

"Okay," was all I said. I didn't want to argue.

I watched silently as he took the child's shoes and socks off and gave him a kiss on the cheek. For the sake of not arguing I kept my mouth shut and followed him into our bedroom.

"Where have you been?" I asked once I closed the door.

He didn't answer and took off his shirt.

"Aren't you gonna talk to me?"

He ignored me and went into the bathroom and closed the door behind him. A few moments later the shower began to run.

It was all I could do not to cry. He'd never been so cold toward me before. I got in the bed and began to pray. I wanted God to fix the mess I created. My marriage had been rocked by this, but I loved my husband and wanted what we had to survive.

Gavin stayed in the bathroom for nearly twenty minutes. He never showered that long. Not without me in the shower with him, anyway. I suspected the extra time was to avoid me.

When he finally returned I moved the bed covers back so he could join me. He froze and stared at me with more disappointment than I'd ever seen. I was nearly crushed.

"I'm sorry, baby," I whispered, and tears slowly ran down my cheeks. "Can we please talk about this? I don't want to fight."

He opened his mouth to say something, but couldn't bring himself to deliver his heart's message. Instead, he picked up his pillow and walked out of the room. Alarmed that he would even hint at sleeping away from me, I jumped out of bed and made it to the hallway just in time to see him go into the guest bedroom. Overwhelmed, I retreated back to bed and cried myself to sleep.

TWENTY-THREE
GAVIN

Things at work went smoothly for the most part over the next few days. I was grateful. The joy of helping others brought a sense of peace and was a comforting break from the tension I felt at home. I could barely stand to look at Dana. The distance I'd put between us by choosing to sleep in the guest bedroom left her both angry and depressed, and I was starting not to care at all about her feelings. She brought it all on herself. She was the one who lied for our *entire* marriage. If I'd done that to her, there was no telling what she would do.

I was mad at her, but I couldn't stop thinking about her. No matter how great things went at work, she consumed the majority of my thoughts. Even now, as I made my way down to the coffee stand, all I could think about was how wrong she was to do something so deceitful—until I saw Parker.

My jaw dropped as she walked toward me from the opposite end of the hall. She was wearing a dress. And heels. *And sheer pantyhose...*

Dddddaaaaannnnnngggggggg!

Ol' girl was looking good! This presentation was far better than the ugly clogs and brightly patterned socks she'd become known for around the clinic. Not that she ever looked bad. She could be dressed in a brown paper bag and everyone would fawn over her. Now, dressed like this, I could, too.

I couldn't help but stare as her shapely legs brought her closer. Finally she noticed me, and a surprised smile came over her face.

"Hey," she said once we were close, and stopped to talk to me.

"Where are you heading off to, all dressed up?" I asked. "I know you can't be working in those clothes."

"No. I have a date," she informed me with a bashful blush. "Well, it's not actually a date. Just a meeting, I guess. It's not a date if it's during lunch, is it? I don't know. There's this guy—He's a doctor, and he works out at my gym. He's been wanting to take me out for a little while now, so I finally agreed to."

"Are you nervous?" I asked. She was rambling. I'd never heard her talk so fast before.

She cringed. "Can you tell?"

"Uh, yeah."

"Ugh, I am," she admitted. "I don't know why. It's just a guy, right? It's just that I haven't been on a date in *sssssoooo* long. Like, over a year, and my game is *so off.* I'm scared I'm not gonna know if he's into me or not."

I gave her a reassuring smile. "You're gonna be fine."

"You think so?" she asked with a pout. Her lack of confidence was cute.

"He wouldn't have asked you out if he wasn't into you."

"Yeah, you're right," she agreed, and chuckled at herself. "I'll stop being so dramatic and go on the date. But seriously, as a friend, tell me what you think of this outfit. It's not too much, is it?"

Oh, no... Did she just "friend" me?!!!

"Well, my wife will tell you that I don't know too much about fashion. But I do know that what you wear depends a lot on where you're going."

"I think he said the restaurant was called La Roux. I've never heard of it. I meant to look it up online last night, but Madison and I just *had to have* a tea party. That little girl drives me crazy. Demanding little diva."

Hearing her daughter's name brought a surprising smile to my face. She was something else. Jonathan talked about her nonstop.

"I think what you have on is fine for La Roux," I told her. "My wife wears something similar whenever I take her there. It's one of her favorite spots in the area."

She gave a sigh of relief, but internally I had none. Who was this guy taking her out to lunch? What exactly did he have planned? Was he cool? How long had he been pursuing her, and what was so special about him that she would give him a chance? Was it because he was a doctor? She wasn't the type that was all about money, was she? No. She was down to earth. But why did I care so much? What Parker did in her life was her business, not mine. I was married. Frustrated, but still married. And she'd just put me in the friend zone. I shouldn't even care.

"Who knows? Maybe it'll be my new favorite place, too," she said with a smile.

I, however, did not want to hear anything else about her date with Dr. Love. I decided to quickly change the subject before I turned into a full-blown hater and verbalized my desire for her date to end treacherously.

"Hey, I've been meaning to ask you how much it's going to cost to replace Madison's glasses."

She was surprised, and smiled sweetly. "Oh, no, Gavin. You don't have to pay for those."

"Are you sure? My son broke them, so I'm responsible. I know those things aren't cheap."

"I'm positive," she insisted. "Her new pair were completely covered by insurance. I didn't have to pay anything."

"Really?"

"Yeah, yeah. Madison's been wearing glasses since she was four, and she's a tomboy. Those were the third pair that she's broken this year."

I grinned, recalling all of the stories about her I'd heard from Jonathan.

"Those kids of ours are something else, aren't they?" I asked with a warm smile. Jonathan had that affect on me. Even when I was tired or in the worst mood, he knew how to bring out the best in me. "I'm not sure if they're back on good terms yet."

"They are. Madison told me yesterday that he told her he didn't like not being her friend anymore, so they made up. She even let him kiss her."

My eyes bulged with shock, and embarrassment, too.

"I am so sorry about that," I quickly apologized, and cringed at the thought of my son putting his lips on her daughter, even after she punched him in the face and they got suspended from school. She must have thought I was raising a wild animal. "I already talked to him about how he's supposed to treat girls, but I'll be sure to talk to him again."

"Will you relax?" She laughed at my discomfort. "We're raising our children right. It wasn't like he slobbed her down. It was on the back of her hand."

Relieved, I breathed easier, but was still concerned. "I guess he's learning something from me. He's still too young to be putting his lips on anybody, though."

"True," she agreed. "But honestly, we're pretty lucky. These days kids their age are getting into all kinds of trouble. It could be a whole lot worse."

It was true, but I couldn't help but shake my head. I remembered what it was like to be in love in elementary school. The first girl who stole my heart was Briana Maxwell. I kissed her, too, and she let me get away with it. Her brother didn't, though. He found me on the playground the next day and whooped my behind. But it didn't stop me. I continued to profess my love for her until she broke my heart by kissing another kid under the slide. I was done with her after that. Hopefully things between Jonathan and Madison would go a lot better.

"Speaking of the kids, are you chaperoning their class field trip this Friday?" she asked.

"Is that this Friday?" It seemed as if I'd only gotten the notice a few days ago, but it had actually been two weeks. So much was going on at home that the trip to the museum had slipped my mind.

"You have other plans?"

"Are you going? I hadn't thought about it."

"I promised Madison I would. You should come, too," she suggested. "It's gonna be an all-day affair. A blast, even."

I rolled my eyes. We knew the only people who were going to have fun were the kids.

"You just don't want to be alone with the rest of the moms," I accused.

"Please don't make me go through it alone," she begged, and leaned against me for added emphasis. "They're going to bore me to death with child safety recall talk. I can't do it!"

"I'll think about it," I told her as we shared a laugh.

"Don't think. Just agree to come," she continued to beg, then checked her watch. "I gotta go. I'm standing here talking to you like I have all the time in the world. I gotta get to my date."

I faked my support by smiling. I really wanted her to spend her lunch hour with me in the cafeteria. We could talk about the upcoming field trip that I'd already decided I was going on, and other things in life. But that would be too much for a "friend."

"Have fun on your date," I forced myself to say.

"Thanks, boo," she said, and twirled to show off her dress one more time before she walked away.

I told myself not to stare, but took a few moments to enjoy the view.

TWENTY-FOUR
DANA

I was in the kitchen putting the finishing touches on a chicken enchilada casserole when Gavin and Jonathan got home. It was my first time making the dish, and I was a little worried about how the tortillas came out. I made them from scratch, and the recipe I found online needed a little tweaking. Still, it looked delicious, and the hour I spent preparing the rice, beans, and guacamole to go along with it weren't in vain.

"It smells good in here," Jonathan said as they walked through the front door. "Smells like..." He stopped and sniffed loudly. "A restaurant."

I peeked my head into the living room and waved at my men. Jonathan smiled while Gavin didn't acknowledged my presence at all. Four days had passed since he found out about my birth control secret, and he was still mad at me. *Still.* He hadn't spoken one word to me since that night.

"Hi, Mommy," Jonathan greeted me as he threw his book bag on the couch. "Did you cook?"

"Yes, sir, I did. But is that where your bag belongs?"

"Oh. Sorry," he apologized, and put the bag in the living room closet before he joined me in the kitchen. "What did you make?"

"Enchiladas," I said proudly, and led him to the counter where the dish was cooling off. "See?"

"Ooooh, Mommy! You made this by yourself?"

"Well, who else do you think helped me? You weren't here."

"This looks good!" he told me, and smiled at me with so much pride. He knew cooking was a challenge for me, and anything I accomplished outside of bacon and eggs was monumental to us both.

Gavin strolled into the kitchen without looking our way and began to go through the mail he brought in with him.

Jonathan noticed his coldness toward me. "Look what Mommy made, Daddy," he said, and pulled him to the food. "Doesn't it look good? It's a chill-a-dees."

"Enchiladas," I corrected him.

"I see," Gavin said nonchalantly to my disappointment, as well as our child's.

"I think it looks tasty," Jonathan said as he looked up at me.

Gavin remained silent. I pretended I wasn't bothered and gave Jonathan a kiss on the cheek for being so sweet.

"Why don't you go wash your hands so we can eat," I told him.

He nodded and scurried to the bathroom a few feet away from us. Gavin went back to the mail as if it were the most important thing in life at this moment.

"*Soooo*.... How was your day?" I asked him.

He continued to sift through the numerous envelopes like he didn't hear me. I wanted to snap at him, but decided to remain pleasant.

"I had a good day," I continued, and began to take dishes out so we could eat. "Things went smoothly at work. Nothing happened to drive me crazy or cause any complaints, so that's good. I wanted to cook for you and Jonathan, so I left early so I could go by the store. Silly me. I rushed to get here and get dinner started so you guys wouldn't have to wait too long to eat, but you guys are home an hour later than usual."

He still didn't say anything. I set the table in silence and prayed so I wouldn't smack him on the back of his head. How dare he be so rude. I ran home from work and slaved in the kitchen to put a decent meal in his stomach, and he didn't even have the courtesy to open his mouth and acknowledge me or my hard work? Being upset with me did not give him license to be a jerk.

"Where were you guys?" I asked.

Nothing.

"Gavin? I asked you a question."

"Oh!" he exclaimed suddenly, and eagerly ripped open a piece of mail while totally ignoring me. "I've been pre-approved for yet *another* credit card! Lucky me!"

"Really?" I asked. "You're not going to tell me where you were?"

"We went to Grandma's," Jonathan told me as he came back in the kitchen. He smiled sweetly, completely unaware of the bomb he just dropped, and sat down at the table.

My eyes flared with rage, but I quickly walked across the kitchen before Jonathan could see them and brought the food to the table. I was mad. More like pissed completely off. Gavin went to go see his mother in the midst of all of this drama, knowing she couldn't stand me! He was such a big ol' mama's boy! He probably ran straight to her lap and cried. *"Mama, she doesn't want to have my baby. She takes birth control. Wah, wah, wah."* I could smack him!!! He couldn't open his mouth to say two words to me, *his wife*, but he could run to Sylvia and talk her ear off?! Was that so? Well, he could let *her* make his enchiladas from now on! And wash his clothes! That's what she wanted, anyway! Maybe he did, too! She probably had Tanya over there, waiting for him, too. That skank.

If I find out Sylvia set him up on any more dates, I'll...

"How do you say that again?"

The cloud of anger before my eyes cleared at the sound of Jonathan's voice.

"Humh?"

"The food," he said with a point. "What's this called again?"

"Enchiladas, sweetie."

He rubbed his hands together. "I can't wait."

"Good, cause it comes with beans. And you have to eat all of them."

His face fell. He hated beans.

"You'll be alright."

I finished getting everything ready and sat down at the table with him. Gavin was reluctant, but sat down, too. I prepared Jonathan's plate, then my own, and purposely left Gavin to fend for himself. He was annoyed by it, but didn't say anything.

"So, what exciting thing happened at school today?" I asked Jonathan.

"Uuuummmm..." He stopped to lick his fingers. "We had a fire drill."

I pretended to be interested while Gavin began to pick over his food.

"Really?"

"Yeah. And Madison was scared of the noise. But I told her not to worry and held her hand."

"I bet you did," I teased him.

He blushed and continued with his story. Gavin remained quiet during the rest of our meal and didn't lift his head to look at me even once.

TWENTY-FIVE
DANA

After dinner I cleaned the kitchen alone while Gavin and Jonathan settled in the living room to work on Jonathan's homework. After they finished we all watched television together while I washed and folded a load of laundry. I realized it was my first time tackling the task in over a year and I became disappointed with myself. I hadn't appreciated how hard Gavin worked to keep the house in order while I tended to my career, and it saddened me that I took it for granted for so long. By the end of the evening I was exhausted and anxious to take a shower and go to sleep. Jonathan had other plans, though. He was wide awake and wanted me to put him to bed instead of his father. I agreed, happy to spend the time alone with him.

After his bath I joined him in the bathroom while he brushed his teeth and flossed. The task took fifteen minutes—a ridiculous amount of time for someone who was missing a few of the small teeth he had. I didn't fuss at him, though. The nighttime antics he carried out to avoid going to bed were always hilarious, and even though we both were dog tired, we laughed together until our sides hurt.

The excitement he had faded away when I tucked him into bed. His face grew long and full of concern.

"What's the matter, baby?" I asked as I fluffed the pillow behind his head.

"Nothing. I'm okay," he tried to assure me.

I frowned at him. "Is that the truth?"

"Yes, but..."

"Bbbbuuuuuttttttt?"

"Mommy, is Daddy mad at you?"

The question startled me, but I remained calm.

"Why do you ask that?"

"It just seems like he's mad at you. Usually he kisses you when he sees you, but he didn't kiss you today, or yesterday when you came home from work. Is he mad at you?"

This kid was too smart. How closely did he watch us?

"Daddy's not mad at me," I told him as I tucked him in. "Sometimes mommies and daddies have disagreements, but it doesn't mean that we're mad at each other."

"Are you gonna get a divorce?"

I gasped. "Where did you hear about divorce?"

"From Madison. And Grandma."

"Grandma?" That witch! What did she say in front of my son?!

"Yes. I heard her say it the last time she came over, and again when her and Daddy were talking after we left the hospital."

Ah hah. So that's where they were. Why didn't she just say that when I called? Disgusting...

"Madison said divorce is when mommies and daddies hate each other and don't live together any more," Jonathan continued. "Her mommy divorced her daddy a long time ago, and she hasn't seen him since she was a baby."

"Well..." This was too much to talk about with a seven year old, but I needed to clarify this. If not, there was no telling what his little friend or corrupt grandmother would fill his head with.

How do I explain this to him, Lord?

"Is that true?" he wanted to know.

"Sometimes," I told him. "But not always. You don't have to worry about me and Daddy getting a divorce. We had a disagreement, but we still love each other. And we love you, too. Okay?"

He nodded, but I couldn't help but see the way his bottom lip poked out. He was disheartened.

I gave him a hug and a kiss on the cheek. "Don't worry, baby," I said. "Everything is going to be all right."

He grabbed onto my hand and held it tightly. "Can I pray for you, Mommy?"

My heart melted. "Sure, sweetie."

He sat up from his lying position and lowered his head, then clasped his small hands around mine before closing his eyes.

"Dear God. Please bless my mommy and daddy, and let them be happy. I don't want another mommy. This one is perfect for me and Daddy, and her chill-adees were good. In Jesus' name. Amen."

I blinked away the emotion that came to my eyes and kissed him good night, then made my way downstairs. Gavin was sitting on the couch, to enthralled with his iPad to notice my reappearance. At least he pretended he was, anyway.

"We need to talk," I told him.

He seemed annoyed that I even spoke to him, and continued to ignore me.

"Hello?" I asked, annoyed too, and waved my hand in front of his tablet to break his concentration. This was getting ridiculous. How long did he plan on staying mad at me? It wasn't like I tried to kill him. Goodness. He acted like I didn't deserve to live. "We gotta figure out something here, because our son is noticing what's going on between us and he thinks we're getting divorced, so..."

He remained completely unfazed.

"Does he have a reason to think that?" I worried.

Nothing.

"Gavin, I'm sorry, alright?" I whined. The silent treatment was killing me. "You haven't said anything to me since the hospital, and I can't take it anymore. I get why you're upset, and I understand. But enough is enough already. We're married adults, and you're acting very childish. Are you just going to ignore me forever?"

He looked up at me as if he were about to go off, but stopped himself and placed his tablet on the coffee table. Relieved that he was finally agreeing to talk to me, I sat down next to him and expressed my joy by giving him a kiss on the cheek.

"I hate it when you're upset with me," I told him. "I can't stand it. I think—"

He stood up abruptly and walked upstairs. I sat with my mouth open, taken aback by his rudeness, and hoped for the sake of our relationship that he would return and apologize. Ten minutes later I was still in the living room alone. Feeling like a fool, I got up finally and followed him upstairs.

I checked to make sure Jonathan was asleep, which he was, then went into our bedroom. Gavin was at the dresser, pulling out a pair of pajama pants.

"I don't want to fight anymore, baby," I told him. "I just want to kiss and makeup, and get things back to the way they used to be."

He remained silent and walked past me into the bathroom. I watched as he got undressed and got into the shower. The clear door gave a glorious view, even though his back was turned to me. He was a beautiful man. So beautiful that I decided to enjoy him. He'd always loved my body. Offering it to him was sure to melt the ice wall he'd built around himself.

I got undressed and made my way over to him. I opened the shower door, but he grabbed it and closed it again with a loud slam. He stared at me with so much anger that I wanted to cry.

"Gavin..." Embarrassed, I covered myself and backed away.

His glare only intensified. I wasn't strong enough to withstand it. I walked out of the bathroom with my head down and closed the door behind me, then put my robe on and sat on the edge of the bed.

He hates me...

I tried not to panic, but this situation was getting far worse than I ever imagined it would. Gavin was becoming cruel. Was what I did really that bad? All I did was take birth control. It wasn't like I secretly ran out and had my tubes tied, or got a hysterectomy and didn't tell him. Having a baby was still an option. Just not one I wanted to take advantage of at the moment. Why couldn't he at least hear me out?

The shower stopped. When he walked out of the bathroom I begged him to forgive me.

"I'm sorry," I pleaded again. "Baby, I am. But what do you want me to do? I can't take back what I did. Can't we just put this past us and move forward?"

He said nothing.

"Can't you forgive me?" I asked.

He stood in front of me for a moment, then slowly walked out of the room.

Again, he was choosing to sleep in the guest bedroom. I didn't even call out after him. It wouldn't do any good, so I closed our bedroom door behind him and got into bed. I fell asleep wondering how it was possible for a married woman to feel as lonely as I did.

TWENTY-SIX
DANA

"Hey, hey, hey!"

I looked up from the stack of paperwork on my desk to see Leah being escorted by a hospital security guard through the warehousing section of my construction site. She waddled slowly with her protruding stomach leading the way, and carried a bag of takeout from Chili's with her as she waved.

"Sissy!" I squealed, and hurried to meet her. "You were thinking about me!"

"Just came to kick it with you," she said as I gave her a hug. The security guard left us alone. "Hope you didn't eat yet. I brought lunch."

"Awh, that's so sweet," I said, and took the bag from her. "What'd you get me?"

"Your favorite bacon cheeseburger." She groaned and rubbed her stomach. "Let's sit down, girl. My feet are killing me."

I led her into my office and let her sit behind my desk. I placed a pillow from the couch behind her back and gave her an extra chair to prop her feet on.

"Thank you," she said with a relieved sigh. "Whew, that's so much better. How you doing today?"

I frowned and gave her a sanitizing napkin from my desk drawer, then gave her a bottled water from my fridge.

"Things any better with Gavin?"

I sat across from her and passed her takeout tray. "No," I answered. "He's not talking to me."

"Awh," she pouted. "Not at all?"

"Nope," I told her. "Not a one mumbling word. I may as well not even live in the same house with him."

She seemed heartbroken by my words. "I'm sorry, boo."

I tried to smile, but only one corner of my mouth lifted. It was pitiful, but better than crying, which was what I really wanted to do.

"There should be a small box in there," she told me, pointing to the restaurant bag. "Can you pass it to me?"

"You going straight to dessert today?" I asked as I gave her what she asked for.

"Better. An onion, soy sauce, and ketchup."

I turned my face away at the mixture she found delight in. "I know you are seriously not about to eat that."

"Watch me," she said proudly.

Nearly gagging, I watched her mix the condiments together with a plastic spoon, dip her whole onion into it, and bite it like it was a golden delicious apple. My horrified expression only delighted her. She smiled and took an even bigger bite.

"Pregnancy is so gross," I told her. "Doesn't that make your eyes burn?"

"No." Her eyes rolled back into her head with sweet satisfaction as she smacked on the vegetable. "This is so good!"

I laughed. I loved my sister. She was so cute with extra weight on her. Even her fingers were round. They matched her face, which was the fullest it had ever been, but I dared not mention it to her. Her emotions were fluctuating, and I didn't want to make her cry, just in case she was feeling self-conscious at the moment.

"So, tell me about Gavin," she said a moment later.

I sighed. "He's not speaking to me. He's been sleeping in the guest bedroom for the past few nights."

"That's not good," she said with a frown.

"What should I do, Leah?"

She took another bite of her onion and thought for a moment. "I'm not exactly sure, honestly. The old me would have told you to take a frying pan upside his head, but the new and improved me—you know, the one who knows Jesus and doesn't want to spend eternity in Hell, or for you to go to jail for that matter, would tell you to take a different route. If I were you, I'd start with prayer. And do whatever Gavin needs you to do to make it up to him."

"Oh, God," I groaned. "He's gonna put me on an allowance and make me cook everyday."

"Well, that wouldn't be so bad," she said as I continued to whimper. "You can do that, sis. It's not that hard. I really don't need to remind you that you did this to yourself, do I? Frying a few chicken wings and scrambling a few eggs isn't too much to do to smooth things over. That man has been good to you, and he is deeply hurt."

I frowned. "You think so?"

"Yes. That's why he's acting like that. But don't stress," she told me. "Just get in your word and concentrate on being that godly wife the bible talks about. Do you remember what Proverbs 31 says?"

"It says a lot," I told her as I opened my food tray. I really didn't need to be reminded. I was pretty sure I fell short in each and every category the virtuous woman exemplified.

"You're right, it does. But the scripture I'm thinking of is verse eleven. It says, 'her husband can trust her, and she will greatly enrich his life.' Trust is a big thing in marriage, and you broke his trust. You have to work on getting it back."

I agreed, but felt completely discouraged. How could I get Gavin's trust back when he wouldn't even talk to me?

"When was the last time you read your bible?"

"I read it," I told her, but we both knew it was not as often as I needed to. When I first became a Christian I read my bible every day. But I was a single woman then, and my career wasn't as hectic. Now I barely had any time for anything outside of work.

"See, this is why you need to come back to my bible study," she told me. "But I'm not gonna fuss at you. Gavin's putting you through enough. But if you wanna make time to come back, you know the door is always open."

I cringed at the thought of being surrounded by the women who attended her home bible study. They were a bunch of judgmental, bible thumping hypocrites who loved to pick on me. But maybe I needed to suck it up and go.

"Oh, shoot!" Leah suddenly yelled.

"What?" I panicked, and jumped to my feet. "Are you okay? Is it the baby?"

"Yeah, I'm fine," she moaned. "The lady was supposed to give me two onions, and she only gave me one," she pouted, then leaned across the desk and swiped the slice out of my burger. Before I could complain, she added, "Leave me alone. I'm pregnant."

TWENTY-SEVEN
DANA

I sat on the edge of the bed and slipped my heels on. I didn't get any sleep at all. I spent the entire night tossing back and forth in bed alone because once again Gavin chose to sleep in the guest bedroom. He didn't even say anything to me when he got up this morning. I could be in here dead, passed away from a sorrowful heart, and he wouldn't have a clue. He and Jonathan were downstairs getting ready for their day, and I was all alone like no one cared about me at all.

He walked into the room suddenly, dressed in a starched pair of jeans and a polo style shirt—not the medical scrubs he usually wore to work.

"Where are you going?" I asked, frowning. Did he have the day off and not tell me?

He looked over his shoulder at me, but didn't answer. My anger flared as he began to rifle through his top dresser drawer in silence.

"I know you heard me ask you a question," I said through tight teeth, and stood to my feet, ready for battle. I'd had enough of this treatment from him. "Answer me."

He dismissed my remark with an obnoxious chuckle.

Tired of being shunned, I marched across the room and slammed the dresser drawer shut. "Stop ignoring me!"

He took a few steps back and breathed heavily. I'd angered him, but he kept his cool by turning away.

"If you must know, I'm chaperoning Jonathan's class field trip to the museum today. Now will you move out of my way so I can get a pair of socks, please?"

Class trip? What in the world is he talking about? Oh, wait. Jonathan did mention something about that. Is that today?

Gavin glared at me with pure irritation. "Can I get some socks, please?"

I blocked the drawer. "Not until you talk to me."

Angered, he tried to move me to the side, but I pushed him, ready to take out my frustrations physically.

"Fine! I just won't wear any!" he snapped at me, and turned to leave.

I ran in front of him and slammed the bedroom door shut. "Talk to me!" I demanded as I blocked it with my body. "We are a married couple! I'm your wife! You need to talk to me!"

"Keep your voice down!" he hissed. "Jonathan can hear you."

"Well, talk to me!"

He rubbed his temples and squeezed his eyes shut. *"What. Do. You. Want. Me. To. Tell. You?"*

"Say *anything,* Don't just ignore me and treat me like I don't even exist."

"Fine," he said quickly, and dropped his hands as he looked me in the eye. "I will tell you that I'm not even sure you're the person that I should have married anymore. The person that I thought I was marrying would never do that you did to me. You lied to me for two whole years, and I thought I was marrying an honest person."

"I said I was sorry," I tried to reason with him. "How long are you going to punish me for it? I tried to tell you that I wasn't ready to have kids, but you wouldn't listen."

"Whatever," he dismissed, and tried to open the door. "Move out of the way. I have somewhere to go."

"See! Like right now! I'm trying to talk to you, to tell you how I feel so we can have an honest conversation, and you're dismissing me again. It's the same thing with you, all the time. You just ignore what I say, like all the times I tried to tell you about your mother. You refuse to listen and just think about what you want!"

He turned around slowly with his mouth open. *"Did you really just say that to me?!!! AFTER EVERYTHING YOU'VE DONE?!!"*

I backed away, scared for my safety. He was so angry that he became menacing. His nostrils flared as his eyes burrowed down on me, and he aggressively took steps toward me as if he were about to hit me.

"You lied to me!" he screamed in my face. "YOU! LIED! Not me! I've *never* withheld anything from you, and you have the nerve to call me selfish?! You don't get to say anything to me! Not about this! Not to me! You lied to me for *two whole years!* I have *NEVER* heard of anything more selfish than what you did!"

"Stop it!" I yelled, and backed into the bedroom door and covered my ears.

"This is what you wanted, isn't it?!" he continued to scream. "For me to tell you how I feel! This is how I feel! I can't stand you!!! You are a trifling, manipulative, disrespectful, vile, and disgusting misrepresentation of a wife! I'm a second away from calling you out of your name and putting my hands on you because I hate you right now! I gave you my love and devotion, and you played me! NOW *MOVE OUT OF MY WAY* SO I CAN TAKE *MY SON* TO SCHOOL!!!"

He reached past me and pulled the door, knocking me to the floor in a ball of hysterical tears. He stormed out of the bedroom and slammed the door behind him while I continued to scream, and didn't bother to stop to see if I was okay.

Downstairs Jonathan asked what was wrong with me, but Gavin only told him to get his things so they could leave. Soon they were gone, and I remained on the floor for nearly an hour, too heartbroken to do anything else but cry.

TWENTY-EIGHT
GAVIN

The bus ride to Daytown's Museum of Science and History took a little less than an hour. Had my thoughts not been totally on Dana and the horrible fight we had before I left home, I would have been embarrassed when my son asked in the hearing of everyone else who'd been sitting quietly why we hadn't been before. As a parent, I should explore all aspects of educational opportunities that were in my reach, but at this moment I could care less about the museum or the ancient artifacts pristinely displayed inside. I left my wife on the floor crying, and Jonathan heard. I felt horrible—as I should have. What kind of man treated his wife that way—especially one who claimed to be a Christian? It was completely wrong, out of my character, didn't glorify God at all, and nowhere remotely close to what I should have exposed my son to. I was embarrassed and ashamed. He seemed to have forgotten all about it now that he was with Madison, though. The two were a collection of non-stop chatter and laughter as soon as we got on the bus. I suppose she got the power she had over him innocently. Her mother often made me forget about my troubles when she came around, too. Our interactions at work were becoming more frequent, and I was starting to believe I could get out of the friend zone if I really wanted to.

"What is wrong with you, Gavin?" Parker twisted around in her seat in front of me so she could look me in the eye. "Are you okay?"

I wasn't sure if she'd been talking to me for a long time, or if she was just now trying to get my attention. Either way, it was extremely inconsiderate and rude.

"It's the kids, huh?" she concluded. "They're distracting. Too noisy. Dealing with one is challenging enough, but times that by twenty-four..." Her eyes bulged before she chuckled. "Bring on the migraine."

I smiled and nodded, but didn't know what she was talking about. I had a feeling the conversation had gone on a little longer than I was aware of, but she seemed satisfied.

"You ready to do this?"

"Ready as I'll ever be," I told her, and waited as everyone began to file out of the bus.

We were sitting in the very back, therefore we were the last to get off. Parker exited the bus before I did, giving me the opportunity to appreciate her tight fitting jeans while she couldn't see my facial expression. Her top, simple in solid white, revealed a small sliver of smooth skin just above her waist, teasing me to the point that my fingertips tingled.

Once we were off the bus, Jonathan's teacher distributed day passes for the museum. We divided into groups and were told that we could roam freely, but were asked to meet in the main lobby at eleven-thirty for lunch.

As soon as we got inside we were greeted by the enormous skeletal remains of a tyrannosaurus.

"So cool!" Jonathan exclaimed, and made a dash for it.

"Boy!" I hollered after him. He knew better than to run inside of a building. Luckily a museum employee stopped him before he could get past the velvet rope that protected the precious bones from his destructive hands.

I excused myself from Parker, who had been walking beside me, and hurried to catch up with him. I then pulled him to the side by his collar and threatened to take him home the very second he pretended not to know how to behave in public. He was so horrified by the notion of it that he didn't stop to consider that we rode together on a bus and I had no way of taking him home.

Once his behavior was in check, I allowed him to admire the dinosaur bones. The rest of our group joined us, and soon afterward we began to take our tour. The children were eager to see everything the museum had to offer, but Parker and I weren't so thrilled. The more enthusiastic parents led the way while we lagged in the back and engaged in small pleasantries until I finally asked her what I'd been anxious to know all week.

"So... How'd your date with that guy go?"

"Ugh." Her face twisted with repulsion, and she shook her head.

"That bad, huh?"

"Bad is not the word. More like disgusting. No, just tacky. Disgustingly tacky, and creepy."

"What? I thought the guy was cool. You went out with him."

"Yeah—one of the biggest mistakes of my life." She rolled her eyes and then held out her arm to stop me. "Can you smile a little harder, please?"

Slightly embarrassed, I put on a straight face. She laughed and we continued to trail behind our group.

"So what happened?" I asked, desperate for details. "The poor guy didn't say anything bad about Houston, did he? What? Did he tell you the truth about your football team?"

"You better watch it," she warned. "If he would have disrespected the Texans I would have had to slap him twice."

I gasped. *"You slapped him?"* That was surprising. Parker didn't come across as violent to me. Either this guy really crossed the line, or there was a degree of feistiness she reserved only for the men she dated. Either way, I was more intrigued now than ever.

"He was a jerk," she explained. "And a complete moron. He doesn't know anything at all about how to treat a lady."

"What did he do?"

"He tried to get frisky with me during lunch. In the restaurant. *In front of people.* And when I told him that I wasn't a whore, he suggested we go to his Jaguar outside in the parking lot."

"Oh, no," I groaned. Man! She did go out with a jerk. But who was I to judge after what I'd done to Dana? "How'd you end up slapping him?"

"He put his hand on my thigh twenty minutes after I met him, as if buying me a salad and a martini gave him permission to access my body."

"Oh, no," I repeated. This fool was an embarrassment to men everywhere.

"I moved his hand and told him about himself," she continued. "He put it back, so I did what I had to do in order to get my point across. I went H-Town on that fool."

I burst into laughter. Parker laughed, too, and covered my mouth with her hand when we got disapproving stares from those around us.

"You're gonna get us kicked out of here. Then Madison and Jonathan will want to kill us. You know there are more dinosaur bones in here, and when he finds out his friends got to see them and he didn't, you're gonna have an emotional child on your hands."

I stifled my chuckles while she shoved me playfully.

"You're glad my date didn't go well, aren't you?"

"No. I just think you're hilarious."

"I know you want to be my only friend," she teased. "Oh, well. That's what I get. I should have known he was creepy from the way he always watched me on the squat machine."

I pretended to gag, but didn't blame him at all. Judging by the way she wore those jeans, I was sure her squats were amazing.

"You went out with him after he did that?"

"I know," she moaned, and covered her face with embarrassment. "I don't know what I was thinking. It's just that I've been here for a while and haven't really met anybody. I've been feeling kind of lonely, you know? The only family I have here is my daughter. She's cool and all, but I don't know how many more Friday nights I can spend making mud pies, re-enacting Michael Jackson music videos, and catching frogs in the back yard."

I chuckled. "You don't have to feel lonely. You know you have friends here."

"Who? You?" she asked sarcastically. "I'm pretty sure your wife doesn't want to spend her Friday nights with me."

No. Dana wouldn't like to spend her Friday nights with me, either. She'd rather be working, or spending a ridiculous amount of money at the mall, but I chose to keep that information to myself.

"So you go out with a jerk?" I frowned. "You're smarter than that. What kind of sense does that make?"

Her expression brightened. "You think I'm smart?"

Confused, I asked, "Does that surprise you?"

"Yes. I didn't know you thought of me that way."

"Well, it's pretty obvious you're not stupid. You have a career you're excelling in, and you're managing to do it all while raising a child. That's pretty amazing. You don't have to settle. Someone will scoop you up."

"If only the rest of the world thought the way you did," she sighed as we continued to walk.

"What does that mean?" I didn't understand why she was doubting herself. She was wonderful. I couldn't imagine who wouldn't agree.

"That you're extremely complimentary and optimistic," she told me. "It's nice to think that I'm this great catch, but I'm no spring chicken anymore. I'm thirty-five years old, and I have a child. All the decent men who wouldn't mind that are already taken. No one wants me for more than a one-night stand." She stopped to keep a safe distance from our group, who was standing at an exotic gemstone display. "At this point, a girl like me has to get what she can when what she really wants isn't available anymore."

She looked into my eyes, and I knew she was talking about me. I was what she wanted that wasn't available anymore. Her indirect boldness was both surprising and attractive, and it was all I could do not to reach out and touch her.

"What is it that you really want?" I whispered. My heart beat faster. I knew better than to toy with fire. Only a select few could get away with it without getting burned. I'd never been so lucky. But Parker was too alluring to simply disregard. She was beautiful, loved to cook, loved children, and wanted to spend time with me. I just wanted her to say my name. If she did, some of the guilt I had about being attracted to her would go away.

"*Gavin...*"

She smiled at me, but her eyes were rebuking. They told me loud and clear not to journey down the road I was tempted to travel. I quickly agreed, and nodded my gratitude. One of us had to have decency. But again, it only made me think more highly of her. She knew how to keep me in check. Every man needed a woman like that.

"I need someone who's available," she told me.

I decided to entertain her thoughts a bit. "What qualities are you looking for?" I asked. Since she knew she couldn't have me, concentrating on what she could actually have would be good for her. That way when the right guy for her did come along, she'd realize it.

"I don't mind if he has kids," she said. "The more the merrier, as far as I'm concerned. As long as I don't have to pay his child support," she quickly added.

"A gentleman. Someone with good sense who knows how to appreciate a woman. Someone who knows that my daughter's safety and well-being are a priority. Someone who will love and treat her like his own. Someone who's loving and respectful, who's decent and has integrity and morals. Someone who makes me happy. I want to be in love. I want to feel butterflies in my stomach whenever I hear his voice or see him walk into the room. I want to go crazy when I can't speak to him, or touch, or feel him. I want to be inspired to be the absolute best that I can for him. I want him to be my motivation to get out of bed in the morning, or my desire to stay in bed as long as he's with me. I want romance, and flowers, and..."

She stopped suddenly and looked away.

"What's wrong?" I asked her.

She became shy and took a few steps away from me. "I'm talking too much," she told me, and dismissed the conversation with a flick of her hand. "I won't bore you with my self-pity."

"No," I stopped her, and grabbed her by her arm. "I like talking to you. You can tell me anything."

"Yeah, right," she said with nervous sarcasm.

"Seriously. There's nothing wrong with transparency."

"At this rate, Gavin, I'll say too much."

She looked down at her arm and I realized I was still holding her. I let go and put my hand in my pocket, suddenly nervous, too.

"Sorry. I didn't mean to grab you," I said after a few seconds of awkward silence between us.

"It's fine," she forgave me. "Let's get back to the kids."

I didn't have to agree. Madison burst out of the group viewing gemstones and ran toward us in excitement.

"*Stop!*" Parker screeched.

The little girl halted.

"What are you doing wrong?"

She thought for a moment, then began to walk. "Mama, where can I get one of those rocks?" she asked when she reached us.

"Do you see Mr. Gardner standing here?"

She nodded.

"What are you supposed to say?"

She studied me for a moment through her new purple and pink glasses. "Hi," she said, and waved.

"*And?*" Parker asked before I could return the greeting.

"Excuse me," she added politely.

"You're excused," I said with a smile.

"Thank you," Parker said to her. "Now, what is it that you want to tell me?"

"I want one of those rocks," she said, and became so excited that she began to flail her hands. "They have a big blue one over there, and I want it. Can you buy it for me?"

"I don't think those are for sale, sweetie," Parker told her. "If we buy them, then no one else who comes to the museum is going to be able to see them. That wouldn't be fun for everyone else who comes to the museum, now would it?"

"Uuuuhhhh," she sucked her teeth. "I guess not. Do they have them at Target?"

Parker laughed and shook her head. "Girl, have you ever seen anything like that at Target?"

"No... Not Target," she pouted. "Maybe a store in the mall?"

"How about you just go back with the rest of your class and enjoy your field trip, okay?"

She slouched, knowing she was being dismissed. "Mama, please?"

Parker batted her eyelashes, a message we both interpreted to mean that Madison needed to get back to her classmates before Parker had to tell her again. The child walked away with disappointment, but cheered up again when Jonathan told her there were pink rocks around the corner.

"That girl is going to drive me crazy," she said, and walked off to catch up with everyone else.

Funny. I was thinking the exact same thing about you.

TWENTY-NINE
DANA

Gavin was overly cruel to me yesterday. When I got home from work he didn't say one thing to me. I used the silent time to pray for us both, and when I woke up this morning my heart was determined to put in the effort to make my marriage work. I remembered what it was like to be single, and all of the things I went through when I was waiting on the Lord to bring him into my life. I didn't want to go through any of it again, or to easily give up on what God had blessed me with, so I was going to fight with all of my might to make up for the hurtful thing I'd done to him. So this morning I got up early and cleaned the house, washed and folded the laundry, and made breakfast. He was sure to love it. French toast, pork sausages, hash browns, and freshly squeezed orange juice. Jonathan enjoyed it so much that he asked for seconds.

To my disappointment, it was nearly noon when Gavin decided to finally get out of bed. Maybe the field trip had worn him out and he needed more sleep than usual. He appeared well rested by the time he made his way downstairs, dressed in a pair of basketball shorts and a muscle t-shirt.

"Good morning," I greeted him from the kitchen table where I was sitting. My laptop was in front of me. I'd decided to get some work done while Jonathan played in the back yard.

Gavin didn't say anything. I closed my laptop and stood up to greet him, but he only walked past me and grabbed a bottled water out of the fridge.

"I made breakfast this morning," I said proudly. "I put a plate in the microwave for you so it wouldn't get cold. French toast, sausage, and hash browns. It's good. I had to make Jonathan save you some. He was going to eat it all up."

He opened the microwave and seemed surprised to find there was actually a plate inside. He pulled it out and took the foil off, giving me hope that my efforts were all worth it.

"This toast is soggy," he frowned, and began to pick at it with his fingers.

Surprised, I quickly went to his side to see for myself. It didn't look appetizing at all, which was far from the way it looked when I first made it.

"It must be the eggs I used. But I can make you a fresh batch. It won't take long,"

I told him, and quickly snatched a skillet out of the dishwasher. "Five minutes."

"Don't worry about it," he told me, and stopped me from turning the stovetop on. "I'm not hungry."

I slouched against the kitchen counter with disappointment. "You have to be. You've slept all morning. Let me feed you, baby. It won't take me but a minute."

"Nawh," he said, and walked out of the kitchen with his water bottle. "I'm going out for a run. When I get back I'll feed myself, the same way I always do."

He grabbed a pair of sneakers from the hallway closet and rushed out of the house. I was hurt, but told myself to remain positive. I really wasn't married to an ungrateful jerk. No. I was married to the wonderful man I prayed for. He was just upset now, and once he got over his anger he would appreciate me again.

"Help me, Lord," I prayed out loud. "Only You can fix this."

I put the skillet away, then emptied the plate of food down the garbage disposal and returned to my work.

THIRTY
GAVIN

I sighed loudly as I looked around the guest bedroom. I was having yet another restless night, all because I was too stubborn to make up with my wife so we could actually sleep together. For the past few weeks I'd been nothing but evil to her. She was trying her hardest to repair what she'd done, but I didn't care. I *wanted* her to feel bad. I wanted her to feel pain. I wanted her to hurt. She'd done me wrong, and she deserved it.

The only problem was that by inflicting pain on her, I was also torturing myself. I couldn't remember a time when I didn't want my wife to cook and take care of the house, and she'd done so every day for the past week. I hadn't had to lift a finger. But instead of thanking her, I found a way to criticize.

"You didn't fold these towels right."

Did I actually care how the towels were folded? Absolutely not. They were clean, which was good enough. But could I let her know that? No. That would be too easy.

"This food needs more salt."

I said that to purposely anger her. It was the same thing Mama told her when she made that meal for her a little while ago. I knew it would get her blood boiling. But did the food really need seasoning? No. It was perfect, and I was honestly happy that I didn't have to come home and cook after working hard all day. I couldn't come out and say that, though. Not right now. I had to make her suffer a little more.

Hot, I kicked the blanket I was under off my legs and spread out across the bed. I was disgusted with myself—a grown man playing childish games like some insecure female didn't even deserve to have a wife. I knew Dana really loved me. Jonathan, too. But she was dishonest. That wasn't something I could easily get over.

I was disgusted, too, because I was sleeping in the guest bedroom of my own freaking house. How dumb was that? I wasn't a guest! But I couldn't be mad at anyone but myself. Dana didn't put me in here. Initially I slept in here because I didn't want to be near her. I didn't even want to look at her, let alone sleep beside her. But when I saw how upset it made her I decided to keep doing it. Now nearly three weeks had passed, and I was over it. Mainly because I was horny.

Being upset with Dana did not negate the fact that she was a beautiful woman. An incredibly sexy, irresistibly seductive, lovely to behold, too desirable to deny woman with all the right curves who knew just what to do to please me. It was a wonder I lasted this long without her goodness. I was about to lose my mind keeping myself away from her. Shoot. I was about to punch a hole in the wall. I couldn't stop thinking about her soft lips. Her breasts. Her hips. The way the line of her back curved as it grew into her behind. Dang! I missed her!!!

This is stupid! Go into your bedroom and make love to your wife!

I told myself I couldn't, and rolled over in bed in a useless attempt to get comfortable. It wasn't going to happen. I needed Dana's fluffy chest to lay on, and her hips to hold on to. Shoot. I even needed to feel her ice cold feet against my legs just to feel some type of normalcy. I didn't even know why I was trying. I wasn't going to be able to sleep until I got what I needed.

Get up. Stop being dumb. Go make love to your wife.

I got out of bed and slowly made my way to our bedroom, being extra careful not to make a sound. Dana and I had managed to keep my sleeping in the guest bedroom a secret from Jonathan, and I didn't want him finding out now.

The room was pitch black when I arrived. I felt my way across the room and turned on the bathroom light so I could see. Dana was knocked out. Her light snoring sounded like sweet music to my ears.

"Dana."

She didn't hear me until I whispered her name again as I got in the bed with her and slowly began to cover her with kisses.

"Huh?" she whispered through a groggy voice, and sat up quickly with her eyes still closed.

I cradled her small face in my hands and kissed her passionately. She was startled at first, but quickly began to kiss me back. She wasn't mad at me. She never was. When I pulled away she had tears in her eyes.

I'm sorry I made you cry, baby. I'm sorry! I never want to hurt you!

I knew I needed to say the words to her, but my pride wouldn't let me, so I kissed her again and made love to her. To my surprise, she was way more eager than usual to please me. We made love for hours before falling asleep in each other's arms.

****

Dana was fully dressed and on her way to work when I woke up a few hours later. Her spirit was clearly lifted. She even seemed to dance as she made her way across the room. The sex we had put her in a good mood. She was glowing.

Sadly, as I watched her, I knew I didn't feel the same way. I wanted to, and felt like I should have after a night of passionate lovemaking, but I didn't. All I could think about was the fact that she was getting ready to run off to her precious career—what she really cared about, and I still didn't have what I really wanted. A baby, and a wife who put me first.

"Oh, you're awake?" She smiled when she saw that I'd been watching. "Good morning, baby," she said sweetly, and walked over to the bed. "Did you sleep okay?"

I nodded.

"Great," she said, and leaned over and gave me a kiss on the lips.

I didn't kiss her back, and she noticed. She pulled away slowly and stared, perplexed by my sudden lack of affection.

"You okay?" she asked.

I really didn't feel like talking. If I said what I really wanted to say, it would only hurt her feelings and start another argument.

"What's the matter?" she asked, and encouraged me to talk by nudging me.

I shook my head and told her to have a good day at work.

"I'll never know what's bothering you if you never tell me. If you never tell me, I'll never know how I can make whatever's bothering you better. Will you please talk to me? I love you, and all I wanna do is make you happy."

Initially I refused to answer her, but I saw how patient she was struggling to be with me. My own curiosity began to gnaw at me, too, so I sat up straight and decided to be direct.

"Are you still taking birth control pills?"

Her face fell. She looked away, and her lips were sealed tight.

Just like I thought.

I rolled my eyes and turned away from her. After *everything*, she still hadn't changed her mind. Unbelievable.

"Gavin," she whined. Her voice cracked the way it often did when she was about to cry. "Please don't be mad at me. I just…"

I was unmoved. The sex we had meant absolutely nothing. I was talking to a stranger. Just some chick who lived in my house and helped me out with my son from time to time.

"I'm not mad," I told her. "Just disappointed. After everything, why would you still be taking them? We weren't even having sex. Are you that afraid of having a baby that even in celibacy you would keep taking them, knowing how I feel about them? What's so wrong with giving me children, Dana?"

"No! No, it's nothing like that at all. It's just…" She became flustered and began to gather her things. "I know why you're upset, and I really want to talk to you about this, but I have a meeting at work and I really can't be late."

Of course. Don't you always?

"I can take a long lunch if you're available," she offered. "Wanna meet me somewhere so we can talk?"

I shook my head. I didn't have anything to say. She'd made her decision, and I was not about to pressure a grown woman to do anything she didn't want to.

"Maybe this evening when we're both finished with work? I can drop Jonathan off with Leah and Marcus so we can spend some time together alone."

"No. It's a school night. He needs to be at home."

"Okay. Maybe tonight, then. After he's gone to bed."

I nodded, but didn't mean it. She kissed me on the cheek and left for work. After she was gone I stared at the door and doubted that things would ever be the same between us.

THIRTY-ONE
DANA

I was in a trance by the time I made it to work. Everyone seemed to buzz by me while I moved around in slow motion. For the first time ever, designing didn't excite me. A marble statue arrived and I didn't even care. I just signed for it and went into my office as if it were simply an office supply delivery unworthy of adoration. My thoughts were completely consumed by how tragic my relationship with Gavin was turning out to be.

This morning was awful. I woke up in such a good mood. I literally sang to myself as I got dressed. Even when I showered and put on my makeup, I had a smile on my face. I thought things were on their way to going back to normal. I assumed that since we had sex he'd decided to let go of his disappointment with me. But then he asked me about those stupid birth control pills. Things seemed even worse now than they were before.

I should have just lied. I should have said, "Oh, no, sweetie. I learned my lesson about those things. I will never, ever take them again because I want to give you all the children in the world." Then things would go back to normal. At least until I got my period again, anyway.

No. That was the wrong thing to do. Lying was what got me into this mess to begin with. I just had to be patient. Gavin would come around.

Hopefully.

Prayerfully...

Ugh. It was dumb of me to believe that just because he came back into bed with me that things had changed. After all, he was still a man, and they all only really wanted one thing. I just didn't think he would ever *use* me for sex. I thought he was better than the other men in my past. Turns out, he wasn't.

I was tired. For the past week I'd been going to work early so I could leave early, just to make sure I had dinner ready for Jonathan and Gavin by the time they got home. Trying to be a career woman and a house wife at the same time was running me ragged. There was no way I was going to be able to keep it up, especially in the middle of taking on such a big project at work. I could barely keep my eyes open, but there was no way in the world I was about to let my career suffer. I'd worked my behind off to get to this point, and I wasn't going to let it slip through my fingers simply to prove a point to my husband. If he loved me the way he demanded that I love him, he would never ask me to do such a thing anyway.

Be that as it may, I couldn't just roll over and let my marriage end, either. I had to fight for it, no matter how disappointed I was in Gavin's actions. Cooking and cleaning was good, but it wasn't what he really wanted. I was going to have to give him a baby.

"Don't throw up," I told myself, and sat down at my desk before I became too lightheaded. "You can do this."

I could have a baby. Women did it all the time. Leah was about to have her third one, and she was still alive. It hadn't killed her yet. She had a lot of experience, and she could help me. More importantly, it wasn't like I was alone. Gavin was a great father. He'd love and take care of the children we would have together. So why was I so afraid?

Just give in, Dana. Give in and give your husband a baby.

THIRTY-TWO
GAVIN

"You messed up again," I told Parker as I looked over her shoulder.

We were sitting in my office coding patient files into the clinic's new system. I'd been training her for the past two hours, and we both were becoming cranky.

"How?" she asked, frustrated.

"You keep logging the patient's information into the wrong spot. All of your therapy recommendations are going to be flagged when you try to send your reports to Dr. Swann, and I really don't feel like hearing it from him today."

A sour expression came over her face. "What are you talking about?"

"Look. You just said Mrs. White needs meds and therapy for a herniated disc in her back."

"Mrs. White has an ankle prosthesis, though."

"*I know*," I sighed. "You coded her information wrong. You need to delete all that and do it over again. You're gonna have her getting arrested at Walgreens for trying to fill a narcotic prescription."

"Ugh!" she groaned.

I rubbed my temples and stood up to stretch my back, then walked around the office to get my blood circulating. My patience was running thin. I was ready to go home and wanted to leave her alone to figure out how to do it herself. I knew she'd be expected to work independently next week, though, and I couldn't let her be ill-prepared.

"What's up with you, Gavin?" she asked as she tabbed her way through the form fields of the program.

"What do you mean?"

"*Wwwweeeelllll...*" she began, and popped her lips with an attitude. "Something is on your mind, and you're too distracted to pay attention to me. I know you didn't just let me sit here and fill out the last ten records wrong just for the fun of it."

I gasped and rushed to the computer. "Girl, I know you didn't," I panicked, and went through her forms. They were all incorrect.

"Sorry," she said shyly. "I thought I was doing it right. You're the one supposed to be training me, so don't blame me."

I groaned again as I returned to my seat. It was Friday, and we had to have the forms completed before we left for the weekend. At this rate we were never going to get out of here.

My phone began to ring. I pulled it out of my pocket and saw that it was Dana. I was in a bad enough mood as it was and didn't need her making things worse, so I silenced it and slipped it back into my pocket.

"Who are you ignoring?" she asked under her breath.

"Pay attention to the forms you're about to redo."

She rolled her eyes and continued to work on the computer. I went over the training with her again until she became frustrated and told me she needed a break.

"Let me ask you something, Gavin," she said after I granted her request. "And don't take this the wrong way. If you feel like I'm out of bounds with this question, you can tell me to mind my own business and I will."

"Was that a disclaimer?"

"I feel like I need one."

Suddenly I was nervous. I knew to proceed with caution.

She looked me in the eye. "Are you happy?"

Now I was offended. "Just what are you trying to say?"

"I'm not trying to be rude," she clarified. "But I can tell something is bothering you. I haven't seen you smile all week, which is really whack, because I actually look forward to seeing that everyday. And I know that was your wife who just called. Not that I was snooping, but the screen on your phone is really big and I saw her name. You're ignoring her calls, and most people in relationships don't do that, so I'm just wondering if you're really happy. 'Cause you don't seem like it."

I was taken aback. No one had ever approached me in such a way—other than my mother, and she never really asked. Her concern was more of an accusation that anything else. But she was my mother, so she could get away with it. Parker, on the other hand, was out of order. We were cool, but asking me about my wife was outside of her jurisdiction.

"You don't get to ask me that," I let her know. "Boundaries."

"I'm not trying to pry," she insisted. "As a friend, I'm just concerned for you."

"There's no need to be. I'm fine."

"Fine and happy aren't the same thing."

I didn't respond, and she correctly got the message that I wasn't going to have the conversation with her.

"Fine. I'll drop it," she said with a hopeless shrug. "All I'm trying to say is that life is too short to be miserable, and I think you should do whatever is in your power to be happy. Trust me. I'm not trying to interfere with anyone's marriage. I just think you're a great guy who deserves to be happy, and if you're not you should consider making some changes. That's all. None of us are getting any younger around here."

I realized that her motives were pure. She was simply concerned for my well-being. Was I that much of a mess that my colleagues were starting to notice? How pitiful had I become? I wasn't falling apart, was I?

"I'm good," I told her. "You just get back to work."

She turned her attention back to the computer. What she said stuck with me, though. Life really was too short to be miserable.

THIRTY-THREE
DANA

I stared into the bathroom mirror and told myself that I was doing the right thing. My hair was big and curly, the way Gavin liked it, and the lace lingerie I spent too much money on was definitely making the statement I needed it to. Red and see through. Nothing was left to the imagination. At. All.

I sprayed perfume on myself and rubbed oil into my legs, then added a few brushstrokes of blush to my cheeks and went back into the bedroom. Rose petals were already on the bed. I'd taken care of that before I jumped into the shower, just in case Gavin came home earlier than he normally did on Friday evenings. I'd already arranged for Leah to pick Jonathan up from school so he could spend the weekend with her. That way Gavin and I could be alone. We needed the time to reconnect. Too much had been happening between us, and I couldn't let it go on any further. It was time to reconcile and make a baby.

I went around the room and began to light the candles strategically placed on top of furniture. Thank God I was smart enough to blast the AC. It was about to get hot in here. I could take the heat, though. It would all be worth it to see his face when he walked into our bedroom.

Normally, Gavin was the one who did things like this for me. Since we'd been together, he'd always gone over the top to display his love for me. Every anniversary, birthday, and Valentine's Day was memorable. Tonight was my turn. I had two more outfits in my closet just like this one, and a fridge full of fresh food to keep him well nourished and satisfied. He was going to need it, especially because I hadn't taken my birth control since the last time we were intimate with each other. It was time to finally make the baby he'd been waiting so long to have.

I finished and sat on top of our bed and waited for Gavin to get home. Unfortunately, it took him over an hour to arrive. By then my mind had wondered to the long list of things I needed to get done at work, and I wasn't really in the mood. However, as soon as I heard the garage door open I propped myself up and put a seductive smile on my face. Gavin called my name out a few times to see where I was, but I didn't answer. I wanted our first interaction to be visual.

"Why didn't you tell me Leah was picking Jonathan up from school?" he asked as he came up the stairs. "A head's up would have been nice. I was at the school looking for him, and now everyone in the front office thinks we don't communicate. You could have at least—"

He stopped when he opened the bedroom door. The sight of the candles and rose petals on the floor caught him off guard. His eyes followed their trail up to the bed, where he found me.

"Hey, baby," I said sweetly, and smiled. *"Welcome home."*

His head twisted to the side as he stared at me. His face twisted, too, as if he were both confused and suspicious at the same time.

"What are you doing?"

A pang of rejection hit me. Hard. In the face. That was not the reaction I anticipated getting from him. Still, I brushed it off and walked over to him.

"I'm trying to make love to my husband," I said, and clasped my hands together behind his neck in a sweet embrace. "I'm sorry if I made you worry about Jonathan. I tried to call you, but you didn't answer. I guess you didn't get the message I left on your voicemail. But that doesn't matter. He's fine, and you're home now. So let's get this party started."

I moved in to place a kiss on his lips, but he forcefully removed my hands and took a few steps backward. This time the rejection pierced my heart.

"I'm sorry," he said when he saw that I was upset. "But what is all this? What are you trying to do here?"

"Do you really have to ask?"

"Yeah," he answered in a demanding way.

I was insulted, but I pushed through it and said, "I changed my mind. I decided not to take the pills anymore. I want to give you a baby."

He rolled his eyes and made his way over to the light switch and totally disregarded my attempts to stop him. The lights came on and he began to blow out the candles.

"What are you doing?"

He ignored me and continued as a light film of smoke began to float through the air.

"Talk to me," I pleaded, and stood in front of him with my arms extended. "Come on. Don't you want this?"

He sighed reluctantly. "Not like this," he said, and walked away from me. "I know you don't want a baby. If you did, you never would have lied to me for so long. Truth be told, if you never fainted that day, you'd still be on those pills."

"But I changed my mind." I was a bit irritated that he didn't think that was possible.

"I don't think you did. Not about this. And I don't want you to do anything you don't want to do. You'll only end up miserable, and you'll resent me for it, and I'm not going to do that to either one of us. Life is too short to be miserable."

"But I want this baby," I insisted, and hated that I was nearly begging. Being with him wasn't supposed to require this much work. "You still want to be with me, don't you?"

It didn't seem like it. He was being downright mean. He wouldn't even look me in the eye. What other reason could he have for suddenly believing having a child with me would be miserable?

"Yes," he claimed, and groaned in frustration as he took a seat on the bed. "I do. Dana, I love you a lot. But we have to work on some things."

I watched him slump over. He still couldn't look at me. His knee began to bounce, a sign that his nerves were on edge.

"Can we talk about those things?" I asked softly.

He grunted and lurched to his feet. "Not tonight. I can't..."

I tried to console him, but he moved away and held his hands up to block my touch.

"Sorry," he quickly apologized. "I don't mean to be mean to you. I love you. I just..." He grimaced and nervously began to crack his knuckles. "I just need some time to clear my head. I gotta get out of here. I'm just gonna go for a drive."

"Baby, why can't we just—"

He walked out of the room, leaving me at the bed completely speechless.

THIRTY-FOUR
GAVIN

I couldn't get into my truck fast enough. The sight of Dana all done up in lingerie irritated the crap out of me. I had to get away, otherwise I was going to say something cruel and hurt her feelings. I'd done that enough already. I wasn't proud of leaving, but I couldn't stand to hear her say that she wanted to give me a child. Why now? Why, after two and a half years of lying about it, would she suddenly change her mind? Whatever she was thinking had to be twisted.

I backed out of the driveway and began to drive into town. My mind was frustrated with how my marriage got to this state. Only a little while ago I was content with Dana. Things weren't perfect, but I loved her and wanted to be with her. Now... I wasn't so sure.

As I continued to drive I began to contemplate what life would be like without Dana. Could I actually divorce my wife? I had no biblical right. She hadn't cheated on me. But was lying about birth control considered a marriage bed violation? Possibly. Or was I reaching?

Don't try to be too spiritual. Just chill and get yourself together.

I wanted to get away. Maybe hang out with a few friends and get a few drinks. Anything to take my mind off the craziness at home. But I really didn't have any friends. My life was all about family. I wasn't about to go to Mama's. Things between us hadn't been the same since I put my foot down about her attacks on Dana, and she was on my mind too heavily right now for me to sit over there and not say anything about her. No. I couldn't hang out with Mama. I couldn't hang out with my in-laws, either. They'd only want to know why I wasn't at home with my wife while they were babysitting my child. No. That wouldn't work, either, so I pulled out my phone and called Deitrick. As soon as he answered I heard a baby screaming in the background.

"What's up, man?" he asked.

"I'm trying to see what's good with you. You got plans for the night?"

"I'm on daddy duties," he said with disappointment. "All weekend, man. What you tryin' to get into?"

Not babies.

"Just got a night to myself. Thinking about maybe hanging out at the sports bar or something."

"Wife working all night again?"

Dang. I hated that everyone knew Dana was a workaholic. I wondered if they all pitied me. Maybe I pitied myself.

"Yeah," I lied. "My kid's hanging out with the in-laws. Wanted to see if you could hang."

"Not at the sports bar," he laughed. "But you can come through to my spot. The baby's with me, but we can kick back for a lil' bit."

"Nawh. That's okay, man," I told him as the baby began to scream louder. "You hang out with your kid and have a good time. We can catch up later."

"You sure?" he asked. "You sound down, man. What's going on?"

"I'm cool," I lied again. "Nothing I can't handle. I'll catch you later."

"All right. Call me if you change your mind. I'll be at the house. Or just come through. You always welcome."

I thanked him and ended the call feeling disappointed, but at least I had his support. I really didn't want to be alone right now, but I didn't want to go back home either. Where did I really want to be?

With Parker.

I told myself not to do it, but I called her. Her number was programmed into my phone for work purposes, just like everyone else's who was on my team.

"Gavin?"

Humph. She had a cute phone voice.

"Hi, Parker."

"Hi. You okay? You sound sad. Is something wrong?"

Man, I must sound a mess. Deitrick said the same thing. What was Dana doing to me?

"I'm cool."

"Awh," she whined. "You don't sound like it. I can hear it in your voice. Are you still upset about... Whatever you were upset about earlier?"

I chuckled. If she knew what I just left in my bedroom she would be blown away.

"I was actually just thinking about what you said earlier."

"What did I say?"

You're playing with fire, man. Don't do it.

"You know. About... Life being too short to be miserable."

"*Oh...*"

"You still feel that way?"

"Yes," she said slowly. "Life is precious. And very valuable. You should live it to the fullest and do whatever makes you happy. If, you know, you are actually unhappy. Are you unhappy?"

"I'm not sure," I admitted after thinking about it. "What are you doing right now? Are you busy?"

"No, no. I'm just here at the house. Madison is at a sleepover with one of her little friends from school, so I have the house to myself."

"Can I come over?"

She was quiet for a moment. I feared that I'd offended her, but she said, "Sure, I don't mind. But are you sure?"

"No, but... I don't want to be alone right now," I said honestly. "I have a lot on my mind and could really use a friend."

"Okay," she told me, and gave me her address.

****

As I walked to the front door of Parker's home I couldn't help but notice the flaws of her property. Before I met Dana my eyes would have overlooked the cracks in her driveway, the split wood around her doorframe, and the plants that needed to be repotted. If she were with me she would point out the countless other imperfections that my amateur eye wasn't skilled enough to notice. I didn't mind them, though. They gave the home a warm vibe, like someone actually lived there and wasn't constantly showcasing it as if it were for sale. I appreciated that. It was inviting.

I rang the doorbell and waited patiently for Parker to answer. She didn't, so I rang the bell again. Finally she came to the door and opened it.

"How long have you been out here?" she asked.

"I just got here," I answered, surprised by her appearance. She didn't have on any makeup, and her hair was twisted into a tousled ponytail at the top of her head. The oversized t-shirt she was wearing hung off one shoulder and was only a few inches shorter than the cutoff shorts she was wearing. A pair of Uggs decorated her feet. I recognized them because Dana had them in every color imagineable, and I always found it to be ridiculous. No one in Texas needed snow boots. They were cute on Parker, though.

"Good," she said. "When I'm in the kitchen I can't hear the doorbell. I just happened to be walking by and saw you out here. You better be glad my curtains were open."

I nodded, then asked, "Can I come in?"

"I guess," she sassed with a smile, and allowed me to enter the house.

I took a few moments to look around as she hurried to the back, out of sight.

"Nice place," I called out to her.

"Thanks," she said. "Come back here with me while I finish cooking."

I walked through the living room and made my way to the kitchen. What I saw was definitely an attraction. Parker was standing in front of the stove, stirring a big pot, and she had a smile on her face. I never saw that at home.

"What you in here messing up?"

"Come look and see."

I joined her at the stove and was surprised to see crawfish inside her pot.

"Are you kidding me?" I asked. "You really do know what you're doing, don't you?"

"Have I ever failed you in this department?"

"No, you haven't." I had to give it to her. It smelled delicious.

"And I never will," she boasted. "It's not ready, though, so we have to wait for a little while longer."

"That's okay. I'll wait," I said, and took a seat at the bar.

She looked over at me and smiled. "I bet you will," she said slyly.

I continued to look around her house and was surprised by how small it was. Then again, it should have been. It was only for her and Madison, and she wasn't grandiose like Dana. Parker was the type of woman who was happy with having enough. Easy to get along with and easy to please. I liked that about her. Despite its flaws, this house was nice, but Dana would never live here. Not without giving it a major makeover that it didn't even need.

"Okay, you're going to laugh at me," she said. "You know how most people drink beer with their crawfish?"

I nodded.

"I don't like it. I drink wine. Weird, right?"

I smiled. "Nawh. I mean, I've never heard of it, but if you like it..."

"I don't know if I'm country or uppity," she laughed. "Would you like a glass? I have soda, too, if you want some."

"Wine will be fine."

She opened the fridge and pulled out a bottle and uncorked it, then poured me a glass.

"Merci."

She poured herself a glass, then lifted it to make a toast.

"To happiness," she said, then tapped her glass against mine.

"Cheers," I said, and took a drink.

****

I went into the kitchen and refilled our wine glasses, then rejoined Parker on the couch to look through more of her photo albums. She had a million of them, and most were filled with pictures of Madison through her vast stages of development.

"You are the *only* person I know who still prints their pictures," I told her as I handed her glass to her.

"You know... I think I am, too," she giggled at herself. "I think people should, though. It's really a lost art. Technology and social media have really taken away from the craft of photography. It's cheapened the value of print, almost."

"What?" I asked with a doubtful tone. "That's not true."

"Yes, it is. Think about it. When was the last time someone actually handed you a picture printed on paper? It's been a long time, right?"

"Yeah, because people just text or email the pictures to me."

"Okay, yeah. But what if you lose your phone? Guess what? You've lost your photos. But if you had it printed, you will have the photos forever. That's why I get mine printed. And, something else people don't think about—when their kids get older, they're going to want pictures of themselves when they were a baby. Are people still going to carry around the cell phone they had from twenty years ago?"

"That's why your phone comes with a memory card."

"Yeah. Until you drop your phone in the toilet. Or in the sink. Or your kid bakes it in their play oven. Yes, Madison did that."

"You are sssssoooooo anti-technology," I laughed, and took a sip from my glass.

"I can admit to that," she said with no shame, and laughed with me as she turned the page. "Hey, do you recognize this child?"

I looked down at the album and was surprised to see a picture of Jonathan. He was standing next to Madison with his arm wrapped around her shoulder, and the two were grinning harder than I'd ever seen.

"When was this picture taken?"

"That's from the class field trip. They were laughing and I just snapped the picture. Came out good, didn't it?"

"Yeah, it did," I said. "Man, look at my boy. He's getting so big," I said with pride.

"They do grow up fast."

"Too fast."

"They can't stay babies forever. But he looks a lot like you."

I chuckled and drank more wine.

Parker studied me for a moment, then closed the photo album and placed it on the coffee table in front of us.

"No more pictures?" I asked, disappointed.

"There's always more pictures," she told me, then took my wine glass from me and placed it on the end table beside her, out of my reach. "We can look at them later. I want to know what's going on with you."

I frowned. "What do you mean?"

"You know what I mean," she said, and looked me in the eye. "I can tell you have a lot on your mind. It's Friday night. It's late... Too late for a married man to be at my house, and your phone hasn't even rang. Now that either means no one is concerned about where you are because they don't care, which I know isn't true because you're still wearing your wedding ring. Or it means that you silenced your phone so you wouldn't hear it ring."

I stared at her. She stared back, unmoved.

"Pretty smart, there, Ms. Parker." I'd actually turned my ringer off when I parked my truck in her driveway.

"I know," she said, and scooted closer to me. "So what's going on? What's troubling you?"

"I really don't want to talk about this, Parker," I told her.

"Are you sure?" she asked. "I don't like to see you like this. Is everything okay with Dana?"

It took me a moment to confess, but finally I said, "No."

She looked sad to hear the news. "It's been going on for a while now, hasn't it? I can tell. These past few weeks at work, you've been different. Not the same upbeat guy that you were when I first met you. I wanted to ask you what was going on, but I figured it was personal and didn't want to pry."

"Yeah, it's pretty personal," I let her know.

"Well, you don't have to share if you don't want to," she told me. "I just want you to be okay."

"I am okay."

She shook her head, then softly said, "You don't seem like it."

I sighed deeply. "I don't want to give too much detail," I told her. "But I will share with you that there was a betrayal of some sort."

"You didn't cheat on her, did you?" she feared

"No, I didn't cheat. I'm not that type of man. And she didn't cheat, either. She's not that type of woman. But what happened was a betrayal, and it hurt. She did it to me, I didn't do it to her. And... quite frankly, I'm having a hard time getting over it."

"Awh.. Gavin..." she pouted, and gave me a hug.

I hugged her back and surprised my own self. I hadn't touched another woman like this is years, and I knew it was wrong. I didn't stop, though. She felt good against me. Her body was soft, yet firm, and felt like a missing piece of my chest that fit right into place. It was nice. *Real nice.*

"Um..." She cleared her throat and pulled away. I didn't want her to, but knew she did the right thing. "It's getting late, Gavin."

"Do you want me to leave?" I wouldn't have been offended if she said yes. It was almost midnight.

"Do you want to?"

"No," I answered honestly.

"Are you sure?" she asked, and looked me in the eye. "I don't want you to have any regrets when it comes to me."

I needed to go home. She knew it, too. But I said, "I'm right where I want to be."

She returned my wine glass to me. "Then you can stay as long as you like."

I took a sip from my drink and draped my arm over the back of the couch, toward her. She slid into the opening and nestled against me as she picked up the photo album again. We began to look at more pictures, and I leaned in close to smell her hair and perfume.

This is nice. Yeah... I could definitely get used to this...

THIRTY-FIVE
DANA

Gavin didn't come home last night. I lost count of the number of times I tried to reach him. It was now six o'clock in the morning and I hadn't heard from him since he ran out of the house nearly twelve hours ago. I couldn't help but think the worst. There was a strong chance he was lying in a ditch somewhere, run off the road by a drunk driver—or even in an alley, attacked and mugged by a thug for the diamond watch I bought him for Christmas last year. Heinous things like that happened to good people all the time. Why would my husband be the exception? He could be in a hospital bed right now, mangled by some horrific accident that left him completely unrecognizable, and the mugger who stole his watch also stole his wallet, therefore he had no identification on him when paramedics delivered his barely breathing body to the hospital. That was why no one called or came by the house to notify me yet.

Lord, please let him be okay...

My mind thought the worst, but my spirit told me that he was okay. It was difficult to believe, though. Gavin had never done anything like this before. Why wouldn't he come home if things hadn't gotten out of his control? Yes, there were several men out there who ran out on their wives, but those men were usually trifling and running into the arms of other women. Gavin wasn't a cheater. Something had to have happened to him. Nothing else explained why he didn't come back home.

I sat up in bed and called his cell phone again. All I got was the same annoying voicemail greeting I'd heard throughout the night.

I hung up and placed the phone on its charger and continued to wonder where he could be. With Sylvia? Of course. She'd always been the other woman in our marriage, hadn't she? But I knew better than to call her. Even if Gavin was with her, she'd lie and say he wasn't just to be cruel, then make some spiteful remark about how I needed to learn how to keep my man at home.

But I *did* know how to keep him at home. Shoot, I busted my butt to keep that man happy. I offered myself to him on a platter and he still ran off. I *was not* the problem.

Maybe he just doesn't want me anymore...

The phone rang. I snatched it and saw Leah's number flash across its screen.

"Is Gavin with you guys? Is he there at your house?"

"Huh?" Leah panted loudly and blew her breath as if she were in pain. "What... are you... talking... about?"

"What's wrong with you?" I asked in a panic, forgetting all about Gavin. "Are you okay?"

"No," she said through a deep exhale. "I'm having... contractions... The baby's coming..."

I gasped loudly. "NO!" I shrieked. "It's not time yet. The baby's not supposed to come for another three weeks."

"I know," she told me through deep breaths. "But... she's coming... and... I need you... to come and... take me... to... the hospital."

"Oh, my God!" I continued to panic, and jumped out of bed. "Where's Marcus?"

She took a deep breath. "He... had a... landscaping job... out of town... I called him, and... he's on his way... The kids are... still sleeping. I... didn't want to... wake them. *Ooooooooowwwwwww!!!*"

"Okay, okay," I told her, and rushed out of bed. "I'm on my way."

THIRTY-SIX
GAVIN

My eyes rolled open slowly as I woke from my sleep and landed on a ceiling I didn't recognize. I tried to sit up quickly, but was stopped by a sharp pain that gripped my neck.

"Ooooohhh," I moaned, and rubbed it as I lifted my head from the backwards tilt it had apparently been in for hours. I had a slight headache, too, as if I'd had alcohol recently.

I realized I was at Parker's house. I looked to my right and found her sleeping against me with her legs stretched out in the opposite direction. Memories of the crawfish we ate last night came back to me, and the wine we drank, too. We looked at photos and talked until the early hours of the morning, but I never went home. Nothing happened, though. We were both fully dressed, and even though her shorts exposed her muscular thighs, I hadn't touched her at all. We didn't even kiss.

Relieved, I checked my watch. 7:47.

Oh, man... What have I done?

Dana was going to kill me. It didn't matter that I didn't cheat. What mattered was that I didn't come home last night, and no amount of guilt she had over her birth control secret would allow me to get away with it.

I didn't want to leave, though. Other than my sore neck, I was comfortable beside Parker. I liked being with her. She was calm and relaxing. I'd never seen her stressed out the way Dana always seemed to be. That was because she was thankful for what she had, and wasn't constantly grabbing for more than what she needed. All she wanted was to live her life and take care of her daughter, and I appreciated that about her. It made her easy to be around. If Jonathan were here, everything would be perfect.

Jonathan...

Crap. I needed to get home. He'd spent the night with Leah, but I didn't know what time she was bringing him back to the house. He was already fearful that Dana and I were getting a divorce, and he'd be worried if he got home and I wasn't there. I couldn't put him through that.

I tapped Parker on the shoulder, but she didn't move. She was completely out, exhausted from working hard all week and keeping me company all night.

"Parker..."

Man. She was even beautiful when she slept. She didn't even snore.

I gave her a firm nudge. She slowly turned her head to face me and sheepishly grinned as her eyes met mine. Embarrassed that she'd been caught sleeping, she covered her face with her hands and turned away.

"Time to wake up," I told her, and softly gave her shoulders a shake.

She took a long stretch and yawned, then curled herself into a ball and nestled against me.

"Not yet."

"Yeah, it's time," I whispered.

She pulled her shirt partially over her face and let it hang over her nose.

"What time is it?"

"Almost eight. I gotta get going."

A low moan came from her. I knew she didn't want me to leave, but she sat up on the couch to free me from the captivity I'd enjoyed for the past few hours.

"Thanks for letting me stay over. Hope I wasn't too much of a bother."

"No, you were fine," she insisted. "I had fun."

"I did, too. I wish I didn't have to leave so soon. I'd hate for you to think I just used you for your wine and food."

"I know better than that," she said, and smiled at me with her eyes as I stood to leave. "You got plans for today?"

I didn't even want to think about what Dana was going to say when I walked into the house. I'd be lucky if my belongings weren't strung out across the front lawn when I got there.

"Don't know," was all I told her.

She stood with me. "Do you feel better now? About... whatever happened?"

"Not sure," I answered, and became frustrated with Dana all over again. But the irritation left as soon as I looked into Parker's eyes again. "I'm glad I got to spend some time with you, though."

The chemistry between us grew stronger as we stood in front of each other. I wanted to kiss her. She wanted me to, I could tell, but forced herself to look away, putting the physical desire we had for one another on hold.

"You better get going," she whispered as she wrapped her arms around herself. "I'm sure you have people waiting on you."

"Yeah, I better go," I agreed quickly, and walked to the door. "Thanks again," I said, and stopped to get one more glimpse of her before I left.

On the way to my truck I pulled my cell phone from my pocket to turn its incoming call notification back on. I was alarmed to find I had twenty-nine missed calls. One from Deitrick, one from Mama, and the rest were from Dana.

My heart dropped. She'd called *that many* times?! Something was wrong.

I called her back in a panic and prayed that everything was okay. Here I was, laying up under another woman, and my wife could have been sick, or in the hospital, or...

Oh, God...

What if it was Jonathan?!

What if Leah got into an accident with him last night, or accidently fed him peanuts? He was severely allergic! What if Dana forgot to pack his EpiPen?!

Oh, no...

What if it was Mama? What if—

"Hello?"

"Dana, is everything all right?" I asked, nearly scared to death.

"WHERE ARE YOU?!"

Oh... shoot. Everything was fine. She'd only called me that many times because she was worried something had happened to me. I ran out of the house last night like a crazy man, and she hadn't seen or heard from me since.

You better hurry up and think of a good lie, fool...

"Where are you?" she asked again when I didn't answer her the first time.

"I... I—I—"

"Why are you stuttering? You have a speech impediment now?"

"No, I—"

"Where were you all night?"

"I—"

"Don't you lie to me. You better tell me *right now!*"

I could hear her fuming through the phone. She gave me a few seconds to explain my absence, but I couldn't say anything.

"Are you in your right mind?" she asked, calm suddenly.

"Uh..." Confused, I answered, *"Yeah."*

"Okay. And you're in good health, right?" she asked sweetly. "No sudden illness or sickness?"

"Uuuhhh..."

I didn't know how to answer. Something was off. This was creepy. She'd never gone from manic to sugary in a matter of seconds before. Had *she* lost *her* mind? Why wasn't she angry anymore?

"Not that I know of..." I told her.

"Okay," she replied in the same tone. "I need you to get to the hospital right now. Leah's having her baby."

I gasped. "What? She's in labor?"

"Yes, and the kids are in the waiting room by themselves. Jessica's watching them, but she's texting on her phone, so you know how that goes."

Yeah, I did. Someone could walk in with a machete and take both Jonathan and MJ hostage and she wouldn't notice.

"Where's Marcus?"

"He went out of town on business, but he's on his way now. *You'd know that already if your brought your behind home last night.*"

She hung up in my face before I could respond. I now understood where the sweetness came from. It was the calm people had right before they unleashed complete mayhem. I had whatever she was about to give justly coming to me. If our actions were reversed I would be just as livid. I had to keep a cool head, though. Otherwise I'd end up needing a hospital room, too.

THIRTY-SEVEN
DANA

As soon as I saw Gavin I knew he'd been up to something foul. I could smell his guilt from yards away. He stared at the ground as he made his way into the hospital waiting room, clearly nervous, as if he didn't trust it to catch his feet. Finally he looked up at me, and when his eyes met mine he quickly turned away. That never happened. Ever. There was only one reason why it would now.

He was with another woman.

I knew it when I talked to him earlier, but I'd fully trusted him up to this point and didn't want to believe he'd actually do that to me. How stupid was I to think that he'd actually gotten hurt. He had me worried for nothing. Now, as he approached me, I was extremely disgusted. I'd put up with antics like this from men in my past, but there was no way I was putting up with it from my husband. He made a commitment to me. We were married, and he knew better.

"Where have you been?" I asked as soon as he was in front of me.

His eyes bulged and looked down at Jonathan and MJ, who were playing a game together on Jonathan's tablet. I stared at him all the more, not caring if the children heard my disrespect, and waited for the answer he owed me.

"Can we talk about this later?"

"No, we are going to talk about it right now."

He sighed and rubbed the back of his head, the whole time looking everywhere but into my eyes.

"Gavin..." I said slowly, and concentrated on keeping my voice down. "You better start talking."

"I was just out."

"Where?"

"Out," he snapped.

"Where did you sleep?"

"Where I slept."

I was outraged, but he stared at me with total defiance, as if I were out of line for demanding to know the whereabouts of my husband. What part of being in a respectable marriage was this?

"You're not going to tell me where you were?"

He stood firm in his refusal and stared back at me with no expression at all.

"I don't have time for this. My sister is having a baby, and I need to be there for her right now. I'll deal with you later," I said angrily, and rolled my eyes at him as I turned and walked away. "Watch the kids."

When I made it back into Leah's delivery room she was lying on her side with a nurse beside her, screaming in pain.

"What's wrong?" I asked. When I'd left her she was fine.

The nurse shook her head. "I think her epidural is wearing off."

I rushed to her side and took her by the hand. She squeezed it with so much power that I thought my bones were going to break. My mouth opened in agony as I prepared to holler, but the nurse rubbed my back and told me I was a great support system. I suffered through it and wished my hand could trade places with Gavin's neck.

****

"Are you ready?" the doctor asked Leah.

"Yes," she groaned through tight teeth.

"Okay, Leah. Push," the doctor told her.

She screamed and bore down as he counted to ten. She sweated profusely and panted heavily, but didn't stop until the doctor cued her that she could.

"Good job!" I encouraged her, and rubbed her leg with my free hand. I no longer cared about the pressure to my hand. I lost feeling in it a long time ago. I kept my head down the entire time so I wouldn't see any of the birth. It was too gruesome. I knew I'd pass out.

The door to the hospital room open suddenly and Marcus rushed in.

"Baby!" Leah screamed at him. "She's coming! You almost missed it!"

"Stay focused," the doctor told her. "Don't get too excited. I need you to push!"

"I am pushing!" she yelled at him, and screamed again.

Marcus moved me to the side and took over hand holding duties.

"You're doing good, baby," he coached her. "Come on. Bring our baby girl into the world."

She burst into overwhelmed tears, and he kissed her on her forehead and began to whisper into her ear.

"Stay with me, Leah," the doctor said. "She's almost here. I need you to push again."

I took a step back to give Marcus more room and caught sight of a large amount of blood at the doctor's feet.

"Oh, God," I said, and became lightheaded as I looked away. "I'm just gonna go..."

"I got it, Dana," Marcus told me. He knew how horrible I was in situations like this.

I gave him a nod and quickly left the room before I could see anything more. I walked into the waiting room and found Gavin asleep as he sat beside Jonathan and MJ, who were too busy playing to notice they weren't being properly supervised.

Why is he so tired? What was he doing all night that kept him from getting any rest?

I kicked his feet, which had been crossed at the ankles, and startled him out of his sleep. The rude gesture irritated him, but before he could fuss I motioned for him to be quiet and join me in the corner.

"Where were you last night?" I asked when we were alone.

He looked away and sighed, but didn't answer.

"I know you heard me," I said as calmly as I could. I really wanted to grab him by the collar of his shirt and demand that he tell me the absolute truth.

"At a friend's," he finally said when he saw I wasn't going to back down.

"What friend?"

"Just a friend," he snapped.

"That's the only answer you're going to give me?"

"That's all you need to know. Nothing bad happened, and everything's cool."

"If everything's *cool*, then why is it such a secret?"

"'Cause you just don't need to know everything, now drop it all right? *Damn.*"

His crassness startled me. What was going on with him? Since when was it ever okay for him to talk to me that way?

"You better tell me right now why you didn't come home last night. I'm not playing with you."

"Dana..." He groaned and rubbed his head. He didn't want to talk, but there was no way I was going to let him off the hook. Not after having me worry all night.

"Are you cheating on me?"

His head snapped in my direction, and he stared at me angrily. "What did you just ask me?"

"Don't play stupid. You heard me. Are you cheating?"

"Man... No, I'm not cheating on you!" he hissed under his breath. "Don't ask me any crazy mess like that. I would never cheat on you!"

"Then tell me where you were!"

"You need to drop it, before you make me mad."

I was ready to slap him. "Do you *really think* I care about you getting mad right now?! Let me tell you something. I will—"

I put my hand over my mouth to hold in the slew of ungodly words that were on the tip of my tongue.

"You are my husband, and I love you very much," I told him after I'd calmed down. "But I'm not going to sit on the side and let you play me like I'm some type of fool. I'm your wife! So the next time you want to stay out all night and not come home, you better make sure you have a change of address form ready, because you will be moving out. I *will not* be disrespected like this again. Do you understand me?"

The door to Leah's room burst open. Marcus bounced out with his hands in the air, praising God as he told us the baby had just been born.

"She's here!" he exclaimed, full of pride and joy. He was so excited that tears were in his eyes. "My daughter's here!" he told us. "April is here! April! And she's seven pounds! Oh, you ought to see her! She's beautiful!"

Gavin and I didn't say anything. We were too focused on being upset with each other to celebrate the arrival of our niece like decent human beings should have. It wasn't until Marcus stared at us with confusion did we realize we were being rude.

"Congratulations," we quickly told him, and I gave him a hug.

He accepted it, but frowned as he watched us. He knew something was wrong.

"How's Leah?" I asked him.

"She's great," he told me. "You go on ahead and see her. You know she's waiting on you."

I turned to go back into her room, and out of my peripheral saw Marcus stop Gavin when he tried to do the same.

"Nawh, bruh," I heard him say. "You stay right here and tell me what's going on."

Yes! Get him, brother! GET HIM!

THIRTY-EIGHT
GAVIN

"Is everything all right?" Marcus asked me.

Irritated that he even asked, I turned away and answered "Yeah," before walking away.

"Don't sound like it to me," he said coolly as he followed. "To me, it sounded like y'all were arguing."

This was none of his business. Besides that, Dana had me beyond pissed off and I needed a moment to collect myself before I went back in the waiting room with Jonathan.

"Wanna talk about it?" he asked me.

"No," I said, but stopped walking.

"All right. I can respect that," he claimed with his hands up in surrender. "I know y'all are grown and married, and what's between y'all is between y'all. But Dana is my little sister, and she didn't look too happy just now. Really, she looked like she was ready to knock your head off. And I got her back, so I'm getting in your business. Now what's going on? Don't make me hurt you, messing with my sister, man."

I dismissed the threat with a head shake. Marcus was just being the over-protective big brother that he always was when it came to Dana. He was cool, though, so I knew I could talk to him. When Dana and I got married he became a big brother to me, too, and I valued his advice.

"What's going on?" he asked me. "Y'all ain't been married long enough to have no real problems, so what's the deal?"

"She just cuttin' up," I said as if I wasn't worried.

He cocked his head to the side, knowing I was lying. "Really, dude?"

Now really wasn't the best time to talk, but I knew he wasn't about to go away. I peeked around the corner to check on the kids, and when I saw they were fine decided to share with him what I was going through.

"You ever just get tired, man?"

"I just drove three and a half hours after working all night."

"Nawh," I said, a bit frustrated. "I mean do you ever get tired of being married?"

His face lit up with the revelation.

"Oooooooooohhhhhhhh... I know exactly what you mean," he said, and gave a nod. "But where did that come from? The last time I saw you, you guys seemed happy."

I hated to admit it, but told him that we hadn't been getting along lately.

"The birth control thing?"

"You heard about it, huh? Leah told you?"

"Yeah, she mentioned it. She was a little upset with Dana about it. I was, too. Disappointed, really. That wasn't a cool thing to do at all."

"See, I have a right to be upset," I declared angrily, and felt vindicated.

"Yes, you do. Dana wasn't honest with you, and she was wrong for that. But..."

"But?"

"Well... Were you really surprised?"

My mouth fell open. "Seriously?!" I thought this man had sense. How would I not be surprised by that? "How would you feel if your wife told you that she didn't want to have your baby?"

"Wait a minute, just calm down, now," he cautioned me. "I know you wanna have more kids and all that, but remember who you married. It's only been two years. The ink on your license is barely dry. When you met Dana, nothing about her said she wanted to have any kids. Shoot, she didn't even like kids until she met Jonathan. And truth be told, I think he's the only one she does like, other than mine. She was all about her career. Don't tell me you thought everything about her would change when you put that ring on her finger. You thought she would all of a sudden embrace all the things she has hated doing her entire life, like cooking, cleaning, and all of the traditional womanly things? I know you weren't that naive, bro."

"No," I argued defensively. "I knew she wasn't going to change into a totally different person. But a wife is supposed to submit to her husband. Ain't that what the bible says?"

"Yes, that's what it says. You are right about that," he agreed with me.

"Ain't she supposed to make me happy?" I asked angrily. "Ain't she supposed to consider me and what I want? Why does it always have to be about her? 'Wives, submit to your husbands,' right? That's what the bible says, don't it?"

"Yes, the bible does say that. But the bible also says that a husband and wife are to submit to each other."

Of course he would take Dana's side. She was his sister-in-law. Besides that, he would never understand what I was going through. His wife just gave him his third child, and she was happy to do it. He would never know the pain I was feeling.

"I know you're mad," he told me. "But this isn't all on Dana. You have to take some fault in this situation, too. You're busy pointing out all of the things that she has done wrong, but what about you, Gavin?"

"Me?" I asked at his audacity. "You don't live in my house. You don't know everything about what's going on, man. I have been a perfect husband to her! She isn't the only one who works. I have a job, too, and I take care of Jonathan, plus the

house, and her."

"All right, G, I don't doubt it," he said, holding up his hands again. "But even in all that, you ain't perfect. You can't be. It's impossible. You're so focused on what she hasn't submitted to, but what haven't you submitted to?"

"You're taking sides," I accused. "You're standing here, talking about I need to submit. I'm a man, and the head of my household."

"Yeah, but you can't have a baby by yourself. It takes two."

"You're taking sides," I continued to insist. "I'm trying to get fair and honest advice from you, man."

"And I'm giving it to you, if you'd listen, *fool.*"

Mad enough to punch a hold in the wall, I stuffed my fists into my pockets and took a deep breath. I realized I was acting the same way Jonathan did when he needed to calm down and took a few moments to get myself together. I was a grown man and too cool to act so childish.

"All I'm saying is that you don't know everything about the situation," I told him a moment later. "There's more to it than you realize."

"All right. I'll give you that," he responded. "But I know enough about the two of you and how you got together to know that y'all can get through this. I know your testimony. I know how both of y'all prayed to God for a spouse, and when you met each other you knew that you were both each other's blessings. I wanna see y'all make it, man. God put y'all together for a reason. And I know you want a baby right now—I get it. But maybe it's just not the time yet. Maybe there are some more things that God wants to do in you both before y'all take that next step. She's only been a mother for two years to Jonathan. It's going to be totally different for her to actually go through a pregnancy. Man, that is a huge experience for a woman. *Trust me.* I've been through it three times with my wife. It's not for the light hearted. Maybe you just need to be content with the son you have already. At least until Dana is ready. If it's meant to be, she'll change her mind about it."

"Says the man with three kids," I quipped.

"Yeah, I got three," he declared. "And I'm telling you, you better enjoy only having one, because three will bring a big change to your marriage and your household. I'm telling you. You better take the time to enjoy your wife the way things are right now. Wisdom is speaking, homie. You better listen."

"But you got three! I only have one. I wish to God that I can experience what you do, man."

He shook his head with disappointment. "You're sitting up here complaining about having only one child. You know how many people wish they could have kids, and can't? My sister is thirty-five years old, only a few years younger than you, and just had a full hysterectomy. Married, but never got the chance to have a baby."

My heart instantly broke for her. In my ranting I never even considered what a woman would feel like if something like that happened.

"Awh, man... I'm sorry."

"Not trying to make you feel bad. I'm just saying that you got it better than you think you do."

"Yeah," I agreed, and felt ashamed of myself for being so self-centered. "You're right about that."

"I know I am. Now, *who is the other woman?*"

My head snapped up quickly from the ground where it had been directed.

"Guilty," he judged. "Who is she?"

"I didn't—I ain't—I—What? I haven't—"

"Boy, you're too holy," he said with a hearty laugh. "You been knowing Jesus for a while and can't lie to save your life, all that stuttering. Who is she?"

"There is no other woman," I insisted.

"You ain't fooling me with that lie, kid. I know it's someone. I can tell by the look on your face. Plus I heard Dana say you didn't come home last night. You didn't wanna tell her where you were, so obviously you were with another woman. Who is she?"

Dang... He's wasting his time landscaping. Should have been a detective...

"Where were you?"

"All right, don't press me," I scolded. "I was with a co-worker. But nothing happened, I promise. We just talked, and it got late. We both were tired and fell asleep. I was in the living room the whole time."

"Y'all were alone? It was just you two?"

"Yes—but *nothing happened.* We just fell asleep."

"Okay. I believe you. But you didn't go over there for no reason. It has to be something going on if you would rather be there with her instead of at home with your wife, especially if you can't tell your wife about it. You better straighten up," he told me sternly. "You play with fire, you get burned. Your marriage is blessed, but that adultery won't be."

"Woah!" I stopped him, offended by the accusation. "No one is cheating."

"Not yet."

"She's a co-worker. That's all."

"You must think I'm new to this. I been married way longer than you, and I'm not a bad looking man, if I must say so myself. I been down the road of temptation before. I know how it looks, and you reek of it. That denial you're entertaining is going to get you hurt. Dana's with you right now, but I know my sister. She's not going to take too much from you, especially now that you're her husband. Whatever you're doing, or not doing... You better make sure she's worth it."

I was suddenly sick with guilt. My brother was telling me the truth.

"Have you ever cheated on Leah?" I wanted to know. He talked as if he had personal experience.

He rubbed the back of his head, uneasy now.

"I came close one time," he admitted, and parted his thick hair with his fingers to reveal his scalp. "You see this scar?"

I leaned over to get a good view of the healed wound. It was about five inches long and looked to have been the result of a very deep gash.

"What happened?" I asked, alarmed. He looked like he'd had surgery or something.

"You'll never know," he told me as he fixed his hair. "Just remember this one thing, if you never remember anything else I ever tell you in life. Our women carry our last names, but they have Jeffries DNA. From one man to another... You don't want to mess with that."

"Oh..." I moaned, and rubbed my own head as my mind ran wild with theories of how he ended up with an injury like that. Thank God they found Jesus.

Be a fence all around us, Lord!

"You okay?" he asked with a chuckle, humored by my unsettled nerves.

"*Me?* You're the one with scars."

We laughed and he gave me a brotherly hug to show there were no hard feelings.

"Take care of yourself, man," he added with a fist bump. "And take care of my lil' sis."

"She's in good hands," I assured him.

"All right. I'm gonna hold you to it, now."

"No need to. I got her."

"Okay. Well you better. 'Cause my wife don't play, either."

"Apparently not," I joked.

He smiled, then said, "Let me get back in here with my wife and new daughter. Go get the other kids, man, and have them come meet the newest member of our family."

I smiled as I watched him bounce back into his wife's delivery room. I was envious, even still, but pressed through it and honored his request.

THIRTY-NINE
GAVIN

Dana only spoke to me twice after we left the hospital. Once was to ask again where I spent Friday night. The second was to tell me I was staying in the guest bedroom until I was man enough to confess. Clearly, she'd changed her mind about wanting to give me a baby. It angered me, but there was no way I would ever tell her that I spent the night with Parker. It was a secret I planned on taking to the grave. Besides, Dana was just as weak as I was when it came to sex. She'd be half naked in front of me again in no time. If not, I knew what to do to get her where I wanted her.

But none of that was on my mind when I left for work this morning. The start of a new week felt promising, especially knowing I'd see Parker again. I looked forward to the exchanges we would share between taking care of our patients. Sadly, when I saw her again, she seemed disturbed.

"Can I talk to you?" she asked with a long face. She'd just knocked on my office door and stood in its opening.

"Yeah," I said, suddenly worried, and put the patient file I was reviewing away as I motioned for her to come in. "Is everything all right?"

"Uuuummmmm..." She came in and closed the door. "It's about the other night..."

I waited for her to say more, but she became curiously silent.

"Parker? What's wrong?"

She took a deep breath. "How did things go when you got home Saturday?"

Oh. She was worried about Dana.

"About as to be expected," I told her, and stood from my desk to meet her at the door. "But that's not anything for you to worry about."

She backed away as I got into her personal space. "See... That's the thing. I kinda am."

I stood still, seeing that she was uncomfortable, and watched as she walked across the room.

"Why?" I asked.

She nervously twiddled her fingers. "I don't want to be responsible for breaking up anyone's home," she finally said.

I sighed, regretful that I'd put her in the position to feel the way she did.

"You're not breaking up my home," I told her.

"You stayed with me all night," she argued quickly. "No woman is going to be cool with that, and she's your wife."

"And that's exactly why you need to let me be the one to worry about her."

"I'm serious," she declared. "I know you guys are having your problems, but I don't want to be in the middle of whatever's going on with you. I'm no side chick, or home wrecker, or second place trophy you keep in your closet to pull out and play with whenever you get bored at home or your wife starts getting on your nerves. I'm better than that, and I'm more than that, and I will not let you—"

"Whoa, whoa," I stopped her, and pulled her to my side so I could hold her. "What are you talking about? *Side chick?* Really? You know I would never treat you like that. Is that what you think is going on here?"

"I don't know what's going on," she pouted, and looked up at me with eyes that were full of worry. "You tell me. What exactly *is* going on?"

I saw how vulnerable she felt and rubbed her shoulders to try to calm her nerves, but it didn't seem to do any good.

"Nothing," I told her, but in my heart I knew it wasn't true. I'd developed feelings for her that were only supposed to be for my wife. But I would never label her any of the names she'd called out, or any other imaginable derogatory term used to describe a woman. I respected her more than that, and she hadn't done anything to lose that respect.

"Are you sure?" she asked.

"Yeah. We're friends," I told her. "That's it. Nothing to feel bad about."

I continued to rub her arms, but she looked away, uneasy.

"You have a son, Gavin," she said a moment later. "I'm a child of divorce, and I know how painful it is. I don't want to do that to him. I'm not trying to break up your family."

"You can't break what's already broken."

She searched my face for a deeper rebuttal, one that would ease her conscious and validate my claim.

"There's no need to feel guilty about what happened the other night because *nothing happened,*" I told her, and gave her a hug. "We're just friends."

Her uneasiness didn't go away.

"Right?" I asked, and waited for her to agree. "We're just friends. That's it. The other night was just one friend helping another friend out. That's all."

She sighed, but said, "Okay," and backed away from me with her head down in disappointment. "If you say so," she added, and opened the door to leave.

"Wait. You believe me, don't you?"

She turned to face me. "If you say we're just friends... *Then we're just friends,*" she told me, and walked away.

FORTY
GAVIN

A few weeks went by with no change between Dana and I. She spent most of her time at work, so Jonathan and I barely saw her. I was still sleeping in the guest bedroom, though now I think she preferred it that way. She didn't even bother to tell me goodbye when she left for work in the morning. The distance between us left the house cold, but it also gave room for things between Parker and I to grow. We'd been spending more time together during our down time at work, and she'd managed to pick up a daily routine of bringing homemade meals for us to share at lunch. We even talked on the phone at night once our kids were put to bed.

Tonight, however, we were on the phone early. She'd made a batch of stew for me a few days ago, and I'd begged her for the recipe every since I partook of the first spoonful. Finally she shared it with me, but after working on it for over an hour I still couldn't get it to taste right and called her for further instructions. Parker, of course, found the misfortune to be very humorous.

"Stop laughing at me," I fussed, even though her giggles were a turn on.

"I told you exactly what to do," she said. "It's so easy. How could you mess it up?"

"I don't know," I pouted, and sampled the stew again. Something was missing. It was close to what Parker made, but not quite what I needed it to be to enjoy it fully.

She continued to laugh.

"You know what's wrong with it, don't you?"

"Yep. But I'm not gonna tell you. I want you to guess."

"Oh, Lord..." She'd been playing this guessing game with me all day. When was her birthday? What did I think her favorite color was? If she were an animal, which would she be? How old was she when she finally learned how to drive? We'd been at it all day, and I'd learned a lot about her. Right now, though, all I wanted to know was how I messed up this stew.

"I added the onions like you told me to," I told her. "And the celery, and tomatoes, and the peppers."

"Yes, that's good."

"What else?"

She snickered. "Keep guessing."

"Ugh. Now you're just being evil."

"Tell you what? If you come over again, I'll make some more. You can sit at my feet and watch me like the culinary student you truly are, and learn from the master."

"Oh, really?!" I pretended to be offended, but laughed inside. She had jokes. Her suggestion actually wasn't a bad one. I wouldn't mind being alone with her again.

I heard the front door open. I stuck my head in the living room and saw Dana enter the house.

"Let me call you back," I quickly told Parker, and hung up the phone.

Dana eyed me suspiciously as she walked into the kitchen. "Who were you talking to?"

"Mama," I lied, knowing she wouldn't want to know anything further about it, and tossed my cell phone on the counter.

"Smells good," she told me. "What are you making?"

"Stew."

"How was your day?"

"Fine."

I was being short on purpose, and she noticed, but didn't start an argument with me about it.

"Where's Jonathan?" she asked a moment later.

"Upstairs in his room, playing."

She leaned against the counter and watched me. "Good. That gives us a chance to talk." She picked up the spoon on the counter and took a sample of the stew. "This is good," she told me, and took another spoonful.

I smiled proudly. "Like it?"

"Yeah," she said, and smacked her lips with satisfaction. "I think it needs some garlic, though."

I looked at the recipe card on the counter. I hadn't written garlic down, but knew that Parker told me to add three full bulbs. That was the missing ingredient.

Irritated, I grabbed them out of the pantry and began to peel them.

"Did I say something wrong?"

"No," I told her, but I was annoyed that she'd ruined the little game Parker and I were playing. There was no telling how long it would have continued. "What do you need to talk to me about?"

"Us," she said, and slowly walked over to the bar and took a seat.

Ugh. Here we go...

"Not really in the mood?" she correctly assumed.

"Go 'head," I told her. "My wife wants to talk, she can talk. I'm all ears."

It took her a minute, but finally she told me, "I really want our marriage to work."

"I do, too."

"Do you, really?"

"Isn't that what I said?"

"Doesn't seem like it," she told me. "Every since you found out about the birth control you've been really cold toward me. It makes me think you don't want me anymore. I'm trying really hard to make up for my past mistake, but you have to help me out here. I can't fix this all on my own."

"That's what you fail to understand," I told her as I continued to cook. "You can't *fix* what you did. There's no way possible to make up for lying to me for our entire marriage. All we can do is move on."

"How?" she asked, frustrated. "You barely even talk to me anymore. What kind of marriage is this?"

"The one *you* created," I answered, and shrugged nonchalantly when she slouched with disappointment. "You're the one who lied, not me."

"I know, but—"

"It is what it is. Don't try to rationalize any further. You made your decision to lie, and now you're dealing with the consequences."

"What's that? A cruel husband?"

I stopped and faced her. "A husband who doesn't trust you anymore. You had my trust, but you broke it. Earning it back isn't going to happen overnight."

"But it's been weeks," she protested.

"Trust has no time table. It happens when it happens."

She wasn't satisfied with my answer. "I'm trying. Can't you meet me half way?"

"Dana..." I huffed.

"Seriously," she told me. "I'll do whatever you need me to. I understand why you can't fully trust me, but you know that I still love you, and I know that we are meant to be together. You're the man for me, and I'm the woman for you. So whatever you need me to do to speed the process along, I will do. Just tell me."

I saw how intent she was on winning my affection back and decided to play hardball.

"Fine," I said. "If this is what you really want, start by being a better mother to Jonathan. Prove how much you love me by loving my son."

"You're calling me a bad mother," she claimed.

"No, I never said that. I just think that if you put half the time into being there more for him that you do into keeping up with the latest fashion, things would go a lot smoother around here."

Offended, she chuckled in disbelief. *"That was low."*

"Hey, you asked," I reminded her, and placed the big spoon I'd been using to stir the stew down in its cradle on the stove. "I need you to be there for him the way that a mother is supposed to. Stop putting your career before him. Pick him up from school from now on, and take him in the morning, too. Also, help him with his homework more."

"You know I can't do that," she told me through tight teeth. "My hours won't allow me to."

"You set your own hours. You're your own boss. No one is going to say anything if you come in later and leave earlier that you normally do."

"No, but my work will suffer. You know I work long hours. You're not being fair. You knew my workload when we got married. You can't hold it against me now because you're mad."

"You also knew I had a son when we got married. You can't use your past lifestyle to escape your present responsibilities. We're married now, and things have to change. I'm not a single parent anymore. I shouldn't be doing it all on my own."

She stared at me coldly, but gave no further objection.

"You know he has a birthday coming up," I continued. "He's been talking about this party he wants to have for months. I want you to take care of all of the arrangements for it. Don't hire a party planner. Do it old school. *You* take care of everything. Use your heart, not your bank card, and give him the best birthday party he's ever had. And he has his open house at school next week. You will be taking him, and you will enjoy every minute of it. You're going to meet his teacher, and his friends, and all of the other parents who come in contact with him."

She frowned at me as if I were being unreasonable, but I stood my ground.

"If you want this marriage, you have to agree to be the woman I need you to be, and the mother Jonathan needs you to be, too."

"Being a mother is more than running errands," she told me. "You're not being fair. You know I have a job, and the project I've taken on at work requires way more of my time than anything I've ever done in the past. You can't expect me to do *everything.*"

"It's your choice," I said impatiently. "I've made my demands. Choose what's more important."

She watched me intently for a moment, then tried to reason with me.

"Look, I know you're frustrated that most of the housework falls on you. I've been helping out lately, and doing the best that I can, but let's be honest. You're home way more than I am. You don't want a wife, you want a servant."

"I resent that comment."

"I resent everything you just said in the last five minutes. You're making this so hard when it doesn't have to be. You want me to be a 1940s housewife, but those women took care of their homes while their husbands went out and worked. I have a job, and I get paid well. More than you, I will add."

"I don't need you to remind me of that," I snapped.

"I'm not trying to insult you, even though you were the one who brought up my bank card. I can't bring home the bacon and be here to fry it up in a pan whenever you get hungry, then wash the pan out, too. There are only so many hours in the day."

"And you spend most of them at work."

She grunted under her breath, her irritation rising. "Why don't we just hire a maid like I suggested a long time ago?"

"Because I'm not married to a maid."

"That's exactly my point!"

I understood, but it wasn't what I wanted.

"These are the things that a wife does, Dana," I told her. "It's what will make me happy. And you need to make love to me every night—starting tonight. No more of that falling asleep crap you pull."

Her mouth gaped with astonishment as she crossed her arms defiantly.

"Are you demanding sex from me?"

"Yep," I said with no shame.

"I'm not doing anything until you tell me where you were that night."

I rolled my eyes when I realized she was referring to the night I spent with Parker. It happened weeks ago, and she still refused to let it go.

"I already told you I'm not talking to you about that—so drop it," I said angrily, and continued to work on the stew.

"I have a right to know," she claimed sharply. "I'm your wife. Why are you keeping secrets from me? We're married, aren't we?"

I ignored her and continued to cook.

"You know what, Gavin? You're full of crap!"

"Am I?" She was getting into a habit of talking to me with disrespect, and I was getting tired of it.

"YES!" she screamed at me. "If I keep a secret, I'm the most horrible person in the world, but if you keep one it's okay. Why? Because you have a penis?!"

"DANA!" I slammed the knife I was chopping garlic with down on the counter and stared at her angrily. *"Watch your mouth."*

"You don't have a right to demand sex from me if I can't trust what you've been up to. I'm not about to subject myself to possibly getting an STD just because you—"

"ENOUGH!" I barked at her. "Don't ask me about that again. Now be a good wife and go upstairs and get our son so he can eat."

She stared at me coldly as her jaw grew tight. Then suddenly, as if controlled by a demon, she marched to the cabinet beneath the kitchen sink and pulled out a bottle of dishwashing liquid.

"What are you doing?" I snapped. "Now you wanna wash dishes? I told you to go upstairs and get Jonathan. See, this is what I'm—"

She popped the top off the cleaner and poured it into the stew. My mouth fell open as she stared at me unapologetically and ruined our evening's meal. I'd pushed her too far. She was capable of dumping my head in the pot next.

"Jonathan!" she called out as she finished off the bottle. Her eyes remained on me the entire time.

"Ma'am?!" our son called out. A few moments later we heard him run down the stairs.

"You hungry, baby?" she asked him with a smile, and tossed the empty bottle into my hands. "You and Mommy are going out to eat tonight. Anywhere in the city you want to go. Just me and you."

"All right!" he cheered. "Daddy, are you coming?"

"Oh, no, sweetie," she answered for me. "Daddy's gonna stay here. He needs some time alone so he can get his mind right."

She walked past me into the living room and joined Jonathan. He asked her if I needed to go see a doctor, but she told him I'd be fine after I spent some time alone and rushed him out of the house.

FORTY-ONE
DANA

I didn't talk to Gavin for nearly a week after he foolishly tried to demand intimacy from me. But after praying about it I decided to put forth an effort to do what he said he needed from me. Even though the way he presented it was idiotic, he had valid points. I couldn't continue acting like my family was self-sufficient. I was a wife and a mother now, and my husband and son needed me. I never intended for my career to be the most important thing, but I'd managed to make them feel that way and needed to make a change. So all week I'd gone out of my way to be home more. I took Jonathan to school for the past few days and picked him up, too. I'd also prepared home cooked meals and took care of all of the household chores. I barely got anything done at work, but Jonathan was happy. Gavin was another story, however. I'd done everything he'd asked me to, other than sex, but he still didn't seem pleased. He barely even spoke to me. I remained as pleasant as I could and continued to beg God to save my marriage. Gavin got on my nerves, but I loved him and wanted to be with him.

I was in the middle of taking a pan of roasted potatoes out of the oven when Gavin finally came home for the evening. Jonathan was at the kitchen table, working on his math homework.

"You're just in time," I told Gavin as he walked through the door, and sprinkled a little salt over the potatoes.

"For what?" he asked.

"Dinner."

"Oh," he said, and walked into the kitchen and gave Jonathan a kiss on his forehead. "What'd you make?"

"Stuffed pork chops, green beans, and potatoes," I answered.

He walked over to the oven and looked over the food. He didn't seem impressed.

"I'm going upstairs to shower," he told me a moment later.

"All right. Hurry up so your food doesn't get cold."

He hustled up the stairs and I put my attention back on our food for the evening. It looked wonderful to me. I didn't know why he didn't seem excited. Home cooked meals was what he asked me for.

"Maybe I should have made gravy," I said to myself. The recipe I found during my lunch break called for it, but I chose not to make any for the sake of time.

Gavin trotted down the stairs a few minutes later with his gym clothes on.

"You're leaving?" I asked, greatly disappointed.

"Yeah. Gonna go shoot some hoops with Deitrick at the gym," he said, and grabbed his sneakers out of the closet.

"Right now?"

"Yeah. He's waiting on me."

"What about dinner? I made all of this food, and Jonathan and I were looking forward to eating with you. We haven't seen you all day."

"Don't worry about dinner. I'll just pick up something on my way back from the gym."

"No, you won't," I argued. *"You're gonna stay here and eat what I made."*

He shrugged as if he didn't care. "Jonathan will eat it," he said with a smirk, and left.

I stood in the middle of the kitchen with my mouth hung open. I couldn't believe he'd just done that to me again. This was the third time this week that I'd hurried home to make dinner and he found a way to weasel of it. Last night he supposedly had to check on Sylvia. The night before he said he had to work late, even though his clinic didn't schedule patients after four o'clock. He was playing a game, and I wasn't putting up with it anymore. There was no way I was going to sacrifice any more of the time at work I didn't have to cook for his ungrateful behind if he wasn't going to eat what I prepared.

"Do you get sad when Daddy doesn't eat your food?" Jonathan asked me.

I looked over at him and sighed. "A little bit, sweetie," I said honestly. "But I'll be okay."

"Well, you don't have to feel bad," he told me, and began to make his pencil dance as he held it in front of his face. "Daddy likes your food. He's probably just still full from the lunch Ms. Parker gave him."

"What?" I asked with a twisted face. Where in the world did that come from? "What are you talking about?"

"Ms. Parker makes him lunch everyday. Or sometimes they go out. He's probably just full."

"Why would your teacher make your daddy lunch?"

He laughed. "Not my teacher. Ms. Parker, Mommy."

I shook my head at him. This boy's antics were too much. Anything to get out of doing his homework.

"You're not watching television or playing any video games until you finish that math assignment," I said sternly. "Stop making up stories."

"It's not a story," he insisted. "Ms. Parker—"

"Back to work!" I fussed, and pointed at his homework. *"Now."*

Frustrated, he slouched against the table and obeyed.

FORTY-TWO
DANA

"DADDY!!!!!"

I lurched out of my sleep at the sound of Jonathan's scream.

"MOMMY!!!! DADDY!!!! MOMMY!!! HELP ME!!!!!"

I jumped out of bed and ran toward Jonathan's room. Gavin met me in the hallway, just as alarmed as I was, and together we found Jonathan in his bed, screaming his head off as hysterical tears streamed down his face.

"HELP ME!!!" he screamed.

"He's having a nightmare," Gavin told me, and quickly snatched Jonathan out of bed by his arm. "WAKE UP!" he yelled at him, and gave him a good shake.

Jonathan screamed again, but opened his eyes. When he saw his dad and I he hid behind his hands and continued to cry.

"You're okay. Shake it off. It was just a bad dream," Gavin told him.

I pulled him into my arms as I sat down on the bed. Gavin didn't like that I babied him, but I didn't care. Jonathan had never had a dream that scared him so much and I wanted him to know that he was okay.

"He was gonna kill me," Jonathan cried, and sniffled loudly as he held on to me tightly.

"Who?" Gavin wanted to know as he sat down beside me.

"The man in the movie."

Gavin and I exchanged confused glances.

"What movie?" I asked.

"The man in the movie with the mask," he said, and wiped his nose.

I forced him to sit up and told him to tell us what he was talking about.

"The man in the movie at Aunt Leah's," he said through his tears.

"Leah let you watch a scary movie?" Gavin asked. I could see the anger that rose within him.

"She didn't know we were watching it," he confessed. "She went to sleep with the new baby in her bed and we watched it on Jessica's laptop."

Gavin rolled his eyes and chuckled. "Oh? So you watched something you didn't have no business watching?"

Jonathan's head hung low. "Yes, sir."

"And now you're having nightmares. Serves you right."

I placed my hand on his thigh to stop him. He was about to go off, and the child had been through enough already.

"Now do you see why your dad and I don't allow you to watch scary movies?" I asked him. "You're too young. They're not good for you."

"Yes, ma'am. I'm sorry," he apologized, and finally stopped crying.

"Go back to bed," Gavin told him, still frowning. "You have to get up for school in the morning."

"Oh no!" he squealed, and squirmed against me with anxiety. "No! I can't go back to sleep! He'll get me! He'll get me! He'll get me! I can't! He'll—"

"What are you gonna do? Stay up all night?" Gavin asked impatiently.

"Can I sleep with you guys?"

Gavin's face fell. He looked over at me, then back at his son, not knowing how to respond. We'd managed to keep his sleeping in the guest bedroom a secret, and he didn't want to disclose it now.

"You don't need to sleep with us," Gavin told him. "You're a big boy. You haven't done that in a really long time."

"I'm scared," he told us, and his little eyes began to tear again. "He's gonna get me when you guys fall asleep!"

"No one is coming to get you!" Gavin fussed, but Jonathan refused to believe it and vowed never to sleep again.

Unable to take it anymore, I finally told him he could sleep with me.

"Dana, I don't think this is necessary. He's—"

"Come on, baby," I interrupted Gavin, and took Jonathan by the hand as I stood up. "You can sleep with Mommy tonight."

Jonathan walked out of the room with me, but stopped just as we got into the hallway.

"Come on, Daddy," he said, and extended his hand toward Gavin.

He stared at us both, but didn't move. Jonathan bounced impatiently, rushing him.

Gavin hesitated for a few moments, then decided to join us.

FORTY-THREE
GAVIN

Jonathan held on to Dana and I tightly as we walked into the bedroom. I really didn't want to join them, but decided to for the sake of my son's feelings. Knowing that we were sleeping in separate bedrooms would only cause him further turmoil.

"Did you lock the front door, Daddy?" he asked me. "And the back door? And the garage? And all the windows?"

"Yes. The house is safe," I assured him.

He quickly got into bed with Dana and snuggled close to her, then looked up at me with eyes that wondered what was taking me so long. I felt awkward, but forced myself to lay beside my family. As soon as I was still he pulled my arm around him.

"Goodnight, guys," he said, suddenly at peace. "Thanks for letting me sleep in here. Because I..."

He didn't finish his sentence. I looked down and discovered that he'd fallen asleep.

"He went that fast?" Dana asked with a chuckle.

"Little knucklehead," I griped, but found myself a little relieved. He'd managed to ease the tension between Dana and I.

"Pitiful thing," she said, and pulled him to the middle of the bed and covered him more with the blanket. "Looking just like you. Even when he's crying."

"Now you know you *ain't never* seen me cry. But all that drama he got from you," I told her as I punched the pillow beneath my head to get more comfortable. "If it were up to me he'd be in his own bed right now, crying in his sleep."

"And you'd be in the other bedroom."

I cut my eyes at her sharply, but she didn't flinch.

"You can go back in there if you want," she added, and flung her hand to dismiss me. "If he wakes up again I can take care of him."

"Don't try to kick me out of here," I snapped at her. She had some nerve. "You aren't at work."

"What's that supposed to mean?"

"It means don't tell me where to go in my own house. Don't try to order me around. I'm not an employee."

"No, *but you are a jerk.*"

I sat up straight and glared at her. "Don't forget that I'm still your husband."

"Whatever," she said with disgust, and turned her back to me.

Satisfied that I'd put her back in her place, I turned away from her, too. A second later a firm pillow hit me in the back of the head.

"*What the...?*"

I turned around and was hit again in the face.

"You're a jerk!" she screamed.

"What is—" I snatched the pillow before she was able to hit me again and threw it on the floor. "What is wrong with you?!"

"You!"

I reached across the bed and covered her mouth. "You'll wake him up," I said through tight teeth as I tilted my head toward Jonathan.

She shoved me away. "You make me sick. Get out of here!"

"You're kicking me out of our bedroom?!"

"Is this *our* bedroom? Are we still married? I thought I only lived here and paid half the bills."

"Ha, ha," I said sarcastically. "Don't be childish."

She rolled her eyes and turned away from me again. "If you want to divorce me, go ahead and do it. I don't want to live like this."

"No one wants to get a divorce."

"I can't tell. You haven't been acting like you want to be married. Not to me, anyway. All you wanna do is hold on to the one thing I did wrong and punish me for the rest of my life."

"One thing? Yeah, right," I scoffed at her.

Offended, she angrily sat up straight and asked me what I meant by my last comment.

"You aren't perfect," I let her know.

"I never said I was."

"You did more than just hide birth control from me. You lied to me for our entire marriage."

"I know that."

"Don't you get it?" I asked impatiently. "You lied to me about *who you are*. I don't even know you."

"No, I didn't, and yes, you do. You just don't know how to *accept* what you don't like, and that's what's making you crazy."

"You did lie to me about who you are. You mislead me. That's the same as lying."

Irritated, she sat back against the headboard and crossed her arms.

"Whatever," she mumbled under her breath after we sat in silence for a few minutes. "You're still a jerk. I've apologized to you a million times already for what I did. I can't apologize anymore."

I knew that I'd hurt her. Her confidence was wounded, and I never realized how much I valued that in her until now.

"I'm sorry," I apologized, and honestly regretted the way I'd treated her. Regardless of her shortcomings, she was still my wife. I knew God wasn't pleased with my actions. "I know I've been mean."

"Yeah, *you have.*"

"I know," I agreed, and shifted so I could look her in the face. She was the most beautiful woman in the world. I was so lucky to have her. How could I be such a fool? "You know I love you, right?"

"You need to act like it, then."

"I'm sorry," I apologized again, and leaned across the bed to try to kiss her cheek, but she pushed me away. I didn't protest. If I were her I wouldn't want to be kissed by me, either.

"We seriously need to talk about a lot of things," she told me.

I suddenly felt overwhelmed and fell against the bed as if I were in agony. I was pretty close. I *hated* when she said we needed to talk. A long lecture usually followed, and a headache, too.

"Don't be like that," she fussed, already knowing my thoughts. "We do need to have an honest conversation, because we can't keep going the way we have been these past few weeks. We'll start hating each other. For real."

I considered her wisdom and realized she was right. "All right," I consented, and took a deep breath. "What you wanna talk about?"

She sat up straighter and looked me in the eye. "Do you really want to stay married to me?"

"Of course," I said honestly. I really did. "But we can't have any more birth control secrets."

"Okay. I promise you that I won't take birth control without you knowing about it anymore."

"But you're on it right now, aren't you?"

"Yes, I am. Because I don't want to be pregnant."

I slouched with disappointment and looked away.

"Hey, I'm being honest," she told me, and grabbed my chin and forced me to look her in the eye. "If this marriage is going to work, we have to be honest with each other, and you have to accept that I don't want to have a baby right now. That's the only way that we will be able to move on."

My feelings toward her softened even more. She was absolutely right. But I couldn't simply move on from my lifelong dream of having a big family.

"I want more kids, Dana."

Sad for me, she said, "I know. But I'm just not ready right now."

I moved her hands away from my face and slid away from her.

"Are you mad?" she feared.

"No," I said with a sigh. "I just wish we wanted the same things out of life. But I guess this is my fault. I should have talked to you about the whole kid thing before we got married to see where you really were about it. It really wasn't fair to assume you'd want kids just because all of the other women I know do."

"I can only be me," she said proudly.

"I know," I said quickly, seeing that she was about to go off. "And I can't ask you to be anyone else."

"Really?" she asked as if I needed to consider the comment again. "So I don't have to cook any more meals that you don't plan on eating again?"

"No. No more," I told her, and was ashamed of myself for being so childish.

She nodded her appreciation. I grinned, relieved that she was at least happy about something, and looked down at Jonathan. The memory of his birth wouldn't allow me to imagine life without more kids.

"Don't you want at least one baby?" I asked her. "Wouldn't that be the best thing in the world? A little mix of me and you, created by God just for us? We can watch her grow up. She'll bring us so much joy."

"Her?" she asked with surprise.

"Yeah," I said proudly. "I want a little girl. And I want her to look just like you. And laugh just like you, and smile just like you," I said, moving close to her again. "Don't you want that?"

She twisted her face initially, but eventually smiled.

"That would be nice," she admitted. "But you're thinking about how cute the child will be. I'm thinking about the pregnancy, and the sleepless nights, and all the time off from work."

Work, work, work. That's all she ever thought about.

"What?" she asked when she saw I was annoyed.

"Our child is more important than whatever building you're trying to make look pretty, Dana."

"I know that," she said, annoyed too. "But my career will be impacted by a baby. Yours won't. So yes, I have to think about that before I agree to have any kids."

"Why?" I snapped. "Goodness, you act like we're broke! I make enough money to provide for us, and you can still work. Maybe you won't have enough money to spend on stupid shoes that cost too much because they're red at the bottom. That's what you're really worried about, isn't it? Your stupid clothes."

"Hold up, wait a minute," she said quickly, and held her hand up to stop my rant while she chuckled to keep her offense in check. "First of all, *Christian Louboutin* is not stupid. Okay? Let's just get that straight. Second of all, I never said money was as issue. I know that we are blessed, so that's not it. I'm just pointing out that my career will be greatly impacted by having a baby, and that's not an option for me right now."

"Wow," I said, blown away by the statement. "Not even for your husband? Really?"

"I know how much you want kids," she said with compassion. "If it were that simple I would have given you one a long time ago. But my career isn't just a job for me. It's my life long dream, and that's not too much to ask *my husband* to support."

"I do support you," I declared. "I have been this whole time! But life can't be all about your career. You're married now, and you have a husband you need to worry about pleasing."

"And by that you mean giving you more kids?"

I sighed as I shook my head at her. "Fine. Forget about it."

"No, that's what you're telling me, right? I need to give you a baby to please you? I can't do that. Not right now."

I refused to admit it, but I understood her argument. She had worked extremely hard to get where she was at right now. The fact that she beat out all of the other companies vying for the hospital remodel proved how stellar she was at what she did. And it had been her lifelong dream. I never wanted to take that away from her. Not too many people were blessed enough to actually pursue their dreams, and she'd mastered hers. I couldn't ask her to give that up. She'd hate me for the rest of her life. But I was her husband. My wants shouldn't have been totally overlooked.

"You gotta meet me somewhere in the middle," I told her.

She thought about it for a moment. "Adoption?"

"No."

She leaned away, offended. "There's nothing wrong with adoption."

"No, there's not. But I want you to have *my* child. You can still work and have a baby. Women do it all the time."

"That doesn't mean they're happy."

"The *child* is their happiness."

She turned to me quickly and stared, offended again.

She doesn't want a baby. Just let it go...

"I'm not saying that it's *totally* out of the picture," she said a moment later, to my surprise. "I just can't bring myself to do it right now. But maybe one day in the future I can consider it."

I gasped, too thrilled with her change of heart to contain it.

"I said *consider*," she pointed out, and laughed when I leaped across the bed and straddled her. "I didn't say yes."

"I'm wearing you down," I boasted, and covered her face with kisses.

She looked up at me and smiled. "You really want me to have your baby, don't you?" she asked, and seemed sad suddenly.

"Yeah, girl. You're my wife. I never would have married you if I didn't."

"But you understand I only said 'consider,' right?"

"I know. But at least there's a possibility. That's better than never at all," I said, and snuggled against her chest the way I loved to before we started fighting. She rested her hand against my head. "When in the future? Like, six months from now?"

"*Uuuggghhh...*"

I looked up to see her wince.

"I was thinking more like two years."

"Two years?!" I bellowed, and covered my mouth quickly when I remembered Jonathan was still beside us.

"Yes, two years," she hissed, and popped my arm for being so loud.

"Ain't nobody waiting two years," I fussed at her. "Are you crazy?"

"That's not that long."

"In two years I'll be forty! I don't want to be forty years old with a newborn."

"What's the difference between thirty-eight and forty?"

"*A lot.* Do you know what the life expectancy of a black man is in this country? Seventy-one. And that's with good healthcare, a healthy diet, and a wife that doesn't nearly give him a heart attack every time she goes shopping."

"Stop," she fussed, and shoved me gently for the jab at her expensive hobby.

"Seriously," I told her. "I've lived half of my life already, and I want to be active with my kids. I don't want to wait anymore."

I could tell that her feelings were hurt. She sank into the bed and her hope for us seemed to dissipate.

"I don't want to put any unfair amount of pressure on you," I said, and gave her a quick kiss. "But two years? Babe...That's a really long time. And that's not even a promise. We could get to the end of that time table and you could change your mind completely and say no."

"Then maybe we could adopt," she said with a shaky voice. I knew she was trying not to cry. "You've said yourself plenty of times that there are millions of kids out there that need homes."

"That's not the same thing," I told her. "You're my wife. I want *us* to create a baby."

"But I have so much going on," she said. "You know my business is going to grow once I'm finished with the hospital. I didn't become a licensed architect for nothing."

"I know, but... Maybe that's just something you'll have to sacrifice for your family. That's what marriage is all about. Love and sacrifices."

"Seems like I'm the only one sacrificing," she grumbled under her breath. "Don't compare having to do housework to me giving away my body and my career."

"It's a lot," I agreed. "And I don't take it lightly."

She thought about it more, then rolled her eyes with frustration.

"What about in eighteen months?"

"Twelve," I bargained.

"Eighteen?"

"Six."

She shoved me again. "You're going in the wrong direction. I'm trying to compromise with you, here. Don't make it harder than it has to be. Two years."

"*Right now.*"

"A year and a half."

"Twelve, and a baby. No considerations. An actual baby."

"A year and a half, and I'll get off my birth control and make a baby with you— *But only if...*"

I lifted from her so I could look her in the eye. She was serious. She was actually going to give me a baby!!!

"You tell me where you were that night."

I was confused at first, but then realized she was talking about Parker.

"Wwwwwhhhhaaaaatttt?" I moaned, and buried my face in her chest. *"Mmmmmaaaaannnn. Not this again."*

"Yes, this again," she said matter-of-factly. "You want me to have a baby, but don't want to tell me where you spent the night? How is that fair? That doesn't even make sense. I'm supposed to be able to trust you."

"You don't trust me?" I asked as I looked up at her again.

"I used to. Before you started spending the night at undisclosed locations."

"You think I cheated on you?" I frowned.

"What else am I supposed to think?"

I groaned, but didn't answer her question.

Rightfully disappointed, she moved me to the side and crawled from beneath me. I knew she was mad, but there was no way I would ever in my life tell her that I spent the night with Parker. There was no need to. Nothing happened, but if she knew I was with another woman things would only get worse between us.

"How about we just give each other a pass?" I suggested after thinking about it for a few minutes.

"To cheat?!" she exclaimed.

"NO!" I yelled, and shook my head at the insanity of the notion. I'd check my own self into an asylum before I presented her with permission to be with another man. "I meant permission to keep one secret from each other."

She narrowed her eyes at me. "What are you talking about?"

"Look, I really don't want to go into details about that night. Things were just crazy, and I made a poor decision by not coming home. But I didn't cheat on you. I never have and I never will. So let's just put it in the past and forget about it, alright? Let that one night be my pass."

She stared at me with even more distrust.

"I didn't cheat!"

"If you say so," she said with doubt. "What's my pass going to be? Can I spend the night with someone else and not tell you about it? Not call or text all night and have you worried sick and not give you any explanation at all?"

"You used your pass already," I informed her.

"I never did anything like that!" she declared.

"You lied to me for two years," I said with a shrug. No further explanation should have been needed. "Don't you think that makes us even?"

"Ugh," she grunted, and flung another pillow at me before turning on her side and facing the opposite wall. "You're not going to ever let me forget about that, are you?"

"That's what the pass is for," I explained. "I'll never mention the birth control again if you never bring up that night again."

She wasn't swayed. I got up and walked around the bed.

"I didn't cheat on you," I told her again as I looked her in the eye. "I'll tell you a million times if that's what it takes. But in order for us to work we have to start trusting each other again. This way gives us a fresh start. We'll be leaving the past in the past and starting things over again without holding anything against each other."

Unsatisfied, she growled under her breath. "You sure you didn't cheat on me?"

"I *did not* cheat."

She glared at me intently, but something inside of her softened, and I knew that she'd decided to forgive me.

"All right," she said with a sigh. "But if I find out you cheated on me, Gavin, I promise I will kill you."

I smiled. "You ain't gon' kill nobody," I said, and gave her a kiss.

"Okay, maybe I won't. But I might cut you, so you better not be lying."

"That, you probably would do," I told her, acknowledging the tiny bit of crazy she had in her that kept me on my toes. "But I don't have to worry because I didn't cheat on you."

I kissed her again and she wrapped her arms around me. I became excited and pulled her legs around me.

"Our child," she fussed, and pointed to Jonathan, forcing me to stop. "How could you forget him? He's only two feet away from us. And you want to have another baby? You're not being very responsible with the one you have now."

"Urgh. Little rug rat always messing up my game," I fussed, and forced myself to be content with simply laying on her chest again. "The things I wanna do to you right now, girl," I said, and nibbled on her ear before I whispered some of them in her ear.

"You're so bad," she giggled.

"Let's go in the bathroom," I suggested, and tilted my head in its direction.

"You better lay down," she scolded me. "He'll wake up."

"He ain't woke up yet, and we been in here yelling and everything," I pointed out, but decided she was right. I didn't want to risk him catching us. He'd really have nightmares, then.

"You forgive me?" I asked, relieved that our weeks of arguing were finally coming to an end.

"Yes. You forgive me?"

"Yes. You love me?"

"Yes. You love me?"

"Always have. Always will," I told her, and slid my hand under her robe. She didn't seem to mind.

"Why did you marry me?" she asked a few minutes later. "It wasn't just to have kids, was it?"

"No," I answered honestly, and was rather surprised by the question. "I married you because I love you and want to spend the rest of my life with you."

She didn't respond. I sat up to study her face. It seemed indifferent.

"You believe me, don't you?"

"Yeah, I believe you."

"What's wrong?" I asked, noticing she seemed bothered.

"I'm fine," she said. "I was just remembering how things were between us when we first got married. We didn't have all this tension. I was just trying to figure out what happened."

"Life happened," I answered for her. "We've just been busy, that's all. Work, and Jonathan, and all of his activities. No one stays newlyweds forever, babe."

"That's not what I mean," she said with a pout. "We were happier. Being busy doesn't make you unhappy."

I thought about it for a moment and realized she was right. Things had changed between us even before I met Parker.

What changed?

"We were both closer to God," I said as the revelation came to me.

Convicted, she nodded sadly.

"We used to go to church all the time, didn't we?" she asked.

"We prayed together all the time, too," I recalled. "And we studied the bible together as a family."

"Remember when we were teaching Jonathan about Jonah?" She laughed, remembering how horrified he was by the thought of being inside a fish. "He was nearly traumatized by that."

I laughed, too.

"Why did we stop?"

"Well, you started working more," I reminded her. "Sundays are really the only days you have left to rest now. And now that you don't go to Leah's bible study anymore, you really haven't been feeding yourself as much spiritually as you used to."

"Yeah..." she agreed, and seemed disappointed in herself.

"But it's not all on you," I told her. "I've been slacking, too. I could still go to church and take Jonathan with me. I've just gotten lazy in that area. I'm sure that's affected the type of husband I've become."

I knew it had. Two years ago I would have never committed the offenses that I had over these past few weeks.

"I'm sure I was a better wife at that time, too," she told me. "Marriage is hard. God has to be in it. Otherwise it won't work."

I looked up at her. "I couldn't agree with you more, Mrs. Jeffries-Gardner. We have to get Christ back in the middle of this thing. Starting this Sunday. We're gonna go to church together as a family."

"Jonathan will be excited," she told me. "I know he misses his friends there."

"Yeah, I'm sure he does. And it'll be nice to see some of the guys there, too. But if we go, that means you're gonna have to be in the bed early Saturday. No later than ten."

"I can do that," she agreed.

"In the bed, and *no work in the bed* with you," I clarified.

Worry came across her face. "Oh..."

"Only me," I insisted, and made my eyebrows dance.

She smiled. "So you're moving back in?"

"There's no place I would rather be at night but next to you," I said, and kissed her again.

Suddenly, Jonathan sat up straight and gasped loudly. *"NNNNOOOO!!!"* he screamed at the top of his lungs. *"OH NO!!!"*

Scared nearly to death, Dana leaped up, nearly knocking me to the floor.

"What's wrong, baby?" she asked him.

He opened his eyes and looked around, then began to frantically pat himself.

"Oh," he said with a sigh of relief. "I thought I peed on myself."

"Ewww. Manners, boy," she fussed at him. "Go to the bathroom just to be sure. I don't need you messing up my bed."

He giggled, but when he didn't move Dana tapped his legs and told him she was serious.

"Hurry up," she rushed him as he slowly crawled over her. "And don't make a mess in there. Keep your eyes open and make sure it goes *in* the toilet, not all around it. And wash your hands *with soap* before you come back in here. No cooties are allowed."

"You know he's not gonna wash his hands," I told her. "Give me a kiss before he contaminates our bed."

She happily planted the sweetest kiss on me that she had in months. I rejoiced inside. It was wonderful to finally have my marriage back.

FORTY-FOUR
GAVIN

Jonathan and I were at home alone, waiting patiently for Dana to come home from work. He was freshly bathed and dressed handsomely in the khaki slacks and blue and white argyle sweater she laid out for him this morning before she left for work. He was excited, too. His school's open house was tonight and he couldn't wait for Dana to take him as she promised. She hadn't been to school with him all year, and he was anxious for her to meet his teacher and all of his new classmates.

The phone rang. The good mood I was in immediately soured. I already knew it was Dana calling with some excuse as to why she couldn't keep her word. I should have known she wouldn't pull through. She was supposed to be home an hour ago, and the open house started in thirty minutes.

"What?" I asked into the phone when I answered it.

"I'm sorry," she apologized with a moan. "Really, I am."

"Yeah, right," I grunted. "You promised."

"Please don't be upset," she begged. "I tried everything I could to get there, but I'm just not going to be able to make it. We had a visit today from the safety inspector, unannounced, and he's making..."

I tuned out her excuses as I watched Jonathan. Once again I was going to have to tell him that his mom was too busy to take part in his life. While she was at work, doing what she loved to do, his entire life was passing her by. It wasn't fair to him.

"You promised you were going to be there for him tonight—and me, too," I reminded her.

"I promise you, this is out of my control. I would never intentionally disappoint you or Jonathan."

I didn't even know why I actually believed things would change. She couldn't even go three days without neglecting us.

"I'm sorry," she apologized. "I have to go. I'm about to get reamed by one of the board members for failing the inspection. Tell Jonathan I'll make it up to him. Promise."

"Yeah, 'cause your word is so reliable around here," I snapped, and hung up the phone before she could say anything else to make me even angrier.

"That was Mommy, wasn't it?" Jonathan asked from the living room. He'd been sitting on the couch, watching television.

I sighed. "Yeah. That was her."

"She's not coming, is she?"

"No, she's not."

"Awh, man," he griped, and threw himself against the back of the sofa in frustration. "I knew she wasn't coming. She always has to work."

"She wanted me to tell you she was sorry and that she'll make it up to you."

He folded his arms across his chest and gritted his teeth. Then, only a few moments later, he tossed his hands in the air and said, "Oh, all right."

"All right?" I asked, surprised. "You aren't mad anymore?"

He sighed. "No. Mommy has an important job. Sometimes she has to miss stuff. She said she'll make it up to me, and I believe her."

I stared at the little boy sitting on my couch and barely recognized him.

"That's a very mature outlook," I told him, and was more than impressed with how fast he was growing up.

"Well," he started, contemplating deeply. "I am about to be eight."

I burst out laughing. He laughed too, amused that I'd become tickled.

"You still wanna go to the open house?"

"Yes, sir," he said with a nod. "I think it's gonna be fun."

"Okay. I'll take you," I told him, and went upstairs to get dressed. On the way I thanked God for my child's forgiving spirit, but resented Dana for him having to have one.

****

Parker's car was the first thing I noticed when we got to the school. She'd gotten a spot in the front, a sign that she'd gotten there early. She was such an attentive parent. She probably wouldn't have missed tonight for the world. Madison was everything to her, and I loved that about her. If only Dana cared half as much about family as she did her business...

"Can we go in now?" Jonathan asked.

I realized I'd gotten lost in my thoughts. I'd already parked my truck and Jonathan had been sitting anxiously, eager to get to the night's event.

"Yeah. Let's go."

We got out of the truck and made our way into the school. Jonathan was greeted with excitement by both teachers and students alike as he proudly led the way to his classroom. I couldn't help but smile as I watched him. He was my kid, and he was amazing.

"Hello, Jonathan," his teacher smiled at him when we reached her door. "Don't you look handsome?"

"Yes, ma'am," he replied, to her amusement.

"It's nice to see you again," she told us both, and handed me a name tag and a pen. "For the other parents," she explained.

I nodded and wrote my name on the oversized sticker, then attached it to my shirt and returned the pen to her.

"There's cookies and punch inside. Jonathan, you can show your dad to your seat. We're about to get started."

We went inside and Jonathan ran to his desk. My stomach flipped when I saw Parker sitting beside Madison, who was drawing on a piece of paper. They both looked up and smiled when they saw Jonathan approach, and Parker gave him a hug.

My heart melted. She cared about my son.

I stood back and watched them interact with each other. She was attentive, and patient, but most of all she was there. That was what I really wanted. A woman who would be there for my child and make him her number one priority. Not her career. There was no way Parker would choose to be at work instead of here tonight. She'd find some excuse to leave and get here.

She looked up suddenly and caught me staring at her. I quickly pointed to the refreshments across the room and made my way over to them. The punch and small variety of cookies and fruits didn't rescue me from my feelings, though. The more time I spent with Parker the stronger they became, and now that she was building a relationship with my son they were undeniable.

I knew it was wrong, especially after making a commitment to Dana to focus on our marriage. I needed to keep my word, even though she'd tossed hers out in less than seventy-two hours. Honestly, I couldn't even be mad at her. She was who she was, and one conversation was not going to change that. No one could help being who we were, especially at this point in our lives. I just had to face it. Dana wasn't going to change her mind about having babies. As driven as she was, if she wanted kids she would have had them by now. It just wasn't meant to be.

My desire for children wasn't going to change, either, and I honestly didn't know if I was willing to live without them. Not when there were women out there like Parker who wanted the same thing I wanted, and wouldn't give me a two year time table to possibly consider making my dreams come true.

I knew I couldn't stay with the refreshments all night, so I grabbed two cups of fruit punch and a few cookies and made my way over to the trio.

"Hey, there's your dad," Madison said to Jonathan, and waved at me. "Is your mom here, too? I thought you said she was coming this time."

"No. She had to work," he told her, and quickly swiped a black crayon from her desk.

"Awh, man. That's too bad."

"It's okay. She has an important job. Sometimes she has to work late."

"Will she be at your birthday party?"

He frowned as he thought about it. "I don't know. I hope so."

"Me, too," Madison frowned, and began to color aggressively with another crayon. "Man, she misses *everything.*"

Out of the mouths of babes...

Parker cringed as I sat down beside her, knowing I'd heard, and gave me an optimistic shrug, not knowing what to say. I told her not to worry about it and offered her a sugar cookie, which she gladly accepted.

FORTY-FIVE
DANA

I was romantically optimistic when I walked into Gavin's therapy clinic. I'd decided to surprise him with lunch to make up for missing Jonathan's open house last night. Things had been much smoother around the house since we had our heart to heart conversation, and I wanted the peace to continue.

This was my first time actually being inside the clinic. As I wondered around trying to find his office I was spotted by Deitrick, who told me Gavin was more than likely already on his lunch break and gave me directions to the cafeteria.

I spotted him sitting at a table in the middle of the crowded room as soon as I walked in. He was engrossed in a conversation with a woman who's back was to me. I approached them quickly, anxious to let him know I was there, but stopped in my tracks when he laughed suddenly and reached for her hand. She placed it on the table and he held on to it as they laughed together.

My stomach fell.

Are they flirting?

His eyes were full of light as I watched them. I hadn't seen him so happy in months. He truly enjoyed his time with her, and to see it was heartbreaking.

He noticed me standing at the cafeteria door just as he was about to continue their hilarious conversation. His smile vanished and he became paralyzed with fear.

Busted.

"Dana?" I watched his lips say.

His companion looked over her shoulder and was just as shocked to see me as he was.

Who is she?! She's freaking gorgeous!

I forced myself to play it cool and smiled as I made my way over to them.

"Hey, baby," he said, and stood to meet me. "What are you doing here?"

"I wanted to surprise you with lunch," I replied, and purposely ignored the woman with him in hopes that she'd somehow disappear into thin air now that I'd arrived.

"Awh. That's sweet, baby," he smiled, and placed a kiss on my cheek as he took the bag I carried away from me. "Thanks."

"It's from that new Mediterranean place downtown that you've been wanting to try out. Kinda my way of making up for missing the open house last night. But it looks like you're already eating, so..."

Awkward silence exchanged between the three of us. Finally I acknowledged her presence with a smile, and as soon as I did I knew I didn't like her. She didn't seem trustworthy. Not at all.

"Oh. I'm being rude," Gavin said quickly, and extended his hand toward the woman. "Dana, this is Parker. Parker, this is my wife, Dana."

"Hi," she greeted as she stood up and shook my hand. "It's so nice to finally meet you."

"Finally?"

She knew me, but I didn't have a clue who she was. Yet she was smiling all in my husband's face. This entire scenario was out of line.

"Yes, Gavin talks about you all the time," she told me. "And of course I just think the world of Jonathan. He's an awesome kid."

I pulled my hand away and stared at Gavin.

"You've met our son?" I asked her while watching him. How was that possible? Was there some family function at the clinic that Gavin forgot to tell me about—along with his friendship with her?

She perked up with surprise. "Yes. I'm Madison's mom."

"Madison's mom?" I asked, and looked to Gavin to see if I'd heard her correctly. "The little girl Jonathan can't stop talking about?"

She grinned while I waited for an explanation from my husband, but he was too caught off guard to provide one.

"That would be the one," she said bashfully. "Madison just adores him, too."

"I didn't know you worked with Madison's mom," I told Gavin with an accusing tone.

"Oh? I didn't mention it?" he asked nonchalantly. "Must have slipped my mind."

I didn't believe the memory lapse was innocent. Not at all. He didn't tell me about her for a reason.

"Must have," I pretended to agree, but narrowed my eyes to show my disapproval.

My stare was making him uneasy, but he tried to shake it off by inviting me to join them.

"Oh, no," Parker objected. "I don't want to be the third wheel. You stay and enjoy lunch with your wife. She's come all the way here to spend time with you. I'll go."

"You sure?" he asked.

Was he really verbalizing his desire for her to stay right to my face?

"Yes," she told him, and widened her eyes to show her disapproval at his objection. "It's no biggie. I'll just catch up with you later."

She closed the food storage container she'd been eating out of, and to my surprise closed Gavin's, too. They were both lime green, clearly from the same set, and filled with the same meal. Baked chicken, corn bread, cabbage, and black eyed peas. It was homemade, but Gavin hadn't prepared anything remotely close to that in months. We didn't drink the brand of cola they both had, either. Nor did we own any lime green food storage containers...

She made this food. She'd spent hours in the kitchen preparing it, and she packed two identical lunches. One for herself, and one for my husband. She intentionally fed *my* husband.

I turned to Gavin angrily, ready to call him out for betraying my trust. How dare he consent to this! It was one thing to let Sylvia get away with it. She was family. *But this chick?!*

Just as I opened my mouth to put them both in their places, I suddenly remembered what Jonathan told me last week.

"Ms. Parker fed him, Mommy..."

Ms. Parker, as in this woman, his new best friend's mother, and not his teacher like I'd assumed.

I watched her and remembered that Jonathan had just started a new school year. Mrs. Parks was his first grade teacher. He was in the second grade now, and I hadn't met his new teacher yet. I'd always been too busy to, like last night when I got the surprise safety inspection. I didn't know any of the new women in their lives. I didn't have a right to be angry about it, either. This was my fault. I'd focused too much on my career and placed my family in this woman's eager lime green food storage container toting hands.

"You know what?" I stopped her. "You guys are already eating. Why don't you just stay and enjoy yourselves?"

"What?" Gavin asked, frowning heavily. "You just got here."

"I know, but I really don't have a lot of time. I have a meeting I need to get to. I really just came to drop the food off and say hello."

"There's a lot of food in here," he stated as he looked into the bag. "You really expect me to eat all this?"

He knew I was lying, but I wasn't about to stay. I'd look stupid interrupting their date, especially in front of his colleagues. I was embarrassed enough.

"I may have been a little overzealous while ordering," I told him. "Whatever you don't eat you can share with Parker, here," I said, and gave her a condescending smile.

"You sure?"

"Yes," I said sweetly. "Enjoy the rest of your lunch. I'll see you at home."

Don't you dare sit down! Don't you dare sit with this woman and send the message that you prefer her baked chicken over our marriage and the life we've built together. Don't you do it!

"Positive?"

"Of course."

You better not sit down. End your lunch with her this instant and walk me to my truck so I can go off on you in private. Hug and kiss me before we walk away together, too, just to let her know that I'm the queen in your world, and never spend time with her again!

"Okay," he said, and returned to his seat.

I'm gonna kill you.

"I'll see you at home," I told him quickly, and stalked out of the cafeteria before I punched Parker in her face.

FORTY-SIX
GAVIN

I watched Dana storm out of the cafeteria and knew I was in trouble. At the very least I should have offered to walk her outside. My clinic was thirty minutes away from Daytown Memorial. She'd come far to see me, and when she got here she found me smiling in another woman's face. Her cool act meant nothing. She probably wanted to kill us both.

"What's the matter?" Parker asked.

"I better go after her," I said. If I ran I could probably catch Dana in the parking lot.

"Why?"

"I..."

I stopped myself. There was no need to explain. Parker would never understand. She was single, and her only marriage didn't last longer than a year.

"Are you okay?"

I shouldn't have sat down. By doing so I pretty much told Dana I'd rather spend my lunch with another woman than with her.

"I need to get back to work," I told Parker, and stood up to leave.

She grabbed my hand, stopping me as I tried to pass her.

"You didn't answer my question."

A doctor at the next table witnessed our sudden physical contact and stared with disapproval. Parker released me and we remained quiet until our nosey audience returned to their own business.

"I'm fine," I told her. "Just got a lot of work to do."

She rolled her eyes. "Are you acting weird because your wife was just here?"

I didn't answer.

"Really? You don't have to run off like we were just caught doing something wrong. We're just friends who work together, and sometimes friends who work together share a meal during their lunch hour. It's no big deal."

I wasn't moved.

"Come on," she continued. "Everything's fine. I know you're not going to make me eat the rest of my lunch alone, especially when this is the meal you begged me to make."

Yes, I did ask her to make it for me, but now that Dana had discovered our relationship it just felt wrong to eat it.

"I gotta get back to work," I told her.

"Will you cut it out, already? It's not like this is an affair or anything. We're just cool. Right?"

She was calling me to a moment of truth. We were more than just friends. Friends didn't feel guilty about being caught having lunch. Friends didn't cook meals for each other every day for simply for no reason. Friends didn't turn each other on.

"Aren't we just cool?" she asked, tempting me to tell her the truth.

"Just cool," I lied, and walked away before she could stop me again.

FORTY-SEVEN
DANA

I was angry and embarrassed when I left Gavin's clinic, but overall I mostly felt blindsided. I had no idea he'd been spending time with someone else. I felt like I'd caught him cheating on me. I no longer had to wonder who he was with the night he didn't come home. I knew he was with Parker. It was obvious, especially since he chose to stay at the table with her instead of walking me to my car like I knew that he knew he should have.

I was such a mess emotionally that when I got back to work I couldn't concentrate on anything. I kept staring at the same mural sketches over and over again until I finally determined I was wasting my time and left. I started to go to the mall, but instead decided to pick Jonathan up early from school.

"How was your day?" I asked him as we got into my truck.

"I had a good day," he told me, and hurled his book bag into the back seat. *"But..."*

I leaned toward him and frowned deeply, signaling him to spill whatever he was afraid to reveal.

"I didn't pass my spelling test."

"Well, you know what that means."

"More homework?" he pouted as we began to drive away from the school.

"Yes. We'll go over the words again tonight. Maybe you can retake the test later this week."

"Okay," he mumbled, and leaned against the door as he peered out of its window.

We rode quietly, and the entire time I kicked myself for not listening when he tried to tell me about Parker. I was so stupid to think he was talking about his teacher! How could I be so dumb?!

"Can I talk to you about something?" I asked him a few minutes later.

He looked over at me and batted his long eyelashes. "Yes, Mommy. You can talk to me about anything."

I smiled. This kid was too cute. I loved that he repeated the same thing I often said to him when he asked me the same question.

"Do you remember the day I was upset because Daddy wasn't eating my food?"

He shrugged and pulled his tablet out of the glove box.

"Awh, man," he pouted after he turned it on. "The battery's almost dead."

I reached into the center console and pulled out the device's charger without taking my eyes off the road.

"Here," I said as he took it. "Are you listening to me?"

"Yes, ma'am."

"Do you remember when you told me that Ms. Parker feeds Daddy?"

"Uuuuummmm..."

"Remember? It was last week when Daddy didn't want to eat the dinner I made for him. You were doing your homework. Remember?"

He shrugged and fiddled with the tablet. "I don't know."

I was irritated, but told myself not to take it out on him. I should have listened to him when he tried to tell me what was going on the first time. I decided to let it go. It didn't matter, anyway. I saw enough with my own eyes to know they were more than just simply friends. A woman that went out of her way to do that much for a man she wasn't with had an agenda.

"I just know that Madison told me that her mom likes to cook for him because they're friends," he said a few moments later. "Her mom likes to cook a lot. All the time. Like, every day."

I shuttered at the double whammy of jealousy and worry that hit me. Of course she cooked every day. She was probably better than me at it, too. And a better mom. She was probably everything Gavin wanted.

"Madison said they were friends?" I asked as if I weren't upset.

"Yep."

"How good of friends?" I asked, and prayed I didn't sound crazy to him.

"Just good friends. They like to talk about stuff."

"What kind of stuff?"

"Just... You know. Grown up stuff."

My heart began to beat faster.

"What kind of grown up stuff?" I asked.

Lord, please don't let me find out that they've been inappropriate in front of the kids...

"You know. About work and stuff," he told me. *"Like...* Helping people learn how to walk again, and stuff like that. That's what they do."

I exhaled my relief. He was only talking about their work duties.

"They're friends, like me and Madison are," he continued. "Madison said that when we grow up we're gonna be like them and have to do stuff together with our kids, too."

"What do you mean by *'do stuff together?'"* I wanted to know.

"Like Ms. Parker and Daddy. Like when we went to the museum."

I flinched. Gavin hadn't said anything at all to me about Parker going to the museum with them. What exactly had I been missing?

"She went on your class field trip?"

I groaned inside. They were together all day that day. Maybe that was the start of their budding friendship. There was no telling what she said to sink her teeth into him.

"Yes, ma'am. And she was at Mark's birthday party, too. The one that didn't have any lions, even though Mark said they would be there. All he had was a monkey."

She went to the museum *and* to a birthday party with him?! Just how many play dates had they been on?!

"Have they been anywhere else with you?"

"No," he said with a shrug. "I don't think so."

Relieved, I exhaled deeply, and discretely wiped the tear that rolled from my eye. My heart hurt. This thing with Parker was way deeper than shared workday meals. In a way he'd been in a relationship with her, and it happened right under my nose. I felt betrayed.

"Mommy?"

"Yes, sweetie?"

"I want dinosaurs at my birthday party," he told me. "A big one, like the one at the museum. Can you do that, Mommy?"

I cringed inside. I already had enough to worry about with Parker, and now I had to find a dinosaur for his birthday party in three weeks. I hadn't even started planning it yet.

I looked over at him and smiled, despite my broken heart. "I will do my best, baby."

"That's all I can ask," he told me.

FORTY-EIGHT
GAVIN

When Dana walked into our bedroom I knew she was mad at me. I put the book I'd been struggling to read for the past half hour down so I cold talk to her, but she ignored me, just as she had all evening. She hadn't even grunted in my direction.

"You okay?"

She acknowledged me with a glance, but nothing more. I watched her closely as she sat on the bed and pulled out a bottle of lotion from her nightstand drawer and began to moisturize her skin.

"Dana? You all right?"

"I'm fine," she finally said, but it was obvious she wasn't.

"Is this about Parker?"

She stared at me angrily, and I knew I'd made the situation worse by saying Parker's name. I shouldn't have even brought her up.

"I know meeting her the way you did earlier was a bit awkward," I continued quickly. "I can understand why an insecure woman would feel threatened by my friendship with her, but—"

"I'm not insecure," she snapped at me. *"Or threatened."*

"Bad choice of words," I quickly admitted.

"That certainly was," she agreed, and rolled her eyes as she put away her lotion. "Just go to bed, Gavin."

"Are you mad at me?"

She snuggled under our blanket and turned away from me.

"I'm just trying to tell you that she's not anyone you need to worry about. We're not even really friends. That's why I never said anything about her. Just associates, which again... is why... you know, I never said anything. But regardless, I should have, and I'm sorry. Do you accept my apology?"

"I really don't want to talk about it, Gavin," she groaned, and pulled the blanket over her head.

"Well, I do."

Annoyed that I wouldn't let her sleep, she sat up and faced me.

"I'm not about to get into some long drawn out conversation with you about this," she said impatiently. "You can't have a wife and a girlfriend, too, so you need to make sure you know which one of us you really want."

Taken aback, I pulled away from her. "I do know who I want," I told her, but I already knew she didn't believe me.

"Just know that I take the vows I made very seriously. When I married you I intended to stay married for the rest of our lives. But if you violate our marriage, I promise you, I am gone. I am not the woman that will stay while my man cheats. I deserve more, and I will be alone before I let you play me. If you go there, you can't come back to me. Understand what I'm saying, because it's true."

Her bluntness was startling, but I was too proud to admit anything further about Parker. But I also knew Dana was telling the truth. I would lose her if I cheated.

"What are you talking about?" I asked, trying to play dumb. "I'm not going anywhere, and I'm not doing anything."

"Don't try me," she warned, then rolled over and turned off the lamp on her nightstand.

"I love you, baby," I told her.

She ignored my words of endearment and went to sleep.

FORTY-NINE
GAVIN

The weekend went by with silence from both of the women in my life. Dana continued to give me the cold shoulder and Parker didn't return any of the three calls I made to her. I figured she was simply too involved with her daughter to get back to me and tried not to think about her too much, but the silence on her end left me feeling a bit neglected.

As soon as I got to work I tried to find her. She wasn't in her office, the cafeteria, the lounge, or the break room. She wasn't at the coffee stand, either. Because I had patients already waiting on me, I decided I'd catch up with her later and made my way back to my office. Just as I rounded the corner I was snatched by my arm and pulled into my team's supply closet.

Angered, I jerked away, but laughed when I saw that Parker was the one who'd accosted me.

"Girl, what are you—"

"Ssshh," she silenced me, and covered my mouth with her hand while quickly closing the door.

"What are you doing?" I whispered.

She wrung her hands together and began to pace back and forth nervously across the narrow closet floor.

"Just be quiet," she told me. "I have a lot that I need to get off my chest, and if you interrupt me it'll only make things harder."

I saw how anxious she was and gave her the floor to talk freely.

She took a deep breath and stood in front of me. "I lied," she said a moment later. "When I told you we were just cool. It was lie. I only pretended I didn't have feelings for you because I was embarrassed that we'd been caught and I didn't want to miss out on our friendship. We're not just cool, Gavin. I like you. Like, as in more than a friend, like. As in borderline possibly falling for you."

I stared at her like she was crazy. What was she doing?! Why was she saying all of this now?! I knew how she felt about me. I felt the same way about her. But we weren't supposed to admit it out loud! What good would forcing ourselves to deal with our feelings do but make us jump over the edge into adultery?! I couldn't do that!

"I know it's wrong," she continued to confess, and followed me as I walked around the closet. "And it's twisted, and it's not right because you're married and we work together, but..."

"We can't do this. *We can't...*"

"I can't help the way I feel about you," she said, and sidestepped quickly so that I had no choice but to face her. "I like spending time with you," she told me as she looked into my eyes. "I'm attracted to you and I want to be with you."

I looked away, suddenly disgusted with myself.

"We gotta stop this," I told her. Things had gone too far. It was one thing to toy with the idea of being with her, but now she was professing her feelings for me and that was unacceptable. "We can't do this. We gotta stop."

She grabbed my arms and forced my hands to rest on her waist. "I... can't," she told me, and looked into my eyes again. She was on the verge of breaking down. "I tried to talk myself out of this all weekend. I can't help the way I feel about you."

"We need to really—"

She stood on her tiptoes and kissed me on the lips. I leaned away, caught off guard, but she pulled me toward her and kissed me full in the mouth.

I lost it. All conviction and reasoning escaped me as I indulged in the warmth of her. She seemed to be the water to my thirst, and I wanted all of her.

I held on to her face as our kisses intensified. She was so soft! She had the sweetest lips, and they were so refreshing! Like the—

Creeeeeeekkkkk...

We gasped at the sound of the door opening. Deitrick stepped into the closet and found our hands all over each other.

"What are you—?"

"I gotta go," Parker interrupted him, and ran out of the room.

Embarrassed, I looked down at the ground and covered my face, humiliated by what just happened.

%#@&!!!!!!!!!

"Ddddduuuudddddeeee..." Deitrick started as he joined me in the closet, and quickly closed the door. *"You're banging Parker?!"*

"No," I told him, and hoped in vain that he'd forget what he just saw.

"You sure? I'm not. Not by the way you had your lips on her."

"Stop. It's not anything like that."

He chuckled, unmoved by my claim. "Whatever, man. You're married."

"I know, and that's why nothing's going on," I said sharply.

"Hey, don't be mad at me. I just came in here to get a wrist brace. You're the one slobbing chicks."

Annoyed, I grabbed a brace from the supply shelf and threw it at him. He caught it and correctly discerned that I wasn't in the mood to play with him.

"I'm just trying to look out for you, man," he said seriously, and tossed the brace back at me. "I need a right-handed one in a large."

Embarrassed, I returned the brace to its storage shelf and handed him what he needed. He accepted it and turned to leave, but stopped suddenly.

"Do you know what you're doing?"

I groaned. "It's not like that, man," I insisted. "You didn't see what you think you saw. Nothing is going on."

"Who you think you're lying to, man? I know the game, all right. I know what I saw. You can say what you want, but we both know what it is. You got a good woman at home. You gon' mess that up? *Over Parker?*"

"Parker's not a ho," I said quickly.

"She knows you're married," he countered. "That don't deserve respect. What's wrong with you?"

I grunted in frustration. I knew he was telling the truth. What we'd done was deplorable. But it wasn't like Parker and I were trying to have a quick romp when no one else was looking.

"There's no affair going on," I told him. "We just got kinda caught up—"

He held up his hand to stop me and opened the door. "Don't explain it to me. Explain it to God, holy man."

I crumbled inside as he walked away. I'd ruined my witness. All of the talks we had about God and spirituality just went down the drain, all because of one incredibly stupid and careless act. I felt horrible, and I deserved to. I hadn't behaved like a Christian for quite some time.

FIFTY
GAVIN

Two days had passed since Parker and I kissed, and my mind stayed on her the entire time. Since then she'd avoided me like a plague. As soon as I left the supply closet I searched all over for her. Finally I found her supervisor, and he told me that she'd gotten sick suddenly and left for the day. The supposed illness had her pretty messed up. She called in both yesterday and today, and again she refused to acknowledge my phone calls or text messages. I knew she was thinking about me, though. I could feel it. Even now, while I laid in bed with Dana beside me, the connection I had with Parker was felt.

I didn't know what to do. Part of me wanted to forget all about her. Just pretend that the kiss never happened and go on from this day forward with work and my marriage as if she didn't exist. That would be the smart thing to do, especially now that Dana suspected something was going on between us. I should just move on and count the entire experience as a huge lapse in judgment and vow never to be so foolish again.

But how could I do that? Our lives were intertwined. We shared more than a kiss. We worked together and our children were best friends. There was no way I could pretend she didn't exist.

I had to see her. I had to talk to her. I was never going to go to sleep otherwise, but more importantly I needed peace of mind. We had to move on from the place of embarrassment and confusion that we were in now.

I looked over at Dana. She was sleeping soundly—as if her marriage weren't on the rocks and she had no worries in the world.

I need to stay right here with her...

She was a good woman, and I knew she loved me. Otherwise she wouldn't put up with my mess. I honestly loved her, too. But she just wasn't Parker.

I have to see her...

The clock said it was 12:52am. I checked to make sure Dana was still sleeping, then got out of bed slowly and crept to the bedroom door.

"Where are you going?"

I froze at the sound of Dana's raspy voice. She sat up slightly in bed and waited for me to answer.

"To the kitchen to get some water," I lied quickly.

"Can you bring me some, too?" she asked. "My throat hurts."

"Okay, baby."

Irritated that I'd been caught, I went downstairs and poured Dana a glass of water. While in the kitchen I remembered the first time I tried to teach her how to cook. Her hemophobia was so severe that she rinsed off a piece of chicken and vomited. She'd come a long way since then. I was proud of her, but I still felt like I'd fallen in love with her representation and not the person she actually was. She led me on to believe that we wanted the same things, and I just couldn't get past it.

I took the glass of water upstairs to the bedroom and placed it on her nightstand. She was sleeping again, which was a relief. That meant I didn't have to acknowledge her. I could still go to Parker's house...

This was my chance.

I took it.

Light as a feather, I quickly made my way downstairs and grabbed my keys, then crept to the garage. I knew its door would wake Dana if I used the remote inside my truck, so I turned the automatic switch off and lifted it slowly by hand. Moments later I backed my truck out slowly, going less that five miles an hour, and didn't turn my headlights on until I was completely out of the driveway.

A rush of exhilaration went through me once I made it to the highway, but conviction soon followed. What was I doing? I left my wife and my son alone in the middle of the night for what? A booty call?

No. This was not a booty call. I would never approach Parker like that. This was only me being desperate to see her because she'd avoided me for two days. That was all.

As I drove to her house I wondered what my life would have been like if I met her before Dana. Would I have fallen for her as soon as I saw her, like I did Dana, or would we have initially only be friends? If so, how soon would we have advanced into something more? Would I have married her? If I did, would we be happy together? How many children would we have? Would I be happier with her than I am with Dana?

The questions were still consuming me when I arrived at her house. Now that I was here I wasn't really sure what I wanted to happen next. What if, after tonight, I decided that I couldn't bear being with Dana anymore? Would I actually leave her for Parker? If I did, would Parker even be able to trust me? If I cheated on Dana, I would do the same to her, right? She wouldn't want a man like that. And what about our children? How would they react to our new relationship? Would they accept it? How would Jonathan feel having his family rearranged again in only a few short years? Would he grow up to hate me for it?

I sat in the truck and continued to go back and forth with my feelings as I stared at the house. The front door opened before me and Parker appeared, dressed in a hot pink cut off shirt that revealed her chiseled stomach as it peeked through an oversized bath robe. Baggy sweatpants covered her lower half, too, and gigantic bunny slippers graced her feet. She used her hand to shield her eyes from my truck's headlights as she stood in the doorway, then closed the door behind her and made her way over to me.

"What are you doing here?" she asked once I rolled my window down. "Are you okay?"

"I couldn't sleep," I told her. "How'd you know I was out here?"

"Your lights," she said, and covered her mouth as she yawned. "They're shining into my bedroom."

I apologized and turned them off.

"What are you doing here?" she asked again. "Do you know what time it is? My kid has to get up for school in the morning."

"I know, and I'm sorry. I just needed to see you."

She looked away angrily. My unannounced visit hadn't pleased her at all.

"You're not happy to see me?"

"You shouldn't be here. You need to go home," she told me, and tied her robe tightly around her waist.

"I'm not trying to disrespect you. I just need to talk to you."

"About what?" she asked impatiently, and stared at me for an answer.

"About us," I said as she shivered. "Get in. It's cold outside."

She looked down at the ground and shoved her hands into the pockets of her robe, but didn't move from her place.

"Come on. I'm not gonna hurt you."

She rolled her eyes and finally walked around to the passenger's side of the truck. I unlocked the door and she climbed in.

"Hey. It's good to see you."

She folded her arms and leaned back against the seat, but didn't reciprocate my verbal gesture.

"You look nice," I added, and touched the ends of her messy ponytail.

She swatted my hand away and warned me with her eyes not to touch her again.

"I've been trying to call you," I said, and watched her closely for a response. "I texted you, too. Several times. But you've been ignoring me."

"I know," she said, and looked away with frustration. "I just needed time."

"For what?"

"To think."

"You couldn't just say that?"

"I don't owe you anything," she said quickly, and glared at me. *"You're not my husband."*

"Is that what you're mad about? The fact that I'm married? You knew that before you kissed me."

"You kissed me, too. And I'm not mad."

"You sure? You seem like it."

She looked away again and grunted under her breath. "What do you want from me?"

"I want you to be cool, like always."

"No, what you want is your wife and me, too, and it doesn't work that way. I saw the way you looked at her when she came into the cafeteria. You love her, and she loves you, too. It's not fair to do this to either one of us, Gavin. I don't want to do this to her. It's not right."

"I know," I griped with frustration, and sighed heavily. "I'm not trying to hurt either one of you, but I can't help the way I feel."

She faced me again. "How do you feel? You're not in love with me, Gavin. Don't pretend to be."

"No, but... I do have feelings for you, and they're real."

"Oh, no," she stopped me. "We're not doing this."

"What? I'm not playing any games."

"This has gone too far. *You're married.* Someone will only end up getting hurt, and I'm pretty sure it's gonna be me."

She closed her eyes and turned away. I realized she was trying not to cry. I never wanted to hurt her, but I'd managed to.

"I'm not trying to take advantage of you," I told her, but it only seemed to weaken her. "Seriously," I said, and reached for her, but she pulled further away from me.

"Just stop," she whispered.

"Do you think I wanted Deitrick to walk in on us?"

"What if it was the head of personnel? Do you know how much trouble would I have been in? We might be unemployed right now. There's a lot more at stake here than just your feelings. I have a daughter to take care of. Who's gonna provide for her if I lose my job? I don't have a fancy interior decorator making all kinds of money living with me. If I don't work, we don't eat. I can't put her in that situation."

"Calm down," I fussed at her. "Nothing like that is going to happen. We just got a little carried away and lost control for a minute."

"A minute? What about right now? You're at my house in the middle of the night," she pointed out. "Where does your wife think you are?"

I didn't answer.

"She doesn't even know you're gone, does she?"

My silence gave me away. She moaned with disappointment.

"Go home, Gavin," she scolded me, and opened her door to get out.

"No," I said, and pulled her arm to keep her from leaving. "Please stay. Close the door."

She exhaled slowly and did as I said. "I'm ending this, Gavin."

"Ending what?"

"Look, I wasn't going to say anything, but I think the best thing for me to do is to take another job. I did some searching and found an opening at the county rehab center. They want to hire me, so as soon as I get back to work I'm filing my transfer paperwork. I'll be taking a pay cut, but I'll still have all of my benefits. I think this is the best thing for me right now."

My heart broke at the news. There was no way I could go without seeing her everyday. Work would be awful without her bubbly personality.

"You can't go to the county," I tried to convince her, and tried to figure out what she could have possibly been thinking.

"I've made my decision."

"No!" I snapped at her. "Do you even know anything about the county center? No, you don't. If you did you never would have considered working there. *No one* wants to work at the country center. That's a step toward hell. The pay is horrible, the working conditions are deplorable. They're always getting sued. Shoot, they don't even have up to date equipment. You may as well try to work out of your garage."

"Don't try to talk me out of it. I'm not going to change my mind," she insisted. "It's the best thing for me to do."

"No, it's not. And you were just gonna go without talking to me about it first?"

"I thought it was the best way to go about things," she said softly.

"I can't let you do that. It's a mistake, and you'll regret it and end up resenting me for it. And why would you take a pay cut? You said yourself that you're a single mom. There has to be another option. One that doesn't involve ruining your career and your paycheck."

"Nothing else is going to work," she tried to tell me.
She was crazy if she thought I was going to let her derail her life simply because we lost control for one minute and a nosy co-worker with multiple baby mamas tried to judge us for it.

"You're not going to the county clinic," I declared.

"What else am I supposed to do, then?"

"I don't know," I replied honestly. "We'll come up with something."

"Something like what?"

"Something like... We just won't let Deitrick catch us anymore. That's all."

"So we'll just guard the door the next time we kiss in the supply closet?" she asked sarcastically while she rolled her eyes.

"Right," I said, feeling stupid. "We won't kiss in the supply closet anymore. We won't kiss each other at all."

She agreed and followed my lead. "No more physical contact. From now on we will just be friends."

"Yes. Only friends. I won't touch you anymore. I won't even talk to you at work. From now on it'll only be in passing."

"We can nod at each other, just so we're not being rude. But other than that, I won't say anything at all," she claimed. "We'll just be work associates. That's it."

"Agreed," I said with a firm nod.

The plan sounded good, but we both knew we weren't going to be able to stay away from each other. We were too close. I couldn't even go three days without seeing her. How was I now supposed to see her at work everyday and pretend that I didn't feel anything for her at all?

"Are we really going to be able to deny each other?" I asked her.

Her eyes closed slowly and she lowered her head.

"Parker?"

She took a deep breath and looked into my eyes.

"Do you really think we can do this?"

"No," she said, and leaned across the truck and kissed me.

FIFTY-ONE
GAVIN

Parker's kisses were aggressive, and her straddle threatened to hurt me if I didn't perform to her liking. I wasn't afraid. I had full confidence in my ability to please her, and I didn't plan on stopping until I saw the final expression of satisfaction on her face.

Her hands were all over me. She felt amazing as she moved on top of me, and between her gropes I stole my own. She wanted me badly. The moans she released as I slid her robe down begged to fulfill me, and I wasn't about to deny her.

My seat reclined. I looked down and saw her hand on the lever and wanted her even more. I took off her top and stared at the lace bra that covered her chest, but before I could snatch it off she pulled my shirt off, too. Then, knowing it would drive me crazy, she pushed me flat on my back and pulled her hair out of its ponytail. It fell around her shoulders as she told me she wanted me. I ran my fingers through it as I sat up for a kiss and unsnapped her bra with a flick of my fingertips.

She gasped and grabbed it before her bare chest was revealed.

"What's the matter?"

She looked out of the window, which was steamed now, and shook her head.

"Nothing," she told me, and kissed me again, though this time I could tell it was forced. Mentally she'd gone to another place, and her embrace no longer carried the same amount of passion that it did before.

I tried to help her focus. I did all the moves I could to entice her, but she groaned in frustration and leaned back against the steering wheel.

"What is it?" I wanted to know. She had the attention of my entire body, so clearly I wasn't the problem.

"Madison," she said with a sigh, and refastened her bra. "She's inside sleeping, and I didn't check on her before I came out here. If she finds us like this... I'm not trying to be a tease. Really, I'm not. But for a split second I just thought about what would happen if she caught us, and... "

"No, it's cool," I told her, and pulled her robe over her shoulders as my excitement dwindled. The sex I thought we were going to have wasn't going to happen tonight, so there was no need to stare at her chest anymore.

"Sorry," she apologized, and slid from my lap into the passenger seat.

We got dressed in awkward silence and she put her hair back into a ponytail.

"I guess I better get back home."

"You can't hit it so you're gonna quit it, huh?" she joked.

"We gotta be at work in a few hours. Are you gonna be there when I get there?"

She hesitated. "Do you *want* me to be there?"

"Do you want to be there?"

"I don't know what I really want," she said after thinking for a moment.

"Yes, you do."

She turned to me slowly with her eyes narrowed. "Fine. *I want you.*"

"But I'm married, right?" I could tell another argument was coming, and I didn't want it. "Do you know what I risked coming over here to see you tonight?"

"I didn't invite you over. As a matter of fact, I told you to go home."

"Yeah, and then you kissed me."

She stared angrily, but said nothing more.

"Just chill," I told her with a softer tone. "Be patient and give me some time to figure everything out, okay. But don't quit your job because of me. I can't let you do that."

"Okay, I won't quit," she said impatiently, and opened the door to leave.

I grabbed her arm. "Give me another kiss."

The demand took away her frustration. She happily complied and got out. I watched her walk away and nearly lost control again. I wanted to run after her, scoop her up in my arms, then carry her into her bedroom and make love to her until the sun came up.

I rolled my window down just as she reached the front door.

"Hey!"

She stopped and faced me again.

"Don't quit on me. I can't take not being able to see you everyday."

"You better hurry up and do what you need to do, then," she sassed, and went into the house.

I fell against my headrest. Suddenly my chest hurt. She wanted me to leave Dana for her, or at least give her a promise that I would. I wasn't quite ready to do that, but it wasn't completely out of the picture, either.

FIFTY-TWO
DANA

I remained motionless as Gavin slithered his way back into our bed. The stench of fruit scented perfume filled my nose, but I kept my disgust for him and the way he smelled within and pretended to still be asleep.

My husband's an idiot.

It was three o'clock in the morning. Did he really think I had no clue he snuck out of our home like some hormonal teenager? If he was half as slick as he thought he was he would have known that he hadn't gotten away with anything. But he was stupid, so I let him carry on like the fool that he was.

His first clue should have been the fact that the bedroom door was closed when he got home. He'd left it open, and when I realized he was gone I purposely closed it so it would wake me when he returned.

Secondly, the glass of water he brought me was now empty. I drank it all and placed it on the kitchen counter, which he should have seen when he came back in the house. Clearly I would have had to wake up to do so and noticed that he was gone. I wasn't a sleepwalker. Had he had any sense he would have known I knew all about his deed.

But no, he wasn't smart enough to think like that. His head was too clouded with whatever he did with Parker. I couldn't even be mad at him, though. Or upset. I was too tired, and I no longer had the energy to worry about him. I didn't want to. I'd done all I could to keep this marriage, but it was obvious he didn't want it as bad as I did. Otherwise he wouldn't have left me and Jonathan at home alone in the middle of the night.

I'm giving this to you, God. Completely.

There was no other way I could keep my sanity. I had too much on my plate to jeopardize it. I was still a mother, and I still had a successful business to run. I couldn't afford to lose my mind behind a man, even if he was my husband—especially when he wasn't worried about me. Worrying about him cost me too many hours at work, and if I continued my reputation and my good name—both of which I had before I even met him, would go down the drain. Then what would I have? Nothing.

From this point forward I was going to put all of my energy into work. No more waiting on him, trying to be the type of woman that he knew good and well he didn't marry. If I worked hard I could catch up and finish the hospital remodel in time. I'd work around the clock if I had to. Gavin was just going to have to accept it, and if he didn't I no longer cared. Everything and everyone else, other than Jonathan, would just have to find contentment without me.

FIFTY-THREE
DANA

I sat at my desk and went over my latest status reports. Amazingly, completing the job on time wasn't going to be as hard as I thought. I was going to have to hire extra hands, make a few substitutions, and work around the clock; but with hard work, prayer, and God's grace, I could achieve my goal.

Feeling encouraged, I put the reports away and went over the list of things I still needed to get done for the day. The most important was planning Jonathan's birthday party. I still had to send out invitations, order party favors, and put together decorations. Mainly I needed to order an amazing birthday cake, and I knew just the person to call.

I picked up the phone and dialed my brother's bakery. He could easily whip up an amazing cake for Jonathan's birthday party. All I had to do was let him know what I wanted.

"This is Sean. How may I help you?"

"Wwwwhhhhaaaattttt?" I teased, happy to hear his voice. "Since when do you answer the phone?"

"Girl!"

We both laughed at his excitement to hear from me. Like myself, he was an overachieving workaholic, and our schedules barely allowed us to spend time together. We hadn't seen or talked to each other in months, but there was no love lost. We wasted too much time in the past fighting over my now openly gay high school sweetheart to let anything come between us now. Whenever we did get together our joy and conversation picked up right where it left off.

"What are you doing, calling me?" he demanded to know, full of laughter. *"Ms. I'm-Rebuilding-Half-Of-Daytown-Memorial-And-I-Ain't-Gon'-Even-Tell-My-Brother."*

"You could have called me," I pretended to fuss. "My number hasn't changed."

"Yeah, right. You know all I'm gon' get is your voicemail. Or Gavin answering the phone, sounding pitiful 'cause you off working somewhere. *How are you doing, girl?!* Oh, my goodness! This is the best thing that could have happened to me today."

I smiled. "I miss you, brother," I said, and wished we were actually talking face to face. "How's work?"

"You know I'm the best baker it town, honey. Ain't nobody 'round here got nothing on me, chile', but maybe Leah. Speaking of which..."

I gasped. "Have you seen April?!"

"Yes! I love my niece!" he beamed. "I'm surprised you were there for the birth. Leah told me, of course. I'm trying to see her more, but you know Mitchell. He's been all over that baby. Whenever Leah brings her by he never wants to let the poor child go back home."

I smiled at the thought. I missed my brother's boyfriend, too. Though he broke my heart a long time ago, I still accepted their relationship and cared about him. I definitely needed to make time to see them more.

"Speaking of children..."

"OH MY GOODNESS!!! YOU'RE PREGNANT?!!!"

I rolled my eyes as he began to shout throughout his bakery. I knew better than to use a segue like that.

"Not pregnant," I announced when he calmed down. "I'm calling about the child I already have."

"Awh," he moaned with disappointment. "I thought I was about to have another niece of nephew."

"Leah might have another one, but you're gonna have to be content with Jonathan from me right now. His birthday is coming up."

"That's right!" he beamed. "I know he's excited. Can you believe he's about to be eight? These kids grow up so fast nowadays."

"That is true," I agreed. "I'm calling because I need a cake for his party in two weeks."

"Sure, I can make it. What kind of cake?"

"Uh, *an amazing one.*"

He burst into laughter. "Dana. Seriously?"

"What?"

"You're gonna need to be a little more specific than that. I'm not simply a baker, darling. I'm an *artist*. I know you ain't coming to me for nothing you can get off the shelf from Duncan Hines, honey."

I suddenly felt overwhelmed. I loved my brother, but he was being dramatic.

"This is for his birthday party, right?" Sean asked when I became quiet. "How many people are going to be there?"

"We're inviting all the kids in his class. Should be about thirty."

"Kids and adults?"

"Uuuummmm..."

"I'll make it big enough to feed a hundred, just to be on the safe side. Now, do you want a 3D cake, a tiered cake, or a cupcake tower? I could do a sheet cake, but that's just too boring for *my* nephew. No, ma'am. He's turning eight and just has to be the talk of the playground, honey!"

"*Oh, Lord...*"

"Yes, call on Him, and ask Him if the kids would like red velvet, chocolate, or white, please."

I couldn't help but laugh. "Sean, I just need something dinosaur themed. You know Jonathan. He never wants much."

"Yeah, he's just like his daddy," he said to himself as he continued to think. "Do you know what colors you want?"

"Uuuuhhh... Maybe green? Aren't all dinosaurs green? Or... brown?"

"Oh, Lord, girl," he sighed. "Just have the planner call me. I'm surprised they haven't already. Or did you try to have someone else make my nephew's cake and they fell through, so now you're calling me?"

"No, that's not what happened. There is no party planner. I'm doing this myself."

"*Why?* Girl, you *go* to parties, you don't plan them. Well, you used to, anyway."

"I know, but..." I sighed, and tried not to become annoyed as I thought about Gavin's demand. "It's what my husband wants."

"Oh, the joys of being a wife," he said as if he understood. "Well, look. You clearly have no idea what you want, so with your permission I'll just go ahead and make what I'm sure everyone will love."

"Thanks," I said, and breathed a sigh of relief.

"The only thing is that you're gonna have to come pick it up yourself."

"You can't deliver it?"

"Girl, his birthday is in two weeks, and you're just now asking me to make it. People have to order my cakes four to six months in advance, boo," he reminded me. "My delivery guys are already booked."

"Ugh," I groaned.

"Hey, don't complain. I'm doing you a favor."

"I know," I agreed, but didn't know how I was going to manage getting across town to pick the cake up the day of the party.

"You still want me to make it?"

"Yeah, yeah. I'll figure something out," I told him, and thanked him for agreeing to make the cake for me. "You're saving my life, here."

"Anything for my sis," he said, then told me he had to get back to work. We said our goodbyes and got off the phone.

The joys of being a wife...

His comment hummed in my ear and made me sad. He probably thought planning a child's birthday party was a joyous task, and for most mothers it probably was. Maybe, had Gavin not forced it on me, I would have found it to be an exciting and pleasing experience. But not today. I had no joy at all, and I hadn't felt any joy in being a wife in a really long time.

My eyes drifted over to a picture of Gavin and I that sat on my desk. It was one of my favorites. Jessica actually took it with her phone, but it came out so perfectly that it looked like a trained photographer snapped it. When I saw it I immediately had it printed and framed. It captured the way he used to look down at me with so much love, even now I could feel it. And I missed it. I used to bask in its warmth every day, but now life just felt... cold.

I still love him.

I refused to think about it. Instead I flipped the picture over and got back to work.

FIFTY-FOUR
GAVIN

"You should come over," Parker told me.

I wished that I could, but getting away wasn't going to be as easy as the last time. It was nearly midnight and Jonathan had been asleep for hours, but Dana hadn't come home yet. She was up to her old habit of neglecting her family by working all day and night. Jonathan hadn't even seen her in three days. He was sleep by the time she got home and still sleeping when she left for work in the morning. I didn't even mention to her how upsetting this was to him. It would only start an argument, and at this point she knew exactly what she was doing. I was actually glad she was gone, anyway. It gave Parker and I time to talk without being interrupted.

"Why?" I asked her through the phone.

"Because I have something I want to give you."

"What?"

"I don't want to say over the phone," she said flirtatiously.

"Bring it to work tomorrow."

"Well... I guess I could, but... Uuuuummmm... I don't think it would be *appropriate*. I think it would make others... *uncomfortable...*"

"What is it?" I asked, though I had a pretty good idea it was erotic in nature.

"I'm a lady. I can't say," she teased me. "But it's really sweet."

"I bet it is."

"It is. You need to come over so I can give it to you."

I laughed, enjoying the idea. We hadn't been completely alone since the night I snuck out, and I was dying to experience her touch again. She knew it, too. We shared too many lustful stares at work for her not to be aware of it, which was why she enjoyed tormenting me like this.

"That's just wrong," I said, still tickled.

"What?" she asked innocently. "I think you'll like it, once you finally get it."

"You better—"

I stopped when I heard the garage door opening and groaned.

"Wifey?"

"Yeah. I gotta go," I hated to say, and hung up the phone after telling her we'd talk tomorrow. She whined, the same way she always did when Dana came home, but didn't argue with me and said goodnight.

A few minutes later Dana dragged herself into our bedroom. Even though she was dressed impeccably, as always, she looked completely worn out. Her eyes were so puffy they were barely open, and dark circles peered through her makeup. She limped when she moved, too, though I'd noticed she'd traded her sky high heels in for a lower pair.

"Tired?"

She shrugged without looking my way and began to undress. Once she was down to her underwear she sprawled across the bed and fell asleep within seconds.

I stared at her for a moment, surprised by how hard she'd worked herself. I hadn't seen her so exhausted in months. Out of compassion I decided to tuck her into bed. She starting snoring as soon as she felt the warmth of the blanket.

I still love her.

Being married to her was nothing like I'd imagined it would be. I was disappointed with her all the time, and we didn't have nearly as much fun together as we used to. I wasn't sure if I still wanted to be with her, but there was no doubt that I still loved her. I knew I always would.

My phone chimed. I knew it was Parker again, and eagerly unlocked it so I could read her message.

Go to sleep and dream about me. Goodnight. ♥

I smiled, thinking about the conversation we ended abruptly when Dana came home. I looked over at her, snoring loudly with her mouth hung open, and knew where I would rather be.

You still wanna see me?

Dana's snoring became louder, and I grew more annoyed as I waited for Parker to respond.

You know I do.

I told her I was on my way, then got up and got dressed.

****

I sent Parker a text message to let her know I'd arrived and waited on the front porch for her to let me inside. A few moments later she opened the door, and I immediately wrapped my arms around her as we kissed.

"Well, hello to you, too," I greeted her after she pulled away and let me inside.

"Glad you could make it," she said, and took a step back so I could take in all of her beauty. She'd traded in her normal relaxed athletic attire for a satin and lace shorts pajama set.

"What do you have on?" I asked, turned off by the ensemble. It looked like something Dana would wear.

"Don't you like it?" she pouted. My lack of excitement was a disappointment to her.

"You look good," I assured her. "It's just not your usual style, that's all. I thought you were more of a t-shirt and sweats kind of girl."

"Yes, but not all the time. I do know how to clean up when I want to."

"Yes, you do," I said while she turned around to give me a view from behind. "But I like you in sweats. Go take that off."

I ignored the thoughts of Dana that popped into my head as I sat down on the couch. I didn't drive all the way over here to think about her. This time was designated for Parker, and that's who I wanted to focus on. The sooner she took the obnoxious outfit off, the better.

"Okay, I will," she told me. "But first I want to give you what I know you drove all the way over here to get."

I looked around nervously and pointed toward the hallway. "You sure your daughter's not gonna hear?"

"You think you're gonna make a lot of noise?" she asked, and licked her lips slowly. "I know I won't. Close your eyes."

I shook my head adamantly, smiling the entire time.

"You're scared?"

"A little bit," I answered honestly.

"I thought you were a big boy," she pouted, and slid the strap of her top down to reveal more of her shoulder. "Close your eyes."

No longer capable of arguing, I did as she instructed.

"Keep them closed," she said, and gave me another kiss on the lips. "No peeking."

I leaned back and covered my eyes. To my surprise she didn't touch me. Instead I heard the refrigerator door open and close.

"What are you in there doing?"

She ignored my question and continued silently, so I told myself to be patient. Whatever she had for me surely would be worth the wait.

"Open 'em," she said a few moments later.

I moved my hands and found a plate of chocolate covered strawberries only a few inches away from my face. A small bowl of whipped cream sat in the middle. She dipped her finger in the topping, then slowly licked if off as she stared at me.

"*Parker...*"

"Weren't expecting these?"

"No," I laughed.

"I said it was something I knew you would enjoy, but not appropriate to give to you at work. You know everyone would be all in our business if I brought these to work. What did you think I was talking about?"

"*I... I mean... I—*"

"Hush up and eat," she said, and fed me a strawberry.

She squealed as I pulled her onto my lap and tickled her. She gave me another strawberry, kissed me, and I began to cover her with my affection. We took our time, but soon found ourselves in the same position we were in before: partially dressed, and eager to take things further than they already were.

"Let's go to my room," she whispered into my ear.

I looked into her eyes as she sat on top of me. She was serious.

"You sure?" I asked, breathing just as heavy while she kissed my neck. "What about your daughter?"

She picked up my hand and began to nibble on my fingers.

She's very sure.

I cursed under my breath as my eyes rolled to the back of my head. "Isn't she gonna hear us? Her room's... pretty close... to yours..."

"I won't make any noise if you won't."

"What if she comes in?" I whispered.

"She won't," Parker told me, and got up from the couch. "Come on."

Under her trance, I stood with her and covered her with more kisses. Anxious to take things further, she pulled me toward the hallway.

"Let's go."

Finally I consented, and placed my hands around her waist as she led me out of the living room. The nape of her neck begged for my lips along the way, and I tenderly obliged.

Just as we got to her bedroom we heard a door open at the opposite end of the hall. Before I knew what was going on Parker shoved me into a nearby room and slammed the door shut.

"What are you doing?" I heard her fuss.

"I have to go to the bathroom," Madison moaned. She sounded half asleep.

I looked at the toilet in front of me and froze. The child was coming this way and would surely freak if she saw me, her best friend's dad, standing in her bathroom in the middle of the night! As soon as she got to school she'd blab the information to Jonathan, who loved Dana too much to keep it a secret. Everything would be exposed, and all of our lives would be ruined!

Lord, please don't let her catch us!

"You're supposed to be in the bed," Parker snapped at her.

"I gotta pee, Mommy," the little girl explained, and her voice revealed how hurt she was by her mother's sternness. She sounded as if she were about to cry.

Panicked, I hopped into the bathtub and hid behind its thick pink curtain. A toy monster truck carrying an array of fake jewels stood parked at my feet, and several dolls with missing heads lounged along the rim as if they were sunbathing at the beach.

"All right, all right," Parker told her. "Don't get all emotional. Just go use my bathroom."

"Why can't I use my own bathroom?"

"Because it's broken."

"I didn't do it," the child quickly let her know. "When I went to bed it was fine."

"I know. I did it," Parker said impatiently. "Now go on in there and use it so you can hurry up and go back to bed. And I don't wanna hear nothing out of you when it's time to get up for school. You know you're not supposed to drink anything after 8:30."

I stayed in the tub and exhaled my relief at Parker's quick thinking. A moment later I heard the door open.

"Gavin?" she whispered.

I peeked my head out of the tub, startling her. She giggled and told me she thought I'd jumped out of the window.

"Maybe I should have," I said as I climbed out of the tub.

"Give me a few minutes to get her back to bed. Then we can pick up where we left off."

"Nawh," I told her. Madison almost catching us was a little too much for me. "I'm gonna go 'head and get out of here."

Her face grew long. *"Nnnnooo,* Gavin. Please stay."

I wanted to, but things had gotten too steamy between us. Madison almost catching us was a sign that I needed to take my behind home.

"I better get outta here. I'm not cool with the kid catching us."

"She won't," Parker insisted.

I silenced her by placing a kiss on her lips, then hurried down the hall as lightly as I could, grabbed my shirt from the living room floor, and rushed out of the house.

FIFTY-FIVE
DANA

I walked into Jonathan's school and felt good about my decision to have lunch with him. It was a little earlier than I was used to eating, but I missed him terribly over the past few days and couldn't let another day go by without spending any time with him. Because I was working around the clock to catch up with work, my long hours only allowed me to place kisses on his cheeks while he was sleeping. The lack of time was heartbreaking, and I was so consumed with thoughts of him that I pulled my phone out every fifteen minutes to look at his photos. Finally Wendy suggested that I have lunch with him. So here I was with a Prada bag and a Happy Meal in one hand and a Quarter Pounder with cheese combo and two small sodas in the other.

I stopped to show my ID at the front office, then followed an escort to Jonathan's classroom. He jumped out of his seat when he saw me and ran to give me a hug. I nearly fell out of my stilettos, but was thrilled he was so happy to see me.

"Are we going home?" he asked as his classmates began to ask who I was and what I was doing there.

"No, I just came to have lunch with you," I told him, and apologized to his teacher for our disruptive reunion. She came over to formally introduce herself, then told me that lunch wasn't for another ten minutes. I apologized again and told Jonathan to go back to his seat while I stood in the back of the room and waited. It really served no purpose. He ignored the math his teacher attempted to teach and continuously turned around and smiled at me.

Once it was time for lunch, Jonathan introduced me to each of his classmates, including the infamous Madison, who happened to look a lot like her mother. I didn't hold it against her and smiled as I shook her hand. Jonathan turned out to be very popular, but it wasn't surprising at all to learn. He had the same outgoing personality his father did, and inviting his entire class to his birthday party next weekend gave him an extra portion of favor with his peers.

He was all smiles as we made our way to the cafeteria. To my surprise, instead of going into the line with the other students who didn't have lunches, Madison followed Jonathan and I to our table and sat with us.

"Did you bring me something to eat, too?" she asked. Her eyes grew big and round at the sight of my burger and fries.

"Oh, your mommy didn't pack your lunch?" I asked with fake concern. "I thought she loved to make lunch for everyone."

Madison stared at me with confusion, and I instantly became disgusted with myself for being shady with a seven-year-old. It wasn't her fault her mother was a tramp. But how off putting was it that Parker neglected her own daughter's nutrition while she made it a point to take care of my husband's?

Wonder if he knows that about Ms. Everything...

"You can have mine," I told her, and slid the food over to her.

"Cool! Thanks!" Madison exclaimed, and shoved nearly half the fries into her mouth with a smile.

FIFTY-SIX
GAVIN

Parker and I tried to keep our flirting inconspicuous during our staff training session, but we couldn't help making eyes at each other from across the room. I wished we were bold enough to sit beside one another, but that would only bring more attention to the chemistry people were already starting to notice between us. We didn't need any added drama, especially after being caught by Deitrick.

"Don't forget about the seminar that's taking place Wednesday," Roxanne, our training coordinator, told us.

Everyone groaned. I looked over at Parker and saw her eyes rolling to the back of her head.

"I know, I know," Roxanne said. "No one looks forward to spending the entire day listening to stuff they already know, but it's important to stay on top of these things."

I slouched in my seat. This training was torturous enough, and we'd only been here for an hour. I couldn't imagine spending an entire day doing this. If it weren't for Parker I would have fallen asleep a long time ago. Watching paint dry would be more stimulating. At least then I wouldn't have to listen to Roxanne's annoying voice.

Finally, we were dismissed. I searched the crowd for Parker, but she'd already been grabbed by a doctor. I lagged behind and made small talk with a few of the interns until she made her move toward the exit.

"Hello, Mr. Gardner," she said slyly when I caught up with her. She kept her head forward and barely moved her mouth when she spoke. "How are you doing today?"

"I'm well, Parker. How are you?" I asked in the same fashion, still trying to keep our interaction subtle.

"Not looking forward to Wednesday, that's for sure."

We took a few more steps and nodded nonchalantly at a few co-workers who passed by.

"I wonder if anyone would notice if we both just happened to be absent Wednesday?" she asked a moment later.

The thought of being alone with her again made me smile. "Just what exactly are you proposing?"

"Oh, I don't know," she said, and slowed her pace. "Nothing illegal or anything. But I have a strong feeling my daughter will come down with something Wednesday. She'll be too sick to go to school. I think she'll be really contagious, too. Some kind of bug..."

"Yeah, I think I'll be sick, too," I said, and coughed as if I was already ill. "I think I'm starting to come down with whatever it is now."

"We both can't be sick. That'll be too obvious," she stopped me. "Maybe something is going to happen to your house. Like a pipe is going to break, and you're gonna have to stay home to take care of it."

I snickered. "I like the way you think."

She released a sigh of satisfaction. "I am pretty smart, aren't I?"

We continued walking and my thoughts became lustful.

"Your place or mine?" I asked.

She grabbed my arm and quickly pulled me into another supply closet.

"Are we doing this again?" I whispered as she checked to make sure no one saw us. I stood closely behind her and placed a kiss on the back of her neck, causing her to shiver with delight.

She turned around and placed her finger over my lips. "Neither."

Confused, I asked, "Neither, what?"

"I had a different plan in mind for Wednesday."

"What's better than spending the entire day with me? Doing this?" I asked, and gave another passionate kiss.

"I was thinking we could do something with the kids."

"They'll be in school."

"I know. But I've been wanting to do something special with Madison. She's been missing our family back home and has been a little homesick. She's fine at school, because, you know, she has Jonathan. But when we're at home I can tell she's sad. Anyway, there's this carnival that just came to town, and I would love to take her."

"During the day?" I asked with doubt. "You're gonna let her miss school for that?"

"Oh, yeah. It'll be fun," she said with enthusiasm. "You never went to a carnival during the day as a kid?"

"No. I went to school. And then I got a job."

"It's awesome. We used to do it all the time. Everyone's at work, so no one is hardly there. You basically get the whole place to yourself. There aren't any long lines, and the vendors are so desperate to make some money that they basically let you rob them. They're very generous. And you know how kids are—very impatient. They'll get to do everything without any bigger kids pushing them around."

I didn't like the idea. It sounded absurd to pull your kid out of school just because you wanted to spend time with them. Wasn't that what weekends and holidays were for? Dana would never do anything like that, and I honestly wasn't about to, either.

"It'll be fun," she told me again, and gave me another kiss. "It's good to take a break from the norm every once in a while and do something fun. Then maybe, after we spend time with the kids, you and I can have some alone time to do what we want."

"I don't know," I told her. "Pulling him out of school?"

"Why not?"

"Because *he needs to be in school,*" I fussed, and stared at her like she should have known that already.

"Let the kid live a little," she argued back, and pinched my arm. "A little extra fun has never killed anybody."

"He'll have all the fun he needs at his birthday party next weekend."

She rolled her eyes and walked away from me with disappointment.

"So now you're mad at me?" I asked, irritated. "Look, if that's how you raise your kid, fine. But Dana and I run a tighter ship. We're raising a little black boy. Nothing is going to be handed to him when he grows up and gets out into the real world. I can't teach him to be a slacker. He has to know what it means to work hard."

"Is that what you and *Dana* think?" she asked, and angrily crossed her arms over her chest. "That I'm raising a slacker? She hasn't even met my kid."

I exhaled wearily. "Why do you like to argue all of a sudden?"

"No one's arguing. But I don't appreciate you throwing your wife in my face—especially when it comes to my daughter. All of a sudden she's a great parent, but how many times have you told me that she neglects Jonathan?"

"That's not what—what I was trying to say—that's not what—"

"Whatever," she said, and walked toward the door. "I gotta get back to work."

I blocked the door before she could leave.

"What's this attitude about? That's how you walk away from me?"

"What do you expect from me? You brag about your wife, then insult me right to my face."

"You're jealous? You know what the situation is. How can you be mad about it all of a sudden?"

"I get it. She's your wife, and I only get you late at night when you feel like sneaking away. Or at work, hiding in a supply closet. Whatever."

"I don't want to sneak around, either."

"Then do something about it!" she snapped at me, and tried to leave again.

"You need to chill," I warned. "You act like we've been having a full-blown affair. We've just been having fun, and it's only been a few weeks."

"And I'm tired of playing."

I lowered my head and rubbed my temples. I didn't feel like going through all of this with her. She was supposed to be the easy one. Being around her had always been relaxing, but now she was starting to stress me out.

"I don't know what you expect me to do," I told her. "Pulling my kid out of school is just stupid."

"Now I'm stupid, too? Thanks for thinking so highly of me," she said sarcastically.

"No, you're not stupid. Just the idea," I explained. "Do you really think involving him in this is smart?"

"*Yes.* He and I need to start spending time together so we can get to know each other better. And I want to hang out with him. He's a cool kid, and the transition needs to be a smooth one. Our relationship *is* going to eventually evolve, right?"

That was a very good question. I wanted it to, but not at this pace. She needed to slow down.

"Right?" she asked again when I didn't answer.

"Right," I responded, just to pacify her.

Pleased for the time being, she smiled and wrapped her arms around my shoulders.

"Good," she told me. "I'm not trying to be mean to you. I just don't want you to start taking me for granted. Or thinking that I'm just gonna wait around while you figure out what you *really* want to do at home. Because I have needs, and they need to be met."

She stood on her tiptoes and kissed me again. She was more aggressive this time, and strategically placed my hands on the parts of her that she knew would entice us both. Before I knew it I had her pressed against the wall with her legs wrapped around my torso. I was moments away from ripping her clothes off when she stopped me and lowered to her feet.

"We'll continue this after the carnival," she told me, and walked out of the supply closet, leaving me stupefied in a haze of frustrated desire.

FIFTY-SEVEN
GAVIN

I stood back in amazement and watched Madison sink basket after basket in the game she was playing. Her mother and I, as well as Jonathan, cheered her on as her point tally soared. She was focused and unmoved by the noise around her, and played hard until the buzzer sounded.

"Twenty-three!" she shouted, and jumped up and down as Parker patted her back. "Pay up!" she told the game operator. *"Pay up! Pay up! Pay up!"*

The man grinned and eagerly handed her the tickets she demanded.

"How many do I have now?" she asked her mother.

Parker quickly counted the tickets. "Fifty-eight."

"I want that elephant up there," she said, and pointed to the pink stuffed animal that had stolen her heart. "But I need a hundred tickets."

"Here, you can have mine," Jonathan told her, and handed her his day's winnings.

"That's so sweet," Parker told him. "Madison, what are you gonna say?"

"Thanks," she said, halfway paying attention to him. "Now how many more do I need?"

Parker recounted. "You got seventy-one now, so you need twenty-nine more tickets."

Madison dug in her pocket and gave the operator another five dollars. It was her last. Parker had given her thirty dollars to spend as she so chose, and for the most part she'd been very wise with it. We'd been at the carnival for over an hour, and other than purchasing a wooden key ring with her name on it, she hadn't spent a dime.

"You sure you want to play again?" Parker asked her. "We haven't even seen all the games yet. What if you see another one you want to play?"

She looked up at her mother with determination in her eyes. "Her name is Billy, and she's coming home with me."

Parker stood back and let her strong-willed daughter proceed. Again, she made basket after basket, but when the buzzer sounded she was nine tickets short of bringing Billy home.

"Sorry, honey," Parker said, sympathizing with her pain. "Maybe next time."

Madison stared at the stuffed animal and I literally saw her heart break. I stood behind her and signaled for the conductor to have compassion and give her the elephant anyway. She'd given him twenty-five dollars after all, and the toy couldn't have cost him more than five. But he shook his head anyway and told me business was business.

"I tried to tell her," Parker whispered to me.

Irritated, I slyly retrieved a five dollar bill from my pocket and dropped it at Madison's feet.

"Is that yours?" I asked, and gave her a nudge as I pointed to it.

She looked down and hollered when she saw the money. "It fell out of my pocket!" she exclaimed as she snatched it from the ground. "I'm bringing you home, Billy!"

She slapped the money down in front of the operator and told him to make sure he gave her a good ball. He started the game for her, and as she began to play Jonathan looked back at me and gave a cool nod, then mouthed, 'I saw what you did,' before facing the game again.

Parker moved closer to me and held on to my arm. I looked down at her and knew she wanted a kiss.

"YES!" Madison squealed. "I got eighteen!"

I pulled away from Parker just as the kids looked for us to celebrate with them. Parker gave Madison a high-five as she received her prize. She threw it high in the air and caught it a second later, then ran off with Jonathan to the next game booth.

"Wild child," Parker commented. "I don't know why she's looking at any more games. She doesn't have any money left."

"Maybe a few more dollars will mysteriously appear at her feet."

"Oh, no. Don't you go spoiling her," Parker told me as we followed. "But thank you for doing that for her. 'Cause Lord knows I would have been hearing about that dang elephant all night."

"No problem. It's no big deal."

"Yeah, it is," she insisted. "That was really sweet. I see where Jonathan gets it from. Just one of those things a girl misses out on not having her dad around, you know? A hero to save the day."

"Hero?" I nearly laughed. "I only gave her five dollars. It's not like I gave her tuition money."

"No, but... I don't know. Maybe I'm being a little emotional... It's just nice to have a man care enough to do something like that for her. Her dad doesn't do anything at all, and here you are taking time off work to be with us. It's something special, and I just want you to know I don't take it for granted. You're a good man."

She kissed the back of my hand, then hurried to assist the kids.

I suddenly became disappointed with myself. This wasn't cool. I had no business being here with Parker, and regretted not following my initial instinct. Parker and I were supposed to be a hidden thing. Now I was out in public with her—*with our kids.* When did I start doing disgraceful things like this? I wasn't Parker's man, and I certainly wasn't her daughter's dad. How did trotting around town with them make me a good man?

"Come on, Mr. Gavin!" Madison called out to me as she waved, eager for me to join them.

I gotta end this before it goes too far...

"Come on!" Parker rushed me. "All four of us can play this one, and Jonathan's talking smack."

"Yep," he said pridefully. "I'm gonna beat all of y'all."

Not wanting to ruin everyone's good time, I told myself I would talk with Parker tonight and went to join them in the fun.

FIFTY-EIGHT
DANA

Wendy sat with me as I went over the discrepancies in her purchase reports and watched me closely as if she were concerned.

"What?" I asked impatiently.

"You don't feel that?"

"Feel what?"

"Your hand. It's shaking."

I observed the aggressive trembling of my limb and became annoyed, then placed the espresso I was holding on my desk and tried to refocus on my work.

"You have got to be more careful when you're entering these digits," I told her, and used a red pen to circle her mistake. "This is a three, but you calculated it as an eight."

She snatched the report from me and looked at it closely. "Fine. It's a three," she reluctantly admitted. "But it looks like an eight, and that's probably because your hand was shaking when you wrote it, like it is now. I love a good coffee like the next chick, but you have got to put all that espresso down. How many have you had today?"

I squeezed my hands to try to calm my nerves, but as soon as I released them they began to tremble again.

"Three," I admitted.

"No, ma'am," she said quickly, and took the drink from me. "It's only twelve o'clock, and I bet you haven't eaten anything all day, either. These are not meant to be a substitute for sleep, young lady."

"I need that!" I fussed, but she pushed my hand away as I reached for it.

"How many hours of sleep did you get last night?"

"A full eight, thank you very much."

"You lie like a rug," she accused. "Tell the truth."

"Okay, three," I admitted, and took my drink back from her. "Don't judge. I need this. You know I've been putting in all of this extra work because I fell behind."

"Yeah, but now you're almost caught up. You can relax a little bit."

"We'll relax when it's done," I told her, and began to put our paperwork away.

"Plus I've been working on Jonathan's birthday party we're having this weekend."

"Oh, that's right," she remembered. "Is he excited?"

"Yes. We invited all the kids from his class, and my brother's delivering the cake. Leah's gonna come over early and help me with the decorations. Did you order that helium tank like I asked you to?"

"Yes. They're bringing it to your house at nine o'clock and said to be done with it by four. Remember? I told you that."

I didn't recall it at all, but dismissed the memory lapse with a shrug. I had more important things to worry about. Like this hospital, and my son, and my husband...

I shook the thought of Gavin away and checked my email, then went over the list of things I still had to get done before I left for the day.

"Are you sure you're okay?" Wendy asked me.

"I'm fine!" I insisted, even though I knew I wasn't going to get everything done.

"You certainly are."

Both Wendy and I looked up to see Mr. Bronson standing in the doorway.

"Your work, I mean," he clarified.

Wendy turned to me and rolled her eyes, not believing his nerve. "I'm gonna get back to my office," she said as she stood up to leave. "I'll just take this with me," she added quickly, and swiped my espresso from my desk. "I'll be back with a water and some food."

I cringed inside for two reasons. The first was because I didn't want to be left alone with Mr. Bronson. The main reason, though, was because I *really wanted that espresso!*

"I didn't mean to run off your assistant," he told me.

"It's okay," I lied. "Can I help you with something?"

"I just came back from a board meeting," he replied as he sat across from me. "We did a walk through of the new construction."

My stomach fell.

"Without me?" I panicked. "The place isn't finished yet. We still have a lot to do, and some of the—"

"Relax," he stopped me. "It was just a walk through, not an inspection. Some on the board just wanted a peek at what you've been doing."

"Oh, no," I groaned, and covered my face in anxiety. They probably were outraged by what they saw. Incomplete walls. Hanging fixtures. A partially built stairwell. There was a method to my madness, but I was the only one who understood it, that's why I never showed my work before it was completed unless it was absolutely necessary. Had I been at that meeting, like I should have been if they were going to inquire about my work, I would have happily told them to schedule a visit with me at an acceptable time. But no. They just did the indecent thing and snooped around on me behind my back!

"No worries," Mr. Bronson told me. "They loved what they saw."

I narrowed my eyes at him. If this was his way of joking, he was an unusually cruel and obnoxious human being.

"I'm serious," he insisted, and covered his heart as if my disbelief wounded him. Finally I believed him, and gave a sigh of relief while he laughed at my pain.

"They loved it," he told me. "They're very pleased, and are assured they picked the right woman for the job. Of course *I* never worried, but..."

He stopped when I gave him a look that suggested he needed to. He took heed to the warning and stood up to leave.

"Just wanted you to know," he told me. "You're doing a fantastic job, and all of your hard work is paying off. Keep it up."

When he left I hopped out of my seat and jumped up and down.

"Yes!" I howled, and waved my hands in the air.

"Mrs. Gardner?"

I gasped and came to an abrupt halt. Mr. Bronson stood at the door and stared at me while I smoothed my skirt down.

"Let's try to keep it professional," he said, and walked away with a smirk on his face.

Humiliated, I returned to my seat and got back to work.

FIFTY-NINE
GAVIN

The rush of adrenaline the carnival's Zipper ride sent through Parker and I was exhilarating to her, but the hysterical screams I released were cause for serious inquiries about my manhood. I was horrified. A grown man now, I wondered how I ever enjoyed such anguish in my younger years. I must have been crazy. I was dizzy and had blurry vision by the time the ride was over, but Parker laughed as though it was the most amusing thing in the world.

"My life passed before my eyes," I confessed through heavy breaths.

She laughed harder and wiped the tears that came to her eyes. "You think the kids enjoyed it?"

Jonathan and Madison were in the compartment in front of us, and thankfully I didn't hear any crying.

"Yeah. They're crazy," I told her, and stared at the metal mesh in front of us so my eyes could regain their focus. "I'm too old for this."

She slid her hand into mine. "Let's do it again."

"Are you crazy?!" I exclaimed, but already knew I would.

We waited patiently as the ride's operator rotated the capsules to release the few of us who were on. The kids got off before us and we followed.

"We want to go again," Parker told the operator.

"Not me," Madison quickly clarified, and clutched her chest to slow her rapid heartbeat. "I am *done* with this ride."

"I'm afraid you all are," the operator told us. "Time to shut it down."

"Shut what down?" Parker frowned.

"The ride. Storm's coming in. Carnival is closing til' it passes."

"What storm?"

He pointed at the dark clouds gathering above us as he handed the kids back the stuffed animals and balloons he'd held for them.

"Didn't you check the weather?" he asked us. "A bad storm is here. We shouldn't have even opened today. I'm surprised anyone is here."

Parker turned to me with a face full of regret. She had no idea a storm was coming, and neither did I. I never checked those things. Dana always did. Apparently we were having too much fun to notice the weather changing around us.

"It looks like it's gonna rain," Jonathan said as he looked up at the clouds.

A bolt of lightning cracked the sky. Madison screamed and ducked behind me.

"That was close," Parker told us, and scooted closer to me. "We better get out of here."

Suddenly rain began to pour down heavily on us. They all screamed and tried to hide behind me for shelter while its fierceness stung every inch of my exposed skin. I yelped at the pain and rushed us off to a nearby booth with an overhang large enough to protect us from the harshness of the storm.

"Oh, no! Our day is ruined!" Madison whined, and held up her now drenched elephant. "Man! Billy's all wet! And me, too!"

I asked Jonathan if he was okay. He told me he was, but I observed the way he was shivering and knew I had to get him out of the rain soon.

"This is my fault," Parker moaned. "I didn't think to check the weather, and I don't even have an umbrella in the car. Now everyone's going to be sick."

Madison burst into tears.

"What are you crying for?" Parker asked impatiently.

"I don't want to go home!"

"We can't stay out here!"

Madison kept right on crying, to the surprise of Jonathan, who stared as if she'd lost her mind.

"I don't want to go home!" she yelled again.

"Stop crying! The carnival is closing. We can't stay out here in the rain!"

"But I don't want to go home!"

"Well, I can't control the rain, so we have no choice."

Madison covered her face with Billy and bent over in tears.

Annoyed, Parker turned to me and shook her head with disbelief.

"I promise you, my child has sense," she said, and checked her watch. "She's just cranky. I let her stay up too late last night, and now it's her lunch time. Hungry and tired is never a good combination."

"I understand," I told her, but gave Jonathan a look that warned I'd have his behind if he even thought about following in Madison's footsteps. He received the message loud and clear.

"I guess we gotta call it quits, guys," Parker told the kids.

Madison forced herself to stop crying and wiped her eyes and nose with her arm.

"Can they come to our house?" she asked her mom with a shaky voice.

Surprised, Parker looked to me for an answer. Apparently liking the idea, Jonathan did, too. When I didn't provide one Parker took my silence as rejection. She told Madison I probably had something to do and that her and Jonathan would just have to play together some other time.

"No, we can go," I told them against my better judgment. I thought it best that Jonathan and I go on home, but it wasn't even past lunch hour yet. His fun had only just begun, and I didn't want to see him mope around the house for the rest of the day.

Parker's face lit up while Jonathan pumped his fist in excitement. Madison was pleased, too. She finally began to smile.

"Are you sure?" Parker asked, but didn't wait for an answer. She winked while the kids began to chat with each other. I could see the appreciation in her face and knew she wanted to show me just how pleased she was with my decision. I knew it was wrong, especially now that I wanted to end things between us, but wanted to see, too.

"Come on, guys," I told them, and grabbed Jonathan's hand as we all dashed to the parking lot.

SIXTY
GAVIN

"Can we go play in my room?" Madison asked Parker as soon as we walked into their house.

"Don't sit on your bed in those wet clothes," Parker said, and tossed her keys on the living room coffee table. "I'll be in there in a minute to pick out something dry for you to wear."

The kids hurried off, leaving us alone. I stood by the door, suddenly nervous, and the mixed emotions of being there with Jonathan expelled an awkward energy. I couldn't even take my hands out of my pockets.

"You didn't get sick from the rain, did you?" Parker asked me.

"I'm fine," I told her, but she knew it wasn't true.

"Are you upset?"

"No, I just..."

"You changed your mind about coming over," she concluded, and frowned heavily to show her disappointment. "You don't want your kid around me."

"It's not you," I tried to explain. "It's just the situation. Skipping school was one thing, but bringing him here... He's probably gonna say something to Dana."

"Well, just tell him not to."

I chuckled at her thinking. If it were that simple I wouldn't be worried.

"Look, you guys are already here, all right?" she said as she flung her purse on the couch. "You may as well chill—at least until it stops raining. You don't wanna drive across town in that mess, do you?"

I didn't need to think about how dangerous that would be. The challenge to get here was scary enough. I could barely see, and the thunder and lightning made all of us nervous.

She took me by the hand and led me over to the couch.

"Relax. After I get these kids situated I'll fix us some tea. We'll sit out here and talk the whole time, and if Jonathan says something to Dana about it, you'll just tell her what it is and she'll get over it."

I said okay, but only to keep her from panicking. She didn't know I'd put her in danger by involving her in my son's life. Dana didn't play those games.

After she got Madison situated she went into her laundry room, only to return later with an overstuffed basket of clean clothes that she dropped at my feet.

"Ya'll are gonna be sick if you stay in those wet clothes, so I emptied the dryer so you can put your clothes in there for a few minutes."

Smart thinking. *A mother's thinking.*

"What are we gonna wear in the meantime?"

She shrugged and rounded her eyes. "Just stay in there until they're dry."

I sighed, but didn't see what other choice we had. It wasn't like she could provide any other solution. Only women lived in this house. She didn't have anything we could wear.

"It won't take long," she assured me.

I called Jonathan and led him into the laundry room and told him the plan. He objected at first, but complied after Parker brought us both towels to cover ourselves with. I leaned against the door, as he instructed, just so no one could walk in on us.

"This is *weird,*" he said as we stood across from the each other.

"But you had fun today, didn't you?"

"Yes, it was fun," he said with a smile as he nodded. "Madison didn't like that Zipper ride, though."

I chuckled with him at the memory.

"You know not to tell your mom about this, right?" I asked.

He stopped smiling. "Why?"

"It's our secret. She doesn't need to know everything."

His face fell, and I saw that he'd become angry. He held his tongue, though, and didn't say anything.

"What's the matter?"

"I thought we weren't supposed to keep secrets?"

Guilt overcame me. I held my head down in shame, but knew I had to convince him to do this for me. I'd have hell to pay if I didn't.

"You're right," I told him. "Normally, we aren't. But this is a different circumstance. You skipped school today, and your mom wouldn't be happy about that if she knew."

He gasped. "I didn't skip school! You told me I didn't have to go today!"

"You agreed to it, didn't you?"

He clenched his jaw and crossed his arms, angry with me. "You tricked me."

"No, I didn't. I just wanted to have fun with you today, that's all. And I thought you'd have fun if Madison came too, so her mother agreed to let her come. You're having fun, aren't you?"

"Yeah, but... *Never mind,*" he grumbled, and adjusted his towel to fit tighter around his waist.

"What is it?" I wanted to know. "You know you can talk to me."

He hesitated, wrestling with himself for a moment, then asked, "Do you want to marry Ms. Parker?"

I nearly gasped out loud.

"What?"

He grimaced. "It just seems like it. She looks at you all weird, like she likes you."

"We're friends."

"I know, but... It just seems like you like her the way you like Mommy. It's weird. And now you don't want Mommy to know about today. I think because you know she'll be mad if she knew."

Dang. This kid was way smarter and more observant than I'd given him credit for. I shouldn't have involved him in this situation at all. I should have kept him in school like I knew I needed to and just let Parker be mad. None of this was worth it. The last thing I wanted to do was teach my son how to be a player.

"Okay. I won't tell her," he promised, but I knew he wasn't comfortable with the decision.

"Don't think of it as keeping a secret," I told him. "Think of it as securing fun days in the future."

He looked up at me with curiosity in his eyes, followed by confusion. *"What?"*

"If you tell your mom, we won't be able to do this again."

"That's fine," he said, and shrugged as if he didn't care. "I had fun, but I like going to school."

Every parent longed to hear those words, and under normal circumstances I would, too. But right now all it did was irritate me. I decided to leave him alone about it for now and we stood in silence while our clothes dried.

Once they finished we got dressed and he returned to Madison's room. I went back to the living room and a moment later Parker emerged from her bedroom. She was wearing a long silk robe and her hair was dripping wet.

"I jumped in the shower," she explained when she saw my curious expression. "My hair had that rain smell. It was driving me crazy."

I stared at her chest, which was wet from her hair, and told myself not to think impure thoughts.

"Feel better now that you're dry?" she asked.

"I'm straight," I said, still ogling.

"Good. I'm gonna fix us some lunch," she said, and went into the kitchen. "Chili dogs sound good to you?"

"Yeah, that's fine," I said, and winced as she bent over to get a pot out of the dishwasher. The light above her cast a glow on her backside.

I want her... really, really, really badly...

****

Parker called the kids into the kitchen and told them their lunch was ready. Hungry, they rushed to their prepared plates, and Jonathan took his to the table and sat down.

"What are you doing?" Madison asked him.

Parker looked up from the pot she was rinsing out to see what the confusion was about.

"Oh, no, sweetie," she told him. "You don't have to eat that at the table. Go on back in Madison's room."

He looked over at me for permission.

"It's cool," I told him from my seat on the sofa. I hadn't moved from the spot since I'd returned from the laundry room.

"Just stay on the floor with it," Parker told him.

He and Madison returned to her room, and Parker brought a plate and drink over to me. I was surprised by how tasty the meal looked. While focusing on the TV in front of me I hadn't realized that she'd toasted the buns and added chopped onions, jalapeños, and shredded cheese.

"Dang, girl. You're a trip," I said, and ate one of the French fries she complimented the meal with.

"Why?" she asked as she went to the kitchen to get her food.

"You make even hot dogs look good."

She giggled as she sat next to me on the couch. "I just wish we could have eaten at the carnival. My mouth was all set for a gigantic turkey leg and a funnel cake."

"This is the next best thing," I told her.

She looked over at me and smiled sincerely. "You always know what to say."

I smiled back at her and began to eat one of my hotdogs.

"Why aren't you eating?" I asked when I noticed she hadn't taken any bites.

"Because I want to show you something."

"What?"

She put her food on the end table beside her and squared her body to face me.

"What are you about to do?" I asked cautiously.

"This," she said, and exposed part of her chest.

I nearly choked on my food. She only giggled.

"What are you doing?" I panicked, and used a pillow to cover her up as I checked to make sure the kids hadn't seen. *"You don't have anything on under there?"*

"Nope," she said, and moved the pillow out of the way. "It's just a little hot in here. Don't you think?"

"Oh, man," I whispered under my breath, and bit my fist to refrain from touching her.

"You've seen one before, right?" she asked as she looked down at herself. "Or have you not seen one so perfect?"

Perfect, it was. Ashamed of myself, I covered my eyes and turned away, but immediately peeked through my fingers and stole another look. She was fine! Fine! Fine! Fine!

"Come here."

I shook my head. "You're trying to get me in trouble," I said, but was too weak to take my eyes off her again.

She moved closer to me and began to nuzzle her face against my neck.

"You smell good," she whispered, and placed my hand on her revealed chest. "How's that?"

I was too shocked to give a response. I'd experienced women throwing themselves at me before, but none like this. The danger of being caught only made touching her more exhilarating.

"You like it, don't you?"

I didn't answer, but didn't move my hand, either.

"Oh, what's that?" she asked as she looked down. "Someone's excited."

I couldn't deny it. She had that affect on me.

Get up, Gavin... Get up...

"I want to kiss you," she whispered, and draped her curvy leg over my lap. "Can I?"

Before I gave an answer, she leaned over and planted one on me.

I'm so weak.

My hands caressed her thigh as she did, and traveled up to her bare behind before she stopped me.

"Not here," she whispered. *"My room."*

"They'll see us," I said through low breaths.

"They're eating and playing video games," she said as she nibbled on my ear. "They'll be occupied for *hours*. Plus Madison knows not to come in my room without my permission. They're not gonna bother us."

She slid off the couch and stood in front of me, then slowly began to back into the hallway. She motioned for me to follow, and when I hesitated she beckoned me with her finger while exposing more of herself.

'Come on,' she mouthed, and walked past Madison's open door as if we were all alone in the house.

I tried to talk myself out of it. I told myself that nothing good would happen if I went in that room with her. We would definitely go all the way, God would not be pleased, and there would be horrific consequences. But the softness of her body still lingered on my hands, and my lips still pulsated from the pleasure of her kiss.

I want to do what is good, but I don't. I don't want to do what is wrong, but I do it anyway...

I got up and slowly made my way toward her bedroom. She stood in front of the door, and I kept my eyes on her as I passed Madison's room. My focus seemed to turn her on more. As soon as I reached her she pulled me into the room and closed the door softly behind us.

"Be quiet," she whispered as she kissed me.

I kissed her back and squeezed all of her. When she couldn't take the excitement anymore she pushed me onto the queen-sized bed that was centered against the back wall.

"Sit," she instructed. "Let me take care of you."

I watched intently as she untied her robe. The thin belt fell to her sides and a sliver of skin was revealed from her neck to her bellybutton. She shrugged to let the robe slip from her shoulders and it fluttered to the floor, revealing all of her.

"Paaaarrrrkkkkkkeeeerrrrr..."

She stood in front of me completely naked, and I couldn't resist kissing her body. Again. And again. And again.

"Don't hold back," she said softly, and began to unbutton my shirt as she looked down at me. *"Please... Gavin, I want you so bad..."*

I told myself to stop. This was crazy! But she looked too good and felt too good to deny. Her body promised to fulfill me in ways that I'd longed for every since I'd known her, and now the opportunity was right in front of me. How could I not take it?

She took off my shirt and straddled me while she covered my chest with kisses.

"I want to take care of you," she said suddenly, and pulled my belt. "Can I?"

She gave the belt another tug, and I knew exactly what she meant. The thought of it was mind-blowing.

"Are you sure?"

"Positive," she said confidently, and lowered herself in front of me.

My mouth fell open with excited anticipation. She unbuckled my belt completely as she squatted before me and slowly pulled it off. I was so aroused by what was about to happen next that I nearly lost my mind. She wasn't worried at all, though, and continued as if there was nothing wrong with what we were about to do. I closed my eyes, unable to take it, and grabbed her hands to stop her.

"If you start, I won't be able to stop you," I warned.

"I know," she told me, and kissed me while she reached for what she wanted.

A loud thud suddenly came from Madison's room.

We froze.

A split second later a piercing cry came from down the hall, followed by the rumble of terrified footsteps as they ran toward us.

"Oh, $#%!!!"* she panicked, and jumped from her position in front of me.

I hurried to cover myself while Parker dove for her robe. The footsteps grew louder as they got closer, and as I jumped from the bed I knew she wasn't going to be dressed in time. She cursed loudly, coming to the same conclusion as I turned my back to close my pants. I snatched my shirt up from the bed and jumped in front of the door just and Madison and Jonathan burst through it, stopping them dead in their tracks before they got an eyeful of what they were too young to see.

"What are you guys doing?!" I screamed at them. My boisterous voice was really a stalling technique to allow Parker time to get dressed, but all of the blood pouring out of Madison's nose had already done that for me. They both shook with fear as she cried hysterically.

"What happened?!" I demanded to know as I put my shirt on.

"It was an accident!" he declared, and stared in horror at Madison. He was sure he was about to get the whooping of his life.

"What did you do?!" I demanded to know, and peeked over my shoulder for Parker. She'd dipped into her bathroom, but came out a moment later with her robe tightly wrapped around herself.

"MOMMY!!!" Madison screamed.

"It was an accident!" Jonathan hollered again.

Parker shrieked when she saw the distress her daughter was in. Her panic only caused the kids to become more upset, and the room became loud with cries and screams from all of us.

"Hold your head back!" I yelled at Madison.

She was too frazzled to listen, so I grabbed her head and forced her to. Blood was all over the lower part of her face, as well as her shirt.

"You need a wet towel," I told Parker.

"In the bathroom, under the sink," she said frantically, and took over head holding duties.

I hustled into the bathroom while Parker asked Jonathan what happened.

"We were playing the game," he explained. "And she got mad because I won and tried to kick me, but I caught her foot and pushed her. Then her face went into the wall."

"I didn't kick you!" Madison argued angrily.

"Yes, you did! You tried to!"

I snatched a towel from the cabinet and soaked it with water, then hurried back into the bedroom and handed it to Parker. Just seeing Jonathan here was too much. I was disgusted with myself, and embarrassed by how foul I'd allowed myself to become. We had to get out of here. *Now.*

"You broke my nose!" Madison screamed at him.

"It's not broken!" Parker fussed, and applied pressure to it while Jonathan continued to plead that he didn't mean to hurt her.

"It's time to go, son," I told him.

"You're leaving?" Parker frowned.

Did she really think I would stay? After this?

"Her nose isn't broken," she told me. "She's just shook up, that's all. And she probably did kick him, so I'm not mad. They're kids. Accidents happen."

"You're supposed to take my side!" Madison yelled at her. "You're my mom!"

"Girl!" Parker nearly grabbed the child by her throat. "Have you lost your mind?!"

Madison quickly apologized, but at this point I'd seen, heard, and done enough.

"Come on," I rushed Jonathan, and pulled him out of the room.

Parker called after me to wait, but I ignored her. She finally caught up with us as we made it to the porch. The rain still poured, but by the grace of God it was light enough for us to leave safely.

"What are you doing?" she asked, becoming angry.

I shook my head and almost felt sorry for her. How could she even ask me that question?

"This is over, Parker," I told her, and turned to leave, but she grabbed me.

"What do you mean, *over?*"

I tossed Jonathan the keys to my truck and told him to wait for me inside. Once he was out of hearing range I turned back to Parker.

"We're done," I told her.

"Why? Are you mad at me? I didn't do anything!"

"My kid almost saw us!"

She gasped loudly. "First of all, I wasn't in there by myself," she retaliated. "Secondly, they didn't see anything, so stop tripping. We played it cool. They don't even know anything. Come back inside."

"It's over," I told her again, and hurried to the truck where Jonathan was waiting for me.

"It was an accident," he told me as soon as I got inside. "I didn't mean to break her nose, and she did kick me first."

"Don't worry about it. You're not in trouble," I told him, and stared at Parker as I started the truck. She stood with her arms crossed and watched me angrily.

"Are you gonna tell Mommy?" he feared.

"Not if you don't tell her about today."

"Deal," he said quickly, and buckled his seat belt.

I did the same and backed out of Parker's driveway. She continued to watch me the entire time, and I knew she wasn't going to make leaving her alone as easy as I wanted it to be.

SIXTY-ONE
GAVIN

I took the next two days off from work, and did nothing but pray, fast, and read my bible. The ordeal at Parker's house left me feeling lost, vulnerable, and graciously spared, and I had to get back to that place in God where I felt confident in my relationship with Him. That only came by repenting, and I'd done it nonstop every since I left Parker's house.

I knew I didn't have to repeat myself over and over again. Jesus heard me the first time I cried out for forgiveness. But the memories of my wrongdoings made it difficult to be unashamed of what I'd done. However, I didn't exactly feel condemned. I knew my sins had been cast away. My heart was actually filled with gratitude. God's grace was amazing, and it kept me from going a step too far. If I'd had sex with Parker there was no telling what would have happened afterward. I could have ended up like David in the bible. His adultery led to a surprise baby and family drama that lasted for the rest of his life. But I was spared, and his goodness protected me.

I couldn't believe I ever even thought about stepping out on Dana. She was the love of my life! The very good thing the bible talked about in Proverbs 18:22. In focusing on her imperfections I did nothing but highlight my very own, and I despised what I'd done to her in the process. That was nothing like me at all. I'd always been loving toward her, and soft-spoken, and caring. But I became so verbally and emotionally abusive that I became another person entirely. And I ended up hurting Parker, too.

But I couldn't even think about her too much. She'd called repeatedly and sent several texts, but I ignored them all, though I knew I owed her an explanation. It wasn't fair to go as far as I did and then suddenly run away without clarifying the reason why. The wrong wasn't solely on her, and she didn't deserve to be made to feel that way, especially when I was the one who was married.

I needed to properly end things with her, but my priority was Dana. The communication between us was nearly nonexistent. I slept beside her every night, but over the past two days we barely said three words to each other. I suspected she knew more about Parker and I than she'd let on, but I wasn't going to bring it up if she didn't. I wasn't stupid. But then again, maybe I needed to come clean in order for us to move on. I longed for the mornings when I woke up and the only thing on my mind was making love to her. We were blessed then, despite the secrets and the lies, and had I not been so foolish our relationship wouldn't be in shambles. I wanted my marriage back, and it was my solemn prayer that the Lord would give it to me.

SIXTY-TWO
DANA

Jonathan's birthday got off to a good start. He woke up early and was in such a good mood that I wondered if he'd somehow gotten into his presents early. He promised he hadn't, so after I made his favorite breakfast I let him open a gift anyway, just to spoil him a bit. He chose wisely. The gigantic box he selected had a skateboard inside. He immediately took it outside to play with, which left plenty of space for everyone to help me get things ready for the party.

Everything was right on schedule. The helium tank came on time, and Jessica got right to work blowing up balloons. Marcus manned the grill outside while Gavin got busy setting up picnic tables and chairs in the backyard. Leah and I spent the rest of the morning decorating the lower level of the house with banners and streamers.

We were in the middle of filling goodie bags when my cell phone rang. Gavin just so happened to be in the kitchen getting a drink of water and appeared repulsed when he heard it.

"That better not be work," he told me. "It's his birthday."

I cringed, already knowing Wendy was the person calling. Everyone else who would reach out to me on a Saturday morning was already with me.

"Hello?" I answered when I picked up.

"Hey, girl," she moaned. "We have a problem."

"What?" I whined.

"The stairwell. Something's wrong with it, and your boy Bronson is acting a fool."

"What's going on?" I asked, and turned away to avoid Gavin's stare.

"Somehow the dimensions got thrown off by five feet. Remember when you made the adjustments to the plans? The team said they followed what you wrote down exactly. But somehow it all got messed up, and now Bronson's having a fit and he says he needs you to get it fixed right now."

"You sure everything's five feet off? That sounds weird."

"Yeah, but... I'm not trying to blame you or anything, because none of us double checked, but you know how your hands shake when you're hopped up on that coffee.

It does make your threes look like eights."

I rolled my eyes to the back of my head and flopped down on the couch. *"Not now, Wendy,"* I groaned. "Can't I just take care of this Monday? We're getting ready for the birthday party. People will be here soon."

"Sorry," she apologized. "The crew is at a work stoppage, and Bronson says he wants you there fixing it now. No excuses."

"I really hate him," I grumbled under my breath, then told her I would be there as soon as I could and hung up.

"No," Gavin said sternly. "You *are not* missing his birthday!"

"It's not my fault," I tried to tell him. "There's an emergency at the hospital and I have to—"

"He's been looking forward to this for months!" he snapped at me. "You need to get your priorities straight! Everything ain't about work all the damn time!"

"Woah! Easy!" Leah yelled at us.

"Stay out of this!" he yelled back at her. "This is between me and my wife!"

Marcus came in from the backyard and heard Gavin's tone. "Hold up, now," he warned him. "Watch the way you talk to *my wife.*"

"Gavin, can you calm down, please?" I begged.

He threw his hands in the air and walked outside, completely fed up with all of us.

"What's got his drawers in a bunch?" Marcus asked.

"Just go handle what you need to handle," Leah told me. "I'll take care of everything here."

"Are you sure?" I asked her. "There are a lot of people coming."

She sighed. "Won't be the first time I bailed you out. Now get, before I change my mind."

"What *happened?*" Marcus asked.

"Just go," Leah told me as she shook her head at him.

I thanked them both, then gathered my things and hurried to the hospital.

SIXTY-THREE
GAVIN

Jonathan ran to the front door when the doorbell rang.

"Madison!" he screamed as he opened it, but slumped with disappointment when he realized it wasn't her. "Oh, it's you, Todd," he said to the little boy standing on the front porch. "Welcome to my house, and thanks for coming to my party."

I tied the balloon I'd just finished blowing up and handed it to Jessica so she could attach a string to it. We had a system going, despite the abundance of people who decided to gather early. If Dana were here she'd be irritated. She always said it was rude to arrive early, and now I knew why. The house wasn't quite prepared, and I felt a little exposed. Then again, that could be because Dana left me to finish taking care of things on my own and I didn't have a clue what I was doing. The children running around like they had sugar and high fructose corn syrup for breakfast had my nerves on edge, and I knew it was only a matter of time before I started barking orders at them all.

Parker was the real reason I was a wreck. I still hadn't spoken to her, and I honestly didn't know what I was going to say when she arrived—especially in a house full of my son's family and friends.

The doorbell rang again, and again Jonathan dropped everything he was doing to see who'd arrived.

"MADISON!" he screamed.

This time it had to be her. There was no way he would be so excited to see anyone else.

I peeked into the living room and watched them hug each other. Apparently all had been forgiven from their fight a few days ago. Parker stood behind them with an oversized box in her hands.

"Happy birthday!" Madison beamed. "Did you get a dinosaur?"

"Not yet. But hopefully."

He let the ladies in and Parker stood nervously at the door.

"Is your dad here?" she asked him.

I blew up another balloon and waved, but didn't go over to welcome her in person. Her optimistic smile faded away.

"Who's that woman?" Jessica asked me.

"Who?"

"Her," she said, and pointed at Parker.

I shrugged as if I didn't know.

"Then why are you staring at her?"

Insulted, I frowned at my niece. "No, I'm not."

"Yes, you are," she insisted, and took the balloon from me.

"Oh, that's one of my co-workers. I thought you were talking about someone else."

She knew I was lying, and didn't appreciate it, nor was she pleased with Parker's presence. She didn't even know her, but scowled at her like she was a whore.

I decided to man up and went into the living room and approached Parker.

"Hi," she said, and placed the gift in my hands. "It's a robot T-Rex. Madison told me he loves dinosaurs, and I remembered from the museum, so..."

She felt my nervousness and it made her uneasy. She fumbled with her now empty hands and slowly teetered back and forth on her heels.

"Oh, yeah. This is great," I told her as I looked at the box. Madison's handwriting adorned its label. "I'm sure he'll love it."

"Well, I hope you didn't get him one already. I tried to call to see if the gift was okay, but... *You didn't answer, so...* Are you mad at me or something?" she asked, and angrily placed her hand on her hip. "Because if you are I really don't understand why."

"Parker, I—"

"Because I didn't do anything to you, and if you think..."

The front door opened behind her. Mama walked in, and I hadn't been so happy to see her in years.

"Mama!" I called out quickly, and ran to her as if she were the resurrected source of my salvation and planted a gigantic kiss on her cheek.

"Well, hello to you, too, baby," she said, and squeezed me tightly. "What's this all about?"

"Oh, nothing Mama," I said, and stole a glance at Parker. She realized my display of affection was a ploy to get away from her and walked into the kitchen, rightfully annoyed. "I just missed you, that's all."

"Really? If you missed me so much, I'd think you would have called. You haven't even come by to see me. I could be dead for all you know."

"Mama..." It was true. I hadn't talked to her in a few days, but that was because I was trying to get my head on straight. "Don't take it personal. Just been busy, that's all."

"Ummm, humh," she said with her lips pressed tightly together. "You can make it up to me later. Right now I have someone I want you to meet." She pulled at the arm of a woman who'd just walked through the door with a toddler on her arm. "This is Lydia and her son, Kingston. She's a friend of mine who just started coming to the church. Lydia, this is my son that I was telling you all about."

I offered her my hand, but she chose to hug me instead and pressed her chest so hard against me that the child in her arms could barely breathe.

"Whoa!"

I quickly pulled away at the violation and saw Mama smile. I instantly knew what she was up to. Lydia was wearing a halter top, hot shorts, and heels that looked like they belonged on a stripper. Who wore that to a child's birthday party? Mama knew better than this! Had Dana walked around the house in this getup she would have went off. But it was okay for this woman to do in front of all of these kids? This was ridiculous.

"Son?"

I held my head down in frustration. She was not doing this to me again. Not after that horrific evening we had with Tanya.

"Isn't Lydia a beautiful girl, Gavin? And she's smart, too. She makes her own handbags."

"I'm really a successful woman," Lydia interjected. "I know it doesn't sound like it, but I can pull my own weight."

"Course she doesn't have much to pull," Mama added quickly. "She's a petite little thing. Look at that tiny waist, son. She doesn't even look like she's had any children, does she? But she has. *And she wants more,* too. Why don't you two have a seat and talk? You know, get to know each other."

Lydia smiled eagerly, but I backed away.

"Let me go check on the birthday boy, first," I told them, and went into the kitchen.

When I got there Parker was waiting on me, so I continued into the backyard and pretended to be occupied with the children who were gathered. Mama and Lydia stood on the back porch and watched me closely, and Parker joined them a moment later.

Oh, Lord... I'm in trouble.

SIXTY-FOUR
DANA

Mr. Bronson and I sat at my desk and went over the adjustments I made to the stairwell design. Because of its structure I only needed to add a few extra support elements, but that was going to be easier said than done. Some of the floor work I'd already finished was going to have to be redone, which hurt my budget. I also had to have it all completed by Wednesday, or else the grand opening would have to be pushed back.

Normally I wouldn't stress so much. I'd been in situations like this before and always came through successfully. But today I was having a hard time. Bronson was breathing down my neck, which made me extremely uncomfortable, and my mind was on Jonathan. I prayed to God that he was having a good time at his party. I absolutely hated missing it, especially knowing how Gavin felt about my absence. I could still see the resentment he had on his face when I left, and it intensified my guilt.

My cell phone rang.

"Sorry, I gotta take this," I told Bronson, and picked it up from my desk. "It's my brother."

He scrunched his face like he didn't care, but I answered anyway.

"What are you doing?" Sean asked me.

"Working."

"Are you guys still having the birthday party?"

"Yeah.... Why?"

"The cake. No one has come by to pick it up yet, and the bakery closes in an hour."

"OH, CRAP!!!" I screamed, alarming Bronson, and covered my face. How could I forget about the cake?! It was the most important part of the party!!!

"Yeah... You forgot."

"Shoot!" I fussed, and stomped my foot. "Oh, no! Can someone deliver it? I'll pay extra. I'll even tip the driver."

"No, I can't do that, remember?" he said as if he were in pain. "I told you that you were going to have to pick it up. All my drivers are out making deliveries."

I recalled our previous arrangement and wanted to kick myself. Bronson shot an annoyed stare at me, so I knew I had to get off the phone.

"Okay," I told him with a sigh. "I'll figure something out."

"You better make it quick. I'm not paying my workers extra to stay open for you."

"All right, fine," I grunted, and hung up the phone. It immediately rang again. This time it was Leah.

"You need to hurry up and get back here," she told me quickly when I accepted her call. "Like, right now."

"What's wrong?" I panicked. "Is Jonathan okay?"

"Oh, yeah. He's fine. It's his daddy that's in here tripping."

I gasped. "What's happening?"

"Who is this Parker chick that's walking around here?"

"What are they doing?" I demanded to know.

"Nothing," Leah told me. "But it's something going on between the two of them, and I don't like it. She keeps watching him, and I think he's avoiding her. They keep making eyes at each other, but they're not talking."

I sighed. "Leah, I don't have time for this. I'm working."

"I know, and you need to get your butt back here and take care of your man, because it's too many whores here trying to take your place. Now it's only so much I can do for you."

"I don't need you to do anything," I said impatiently.

"Are you sure? Because your mother-in-law just came in here with some half-dressed woman."

I stopped what I was doing. *"WHAT?!"*

"Yep. Just tacky. I'm just giving you a head's up."

I groaned and thanked her for letting me know, then hung up the phone.

"Everything all right?" Bronson asked when I began to massage my forehead.

"Yeah, it's just..." I tilted my head back in hopes it would alleviate some of the pressure I was feeling. "My son's birthday is today and there's a party going on at my house. But of course it's all falling apart because I'm not there."

He sat up straighter, surprised and suddenly interested. "I didn't know you had a son."

I nodded and exhaled slowly.

"How old is he?"

"Eight," I replied, and tried not to think about him as guilty tears came to my eyes. I hated that I was missing his big day. I was his mother, and I should have been celebrating with him, but instead I was at work. *Again.*

"I have a son, too, you know? Two, actually. And a daughter."

I nodded as if I really cared.

"Yes. They're older. Ten, twelve, and sixteen. Let me tell you, if there is one thing I regret, it's spending too much time at work. I missed a lot of special moments. Like birthday parties..."

Okay... Not really making me feel any better...

"Go home," he said suddenly.

I stared, unsure if I heard him correctly.

"Go," he said again, and cocked his head toward the door. "Get out of here and go be with your family. And tell that son of yours that I said happy birthday."

I clutched my chest as I gasped. *"Really?!"*

"Go! Before I change my mind and make you stay."

I lifted my head toward heaven and gave God a moment of nonverbal worship.

"Thank you!" I shouted at Bronson, and gave him a gigantic hug. "Thank you so much!"

"Whoa... Easy," he cautioned me as he straightened his clothes. "Let's not make things uncomfortable, here."

"Sorry," I quickly apologized. "I'm just... It's my baby's birthday..."

"No need to explain. I'll hold off the vultures for today, but you better have that stairwell done by Wednesday morning, young lady."

I already had my purse and keys in my hand and was halfway out of the door.

"Absolutely! You don't have to worry about me. It'll get done," I told him, and hurried to pick up Jonathan's birthday cake.

SIXTY-FIVE
GAVIN

So far Dana's party was a hit. Jonathan was having the time of his life, and so were his friends and their parents. I had no idea she'd invited so many people, but it made avoiding Parker easier—and Mama and her friend, too. The party had been going strong for over an hour and I'd managed to get away without saying much to either of them, though I suspected Leah could tell something was going on between Parker and I. She'd noticed a few awkward exchanges between us and didn't seem too pleased.

It was almost time to eat, so I went outside to check the food table. Leah and Marcus had done a good job of preparing everything. Burgers and hot dogs sat in heated trays, and vegetables remained cool in covered bins. The table was stocked with condiments as well, but somehow the paper napkins had been forgotten.

I returned to the kitchen and snatched a few of the dinosaur themed packs Dana purchased last night from the pantry. When I closed the door Parker was standing on the other side.

"So you're just not going to say anything to me?"

I anxiously looked around the room, fearful that someone had heard. Luckily we were alone in the kitchen, though several adults were gathered in the living room only a few feet away.

"You don't know me now?" she continued. "You freak out about what didn't even happen, and now you can't even talk to me anymore? Is that what's going on? *I'm supposed to act like you didn't just see me naked the other day?*"

I grabbed her by her arm and pulled her to the laundry room.

"Are you crazy?" I asked angrily as I pressed her against the door.

"No. I'm pissed off at you!"

"Keep your voice down."

We looked around the corner to make sure no one heard our outburst.

"I know I was wrong to ignore you for the past few days," I told her once I knew the coast was clear. "Especially after what happened between us. But I just needed some time to be alone."

"You mean some time with *your wife?*"

"No. Time alone to think about things. Get my head on straight. Things were just getting out of control. You should be able to understand that. It wasn't that long ago that you were giving me the cold shoulder. Remember?"

"That was before we started our relationship."

"*Relationship?* We were never together."

Her face fell suddenly. "You're breaking up with me?"

"I was *never* with you."

She stared at me as if I'd all of a sudden started speaking a foreign language. She slowly began to sink into herself with each second of silence that passed.

"I'm sorry," I apologized, trying to ease her pain. "But you know I have a wife. I'm sorry if you thought it was more than a physical thing, but that's all it was and it's time to let it go. Sorry if you got hurt in the process."

I shrugged, not knowing what else to say, and began to walk away.

"Why are you lying?"

A woman entering the kitchen stopped and stared at us. I smiled as if there was nothing to see, and once she was gone I faced Parker again.

"You know we have a connection," she told me. "We talk on the phone every night—well, until the other day we did. That's not just a physical thing. We mean something to each other."

"You need to—"

"What about all the times we kissed?" she continued. "Huh? Yeah, I knew you were married, but so did you when you showed up at my house in the middle of the night. Don't you dare try to pass me off like I was some booty call. That's so whack, Gavin, and you know it. What about all the fun we had at the carnival? I brought my daughter around you! That's not just a physical attraction, so don't come at me like I'm some ho you just used to get off."

"I'm not!" I was beginning to lose my patience with her. This was not the time or the place to talk about this, and she knew it.

"The way you held me the last time we were together—that was something. Men don't hold women like that unless they mean something to them."

"Parker!" I snapped, and grabbed her arms. "*Stop it!*"

She sneered at me, fully disgusted. "You are full of crap. So you suddenly have a conscious, because, what, *it's your son's birthday,* now you all of a sudden don't want me anymore? You're just throwing me away? I'm a person! I'm not here just for your sexual pleasure. I thought we were friends."

I'd hurt her, and I regretted it. Out of guilt I rubbed her shoulders to try to ease the pain.

"I know," I said, but I could see she didn't believe me. "That's why I want to end things between us. I've decided to work on things with Dana, and it's not fair to keep holding on to you, too. I'm sorry."

She stared with disbelief, then slapped me hard across the face. Saliva flew out of my mouth, and the entire side of my head felt like a torch had been lit next to it.

Did she just slap the spit out of me?!!!

"#@&! you, Gavin," she growled angrily, and shoved me before turning away.

I rubbed my face and pulled her into the laundry room before she could get away.

SIXTY-SIX
DANA

When I made it home I was annoyed to find the driveway full of vehicles. There wasn't even space along the street in front of the house to park.

"Urrgghh!" I moaned, but I was happy my baby had a good turn out for his party. *"How am I gonna get this cake inside?"*

I twisted in my seat to get a good look at the oversized box covering the gigantic cake Sean made for Jonathan. He went above and beyond, but I should have known he would. He always did when it came to family.

I parked in the closest available spot and made my way into the house. It was packed. There were children running everywhere, and adults mingled together in small groups throughout the living room and kitchen. I invited thirty kids, but didn't take into account their siblings. That mistake nearly doubled the number of underage liabilities reeking havoc on my nice things.

It's for Jonathan, Dana. It's for Jonathan.

"Well, look who finally decided to show up to her son's birthday party."

A chill went through me at the sound of Sylvia's voice, but I forced myself to smile before I turned around to face her.

"Hi, Sylvia," I said, and held my breath to keep from vomiting as I gave her a hug. "So nice to see you."

"I'm sure," she said, and managed to give a smile with her turned up nose. "I have someone I'd like you to meet. Dana, this is my friend, Lydia. Lydia, this is Dana."

The partially dressed woman beside her smirked as she extended her hand. I didn't shake it, but instead looked at Sylvia like she was crazy. Was she really doing this again? At my son's birthday party? Didn't she learn her lesson the last time?

"Aren't you going to be polite?" Sylvia asked me. "Lydia's a guest in your home."

"Bye, Sylvia," I told her, and walked into the kitchen. I didn't have the energy to deal with her anymore, and didn't even want to.

"Hey, Aunt Dana," Jessica greeted me as soon as she saw me. She was sitting at the table eating a hot dog.

"Hey. Where's your mom?"

"Upstairs, feeding the baby."

I looked around the room. "Have you seen Gavin?"

"He was here a little while ago. Maybe he's outside with Daddy."

I went to the back porch and looked over the back yard, but didn't see a sign of Gavin anywhere. Annoyed, I walked back into the kitchen just in time to see him walk out of the laundry room with Parker.

My face fell. So did his.

I stared at him, then her, but neither one of them said anything.

"It's not what it looks like," he told me. "We were just talking. I—"

I walked away before I attacked them both.

Really?! You sneak around with that whore in my house?! In front of all of these people?! Right to my face?!!!

As I walked into the living room I noticed Sylvia and her trampy companion watching me, eager to continue the conversation I walked away from. Refusing to give them the satisfaction, I made a quick about face into the back yard again and grabbed Marcus.

"Hey," he smiled, and seemed relieved that I was back.

"I need your help," I said quickly, and signaled for him to follow me.

"What are we doing?" he asked.

I noticed his long legs had to trot in order to keep up with me and slowed my pace.

"I need help with the cake," I told him as we walked around the house.

"Oh, how did it come out? Sean said he was going all out for you."

I chuckled under my breath. "Yeah, he went a little too far out," I said. "You'll see."

When we got to my truck I unlocked the back and slowly opened the door.

"Good googly moogly!" Marcus nervously exclaimed when he saw the towering cake box.

"He made a 3D tyrannosaurus."

His eyes widened with amazement.

"The thing is nearly four feet tall," I continued. "And it's super heavy, which is why I need your help."

"This thing is huge. We might need some help to get this in the house. Let me go get Gavin to—"

"No," I snapped. *"We don't need him."*

He stared with curiosity, and I could see the wonder in his eyes, but thankfully he didn't ask any questions.

"Let's get this cake inside," he told me.

I took the foldaway box that covered the cake away and stashed it in the backseat. I wanted Jonathan to see the dinosaur when we walked in, as well as everyone else—especially his evil troll of a grandmother, and stand in awe.

"Ready?" Marcus asked.

I nodded and helped him slide the cake out of the truck by its base. It was way heavier than I imagined, and the weight of it made me nervous.

"You sure you don't want to get Gavin?" he asked again as he adjusted his grip on the cake.

"We can do this!"

"Okay," he said reluctantly, and together we made our way to the house.

The walk across the yard was more difficult than any I'd taken before, and by the time we reached the front door we both were sweating. My legs felt like they were on fire and my knees threatened to buckle beneath me.

"This cake better be good," he griped, and took a deep breath. "How are we gonna get the door open?"

I inched forward and kicked it.

"Shoot!" I fussed when I saw the mark I made, and had to kick the door again when no one answered.

Finally, after three more kicks and a yell from Marcus, the front door opened. A child who looked to be about Jonathan's age stood before us, and his face filled with awe at the sight of the exquisite cake.

"How cool is that?!" he exclaimed.

"Can you move out of the way, please?" I asked as patiently as I could. My hands were so sweaty they were starting to become slippery.

"Sorry," he quickly apologized, and shuffled to the side so we could walk into the house.

The living room filled with adoration as we crossed over the threshold. Sean's creation left everyone amazed, and the commotion caused everyone to gather from the kitchen and backyard.

Jonathan burst through the crowd as everyone clapped. "Is that a real cake?" he asked, not believing it could be true. "It's a dinosaur!"

"It is, baby!" I told him. "Happy birthday!"

Everyone congratulated him as Marcus and I began to make our way to the kitchen table. Suddenly the heel of my shoe buckled. I stumbled and the cake slipped from my hands. The room erupted into startled gasps and horrified screams as the dinosaur smashed to the ground and crumbled into a heap of ruined pieces.

"Oh no!" I screamed, and jumped to my feet, but slipped on a glob of icing and landed right in the middle of what remained of the cake.

The room became devastatingly quiet. No one moved. They all stared with shock and embarrassment for me as I sat, like the clumsy uncoordinated fool that I was, in the pile of delicious remains. Icing was everywhere. It'd even managed to get inside my shoes.

I was humiliated.

I wanted to die inside. Everyone felt sorry for me, even the children, and I hated their pity. My heart broke completely when my eyes locked with Gavin's. He didn't move to help me at all while he stood beside Parker and watched the complete mess of a mother and wife I had become. But why would he move to help me? He had the woman he wanted with him. I was just the one he strung along because he just so happened to have met me first. She probably could have made this cake herself, and she would have known how to get it into the house without ruining the party for everyone. Of course he didn't want me anymore. I was a cake dropping klutz who couldn't even give a child a birthday party!!!

"Dana, you okay?" Marcus asked, and helped me to my feet. I slipped again, but another parent extended their hand to keep me from falling. Once I had my balance I ran upstairs with tears streaming down my face.

SIXTY-SEVEN
GAVIN

My heart broke as I watched Dana run upstairs, and I immediately chased her into our bedroom. I found her sprawled across the bed with her face buried in a pillow, crying her eyes out. I closed the door behind me and nearly broke down at the sight.

I did this to her.

I'd never seen her broken like this before. Not only was she crying, but the icing all over her was ruining our very expensive bedding. I knew how much she spent on it, and I knew she did, too. Not caring about it anymore proved how distressed she was.

"Just leave me alone," she moaned through her tears.

"I can't do that," I said softly. "I want to make sure you're okay."

"Are you sleeping with her?" she asked a moment later.

The question surprised me, but I didn't run from it.

"No."

"Did you sleep with her?"

There was a knock at the door.

"Can I come in, please?" Jonathan asked from the other side.

"Go back downstairs to the party," I called out to him.

"No. I need to check on Mommy."

"What did I say?" I asked him impatiently.

Dana sat up and forced herself to stop crying. "Let him in," she instructed me, and used the backs of her sugar coated hands to wipe her eyes.

"You sure?" I asked.

She nodded and continued to wipe her face, so I opened the door. As soon as Jonathan saw her he ran and jumped into her lap and gave her the biggest hug I'd ever seen from a kid.

"It's okay, Mommy," he told her, and kissed her cheek. "You don't have to feel bad about the cake. I saw it and it was really cool, and I'm having a lot of fun at my party."

"Awh, baby," Dana said, and burst into tears all over again.

"Don't cry, Mommy," he begged her, and wiped her tears.

"You are the sweetest kid," she told him, and hugged him closely.

"Can you please come back downstairs with us? No one is mad that there's no cake. We can eat cookies."

Madison ran into the room suddenly.

"Ms. Gardner, you don't have to cry," she said. "My mom can go get a cake from the store."

"Oh, I bet she's just dying to," Dana said cynically, though the children were too young and naive to notice.

"She doesn't have to do that," I quickly told Madison.

"What's going on in here?" Leah asked anxiously as she hurried into the room. "There's cake all over the floor downstairs, and the..." She stopped when she saw Dana's appearance. "Are you okay?" she asked, horrified.

"She's fine," I told her. "I need some time alone with my wife. Can you leave us alone, please? And take these children with you."

"Oh, no!" Jonathan whined, and poked his lip out. "I want to stay with Mommy," he said, and hugged her again.

"What did you do to my sister?" Leah asked, and squared her shoulders at me.

"I didn't do—"

"I'm fine," Dana said quickly.

Leah didn't believe her, and threatened me with her eyes before instructing the kids to come with her. Madison quickly obeyed, but Jonathan didn't move until Dana told him he had to. He slumped away from her and didn't appear to feel better until Madison took him by the hand.

"I'll take care of everything downstairs," Leah told us on her way out. "Stay up here as long as you need to. Just holler if you need me."

I thanked her, and in return she rolled her eyes and slammed the door in my face.

"Everybody's mad at me," I said a moment later, feeling helpless.

Dana had no compassion for me, and I honestly couldn't blame her. Not knowing what else to do, I sat down beside her on the bed.

"Baby, I—"

The tension in the room forced me to eat my words. We sat in silence for nearly ten minutes. Finally, unable to take it any longer, I scooped a dollop of icing from the bed and swiped it across her nose, thinking it would make her laugh.

"It's not funny," she whispered, and returned the topping to the bed. *"None of this is funny."*

She got up slowly and walked into the bathroom. I joined her a few minutes later and found her crying. She'd taken her dress and shoes off. Only her bra and slip remained, and I was surprised to see the icing had managed to seep through her dress and onto her skin. She had a towel in her hands and used it to clean her face, and more had been gathered in preparation for a shower.

"I can't take any more of this, Gavin."

"I know," I said, and was truly sorry for how far I'd pushed her.

"Did you sleep with her?" she asked me again.

"No," I answered, and decided to be totally honest. "But I thought about it. And came pretty close, too."

"Oh, God," she whispered, and turned away at the information. "And you have her in our house? In front of our son and our whole family..."

She lost hope for us. I watched as it evaporated from her eyes.

"No," I begged quickly, and grabbed her arm. "Don't leave me. I don't want a divorce. I don't want to live the rest of my life without you."

"Take *your hand* off of me."

"I'm not gonna let you divorce me," I told her, and held her as she cried and asked me how I could do this to her.

"I don't know, baby. I'm sorry," I apologized.

She pulled away and slapped me. The sting of it went through my jaw and rattled the nerves of my teeth, but I didn't whine or complain. I deserved it. I deserved for her to hate me.

"I'm done with her. I cut it off. That's what I was doing in the laundry room when you saw us earlier. It's done. We're done. It's through."

"Don't lie to me, Gavin!" she screamed, and punched my chest repeatedly until she fell onto it in tears. "I hate you! I hate you so much!"

"I know, baby," I said, and hugged her again while I kissed the top of her head. "I know, and I'm sorry. I lost my head and my good judgment for a period of time, but I know what I want now. I want you. I want us. I want our marriage."

She cried for a few minutes, then pulled away slowly and looked me in the eye.

"You better tell me everything," she said through tight teeth. *"Everything."*

I knew I had to. Our secrets were tearing us apart, and if any more came out I knew we wouldn't make it. So, with pain in my chest, I gave her the entire story.

SIXTY-EIGHT
GAVIN

Dana and I never made it back to the party. We stayed in the bathroom and talked for nearly two hours until Leah knocked on the door and told us all of the guests had left. She correctly sensed that Dana and I needed to be alone and offered to take Jonathan to her house for the night, and we gladly accepted. Once we were completely alone we voyaged downstairs to try to clean up the leftover mess from the party. Our conversation switched back to how betrayed she felt over my dealings with Parker and the cleaning never got done.

The dialogue was the most painful I'd ever had in my life. She slapped me a few times, punched me a few times, and even got in my face and screamed. We both cried, but by the grace of God we got through it. After that we decided to pray, and for the first time in months we opened our bibles and studied together.

We were exhausted by the time we were finished, but too much was at stake for either of us to fall asleep. We stayed up until the early hours of the next morning discussing what we needed to do to improve our marriage. I expressed that I needed her forgiveness, and she let me know it wasn't going to come easy, which I accepted. I acknowledged the pain I caused her and told her I was willing to wait as long as she needed me to. She in turn told me that I needed to put my mother in her place once and for all. Lydia's appearance at Jonathan's party poured salt on a wound that hadn't healed yet, and she couldn't go through any more of Mama's torture. The disrespect left me with no choice but to deliver an ultimatum, so after getting a few hours of sleep we went to Mama's house for a visit.

"Well, this is a pleasant surprise," she said as she opened the door. "What are you doing here?"

"We need to talk to you," I told her as I held on tightly to Dana's hand.

"Everything all right?"

"We're fine. Physically, anyway. But... We need to talk to you."

She stared at us both, then allowed us to come inside.

"Where's my grandbaby?" she asked as she closed the door behind us.

"With his aunt and uncle," I answered. "We need to have this conversation alone."

"I see," she said, and moved past us into the living room. "Well, if I'd known you were coming I would have stopped by the supermarket. I don't have anything to eat. I was gonna go later."

"We're fine."

She rolled her eyes as she sat down in her rocking chair. I noticed that she hadn't spoken to Dana yet. Dana hadn't said anything either, but at this point that was probably a good thing.

"So," Mama began as we sat on the sofa. "What do you need to talk to me about?"

"Us."

"Me and you?"

"Me, you, and my wife," I clarified. "The three of us and the dynamics of our relationships."

She slouched and sighed. "What is it now?"

I felt Dana stiffen beside me, but she remained cool and kept her mouth closed.

"Mama, Dana and I have been married for almost three years now."

"I know that," she said impatiently. *"Barely."*

I sighed. She was starting early.

"No, not *barely*. We've been married this entire time," I corrected her.

"Okay. *And?"*

"And it's time for you to stop disrespecting her."

She smacked her lips. *"Ain't nobody disrespecting that girl."*

"We didn't come here to fight," I quickly let her know. "We're trying to resolve the issues that we have, because we do have issues, and all the drama has to stop. I can't take it anymore."

"What drama?" she asked innocently.

"Like you calling me a girl," Dana interjected. "I'm a grown woman, and I have been the entire time you've known me."

Mama twisted her face, and I knew she was about to go off. I held my hand up to stop them both.

"Let's remain calm," I gently suggested. "We can't resolve anything if we start acting crazy."

"She's the one with the problem. Not me," Mama claimed.

I wasn't about to let her get away with that. Not after yesterday.

"Okay, Mama. So why did you bring Lydia to our house?"

"Lydia? Oh, she's just a girl at the church that needs a mother figure, that's all. She's really sweet and she has a baby, so I thought it'd be nice to invite her to the party."

"Without letting me or Dana know? After the whole situation with Tanya?"

"I didn't think it would be a big deal," she said passively, but her anger was obvious. "Is that what this is all about? I can't help it if the woman you married is insecure, son. That's your job to build her self-esteem. Not mine."

Dana chuckled at her audacity.

"This isn't a game," I fussed, and stared coldly so she's know just how serious I was. "I need you to start respecting my wife, or else Jonathan and I won't come around anymore."

Her mouth fell open. "Just what are you trying to say?"

"Exactly what I just said."

"I am your mother!" she snapped.

"And Dana is my wife."

"She doesn't come before me!"

I reeled back, shocked by her words. Dana sat back on the couch and crossed her arms and legs with an annoyed "I told you so" expression stamped across her face.

"Mama... Yes, she does."

She objected with an eye roll. I had to take her by the hand and look into her eyes before she would listen any further.

"You are my mother," I told her. "And I'm your son. That will never change. But I'm a husband now. The dynamics of our relationship has to change, or else our family won't make it."

"Nothing has to change. We are who we are, and when she married you, she married your family, too."

"No the hell I didn't," Dana objected, and looked at Mama as if she were senile. "Show me that scripture in the bible. Please, I really would like to see it."

"Yes, you did! He and I were family first. I'm his mother," Mama argued.

"But you don't come first anymore," I stopped her. "My priority is my wife. I'll always love you, and you know I'll always do what I have to in order to take care of you and protect you—"

"As you should," she interjected.

"I wouldn't be a good son if I didn't," I added. "But if I keep allowing this I won't be a good husband, either. And I can't have that, Mama."

She looked over at Dana with piercing eyes, and I knew she saw her as an enemy.

"Why are you looking at her like that?" I asked. "She didn't do anything to you."

"She came and took you away from me," she said, and water came to her eyes. She struggled to keep her tears in.

"No, she didn't," I said softly, and kneeled before her so I'd have her undivided attention. "I pursued *her*. I asked *her* to marry me. It wasn't the other way around. I chose *her*. She didn't choose me. She's the woman that *I* picked to stand by *me.*"

"But you didn't know what you were doing," she insisted. "She tricked you. Hoodwinked you, with her lil' body and all them fancy clothes she like to wear. She fast."

Dana chuckled behind us with disgust, and she had every right to be offended. Mama talked about her as if she were some whoremongering witch who put a spell on me.

"That's not true," I told her. "Dana's a godly woman. She didn't do anything but be the person that she is and I fell in love with her. Jonathan did, too. Yeah, she's different," I acknowledged. "She don't really cook much, and she's not into housekeeping. She's a business woman, and that's something to get used to where we're from. But that's what makes her who she is, and I love her."

She was starting to understand, but she still refused to accept it. She shook her head at me and pulled her hands out of my grip.

"You made a mistake," she told me. "Just like you did last time."

My eyes closed slowly at the insult. There was no need to bring up my ex-wife. Mama was just being evil now.

"Don't make this situation harder than it has to be," I told her.

"There ain't nothing hard about it," she insisted. "I'm not the one with the problem. It's y'all."

I sighed deeply. I didn't understand why this had to be so difficult.

"Can't you just respect my choice, Mama?" I pleaded. "Out of love for me, can't you do that?"

"Why would I do that?"

"Because I'm asking you to."

She took me by the hand and leaned in close as she looked me in the eye.

"Baby... *You might as well give that up.*"

I leaned away in disappointment as I finally began to understand. Mama never liked Dana because she never *wanted* to. She didn't want me to ever get married again. She liked things the way they were when she had Jonathan and I all to herself, and that's how she wanted things to be forever. She was toxic, and for the first time in my life I was thoroughly disgusted by her. Did she really think I was going to live alone just to please her? Was I supposed to be a single parent, live sexually frustrated, and take on all of life's responsibilities on my own just to make *my mama* happy? What the... *I WAS A GROWN MAN!!!* What about my happiness? Dana was my blessing, and I WAS NOT about to give her and all of her goodness up for my mama! She was wrong for even wanting me to.

"I'm not doing this anymore," I told her. "Until you respect my wishes and treat my wife differently, you won't see me."

Mama tried to object, but I stood up quickly and cut her off.

"Let's go," I told Dana. *"Now."*

She didn't move, but stared at me with worry. "Are you sure?"

"Yes," I said, and took her by the hand. "This is ridiculous, and you don't have to put up with it anymore. I'm embarrassed I forced you to for this long. Come on. I'm taking you home."

"But we—"

"Now!" I rushed her, and jerked her to her feet. I was three seconds away from going completely off on Mama, and if I said what was on my mind she would never forgive me.

"Gavin, wait. Let me—"

I moved so fast that I nearly dragged her outside to the truck. I realized that my anger caused me to squeeze her wrist too hard when she winced in pain.

"Don't leave like this," she begged when I released her. "Don't throw away your relationship with your mother on account of me."

"I didn't throw it away. She did," I let her know.

"Just give her some time," she told me. "You guys can reach some type of compromise. I know what it's like to grow up without a mother and a grandmother. I don't want that for you and Jonathan."

Her voice quivered, and I saw she was trying not to cry. It only proved how much she really loved me.

"You would put up with Mama and all of her craziness for me?"

"I don't have to be around her," she said. "I'll just stay home whenever you guys want to see each other. She never has to come to our house."

"No." I shook my head and opened the door for her. "I'll never go anywhere you aren't welcomed and appreciated. We're one, babe. *Therefore a man shall leave his father and mother, and cleave to his wife, and the two shall become one flesh.* I'm not going anywhere without you."

A tear fell from her eye. She wiped it away, then looked up at me with so much pride.

"I love you, baby."

"I love you, too," I told her, and gave her a kiss. She got in the truck, and we left.

SIXTY-NINE
DANA

After the emotional meeting with Gavin's mother, neither one of us had the energy to say or do anything but get into bed and go to sleep. Now that we were both awake we still didn't have too many words to share. I was still mad at him about Parker, but I saw that his disagreement with Sylvia had hurt him and allowed him to rest against me for comfort. I hated being the source of their split, but she really gave him no other choice. When I told him she'd come around eventually he told me not to hope. He knew his mother and doubted things would ever change.

My stomach growled suddenly. Embarrassed, I covered it and hid my face. Gavin only laughed and asked if I was hungry.

"Yes," I admitted. "It's late. We haven't eaten yet."

"I'll make something to eat," he said, and slowly got out of bed. "Whatever you feel like eating. Then we have to clean this house up. The backyard is a trifling mess. We need to call Leah, too, and see what time we need to pick Jonathan up. He has school in the moring."

I agreed and told him I wanted waffles and bacon.

"Waffles and bacon it is," he said, and went downstairs.

I stayed in the bed and tried to relax, but my attempts were ruined when Gavin's phone chimed as it sat on the nightstand. My gut told me Parker was the one texting him, and when I checked I discovered I was right.

I wanted to call Gavin back upstairs and go off, then smack him in the head with his phone. However, I forced myself to calm down. There was no need to panic. If Gavin still wanted to carry on with her he never would have told me about it. She was the past. The *very recent* past, but she was still the past. I had to accept that.

The phone chimed again.

I tried to ignore it, but my anger got the best of me. I snatched the phone and tried to unlock it, but he'd changed the device's password.

"Shoot," I grunted under my breath. "What could his password be?"

Gavin was smart, but he wasn't very creative, so I knew it had to be something simple. The last password was Jonathan's birthday. Maybe the new one was mine. But he wasn't thinking about me when he changed it. If he was he never would have been so secretive, so he wouldn't have used our anniversary, either...

His birthday.

I typed it in and the screen unlocked. I was almost ashamed of how simpleminded he could be at times. How he made it through life before me I would never know. I was his *help meet*—and praise God! The man really did need my help! No wonder he fell into the hands of Parker. He was a complete fool without me.

The messaging app opened immediately, and I saw a long conversation between them. I knew I wouldn't be able to take reading them all, so I focused on the last two.

Call me, please. I miss you.

I haven't been able to sleep. I need to see you.

She still wanted him, and was refusing to bow out.

It was time to go to war.

In the past few months this woman had come into my life and disrupted my family. Gavin played his part, but there was no reason for her to continue to contact him now. I'd let her win too many battles, and now she was cocky. She thought if she continued to peck at my marriage she'd win my husband, and I wasn't about to let that happen. It was time to demolish her once and for all.

Can't. Wifey.

I sent the text, pretending to be Gavin, and waited for her to respond. It was devious to pretend to be him, but she was the one who started this. It was time for me to finish it.

Can you meet me somewhere? I really need to see you.

"Get over yourself," I whispered at her response, and nearly gagged when she sent a broken heart emoji. I remained cool, however, and asked her where she wanted to meet.

The park down the street from the kids' school. Bring J so he can play with Madison while we talk.

Ooohh! The nerve of her! She was going to continue to involve my son in this?!!! *Really?!!!*

I wanted to call her and go off, but knew in order to be effective I had to stay calm and collected. I told her I would be there in thirty minutes and got up to get dressed.

****

I told Gavin I needed to run to the store to pick up a few feminine products so he wouldn't ask any questions about me leaving the house so suddenly. I covered my tracks by deleting the text exchange between Parker and I, and to be extra vindictive I drove his truck so she'd think I was him when I arrived.

The plan worked. As soon as I pulled up Parker put away the book she was reading and waved, but her happiness shattered when she saw me. I smiled eagerly at her disappointment and made my way over to her peacefully while she sat with gloom and doom all over her face.

"Surprised to see me?" I asked as I sat down beside her. "Expecting someone else?"

I could feel how scared she was. Though her movements were barely visible, I noticed the indecisive twists and turns she took as she squirmed, undoubtedly trying to decide if she should run or face me like the woman she'd been pretending to be this entire time. I enjoyed it. It gave me further confidence, and she deserved every bit of torture she felt.

I crossed my legs in her direction and looked her straight in the eye.

"I don't believe in wasting time, so I'm gonna get right to the point. Stay away from my husband."

Her mouth fell open. *"Excuse me?"*

"Don't play dumb. I know all about what's been going on between you and Gavin. He told me everything, including the fact that he told you things were over between the two of you. Don't text my husband anymore. Or flirt with him, or do anything else to disrespect me or my marriage again. Do you understand me?"

"I don't know what you're talking about," she claimed.

"Yes, you do. And if you try to involve my son in your little schemes again, or even come near him for that matter, you will have a real problem on your hands—and trust me, that is not what you want."

She scoffed at me. "Are you crazy? That sounded like a threat."

I smiled to keep from slapping her.

"Look, we can be mature adults about this, or we can play games like little children. I know what you're trying to do, and it ends now. Don't contact my husband any more, and don't use my child in any more of your games. I promise you, *you don't want any more problems with me."*

She tried to stare me down, but I didn't budge. She finally realized I would get physical with her if she wanted me to and backed away from me.

"What about our kids?" she asked. "They're best friends. Are they just not supposed to see each other anymore?"

"Oh, please," I said, and nearly laughed in her face. "They will see each other enough at school."

Unable to argue, she looked away and kept her mouth closed.

Yeah. Let it go.

"Are we done here?" I asked her.

I could tell by the way her jaw clenched that she was angry, but I didn't care. She had some nerve getting upset, knowing she'd snuck around with my husband behind my back. She was lucky I was a saved woman now. Jesus wouldn't be pleased if I wrapped my hands around her neck and squeezed until her eyes popped out, or grabbed her by that pretty hair of hers and slammed her face into the ground in front of her child.

"Are we done?" I asked again, louder this time.

"We're done," she told me. "I'll leave Gavin alone. I'm not into sharing my men, anyway."

I chuckled. We both knew that if she could get a man she would have never went after mine. But there was no need to point that out. She'd tried, but I won. Nothing else needed to be said.

"Good," I told her, and stood from the bench.

As I walked away Madison spotted me from across the park. She stood up from the pile of mud she was building and ran in my direction.

Oh, no... NNNNOOOO!!!!

She was filthy. Her clothes were smeared with dirt and grass stains, and her hands were covered with it. And they were coming for my white Roberto Cavalli jeans!

"Hi, Ms. Dana!" she squealed when she reached me, and wrapped her dirty hands around my waist in a hug. "I didn't know you were coming today!"

When she pulled away a large smear of mud appeared on my thighs. My beautiful jeans were ruined, but the child didn't even notice. She looked up at me and smiled as if she hadn't done anything wrong at all. What the heck was wrong with her?! I could get down and dirty with the best of the best, but I never, *ever* sacrificed my fashion for it! How was Parker raising this child?!!!

I forced myself to seem excited with a laugh. "Hi, Madison. How are you, dear?"

"Good," she said innocently. "Where's Jonathan? Is he here?"

"No. He's at home. I just came to talk to your mom."

"Oh." She seemed disappointed as she looked back at Parker, who was watching us closely. When she faced me again she noticed the mess she'd made.

"Your pants are dirty," she told me, pointing.

"Yeah," I said, and forced another laugh. "They are. But you take care, sweetie. Okay? And behave yourself."

"Okay. See you later," she told me with a wave, and bounced back to her pile of dirt.

I looked over my shoulder and sent Parker an evil stare, then went back to my truck. If I never saw either one of them again in my life I wouldn't feel bad about it at all, and I was perfectly okay with feeling that way.

SEVENTY
GAVIN

I was tired when I walked into the house, but when I saw my family I suddenly felt rejuvenated. It had been a trying week, but I was a blessed man, and had to take a moment to thank God for saving my family.

"Hi, Daddy," Jonathan smiled at me from the kitchen table. "Mommy, Daddy's here."

"I see," she said, and looked up from the table where she'd just placed a large salad bowl. "Hi, honey."

My heart melted when she smiled at me. Two months had passed since I confessed my transgressions with Parker, and I hadn't received much warmth from her. I knew I had a long way to go before she would fully be able to trust me again, but to see her smile was everything.

"You making dinner?" I asked as I joined them.

"Nope," she answered proudly. "I just made a salad. I ordered pizza."

"Sounds good to me."

I honestly didn't want pizza, but kept that comment to myself. She'd cooked twice this week already, and had every right not to be in the mood to do so tonight after working hard all week. After all I'd done, if she never wanted to cook a full meal again I would never utter a word of complaint. But over the past few weeks we'd managed to reach several compromises that worked for both of us.

For starters, she promised that as soon as she finished with the hospital next week she'd bring her schedule down to only forty work hours a week. She also agreed to put a nice portion of her check into savings, strictly for my comfort, as long as I agreed to keep my mouth closed about how much money she chose to spend on clothes. I, in turn, agreed not to pressure her about having a baby anymore. She'd let me know when she was ready, and if she decided it just wasn't for her I would accept it. I also had to hand over my phone for her to go through at any time with no protest. We took equal shares of the household chores and both helped Jonathan with his schoolwork.

"I'll get the plates," I said, and moved over to the cabinet.

"Grab cups and utensils, too," she told me. "How was work?"

"Work was..."

She looked up suddenly when I didn't finish my sentence.

"Interesting," I finally said.

"Interesting?"

"Yeah..."

I debated whether or not I should tell her about Parker. Today was her last day at the clinic. The news came as a shock to me, but apparently everyone else knew. When she stood up at our staff meeting and announced that she was moving back to Houston no one seemed surprised. We hadn't talked since Jonathan's birthday party, but I was kind of sad to see her leave. I knew it was because of me, and I felt horrible. I'd really hurt her. When she said goodbye she couldn't even look at me.

"Babe? What happened?" Dana asked.

I shook my head nonchalantly. "Just work. Nothing to even think about, really."

She gave a nod of understanding and continued to help Jonathan with his homework. I watched them from the counter until the doorbell rang.

"Pizza's here!" Jonathan yelled.

"Was it really necessary to scream?" she asked, and covered her ears.

"Can I still pay for it?" he asked without apologizing.

She nodded and he jumped up from the table so fast that he nearly knocked his chair onto the floor.

"Slow down. There's no need to rush!"

He snatched the fifty dollar bill that was sitting on the counter and sprinted to the front door.

"Wait, boy!" she fussed, and chased after him. "The pizza man night be crazy or something. You don't know."

He waited for Dana to open the door for him. I watched with pride as he handed the delivery guy the fifty dollar bill and calculated the change he was owed in his head the way Dana taught him how to. Apparently it was a skill she learned during her early years of shopping. Whatever worked. He was now making excellent grades in math, and I appreciated it.

When they came back into the kitchen I took the pizza from them and prepared everyone's plates while Jonathan went into the restroom and washed his hands. Dana poured our drinks, and a moment later we all sat down to eat as a family.

"Do you wanna say grace?" Dana asked Jonathan.

"Let's let Daddy do it," he suggested.

Dana smiled, liking the idea. I did, too.

"Thanks, son," I said, and we joined hands as we bowed our heads. "Thank you, Lord," I said, and became filled with immense gratitude. "For my son, and for my wife. For... my family."

Dana squeezed my hand as I struggled to keep myself together. I opened my eyes and found her watching me. Jonathan grew concerned, too, and looked up to check on me.

"Daddy?" he asked when he saw my tears. "Are you okay?"

I laughed and nodded. "Yes, son. I'm just really happy."

"Because of pizza?"

Dana began to laugh with me. "Yeah, he's really hungry."

"And thankful," I added.

He pouted. "Okay, but... Do you really need to cry about it? It's just pepperoni."

Dana and I laughed again, and I finished the prayer so we could eat. Afterward we enjoyed our meal over a pleasant conversation. The entire time I thanked God for his grace and mercy, and for loving me enough to allow me to keep the blessing I so foolishly almost gave away.

The End

For more from the author,
visit

www.LaShandaMichelle.com